...vels *The Agincourt Bride* and *The Tudo...* e followe... ...he life of Catherine de Valois, Queen Consort to the conquering King Henry V and, with the Welsh squire Owen Tudor, founder of the Tudor dynasty. In *Red Rose, White Rose* Joanna focuses on a time of great turbulence in England and the eventful life of one of the fifteenth century's most powerful women, Cicely Neville, mother of Edward IV and Richard III.

Joanna is married and now living in Wiltshire, with an extended family and a wayward Irish terrier. She welcomes contact on Facebook (Joanna Hickson) or Twitter (@joannahickson).

By the same author

The Agincourt Bride
The Tudor Bride

RED ROSE, WHITE ROSE

JOANNA HICKSON

HARPER

Harper
An imprint of HarperCollins*Publishers*
77–85 Fulham Palace Road,
Hammersmith, London W6 8JB

www.harpercollins.co.uk

A Paperback Original 2014
1

A catalogue record for this book
is available from the British Library

ISBN: 9780007447015

Typeset in Birka by Palimpsest Book Production Limited,
Falkirk, Stirlingshire

Printed and bound in Great Britain by
Clays Ltd, St Ives plc

MIX
Paper from
responsible sources
FSC™ C007454

For my intrepid and lovely sister Sue

(1) MARGARET STAFFORD m. **RALPH NEVILLE,** m.
(daughter of Hugh Stafford, *1st Earl of Westmorland*
Earl of Stafford)

JOHN NEVILLE m. **ELIZABETH HOLLAND** + *7 others*

RALPH, m. **ELIZABETH** **SIR JOHN** **THOMAS** *4 girls*
2nd Earl of **PERCY** **NEVILLE** **NEVILLE**
Westmorland

'JACK' NEVILLE

RICHARD 'HAL' m. **ALICE** **ELEANOR** m. **HENRY PERCY** **ROBERT,**
Earl of Salisbury **MONTAGU** *Earl of* *Bishop of*
Northumberland *Salisbury*

RICHARD 'DICK', *had issue*
Earl of Warwick

\>\>

EDWARD 'NED' m. **ELIZABETH** **CICELY** m. **RICHARD,**
Baron Bergavenny **BEAUCHAMP** **Duke of York**

See separate York tree

(2) JOAN BEAUFORT
daughter of John of Gaunt,
Duke of Lancaster

The HOUSE of NEVILLE

>>

'WILL' *m.* **JOAN**
Lord   **FAUCONBERG**
Fauconberg

ANNE *m.* *HUMPHREY*
Duchess of   Earl of Stafford
Buckingham

JOAN   ELIZABETH   **ALYS**   *HUMPHREY*   *HENRY*

5 other children were born
to Ralph & Joan before Cicely

CUTHBERT OF MIDDLEHAM
(illegitimate son of Ralph Neville)

Names in bold feature as characters in *Red Rose, White Rose*
dy = died young

EDMUND OF LANGLEY   *m.*   *ISABELLA OF CASTILE*
1st Duke of York   *& LEON*
(5th son of King Edward III)

EDWARD,   *CONSTANCE*
2nd Duke of York

                                      no issue

no issue

ISABEL *m.* *HENRY BOURCHIER*
                        Viscount Beaumont
                        Earl of Eu

had issue

premature son   **ANNE**   *m.*   *'HARRY' HOLLAND*
(died at birth)   **Duchess of Exeter**   *Duke of Exeter*
                (b. 10/8/1439)   *(b. 27/6/1430)*

\>>

ELIZABETH   **MARGARET**   *WILLIAM*
(b. 22/4/1444)   *(b. 3/5/1446)*   *(b. 7/7/1447 dy)*

Names in bold feature as characters in *Red Rose, White Rose*
dy = died young

The
HOUSE of
YORK

RICHARD   m.   *ANNE MORTIMER*
Earl of Cambridge

RICHARD   m.   **CICELY NEVILLE**
3rd D. of York   **(b. 3/5/1415)**
(b. 21/9/1411)

>>

HENRY   **EDWARD**   **EDMUND**
(b. 10/2/1441 dy)   **Earl of March**   **Earl of Rutland**
                       (Edward IV)   *(b. 17/5/1443)*
                       (b. 28/4/1442)

JOHN   **GEORGE**   **RICHARD**   **URSULA**
(b. 7/11/1448 dy)   **Duke of Clarence**   *(Richard III)*   *(b. 2/7/55)*
                       (b.21/10/1449)   *(b. 2/10/52)*

The ENGLISH ~ROYAL FAMILY

EDWARD III OF ENGLAND   m.   PHILIPPA OF HAINAULT

EDWARD
Prince of Wales

WILLIAM
dy

LIONEL   m.   **ELIZABETH**
Duke of Clarence   of Ulster

RICHARD II

no issue

PHILIPPA   m.   **EDMUND**
Countess of Ulster   **MORTIMER**
Earl of March*

MORTIMER
succession

JOHN BEAUFORT
Earl of Somerset

HENRY BEAUFORT
Cardinal

THOMAS BEAUFORT
Duke of Exeter

no issue

JOHN BEAUFORT
Duke of Somerset

EDMUND BEAUFORT
Duke of Somerset

MARGARET BEAUFORT   m.   **EDMUND TUDOR**
Earl of Richmond

HENRY VII (TUDOR succession)

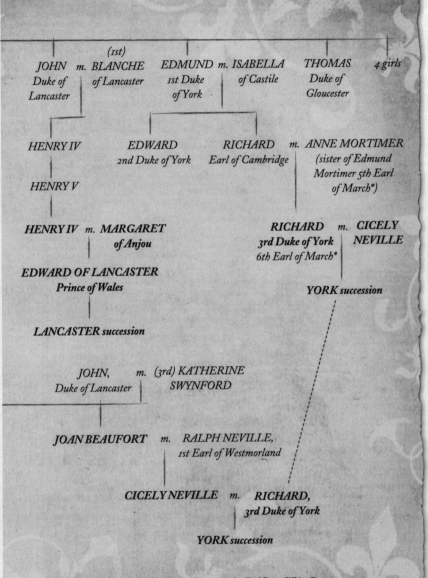

JOHN *m.* BLANCHE (1st)
Duke of   of Lancaster
Lancaster

EDMUND *m.* ISABELLA
1st Duke   of Castile
of York

THOMAS   4 girls
Duke of
Gloucester

HENRY IV

HENRY V

EDWARD
2nd Duke of York

RICHARD *m.* ANNE MORTIMER
Earl of Cambridge   (sister of Edmund
Mortimer 5th Earl
of March*)

HENRY IV *m.* **MARGARET**
of Anjou

EDWARD OF LANCASTER
Prince of Wales

LANCASTER succession

RICHARD *m.* **CICELY**
3rd Duke of York   **NEVILLE**
6th Earl of March*

YORK succession

JOHN,   *m.* (3rd) KATHERINE
Duke of Lancaster   SWYNFORD

JOAN BEAUFORT *m.* **RALPH NEVILLE,**
1st Earl of Westmorland

CICELY NEVILLE *m.* **RICHARD,**
3rd Duke of York

YORK succession

NB. Names in bold feature as characters in *Red Rose, White Rose*
* The March inheritance gave Richard of York two lines of succession
dy = died young

England, Ireland
& Northern France
15th Century

IRELAND

Carrickfergus

Dublin

North
Sea

Newcastle
Brancepeth · Durham
Penrith · Raby · Aycliffe
Middleham
Sheriff Hutton
Sandal Magna · York
Conigsburgh
Penrhyn · Chester · Tattershall
× Blore Heath
ENGLAND
Ludlow · Maxstoke · Fotheringay
× Mortimore's Cross
Pembroke · Ampthill × St Albans
Lampbey · London
Cardiff · Windsor
Dover

Calais

English Channel

Rouen

Paris

FRANCE

PROLOGUE

**Provins, County of Champagne,
France, 1275**

At first there was only a subtle hint of fragrance borne on the breeze, an exquisite teasing of the senses. To the knight on his weary warhorse it was like the breath of God, lifting the hairs on the back of his neck and stirring the golden leopards on his banner.

'It is the scent of roses!' he cried to his companions. 'In the Holy Land we called it God's Incense.'

When the cavalcade breasted the hill ahead he reined in his horse with a gasp of wonder. All over the wide plain below stretched a carpet of red roses, covering the earth as far as the eye could see, as if a celestial gardener had scattered divine seed. The knight gazed in silent awe, struck by the power of the symbolism laid before him; that the single rose, an object of beauty and simplicity could, when massed with a myriad others, become a potent force, a source of mystery and strength. The words of a hymn sprang into his mind, which he had heard sung in the dust and heat of the Holy Land by choristers in his crusading army.

> *There is no rose of such vertue*
> *As is the rose that bore Jesu,*

For in this rose contained was
Heaven and earth in a little space.

'If there is a heaven on earth,' he declared, 'it is surely here.'

The knight was Edmund, Earl of Lancaster, crusader brother to Edward I, King of England and known throughout Christendom as Edmund 'Crouchback' or 'The Cross-Bearer'. Returning through France from his crusade, he was making a mercy mission to Provins where the Count of Champagne had recently died, leaving his young widow and their baby son vulnerable to abduction by neighbouring barons, eager to acquire access to the great wealth generated by the famous rose fields.

Grown from a single root brought back from Damascus by an earlier crusader, the precious roses were not just objects of beauty, they were an industry. Their dried petals became shards of perfumed sunshine to freshen the rushes on a rich man's floor; their floral essence could be distilled into attar of roses to perfume a lady's breast or diluted into rosewater for bathing and cooking; rose leaves were pounded into healing poultices and even the prunings, with their long, sharp thorns could be woven into fences for protecting flocks and crops.

But it was the rose of *'vertue'* that Edmund held in his mind when he first encountered Blanche, the lady in distress. Wearing white robes of mourning, she held her baby in her arms and her face was sweet and troubled. 'The Blessed Virgin has answered my prayers,' she sighed as he kissed her hand. By the next rose harvest Edmund and Blanche were married and the red Damask rose became for him a talisman, a badge of honour which he bore on his shield and gave to his favoured followers; the Red Rose of Lancaster.

A hundred years later another Edmund, younger brother to the great John of Gaunt, Duke of Lancaster, was created Duke of York by their father, King Edward III. This Edmund aimed to better his brother in all things, including the heraldic symbol of his dukedom. He could not have the red rose so he chose the white, the lovely wild rose of England with its five creamy petals and fierce, hooked thorns. He declared the white rose superior to the red because it was native to the soil it grew in, spreading over the hills and valleys of England in great tangled brakes, delighting all with its airy fragrance and spangled masses of blooms but repelling any who tried to seize it. Edmund had his minstrels compose a song in praise of the white rose:

> *Of a rose, a lovely rose*
> *Of a rose I sing a song.*
> *Lyth and lysten, both old and younge*
> *How the white rose becomen sprong,*
> *A fairer rose to oure leking*
> *Sprong there never in kynges lond.*

During the next century, in the battle for supremacy between Lancaster and York, the red rose and the white were to scratch a bloody trail across the 'kynges lond', leaving England blighted and bleeding.

PART ONE

County Durham, England
Spring 1433

1

Langleydale, Co Durham

Cicely

I breathed deeply of the scented air that swept off the Teesdale fells. It carried the chill of snow-capped mountains and the smell of juniper. When I was a small child my father had perched me in front of him on his great warhorse and taken me out on the moors to teach me the names of the peaks and pikes that rolled towards the horizon to the north and west of our home. Now I identified them one after another all the way to Cross Fell, misty blue in the distance; Snowhope, Ireshope and Burnhope, Holwick, Mickle, Cronkley and Widdybank. Their names sang in my head like a psalm, accompanied by the moan of the wind over the rock-strewn slopes and the cries of the birds that haunted them.

When I turned my mare's head to the east, her ears framed a view even more familiar. Each beck and stream from those high moors fed into the River Tees, which flowed through a valley ever-wider and greener as it meandered towards the coast. Dominating the upper reaches of this fertile basin was Raby Castle, the ancestral home of the Neville family – my family. Renowned as one of England's great northern fortresses, Raby's nine massive towers sprawled below me like the giants of legend; they loomed over the meagre mud-plastered cotts of the village beyond its moat. I had lived most of my seventeen years within those soaring walls. To my mother it was a palace, a great haven of security and splendour demonstrating infallibly the enormous wealth and power of the Nevilles, but to me it had become a prison. Often I had felt like a caged bird longing to fly. It was wonderful to be out, after a winter confined by its grey stones, up high above Langley Beck, relishing the wind in my face and the trembling anticipation of the hooded falcon on my fist.

'Look lively, Cis! Stop admiring the view and start working that bird of yours.'

It was my brother who spoke. We Nevilles were a numerous family and I could count six brothers who still lived; some I liked better than others. Three of them were out hunting with me on that March morning, but this particular brother held a special place in my life. Dark and even of temper, Cuthbert was my personal champion, five years my senior and sworn to protect me for life by an oath made to our father before his death. He was an expert swordsman, had enormous skill with the lance and a physique unsurpassed among the knights of the Northern March. Nevertheless I did not let him order me about.

'Selina will fly in good time, Cuddy, when the dogs put up some partridge. I do not fly her at inferior prey.'

His baptismal name was Cuthbert, after the great hermit-saint of the Holy Isle whose bones lay only five and twenty miles away in Durham Cathedral, but I used the nickname he had earned among his fellow henchmen at Raby for his close affinity with horses. Not only was Cuddy the local name for the saint, it was also one of the many northern words for a horse, particularly the small, strong, nimble pony which carried men and goods over the treacherous terrain of the border moors. Cuddy had the knack of getting a good performance out of even the most stubborn nag. It would not be boasting to say that I sat a horse as well as he did, since it was Cuddy who had taught me to ride, and I rode astride from the very first lesson, despite the disadvantage of wearing skirts.

His reaction to my protest was indignant. 'Huh! It will be a miracle if your merlin brings down a partridge. They are twice her size.'

We were hunting game for the Easter feast that was just over a week away. The birds would hang until then to intensify their flavour, while we Christians completed our Lenten fast. Cuddy preferred chasing stag. On this hunt he was acting as my body-guard and the captain of our armed escort. He carried no hawk and, in my opinion, knew little or nothing about them.

'You may think that, big brother, but Selina can bring down snipe, which are the same size as partridge and fly a lot faster.'

I dropped my reins briefly to remove the crested hood from the little bird on my other fist and felt her claws clench expectantly over the thick leather gauntlet that protected my hand and wrist. Released from the imprisonment of the blindfold, the falcon blinked and her yellow eyes began to dart about, filled with anticipation at the sight of the moor and the busy spaniel quartering the heather ahead of us. My palfrey pranced excitedly as I gathered up the reins and I bent to murmur calming words in her ear.

In a loud explosion of noise a covey of partridge burst up from the ground. 'Climb, Selina, climb,' I yelled, releasing the merlin's jesses and sending her off my fist as the game birds sped away from us, swerving and tumbling in panic.

For a few joyful seconds I watched the powerful beat of my falcon's wings as she scaled the wind, gaining height for her stoop and then the spaniel let out a throaty growl of warning, which crescendoed into a volley of barks. Only twenty yards away half a dozen men wearing protective canvas jacks and wielding an assortment of rustic weapons rose as if from nowhere, like demons from the underworld, and ran snarling and yelling down the slope towards us, leaping over the straggling heather which had so successfully hidden their presence. They must have belly-crawled from the cover of the stunted trees that grew in a rocky cleft nearby, where the beck tumbled down a steep part of the fell-side.

Cuddy drew his sword. 'Holy St Michael – reivers! They're after the horses. Ride, Cis – ride for the castle! Stop for nothing. I'll hold them off.' He wheeled his horse to face the oncoming foe and charged at the front-runner, yelling the family call-to-arms. 'À Neville! To me!'

From the corner of my eye I spied the first reiver fall as I set my horse's head down the slope. There I saw my other two brothers, Will and Ned, throw off their hawks, draw their weapons and urge their horses into a gallop, hurtling past me to give Cuddy support and returning his warcry, their mouths wide, faces twisted into angry scowls. Pounding up the hill behind them, yelling defiance, came our escort of half a dozen armed horsemen.

Reivers were the universal enemy, even here on the southernmost edge of the Northern March. Within the miles of untamed territory between Scotland and England known as the Debatable Lands, title to land and property was hotly contested and the rule of law rarely successfully applied. Gangs of bandits operated freely and internecine feuds abounded but however much they fought amongst themselves, English landholders and their tenants were united in their hatred of the Scottish reiver clans – Armstrongs, Elliots, Maxwells and Johnsons, to name but a few. These rampaging villains swooped down from the hills without warning, sometimes in a large troop to raid a whole town or village, sometimes in a small posse to grab whatever plunder they could, robbing travellers at random, raiding a single farm or rustling a herd of cattle and driving the beasts to a secret muster deep in the mountains.

Cuddy had automatically assumed that these particular bandits were after our horses, a valuable commodity, especially when of good breeding and training as ours were. Since he and I had strayed a small distance from the rest of the hunting party perhaps they had not realized how many of us there were nor how well armed and skilled in combat. Considerably older than me, my brother William was not only a knight of some renown but held estates and a seat in parliament as Lord Fauconberg and had been accompanied to the hunt by a number of his young retainers, including the brother next to me in age, nineteen-year-old Edward, known as Ned. In this part of the world no knight or squire ever rode out in less than half-armour, belting on his sword and carrying a mace or battle-axe slung from his saddle-bow, so I was confident they would make short work of the attackers. The hunt servants, unarmed except for their hunting knives, obviously thought the same because they called in the dogs and retreated only a short distance before turning back to watch the skirmish. Despite Cuddy's order to ride non-stop to Raby, I was tempted to follow suit, hoping to lure back my precious merlin Selina from wherever she had found a safe perch. However, even as the notion entered my head my own situation suddenly became perilous.

We had misjudged these reivers. They were not a small band of snatch-thieves willing to risk their lives in the hope of securing one or two valuable horses; they were a gang of bandits seeking an even richer reward. As I galloped past a grove of gnarled ash trees rooted in a sheltered hollow, six wild men mounted on ponies burst out from their cover to block my path. My speeding mare threw herself back on her haunches to avoid a collision and within seconds I found myself surrounded.

I wheeled the mare around, looking for help, but quickly realized that this ambush had been carefully planned. The smug grins on the faces of the surrounding horsemen confirmed this.

'They will not see us, lady. We are hidden by the hill, so best to come quietly.'

The speaker's face was disguised with dark, caked mud and he wore a dented metal sallet on his head, its visor pushed up. A camouflage spray of myrtle leaves tied over the helmet shadowed his eyes so that he resembled the evil green man depicted in church carvings. His cocky smile revealed rotting teeth. Despite my fear I felt a fierce surge of anger.

'I do not know who you are, villain, but I am a Neville and Nevilles do not "come quietly",' I said, and throwing back my head, echoed the family warcry I had heard so recently on my brothers' lips: 'À Neville! Cuthbert, to me!'

The evil green man spoke sharply to his companions and a large, callused hand was clamped over my mouth from behind me. At the same time another man snatched the reins from my hands as yet another pulled my arms back and wound a cord around my wrists, tying them tightly together.

'We ride!' shouted the leader and all at once I found myself desperately struggling to remain in the saddle as, corralled in the midst of their horses, my mare was forced to bound clumsily up the steep side of the hollow. But once I had caught my breath and clamped my thighs to my horse's sides, I realized that although my hands were tied my mouth was still free and I took advantage of the fact, renewing my screams for help, albeit in shrieks and jerks from my mare's hunched leaps. A loud oath came from the leader and as soon as we reached flatter ground he held up his hand for a halt. I continued shouting while he kicked his horse up to mine, scrabbled in the front of his battered gambeson and finally pulled out a filthy kerchief.

'For a well-born lady you screech like a fishwife but this should shut you up,' he growled and retaliated by spitting into the kerchief before using it to gag my screams.

I twisted my head this way and that but without the use of my hands I was unable to prevent him pulling the damp, stinking cloth between my teeth and tying it at the back. My shouts were reduced to muffled moans and then silenced altogether as I retched at the foul taste on my tongue.

'Calm down, my lady,' the man sneered, 'or I will have to throw you over my pommel and that will make a very painful ride.'

Forced to inhale through my nose, my eyes bulged as I fought to draw the air into my lungs. I knew I would have to stop struggling if I was to keep breathing and so although I glared daggers at him, I stopped grunting and wriggling.

His lip curled in contempt. 'That is better. Right – onwards, comrades – to the forest!'

He set off again at a fast pace but as we began to climb more steadily on a drover's track, I found it easier to stay in the saddle. And now I knew where we were headed – to Hamsterley Forest on the northern side of the dale. I also knew that if we got there the chances of my being rescued were minimal. It was ancient forest, deep and impenetrable. Even if a hue and cry were raised, it would be hours before the blood-hounds found my trail and beyond the forest the terrain was full of hidden ravines which I did not doubt that the reivers would know intimately. By using them as cover they could hustle me over the River Tyne and beyond Hadrian's Wall before a search party got near. I tried to look back for any sign of help but very nearly fell off in the attempt and gave up in favour of staying on my horse.

'Looking for a knight in shining armour, lady?' lisped the reiver leading my mare. Under the brim of his ancient kettle helmet were bloodshot eyes, a wrinkled brown face, and a tooth-less grin. He looked about seventy, but with only rough sackcloth for a saddle he stuck to his steed like a limpet. 'There's none of their like around here,' he went on. 'But dinnae worry, all we want is a good price for your horse and a queen's ransom for you. And mebbe you might dance for us a bit, eh? He-he!' He found this notion so amusing that he made himself cough and splutter.

That use of the word 'dance' had a sinister ring to it and I wanted to smack the grin off his face, but all I could do was stick out my chin and fix my eyes on my mare's forelock, willing her to avoid all hazards, since I could not steer her.

Another loud stream of oaths from the leader silenced the bearded man's mirth but they were not aimed at him. On the crest of the hill, our path was crossed by a drove-road that ran from west to east, and that very knight-errant I had been mocked for seeking was approaching the junction, closely followed by a dozen men-at-arms. I could not believe my eyes. The chances of meeting a fully armoured knight and his retinue on a drover's path in any season were almost nil, yet there he was. As soon as he sighted the reivers he drew his sword, obviously as surprised to see them as they were to see him.

The green man did not hesitate. He knew when the odds were stacked against him. 'Run for it, lads,' he yelled, clapping his heels to his pony's sides. 'Every man for himself. Dump the loot.'

In different circumstances I might have been offended by being described as 'loot' but at that moment there was pandemonium as my captors galloped away in all directions and my mare plunged off the path into the maze of rocks, lose scree and whin that formed the terrain of this high fell country. Horses are herd animals and naturally follow their leader but which other horse to follow my mare did not know and I could not help her, being gagged and tied, so she skidded and skittered and plunged and it was only a matter of time before she lost her footing and fell, tossing me off into the middle of a patch of gorse, which luckily broke my fall.

Having all the air knocked out of your lungs when wearing a gag creates a desperate situation. For several long minutes I wheezed and coughed and feared I might lose consciousness but eventually I managed to force enough air into my deflated lungs to pay attention to my plight. All around me I could hear the cursing of men and the clatter of stones as even the reivers' agile dale-trotters tripped and slithered over the treacherous ground. My own mare lay a few yards off, hooves thrashing as she writhed and twisted, trying to get to her feet. When she finally managed it she stood on three legs, her sides heaving. There was no doubt she was lame; perhaps her leg was broken. Even if I could have caught her she was no longer rideable and, anyway, I doubted if I could mount without the use of my hands.

I set about trying to extract myself from the gorse but my

skirts had become entangled and sharp prickles pierced my clothes and scratched me painfully. When I stopped struggling to take a rest I noticed that the sound of the chase had diminished and the cries of birds were once more audible in the air. A few loose stones rattled close by and I felt a presence looming over me. Tipping my head back I found myself staring up at a richly trapped horse with a knight in armour on its back. Clearly the fighting was over because he had removed his helmet. Thick, neatly cut flaxen hair framed a suntanned face distinguished by a high brow, a straight nose and a pair of piercing grey eyes. He bowed politely from his saddle.

From my prone position almost anyone would have looked imposing but when he dismounted, making little of the encumbrance of steel-plate, I saw that he was tall and broad-shouldered, the belt on his jupon lying low on slim hips; but my attention was caught by the jupon itself: blood-red and cross-slashed by a white saltire cross, at its centre a black bull's head. The X cross and the black bull were devices I knew. I did not recognize his face but this could only be a Neville knight.

Incongruously, he bowed. 'God save you, my lady, are you hurt?'

My temper flared. Manners were one thing, I thought, but was he blind? Could he not see that I was gagged and tied? He must have seen the anger blaze in my eyes for he quickly bent and untied the filthy kerchief, pulling it from my mouth and gazing at it with distaste before throwing it away into the gorse. 'That does not look pleasant,' he said and beckoned to someone beyond my eye-line. 'Bring a wine-skin, Tam,' he ordered. 'Lady Cicely needs a drink.'

My eyes widened. So he knew who I was, even though I wore no distinguishing badge. My heart missed a beat as he drew his dagger but he hastened to reassure me. 'I will not harm you. It is to cut your bonds.'

With relief I felt my wrists fall apart and I was at last able to haul my skirt off the clutching bushes and clamber to my feet. I noticed several rips in my clothing where the gorse had done its damage but worse was the taste in my mouth, as if my tongue had been dragged through a midden. I stood gasping at clean air like a stranded fish and rubbing my chafed wrists.

Being taller than average I could meet Sir John's enquiring gaze straight on. 'I cannot thank you enough for your intervention, sir,' I said, embarrassed that my voice emerged in a frog-like croak. I cleared my throat. 'I was out hawking with my brothers and fleeing from one pack of reivers when another gang ambushed me. Did you catch any of them or see any of my hunting party?'

The knight ignored my questions. 'Was it you or the horse they were after?'

I drew myself up. 'One of them boasted that they would get a good price for the horse and a queen's ransom for me.'

He raised an eyebrow. 'Is that so? I heard you were soon to be a duchess but is not "queen" aiming a little too high?'

For a stranger he was far too knowledgeable. I was about to demand his name when the young squire Tam appeared at my side offering a wine-skin and suddenly the evil taste in my mouth was of vastly more importance. Murmuring thanks I sucked at it greedily, swilled the wine around my mouth and, abandoning good manners, turned away to spit it into the gorse.

The knight indicated my injured horse standing nearby, three-legged, her head drooping. 'I believe you would hold your price, Lady Cicely, but I fear the same cannot be said of your mare.'

This was the second time he had used my name and title

and I was becoming irritated. 'You have the advantage of me. You seem to know who I am but I do not know you.'

His smile transformed him from merely good-looking to strikingly handsome. A complete set of even white teeth was seldom to be seen in a fighting man, which he so obviously was. 'But you know I am a Neville from my jupon,' he said, placing his hand over the black bull on his chest. 'Sir John Neville of Brancepeth, brother to the Earl of Westmorland.'

'Ah.'

It was a shamefully inadequate response but the revelation had given me a severe jolt. I had not shared the conversation in my mother's solar for the past three years without hearing a great deal about the present Earl of Westmorland *et al.* Far from being rescued by a knight in shining armour, I may have escaped from the cauldron only to fall into the fire.

2

Weardale and Brancepeth Castle

Cicely

'Y̶ou appear disconcerted, Lady Cicely,' said Sir John.

I made no response, merely staring at him, my mind filling with random memories and snippets of information. The Nevilles were an extremely large family and I was woefully ignorant of the undercurrents that steered the relationships within it.

'As I see it, we have only one problem,' Sir John went on, ignoring my bewilderment and addressing the immediate practicalities, 'your horse cannot be ridden and my destrier is the only one strong enough to carry two people. So I hope you will accept a lift from me, unless of course you prefer to walk.'

I looked around. The knight's retinue had been moderately successful; none appeared injured and two of my recent abductors now stood with their hands bound, the ropes tied to the panniers on either side of the sumpter horse which carried the knight's baggage. One of them was the wizened man but I could not see the face of the other, nor could I see their ponies. Wherever the two captives were being taken, they were clearly going on foot. I had no intention of doing the same.

'The last time I rode on the pommel of a knight's saddle it was in front of my father,' I said, 'when I was seven.'

Sir John turned to the young man who had brought the wineskin. 'Tam, get my bedroll and tie it over the front of my saddle. For the comfort of Lady Cicely.'

I had lost my hat in the fall and my unruly hair was loose, tumbling down my back and no doubt tangled with spikes of gorse. In my torn skirts and mud-stained riding huke, with my wild mass of auburn hair, I was conscious of looking more like a camp follower than a future duchess. I remarked pointedly, 'If someone could find my hat in the gorse, it would prevent my hair blowing in Sir John's face while we ride.'

As I had hoped, Tam glanced up from his task. 'I will find it for you, my lady,' he said with a shy smile. He did not wear a knight's spurs and I guessed he was no more than twenty.

I smiled back and thanked him but Sir John frowned. 'Make it quick, Tam. We must be going.'

This prompted me to ask the question uppermost in my mind. 'And where *are* we going, Sir John?'

'To Brancepeth of course,' he replied tersely.

Brancepeth was Lord Westmorland's castle, some twenty miles distant, on the road to Durham. It was not the answer I wanted to hear. 'Surely Raby is more or less on the way?' I pointed out.

He shook his head. 'It is a detour and I must get to Brancepeth before nightfall. I will send a message with one of my men to let your mother know where you are.'

I forced a smile. 'Thank you, Sir John. My mother will be relieved. I hope the present Countess of Westmorland will not object to accommodating a guest from Raby.'

Ignoring my remark he turned impatiently to inspect the squire's efforts with the bedroll. 'That will do, Tam. Now fetch

Lady Cicely's hat and let us be on our way. We will leave her injured horse here. Without doubt there will be a search party and they will find the mare.'

When Tam stirruped his hands to help me mount the destrier, Sir John looked surprised to see me settle myself astride the padded pommel, arranging my skirts modestly on either side of the horse's withers. However he made no comment and swung himself quickly up behind me. The rest of his retinue fell into line, Tam leading the sumpter with the two prisoners attached. Since we could only progress at their walking pace I had to concur with my companion's assertion that we would hardly reach Brancepeth castle by dusk.

In addition to the discomfort of riding on the pommel, I felt ill at ease at being thrown so close to this undeniably attractive man. Not since my father's enthusiastic embraces during my childhood had I ever been physically so close to any male, even my brothers. It was impossible to avoid contact with him and I confess that I found it disturbingly exciting. Sir John remained silent behind me and, clinging to the mane of his big bay stallion as it sidled and pecked at the unaccustomed weight, I distracted myself by mentally analysing my situation. Brancepeth Castle was the seat of Ralph Neville, second Earl of Westmorland, and it should follow that I would be kindly treated there and returned as soon as possible to my home at Raby. But recent family history told me that this was far from certain.

At first sight the dispute between the Nevilles of Raby and the Nevilles of Brancepeth appeared to arise directly from my father's death, but what was actually at the root of the family feud was my parents' marriage. For both it had been a second marriage. My father had already sired seven children, and his first wife died giving birth to the eighth. I do not know what caused the death of my mother's first husband, only that she was a widow at eighteen with two young daughters. And so there were already several infants in the nursery at Raby even before she and my father added another eleven children – theirs was undoubtedly a passionate love match. It would have been thirteen if twin boys had not sadly died within hours of their birth and almost taken our mother with them. I was the youngest of the family and I knew that the man whose saddle I now shared was my father's grandson. The fact that I had never met him before was some indication of the distance of our relationship, even though as blood kin we should have had a close affinity. Paradoxically and through no fault of our own, we did not.

Although he had been dead for seven years, I still thought of my father as a giant among men, in every sense of the word. He had, indeed, been extremely tall – a head taller than most of his fellow noblemen, a physical feature I had inherited, being as tall as most men and towering over many. He had also been considered clever, charming and ruthless, a skilled soldier and one of the most successful military and political tacticians of his generation. However, when it came to writing his will his tactics had been, let us say, questionable. The Westmorland title had perforce to follow the senior male line but, controversially, he left most of his property to his second wife, my mother. Therefore while Sir John's older brother Ralph, the second Earl of Westmorland, held and resided at Brancepeth Castle, my mother held the three other Neville palaces, Raby and two vast castles in Yorkshire, together with all their manors and other sources of revenue. As may be imagined, this arrangement had not gone down well with the Nevilles of Brancepeth, who resented what they called blatant favouritism and frequently found ways to express their resentment and press home their claim to a greater legacy. My fear was that I might be used as a tool to further their cause.

After plodding in silence across high moorland tracks for a couple of hours, passing several well-fortified farms, we dropped down into a dale where a small but sturdy castle stood sentinel over a bridge spanning a fast-flowing river. The crossing was guarded by a posse of men-at-arms, who saluted Sir John. As we rode through, one of them shouted a bawdy comment about the knight's 'saddle-doxy' which Sir John studiously ignored but which had the effect of breaking the tense silence that had developed between us.

'I must apologize for the guards' uncouth manners, my lady,' he said when out of their earshot. 'They do not recognize you or they would not dare.'

'Whose men are they?' I asked. 'And what castle is this?'

'It is Witton Castle, held by Sir Ralph Eure, a tenant of my brother the earl. We have just crossed the River Wear.'

'Only half way to Brancepeth then?' I glanced at the western sky, where clouds were already blushing faintly pink.

I could not see Sir John's face but I felt him tense in the saddle. 'Yes, we make slow progress – too slow for my liking.' He turned to beckon the squire forward. 'Take the reivers to the captain at the Witton guardhouse, Tam. Sir Ralph can keep them in his prison until the session judge comes to Durham. We will water the horses while you sort it out.'

I watched the old reiver, the wizened man who had earlier held the reins of my mare, as he stumbled away behind the sumpter horse. No longer grinning, he now looked weary and desperate. I thought he would be grateful to sit down, even in a stinking dungeon, and very nearly summoned a pang of sympathy, until I remembered his sinister remark about me doing a dance. There was no doubt in my mind that he would have had no sympathy for me had I been subjected to whatever pain or humiliation 'dance' was a euphemism for. At least I had escaped the 'dance', whatever the unknown future I was riding into might have in store.

Presently we joined a well-trodden highway where a milestone indicated seven miles to the city of Durham, and I knew that we were nearing Brancepeth. This was mining country and the high moor above the road to the north was peppered with numerous adits, holes that had been opened into the hillside, and a web of paths leading between them, worn by the feet of miners and the wheels of the carts. They wove a pattern across the winter-brown grass of the slopes down to the river where the coal was brought for transport to the coast. I knew that these mines were an important source of income to the Brancepeth estate; without them the earl would have been even more impoverished than he claimed to be.

Before the end of our journey I became sleepy and, despite my best efforts, must have slumped back against my companion who punctiliously nudged me upright again. 'Take care you do not slumber, my lady, in case you fall from the horse,' he said. 'It is not far now.'

'Talk to me then,' I urged irritably. 'Tell me why you happened to be riding that drover's track when you rescued me from the reivers.'

I thought he was going to maintain his stubborn silence because there was a lengthy pause before he launched into his reply. 'The young man, Tam, who found your hat, is the Clifford heir and a ward of the earl's. We had been attending a Halmote – a manor court – at Brough Castle and, if you want the truth, we

24

always take the high route over the moors because that way we avoid crossing Raby lands. Surely you must realize that the sight of your home is like a red rag to the Nevilles of Brancepeth.'

Despite the grim tone of his remark I smiled, thinking of the black bull badge on his chest. 'A red rag to a bull; yes, I see.'

'No!' His voice was angry. 'I doubt if you do see, Lady Cicely. My brother is the second Earl of Westmorland – your father's heir. Yet he has been deprived of the heir's rightful inheritance. He should have tenure of the entire legacy of Westmorland – all its lands and all its castles. *All* of them – and the income they provide. And it should be up to him as their lord how those lands and castles are occupied and stewarded. Instead he was left only one seat – Brancepeth – and not even enough manors to provide his immediate family with homes and livelihoods. He and his dependents have been slighted and disinherited by your overweening, greedy mother.'

Now it was my turn to be angry. True, my mother was proud and sometimes haughty but she was a great lady of royal blood, a granddaughter of King Edward the Third, and I could not brook her being held in contempt. 'My mother has served the honour of Westmorland more profitably than any of the present earl's family and it is hardly chivalrous to speak thus of a great lady, Sir John.' I laid particular stress on the 'sir'.

'Which is why it is better if we do not speak at all,' the knight snapped back.

After this a heavy silence prevailed once more until we came within sight of our destination. I knew the history of Brancepeth from my childhood lessons. An advantageous union three hundred years ago had brought the manor and its castle into the Neville family when Geoffrey de Neville, grandson of William of Normandy's Admiral of the Fleet, had married

Emma, the heiress of Bertram Bulmer of Brancepeth. Heraldic wordplay on the Bulmer name had brought the black bull device into the Neville crest. It was an alliance which had marked the start of Neville dominance over the sprawling County Palatine of Durham. Many times had the warlike Prince Bishops of Durham taken up arms to defend the English border against the Scots, but bishops came and went by papal appointment, whereas succeeding generations of Nevilles had dug their roots deep into the denes and dales, establishing themselves among the clutch of great marcher clans on which successive kings of England relied to defend the northern fringes of their realm.

Brancepeth was a four-square fortress; its thirty-foot-high curtain enclosed a hall, chapel and bailey with a sturdy tower at each corner and a formidable gatehouse protected by stout barbicans. Defensively perched on the edge of a steep-sided dene or gorge, through which a fast stream flowed, its ochre-coloured stone was blackened by soot from burning the coal mined on its demesne and it loomed dark and grim in the deepening twilight. We approached through a closed and quiet village, where I could picture the villeins clustered around their hearths, filling their bellies with their evening meal. My own stomach rumbled at the thought. Only a few spluttering torches lit our way under the gatehouse into a flagged courtyard where a flight of steps led to the arched entrance of the great hall. There was a loud rattle of chains as the drawbridge was raised behind us; a sinister sound in the gathering gloom.

Sir John dismounted and helped me to do so, speaking to an eager page who had rushed forward to hold his stirrup. 'Tell the countess there is a guest. Lady Cicely Neville. I will bring her to the hall.'

As the page hurried away up the steps I saw a mop-headed

little boy wriggle from the clutches of his nursemaid and scurry towards us, ducking and weaving through the confusion of horses and men, his little face bright with curiosity.

'You have brought a visitor, Uncle,' he said in a high, sibilant voice. 'Who is she?'

With a frisson of pleasure, despite myself, I saw the knight's transforming smile once more as he greeted the boy with an affectionate cuff on the shoulder and a mild rebuke. 'Where are your manners, Jack? Make your best bow to your kinswoman Lady Cicely Neville, and then you may take my helmet to the armoury.'

Pink-faced, the boy bent his knee and bowed his head to me, shyly keeping his eyes lowered. I guessed he must be the heir of Westmorland, whose birth I remembered being discussed with some surprise at Raby – surprise because it demonstrated that the earl, commonly described as a cripple, was not entirely disabled. The little boy proudly took the proffered helmet and carried it away, staggering slightly under its weight, and Sir John and I both watched his progress. He was closely followed by Tam Clifford leading the laden sumpter and the knight's weary warhorse to the stable, a long timber structure built against the high perimeter wall.

All around us was clatter and chatter as the retinue dismounted and began leading their horses away. Reverting once more to cool courtesy, Sir John indicated the narrow stone staircase which hugged the hall wall. A pair of helmeted halberdiers guarded the iron-bound oak doors that stood open at the top. 'Will you enter, my lady?'

His stern expression deterred any thought of refusal but as I ascended I felt the first stirrings of alarm, wondering what I would find within and when I would ever descend. Sir John's armoured feet rang threateningly close behind me on the stair. We passed through the iron-bound doors into an ante-room, then up a shorter and wider stone stairway, through a carved wooden screen into a long, high-beamed hall warmed by two blazing fires, one on the dais at the far end and another under a carved hood in the body of the hall. As we entered, a lady dressed in a crimson fur-trimmed gown and a cream linen wimple emerged from a privy door onto the dais. A deep frown creased her brow and her thin mouth was set in a downward curve. She made no move to greet us.

Apart from a servant tending the fires the three of us were alone in the large room. If a meal had already been served there was no sign of it and the trestles had been cleared. Two cushioned chairs were set near each hearth and various wooden coffers and benches lined the walls, which were hung with dusty tapestries depicting aspects of the chase. Fading light seeped through high-set shuttered windows and guttering torches filled the room with sinister shadows. My anxious gaze met no reassurance.

His hand firmly on my elbow, Sir John drew me towards the dais and the frowning lady, who glared down at me. 'Lady Cicely, may I present my sister-in-law, Lady Elizabeth, Countess of Westmorland.' While I made an equal's curtsy he turned to her. 'This is Lady Cicely Neville of Raby, sister. She was the unfortunate victim of reivers who attacked her hawking party out on the moor. I was obliged to come to her aid.'

Lady Elizabeth voiced none of the customary words of greeting. 'But were you obliged to bring her here, Sir John?' she asked, blue eyes frosty in the tight frame of her wimple. 'She is hardly welcome.'

Stung by this insult I protested. 'Believe me, Lady Westmorland, I would have been more than happy to return immediately to

Raby but this gallant knight insisted we come first to Brancepeth.' My use of the term 'gallant knight' was laced with irony.

'I am astonished to learn that your mother allowed you to venture on to the moors at all.' Lady Elizabeth's tone was as sharp as my own. 'I should have thought the dowager countess would be more protective of her precious duchess-to-be.'

I freely admit that I am quick-tempered and I showed it then. 'You seem determined to offer me nothing but scorn, my lady, but at least I am here to defend myself. I consider it churlish to slight my mother when she is not.'

The countess seemed to gather herself up, like a goaded cat, her whole body shaking with repressed rage. 'Churlish! It is she who is churlish in the extreme and remains so while she holds lands and castles that are my lord's by right. There is no welcome for one of Joan Beaufort's children under this roof while she lives under a roof that is legally his and withholds from him lands and revenues that should be his also.'

She swept down from the dais and stalked past me to the great hearth with the carved hood where she seated herself in one of the two chairs placed there. I started to follow, fulminating. I was only vaguely familiar with the terms of my father's will but I did know that commissions of inquiry in both London and Durham had confirmed its legacies and settled its terms.

I turned angrily on Sir John. 'Since I am declared unwelcome I should be given the courtesy of a horse and an escort and allowed to leave. Or am I, in fact, a hostage, sir?'

The knight denied me eye contact and shrugged. A squire had entered the hall and began removing Sir John's armour, kneeling to unbuckle the greaves from his shins. 'I have sent word to Raby that you are here,' Sir John said. 'We must wait and see how your family construes the situation.'

'I imagine their "construing" will depend on the content of the message you have sent,' I retorted.

As the corselet was lifted from his shoulders a faint smile flickered across the knight's face and was gone. 'Indeed it will, Lady Cicely. To be precise then, I have told the dowager countess that you are free to leave as soon as we hear that the castles of Middleham and Sherriff Hutton have been handed over to my brother's agents.'

These words fell between us with the impact of a cannon shot. Middleham and Sherriff Hutton were the two vast Neville estates in Yorkshire, the original foundation of the family's assets. Lady Westmorland gave a little crow of delight; her hand flew to her mouth and her eyes began to glitter with gleeful excitement.

I exploded with fury. 'So this is your idea of chivalry, Sir John! This is how you help a lady in distress? I think your fellow knights would call it dishonorable extortion.'

He met my anger impassively, his expression veiled. 'We shall see,' he said coolly. 'Some might say that extortion has been practiced on me and mine, rather than *by* me.'

I fell silent, still hostile but bereft of words. By now the industrious squire had removed all elements of the knight's armour and gathered them up for removal and cleaning. Sir John stood in his doublet and hose but made no less an imposing figure, tall and lean with well-muscled shoulders and the powerful thighs of a man who could control a war stallion through day-long combat. He also had the air of one embarking on a venture with some relish, anticipating the challenge ahead. The squire returned with soft leather shoes and a blue, fur-lined gown which he proceeded to help Sir John put on.

Eventually I broke in with a request. 'Perhaps the next time you send anyone to Raby they would inquire after my bodyguard.

When last I saw him he was tackling a band of cut-throat reivers single-handed. I would be grateful to hear how he fared.'

Lady Westmorland's response to this cut the air like a knife. 'You show great concern for a servant, Lady Cicely. I wonder what my cousin would think.'

At first I did not follow her train of thought. 'Your cousin? Oh, do you mean the Duke of York?'

The countess nodded. 'Yes, your betrothed. Perhaps you did not know that I am Hotspur's daughter and my mother was a Mortimer, like his. I wonder how happy his grace would be to hear you so excessively concerned for your bodyguard.'

I resented her implication. 'Of course I am concerned!' I cried. 'It is my brother Cuthbert I speak of. I suppose I may show concern for a brother without offending against any code of conduct?'

Lady Westmorland's lip curled. 'Ah – the late earl's unfortunate by-blow.'

'Unfortunate!' I echoed, incensed. 'I am sure that even Sir John would allow that, illegitimate or not, Sir Cuthbert of Middleham is one of the finest knights on the Western March.'

I swung round to seek the knight's endorsement but my use of Cuddy's full name had touched a raw nerve in the countess. 'Marie! Not just a by-blow but a *Middleham* by-blow. He certainly spread himself far and wide, your father.'

'Enough!' Sir John's face had darkened; his grey eyes were narrow beneath knitted brows. 'Let us speak no more of such things. Is there no refreshment for returning travellers, my lady? I am starving!'

The countess rose from her chair, her expression sulky, but she snapped her fingers at the servant who had been stoking the fires. 'Go, boy! Fetch food and wine for Sir John.'

'And for Lady Cicely,' added her brother-in-law as an after-thought. 'She will also need a bed somewhere safe, sister. I am sure that can be arranged.'

He had fixed the countess with a steely gaze and she held it for several seconds as if tempted to deny him but then nodded briefly and made for the exit to attend to his request. I wondered why she had no lower-ranked female companion to whom she could delegate such a task but supposed that none could stomach her sour disposition. Certainly I had no desire to be beholden to such an unpleasant hostess but although my stomach was rumbling with hunger I needed other bodily relief more urgently. As she passed by me I adopted a placatory tone.

'Lady Westmorland, I have been riding since morning and would be grateful for the use of a guarderobe.'

I have an audible voice, low and clear, but to my consternation the countess made no acknowledgement and disappeared under the screen arch in a swirl of skirts. I felt my cheeks burn.

Sir John gave an apologetic cough. 'My sister-in-law cannot have heard you. I will summon a female servant to show you the way,' he said. 'There will be refreshments when you return.'

Of necessity there is always a guarderobe or latrine off every great hall but I was not shown to one so close by. Perhaps being mainly for the use of visiting knights and their retinues it was not considered suitable for ladies. Instead a hatchet-faced serving wench led me two flights up a spiral stair built into the thickness of the wall, which ended in a small tower chamber bare of furniture but with a small guarderobe leading off it. Although I was used to an upholstered seat rather than cold wood, at least I could not complain about the latrine's cleanliness. After making use of it I spent a few minutes attempting to remove the gorse twigs and prickles still stubbornly attached to my clothes and hair, observed with dumb curiosity by the servant, who made no attempt to help.

On my return to the hall I encountered an influx of young men, all seating themselves noisily at a newly erected and cloth-covered trestle-table. Among them I recognized Tam and the squire who had removed Sir John's armour. Two pages stood by with bowls and napkins for hand-washing. There was no sign of Lady Westmorland but Sir John had been joined at the dais fire by a thin, pale-faced individual well wrapped in fur-lined robes and seated in a curiously constructed chair equipped with a foot-rest and slots for carrying-poles. I approached them hesitantly, unsure of my welcome.

'Ah, here is our visitor,' said Sir John, catching sight of me and beckoning me onto the dais. 'Lady Cicely, allow me to present my brother Ralph, Earl of Westmorland.'

'My lord of Westmorland.' I made the required acknowledgement with little enthusiasm in either voice or curtsy.

'Well, there is no disputing your Neville breeding, my lady,' responded the earl, showing more amiability than his wife. 'You are nearly as tall as John here.'

'She is Lady Joan's youngest,' remarked Sir John.

His brother glanced at him sharply. 'The Beaufort's youngest?' he repeated. 'I thought that one had married the Duke of York.' He made a seated bow in my direction. 'You must forgive me for not rising, your grace. I am unable to trust my legs.'

'She is not "your grace" yet, brother. That is a betrothal ring on her finger, not a wedding band.'

I glanced down at my right hand, where the big polished cabochon diamond glinted even in the gloom of the ill-lit hall. 'I am not yet married, my lord, no. But I am surprised to hear

Sir John call me a visitor. I believe hostage would be a more accurate term.'

'Hostage?' Lord Westmorland looked up at his brother, one eyebrow raised. 'What does she mean, John?'

The knight shrugged. 'I have sent word to her mother that she will be returned to Raby only when Middleham and Sherriff Hutton are yours.'

His brother held his gaze for several seconds, blinking slowly, before bursting into delighted laughter. 'Ha! She is right, she is a hostage. I do not know how you came by her, John, but you have clearly made good use of your windfall. You are the pillar of my house, brother, indeed you are.'

This was too much for me. I cut through his offensive laughter with a voice like flint. 'I would have expected honourable treatment from a man of nobility, my lord! But clearly I am mistaken.'

The earl reduced his mirth to a smile. 'I see no dishonour in demanding ransom for a noble prisoner, Lady Cicely, and you are certainly that. Daughter of an earl, betrothed to a duke – and what do they call you in these parts? The "Rose of Raby", do they not? Your mother's favourite child. Oh yes, the dowager will give much to see you back safely under her wing. I believe I can look forward to taking possession of my rightful inheritance very soon.'

This mocking speech had brought me close to tears but I forced them back. I knew enough about the senior branch of the Nevilles to appreciate that life had not been kind to them. The stories of the present earl's childhood accident – a fall from a horse which had weakened his back and gradually robbed him of the use of his legs – and the unfortunate death of both his parents within a year of each other were well known in the north-country, as was the vast discrepancy between the grand-paternal legacies to him and those to my mother. Also, not only had my father left the bulk of his estates to our side of the family, while enjoying a flush of royal favour in his later years he had secured marriages and titles of much higher rank for his second family than his first and the best match of all had been won for me. Richard, Duke of York was the richest nobleman in England and, having reached his majority in September of the previous year, had spent the intervening months establishing his claim not only to the York estates but also to those of his cousin Edmund, Earl of March, his mother's brother, who had died without issue at about the same time as my father. Ever since I had known him, Richard had been looking forward with a fervent appetite to petitioning parliament for his vast inheritance and, if I am honest, I shared his eagerness, having desires and ambitions of my own. In that respect I was my father's daughter and he had made a perfect match, for Richard of York was no prouder or more ambitious than Cicely Neville.

What the Brancepeth branch of the family did not know – at least I certainly hoped they did not – was that the day was fast approaching when Richard of York would come to Raby to claim me as his bride and it would be unfortunate to say the least if, when he arrived, I was not there to marry him. I could imagine the heated debate that would take place between my mother and those of my brothers who were available; the urgent necessity of my return balanced against their united determination not to cede one stone or acre of their inheritance to the other side of the family. I would doubtless have found it funny if the situation did not make me feel like a scrap of meat being fought over by snarling dogs.

3

Raby Castle

Cuthbert

My half-brother Hal paced the floor of Countess Joan's salon, his face displaying anger and fatigue in equal measure. He had ridden through the night from his castle at Penrith to attend this family summit meeting, gathered twenty-four hours after Cicely had vanished off the moor and twelve since the ransom note had been received from Brancepeth.

'You have indulged the girl too much, my lady mother, and this is the result.'

Only Hal dared to address the majestic Dowager Countess of Westmorland in such an admonitory tone. Her eldest son, the first of the thirteen children she had borne to the late earl, he was the only one to whom she deferred because he had inherited our father's air of authority, though not his devastating charm or extreme height. Richard Neville, Earl of Salisbury, was known in the family as Hal for reasons that went back to the establishment of the Lancastrian dynasty at the turn of the century. Having been baptized in honour of King Richard the Second, who had granted my father both the earldom of Westmorland and the marriage to his cousin, Joan Beaufort, the name became an embarrassment when Henry of Lancaster forced King Richard to abdicate in his favour – and so the baby Richard Neville quickly became known as Henry instead, or Hal for short. However, by the time he came of age, the name Richard was no longer out of favour and he used it officially, but within the family Hal had stuck.

Nicknames seemed to haunt Hal though. At court, where he served on the king's council, I had heard him called Prudence behind his back, because of his strategic and cautious approach to everything. It was my guess that had Hal been at Raby, Cicely would never have been allowed out on the moor to hunt so close to the date of her wedding.

Now his attitude was starkly pragmatic. 'If Richard of York hears of this he will repudiate the marriage and then Cicely might as well go straight to the nearest convent. She will be damaged goods.'

Seated in her gilded chair beneath a baronial canopy embroidered with the Beaufort portcullis crest, the dowager countess looked weary and distracted, but she retained her composure in the face of her son's anger. 'None of our retainers will dare to breathe a word of it, even if they become aware of Cicely's precarious situation,' she said. 'York will never learn of it as long as we can get her back before his harbingers arrive and that cannot be for two more days at least. What is your plan to gain her release, Hal?'

Her son gave an exasperated sigh and let his gaze sweep the assembled company. 'You let her leave the castle, mother, and Will and Ned let her ride into the arms of reivers. None of you seems to have covered yourself in glory over the matter and now you call me in and expect me to wave a magic wand and sort out the mess. Well, it will not be that easy.'

I suppose I should have been grateful that I was excluded from his list of blame but I knew that did not exempt me from responsibility; rather it indicated that Hal did not recognize my right to be in the room, for Lord Salisbury was a stickler for rank and protocol. I was baseborn and in his eyes a bastard could never be considered of rank, even one who had been accepted into his family household as a child, was reared with his brothers, and had earned the accolade of knighthood during a campaign on the Western March toward Scotland, of which he was Lord Warden. Although we were brothers, Hal Neville and I were not exactly friends.

Anyway I did not escape entirely.

'It was Cuthbert who told her to ride for Raby.' This helpful remark came from Ned, the brother closest to Cicely in age and another whom I did not count among my supporters. 'Otherwise she would not have become separated from the rest of us.'

'Cuddy was obeying orders,' Will Neville cut in, the only one of my brothers who used Cicely's nickname for me, a man on whom I could always rely to take my part. 'Do not try and blame him for our mistakes. The reivers should never have got so near us. We should have kept scouts out all the time, not called them in when the hunting started.'

'Dogs cannot flush out birds while scouts are tramping all over the moor,' protested Ned. 'There would be nothing there to hunt.'

'Oh stop bickering!' cried the countess, fixing Ned with pale-blue eyes narrowed and glittering with unshed tears. 'The whole world knows that Cuthbert would die for Cicely. He is as distressed as any of us by her perilous position. Nor can we lay all the blame on Sir John Neville because it was he who rescued Cicely from the reivers. Had he not, her fate might have been even worse. No – if we are fixing blame we need look no further than the man who unfortunately bears the title your father worked so hard to achieve.'

Countess Joan used an exquisite lace kerchief to dab her cheek where a single tear had escaped her control.

'You are right *sans doubte, Madame ma mère.*'

Young Ned had pretentions of grandeur and often used outdated Anglo-French phrases in order to stress the ancient Neville connection with the conquering Normans who had subdued England four hundred years ago. The rest of us were content to use English, the only language commonly understood and spoken by everyone in the north.

'The devil twists a body which contains a twisted mind,' Ned persisted. 'We should attack Brancepeth with all force before that son of Beelzebub takes it into his warped mind to send a ransom demand to Richard of York. That would ruin Proud Cis's prospects for certain!' Despite his call for instant military attrition, Ned also sounded positively gleeful at the idea of Cicely being rejected by her wealthy bridegroom.

Will was indignant. 'Neville cross swords with Neville? No! That is a recipe for disaster. Besides, Ned, there is no reason why anyone should have a warped mind simply because his body is not perfect, or vice versa. My Jane may be feeble-brained, but she is the most kind and loving of females.'

Will's wife was Jane Fauconberg who, when she married him at sixteen, had literally been a childlike bride with the mind of a girl of six. Nevertheless she had brought him, an otherwise impecunious and untitled younger son, the extensive Barony of Fauconberg. Those who objected that the marriage was distastefully mercenary and wholly against nature were confounded by the affection and care Will displayed towards his spouse and her clear love for him. Love had been rewarded, and their marriage was confirmed as legal and consummated when she recently became pregnant with their first child at the start of the year. Needless to say, Will was hoping for a healthy boy to inherit the barony, having already proved his own ability to father sons by siring two with his resident mistress.

Ned was scornful. 'You are as soft in the head as your wife, Will,' he sneered. 'Anyway, I say attack is the only option – preferably today.'

I waited to see which way Hal would jump. Surprisingly, for a man of the sword, he sided with Will and his mother. 'I do not agree,' he said firmly, turning his back on Ned's angry glare. 'We do not have to fear for Cicely's honour or her safety. Westmorland and his brothers may be thorns in our side but they are not the monsters you paint them. It is our sister's reputation we must protect. Richard of York will be keenly aware, as I am, that a young girl who has not been permanently under the protection of her mother or some other responsible female can be considered damaged goods. If he perceives Cicely's abduction as a way to free himself from his obligation to marry her, the king's council would support him because they are looking to strengthen England's crucial alliance with Burgundy. A marriage between a scion of Burgundy and an English royal duke would re-point its masonry.'

He moved nearer to the countess's canopied chair and knelt down before her in the guise of an earnest appellant. 'We cannot allow that to happen, my lady mother. Although I know you remain sensitive in the matter, I think we should appeal to Eleanor to intervene. She must surely have considerable influence with Lord and Lady Westmorland.'

Lady Joan's face set in an icy stare and her knuckles grew

white on the arms of her chair. Strictly speaking, she was no longer required to wear mourning for her late husband but, by payment of a hefty sum to the royal exchequer, she had obtained permission to remain unmarried and she still favoured widow's weeds. In her gleaming black minerva-trimmed gown, relieved only by the high neck of her white linen kirtle and veil, she resembled an affronted abbess about to address an offending novice.

'No, my lord, under no circumstances! Eleanor made her bed with Percy and she must lie in it. I have nothing to say to her.'

Eleanor Neville, the eldest daughter, had eloped at sixteen with one of the Raby henchmen esquires, to be married by a hermit-priest in his cell deep in the Northumbrian borderlands. In a romantic turn of events it transpired that the apparently humble squire was, in fact, Henry Percy, heir to the earldom of Northumberland, who had been living incognito ever since his father and grandfather had forfeited their titles and estates by rebelling against the first Lancastrian king, Henry IV. Young Percy had wooed and won his lady in a fashion which might have thrilled a troubadour but had horrified and offended Lady Joan, who had never forgiven Eleanor, notwithstanding her chosen swain proving to have a status equal to her own. Family pride had induced the countess to intercede with her nephew, the newly crowned King Henry V, to get the young earl reinstated, so that her daughter could at least obtain the rank to which her birth entitled her, but the unforgiving dowager had never again set eyes on her runaway daughter, nor on the seven grand-children Eleanor had provided her with.

Now she reinforced her objection. 'Besides, as I understand it there is little love lost between Lord Northumberland and his sister, the present Lady Westmorland. She too disliked the manner of his marriage. I doubt if they communicate.'

Salisbury rose from his knees and stepped back speechless, merely shrugging his shoulders with a sigh.

'So much for family loyalty,' commented Ned with a grin. He made a sketchy bow in the direction of his mother's chair. 'If that is the best we can do I will take my leave. Cicely had better take her future into her own hands for it is apparent that no one here is going to bend over backwards to help her.' He tossed a withering glance in my direction. 'Least of all her much-vaunted champion, Cuthbert.'

I bit back a retort as the countess rose, indicating that as far as she was concerned the meeting was over. 'At least we can pray. I shall be in the chapel and do not wish to be disturbed unless there is an emergency,' she said, sweeping her dark skirts around her feet and heading towards her privy door, trailing a drifting fragrance of attar of roses in the air and causing an ornate heraldic banner to billow on the wall. The banner quartered the red rose of Lancaster with the Beaufort portcullis and was bordered in blue and white; her own personal standard.

Lady Joan made a small gesture as she passed me, indicating that I should follow her out but before closing the door behind us I heard Ned remark dryly, 'Praying is all she will do. There will be no property concessions, that much is certain.'

The private chapel at Raby was a small gem. Intended only for the use of the Neville family and their distinguished guests, it had been built by the old earl's father, but Ralph Neville himself had commissioned the colourful frescos on the walls which celebrated the family's rise to power. On an azure sea sailed the three-masted ship from which Admiral de Neuville had commanded the fleet which brought Duke William's force from Normandy to invade England; beside that a scene of knights and archers in close combat depicted the famous Battle of Neville's Cross, when the Scottish king had been taken prisoner on the moors outside Durham; and finally there were scenes showing masons working on the soaring walls of Raby castle, confirming the establishment of the Nevilles among the premier barons of England. At the chancel end of the nave stood a beautiful rood screen carved from Ancaster alabaster and adorned with images of local English saints especially revered by the family; St Cuthbert, St Hilda, St Aidan and St Godric.

Lady Joan led me down the nave and paused by the screen. 'You were named for St Cuthbert,' she reminded me, 'but my lord's favoured saint was this one, Godric the crusader.' She laid her hand on a fold of the saint's stone robe. 'A few weeks before your father died he brought me here and, despite his pain, he managed to kneel before this statue, though his wounded leg stuck out like a broken branch. Then he prayed aloud, asking the saint for guidance but I knew he was really consulting me.

'"The surgeons want to cut off my leg," he said. "You fought the devil, Godric. Standing waist high in the waters of the Wear, you battled the Anti-Christ for a day and a night. Tell me, God's stalwart soldier, what must I do to combat Satan's demons that fester in my leg?"'

The countess turned away from the screen and addressed me directly. 'Ralph did not have the strength to continue and I finished the prayer for him. I begged St Godric to allow my lord to remain a true knight, proud and upright and to carry his sword in Christ's name. Not to let him stand before God a cripple.'

'Oh, my lady,' I croaked, shocked to hear that word applied to the father I revered. 'What did my father say?'

'He understood. He smiled at me through his pain and said, "So be it. I am sixty-two. I have lived my life. I will go to the Creator as He made me, with every limb intact. It shall be as it shall be. May St Godric give me the strength to bear it."'

I stared at her, bewildered. 'You believe that cripples are the devil's acolytes? That the present Lord Westmorland is a disciple of Satan?' I asked.

'Yes. But I believe he can be confounded by a miracle. There was no miracle for my lord Ralph but I will pray for one for Cicely.'

With that Lady Joan went to kneel down at the plush prie Dieu which had been specially placed for her in the chancel beneath an image of Our Lady. I hesitated, wondering why she had required my presence but all became clear when she began to pray aloud. 'Holy Marie, Mother of God, be with my daughter Cicely in her hours of trial. Show her the way to escape her captors and let there be a strong hand to help her when your miracle has been fulfilled.'

I understood now. Lady Joan did not make specific requests of her vassals because she did not want to be disappointed if they failed to fulfil her wishes, but if they could be made to know those wishes indirectly then neither she nor they could lose face in the event of a failure. I was being given clear instructions to make it my business to act as spy and support for Cicely in any way I could, without involving the others. In other words, I was to perform the task that Lady Joan herself would have done, were she young and a man.

As her prayers dropped to a low murmur, I bowed to her apparently oblivious back and walked out of the chapel as quietly as my hard leather soles would allow. I never wore the soft-soled shoes affected by my brothers in their domestic life. It was part of my vow as a knight-champion that I remained constantly ready for action. To that end I carried a hidden blade, even when carrying arms was not permitted. All I had to do to begin my appointed task was collect my saddle-bags, my short sword, my helmet and my habergeon, the light body armour that protected throat and breast without hampering silent movement through any terrain; and, of course, my horse. I would wear no symbol of affinity but cease being a Neville knight and become an anonymous mercenary soldier of fortune; one that could mix with others of like kind.

However, before any of that I had to seek out one other person. I found her in the inner garth, a small and private walled pleasure garden. It afforded fresh air but there was little grass evident because the sun barely penetrated the high walls of Raby's inner court, and so it was laid out with gravel paths, small evergreen bushes and painted wooden posts carved into heraldic beasts. At the far end was a sandy square reserved for bowling, where a girl in a green kirtle and a pretty lace-trimmed coif was throwing a stick for a little brown and white terrier.

Hilda Copley was the daughter of a local knight, who had arrived at Raby five years before to be a companion for Lady Cicely. The two girls had shared lessons, leisure activities and even a bed ever since, and I knew how anxious Hilda would be about Cicely's continued absence. Besides, having taught both of them horsemanship and the rudiments of archery and self-defence, I was as close to Hilda as I was to Cicely, except that I was not Hilda's half-brother and to me that was a very important difference.

When she saw me at the garth gate she abandoned the dog

to his stick and ran towards me, skirts flying, a sight I greeted with a wide, appreciative smile.

'What are you smiling about, Cuddy?' she demanded excitedly. 'Has Cicely returned?'

'No, I fear not,' I admitted. 'Lady Joan wants me to spy out the situation in Brancepeth so I am about to leave.'

Hilda's dark brows knitted in vexation. Usually I loved it when her pretty face creased in a frown and her brown eyes glinted in challenge but on this occasion I knew she was about to dispute my unquestioning obedience to Lady Joan – not a subject I was prepared to debate with her – so I forestalled her protest.

'No one else seems to have any idea how to grapple with the problem so I am more than willing to go on a fishing expedition. At least I can travel unrecognized and ask questions in places where the Nevilles would not go. It might just yield results. God knows, something has to.'

The light of battle died in Hilda's eyes and she became practical. 'Some*one* has to,' she amended, favouring me with faint twitch of the lips, 'and Cicely can always rely on you.' She did not add 'more than the rest of her brothers' but I could hear the unspoken words in her tone of voice.

She whistled sharply and the terrier came running up and dropped his stick at her feet. 'Caspar is pining for his mistress,' she revealed, picking him up and tucking him under her arm. 'I thought a bit of exercise would cheer him up.'

Caspar was Cicely's dog, used to following her everywhere except of course to the hunt, when the big alaunt hounds would probably have eaten him for dinner.

'I expect Cicely is missing him,' I remarked, falling into step beside Hilda as she walked towards the gate. 'Are you going to feed him now?'

'Yes, why?'

'Well, I thought if you were going to beg some scraps from the kitchen for Caspar you might also acquire some supplies to sustain me on my travels.'

I was rewarded with a cuff on the arm. 'So that is why you came to find me. And I thought it was for a sight of my bonny brown eyes.'

'So it was,' I protested, feeling the blood rise in my cheeks. 'And your way with the kitchen staff.'

Hilda stalked off ahead, affecting indignation. The terrier's tail wagged dismissively at me from under her arm. 'Hah! Well, I suppose Caspar *might* spare you a bit of gristle.'

4

Brancepeth

Cuthbert

I took the moorland route to Brancepeth and rode in bright sunshine, my horse trotting easily over grassy sheep tracks. The dry conditions meant I could let my mind wander, considering the reasons for my unquestioning obedience to Lady Joan; the obedience which the spirited Hilda found so hard to comprehend.

Hilda was not illegitimate. She was the true-born daughter of Sir William Copley, late tenant of one of the closest of Raby's many manors. Even as a young child, while her father was still alive, she had often been to Raby, making friends, especially Cicely who was nearest to her in age. I had often encountered her when I was a boy, but by the age of eleven I had begun serious training military training and grown scornful of little girls with their dolls and giggles. Now, of course, it was a different matter.

I do not remember precisely when I began to notice that Hilda had grown from a cheeky little girl into a dark-haired temptress, but it must have been during the summer that I started to teach her and Cicely how to shoot an arrow. I found something intensely appealing about the way Hilda tilted her chin before she hauled back on the bowstring, and when she flexed her arm and pulled I felt a blood-rushing response to the thrust of her budding breasts against the fabric of her bodice. She was thirteen and I was not yet twenty. During the three years since then, my teenage lust had turned into something more controlled, but my heart still missed a beat whenever I caught sight of her.

Since then, too, her father had died and her eldest brother Gerald had inherited the manor of Copley. Young Gerald had been one of my fellow henchmen at Raby, sharing the training, both military and social, that was intended to turn us into fierce and faithful Neville knights. As youths we had been quite good friends until I began to receive more senior and responsible posts than he did, a situation he judged to be due to favouritism. That was when he began to cast snide remarks in my hearing about 'bastard blood' and 'bum-licking by-blow', insults I managed to ignore. But when he got wind of my feelings for his sister his antipathy grew more sinister; there was ample opportunity on the practice ground for knocks and thrusts to result in real wounds inflicted accidentally-on-purpose. I had been much relieved when his inheritance took Gerald back to the manor of Copley, but before he left he made it abundantly clear to me that if any word reached him linking my name to Hilda's, violent retribution would follow. Our paths had not crossed since but I knew that, apart from when he performed his knight's service on the Scottish border, he was never far away.

The stain of bastardy was the glue that bound me to Lady Joan; not that she ever used that word. It was the reason I gave instant and unquestioning service to her. Very soon after my arrival at Raby I had been surprised and perturbed to be summoned to the countess's tower and admitted to her private quarters. In the room she called her salon I was dazzled by the light that streamed through half a dozen diamond-glazed windows and awestruck by the opulence of the furnishings. Until then, I had known only the interior gloom of my family's fortified farm high up in the dale above Middleham Castle, and its rough-hewn table and benches. Lady Joan's sumptuous silk hangings and polished-oak chests and chairs were a revelation to me and I needed no nudging from her chamberlain to fall instantly on my knees before her raised and canopied throne. I was convinced I must be kneeling at the feet of a queen.

'You are welcome to Raby Castle, Cuthbert.' Her soft, aristocratic tones sent nervous shivers down my spine. 'You may be surprised that I have sent for you but we have much in common, you and me. Like you I was baseborn and grew up under the shadow of illegitimacy. I know it is not an easy road to walk. I was lucky. My father eventually married my mother and was powerful enough to have her children legitimized. That will not happen to you and yet you too are lucky because you have impressed your father with your strength and intelligence. He will see to it that you receive the training necessary to join the elite force of Westmorland men-at-arms. But because you are his son he has asked me to ensure that you also receive an education and learn good manners, and so you are to join my sons and daughters at the appropriate lessons. I trust you will take advantage of this opportunity and repay our generosity with true loyalty.'

Under her gracious azure gaze I blushed furiously and mumbled some words of gratitude, turning the new homespun hood which my mother had made for me round and round in anxious fingers. At ten years old I needed no urging to pledge my loyalty to this beautiful, fragrant, splendidly jewelled lady. I wanted to prostrate myself before her and let her trample me under her satin-slippered feet but instead I bowed my head and tugged at the fringe of hair on my forehead. 'Oh yes, my lady, I will,' I said and, true to my word, I had repaid her over and over again and was even now continuing to do so.

At Brancepeth a posse of Raby men-at-arms was now camped in the shelter of a tree belt, well back from any archers' arrows fired from the castle walls. Hal had seen to that at least. As I was wearing no insignia that might be recognized from the battlements, I went to speak to the sergeant in command but I took care to remain in the shadow of the trees. He reported no activity at all that day and, with dusk fast approaching, did not expect any. This puzzled me as Brancepeth was not under siege, but my curiosity was met with a shrug from the sergeant; his instructions were to keep out of arrow-range and log any activity. I took myself off to the village where I hoped to find looser tongues.

In the main street I promised a halfpenny to a loitering lad to mind my horse and he directed me to the alehouse, identifiable by a desiccated evergreen bush hung over its door. It was the usual low-roofed, smoke-filled, mud-floored hell-hole; a meeting place for unmarried local villeins with a farthing to spend, thirsty black-faced colliers from the nearby mines and weary travellers from the west who could not quite make it to Durham before curfew. I hoped it would be assumed that I fitted the last category. There was no room near the fire so I took a seat on a corner bench beside a man wearing the Neville bull on his jacket and signalled the pot-boy to bring me a mug of ale.

'You must be a local resident, sir,' I said politely, indicating my neighbour's livery badge. 'That is the Neville bull, is it not?'

The man's grin revealed only three or four blackened teeth. '*Brancepeth* Neville, sir. The other lot, with their fancy sailing ship, do not show their faces here.'

I affected ignorance of Neville business. 'Oh? Why is that?'

He rubbed his thumb and forefinger together with a knowing look. 'Family feud, sir, over land, coin and castles. Rich men's pickings.'

The pot-boy arrived with my ale in a banded wooden mug and I tossed him a farthing. 'You seem very knowledgeable about the lord's affairs,' I prodded, taking a long gulp of the thin liquid. It was stale but not unpleasant.

He puffed out his chest. 'Well I should know something since I work at the castle.'

With teeth like his I doubted if he worked in the private apartments but I decided flattery would aid my cause. 'You must have a senior position, sir, if you can leave after dusk. When I rode past the drawbridge was up and the portcullis well and truly down.'

The man pressed his finger to the side of his nose. 'There's more than one way in and out of that place,' he confided. 'If you know the guards you can slip out the back. The lord's brothers went that way very early this morning. I was returning from plucking a nice plump hen last night, if you get my meaning, and I saw them leave.'

I tried hard not to show my surprise at this information. 'Off hunting vixen, were they?' I suggested with a smirk.

He pursed up his lips, looking doubtful. 'I reckon not. They had some skirt with them. There's been a mystery woman staying and they fired one of the gatehouse canons at a troop from Raby which arrived this afternoon. Something to do with the family rift it seems. I work in the stables and one of the countess's palfreys was missing from its stall but Lady Westmorland is still in the castle.'

Now the hair rose on the back of my neck. Was it possible that Cicely had been moved from Brancepeth and, if so, where had they taken her? Or had she persuaded her kidnappers to let her go and if so, again, where was she? I downed the rest of my ale hurriedly and stood up, excusing my hasty departure. 'I need to get back to my horse before the lad I left it with realizes it would fetch more than I've promised him. Thanks for your company, my friend.'

'If you need a bed I know a nice clean widow in the village who would share hers with you for half a groat.' A big wink and another gap-toothed grin accompanied this offer.

I shook my head. 'Not tonight, regrettably, I am on a pilgrimage.' I saw his eyes pop with astonishment as I turned away and fought my way through the smoke and bodies to the door. Outside I smiled to myself and breathed the fresh night air with relief. The boy was still holding my horse and scampered off with glee, biting at the half-moon of silver I had given him. My stomach urged me to eat before following up on the information I had just received, so I set off, leading the horse, to seek a place to let him graze while I raided the saddle-bag supplies Hilda had procured for me.

In a far corner of the Brancepeth churchyard, I hobbled my horse and let him loose, then settled down on a gravestone to enjoy a substantial cheese pastry in the light of the rising moon. The church was dark; not even the flicker of a votive candle showed through the leaded windows of its rounded arches. Either they were shuttered or else the priest was gone for the day.

I could hear my horse munching his way around the graves and the occasional clink of his metal shoes as they struck a stone edge. I wondered what Cicely would be doing at that hour and where she would be laying her head. This would be the second night she had spent away from Raby. If she was no longer at Brancepeth would she even have a bed, or might she be confined in some cave up on the moors, or forced to sleep in a forest hut, hidden from prying eyes? If so, she would be uncomfortable and frightened but the worst aspect for her would be thinking that her family had entirely abandoned her. Cicely was not used to being belittled or ignored. Although she hated her brothers calling her Proud Cis, she was fiercely aware of her lineage and expected the deference due to a potential duchess. I wondered how she would have reacted if her 'hosts' had treated her with anger or disrespect. Might her removal from Brancepeth be due to them inflicting some form of retribution or induce-ment? A sense of the urgency of my mission escalated as I contemplated her position. I did not believe that the present earl would allow any physical harm to come to a female who was, after all, his close relative, but revenge could be achieved in many devious ways, particularly through damage to such a valuable young girl's honour and reputation.

I consumed the last morsel of the pastry whilst considering what form that damage might take and disliking the turn my thoughts were taking, when my meditations were interrupted by the increasingly urgent sound of human copulation coming from the deep shadow of one of the church buttresses nearby. Copulation or rape, with a crescendo of climactic grunts coming from the male participant and what I took to be wails of increasing protest from the woman. I was in half a mind to intervene but held myself in check, conscious of my own invidi-ous position. To become involved in any sort of incident in Brancepeth would inevitably destroy my anonymity and put paid to any chance I had of assisting Cicely – and might even lead to my own imprisonment.

Quashing feelings of guilt, I crept off to collect my horse and buckle on my saddlebag, but I had not made sufficient allowance for the woman's distress. Hardly had I removed the hobble and re-bridled the courser when the grunting ceased, but to my dismay the protests of the unfortunate girl redoubled, and she crawled out of her dark corner into the moonlight, tugging her skirt down and screaming at her still-hidden companion.

'You foul beast! You should be whipped. You promised me silver. Just a quick feel you said – then you force yourself up my arse! You are a liar and a pervert.'

By this time the moon had risen above the trees surrounding the churchyard and its soft blue light beamed down on the girl. She might have been pretty, had not her face been twisted into an ugly expression of hatred and anger. She looked no older than Cicely; too young, I thought, to be whoring herself in a churchyard, even for a shilling. I couldn't help feeling compassion for her. Not only had she been cheated out of the promised silver, she had also been abused by a bully and a pederast. Her abuser, however, must have been brazenly confident of getting away with it, even to the extent of using the churchyard for his dirty work, when fornication and particularly buggery were carnal sins which could lead to the consistory court, a whipping and a public penance. Then the man himself stepped out of the shadows and my lip curled. It was my erstwhile bugbear, Hilda's unpleasant and vicious brother, Sir Gerald Copley. I clenched my fists, itching to punch his teeth in, but he had not seen me and I wanted to keep it that way. Neither I nor the horse moved.

Gerald was grinning lecherously while adjusting the codpiece flap of his hose. 'You stupid slut,' he said and aimed a kick at his crouching victim, sending her sprawling. Her screeching redoubled and she scrambled to a gravestone and hauled herself to her feet as he continued to berate her. 'You have the brains of a frog and the backside of a donkey. Why would anyone pay you a shilling to use that spotty arse? And why would any man risk getting a bastard by taking the front door? Bastards are the devil's spawn. They should be strangled at birth.'

Sensibly the girl decided to retreat rather than risk another vicious kick. She gathered up her skirts and lurched off into the darkness, but not before she had aimed a gob of spit at him so large that I could see it glint in the moonlight. Gerald growled angrily and made as if to chase after her but took only a couple of threatening steps before stabbing the two-fingered witch sign at her and letting her go. From the deep shadow of the trees I watched him adjust his doublet over his sullied hose and saunter away between the graves to the churchyard gate. And I made a silent vow that if ever I encountered Gerald Copley in any kind of confrontation, whether on my side or the other, I would sink my dagger in one of his strutting buttocks. It would be in retribution for his remarks about bastards as much as for his callous mistreatment of a defenceless young woman.

5

From Brancepeth to Aycliffe

Cicely

My first night at Brancepeth had been short and sleepless. Seated at one end of Lord Westmorland's high table I had forced myself to eat a little of whatever was offered to me but although I was hungry, I seemed to lose my appetite as soon as food touched my tongue. Rather pointedly I thought, the countess remained absent but the earl had attempted to engage me in conversation. However, as I felt no inclination to indulge him our intercourse had been brief and stilted and afterwards Sir John had escorted me back up to the tower chamber in brooding silence. As we climbed the stair from the bustling hall a sudden sense of loneliness engulfed me. Coming from a large family and a castle that teemed with activity like an ant's nest, the prospect of a night locked away alone terrified me. There had been no response from Raby to Sir John's ultimatum and the feeling of abandonment was overwhelming. All my life I had had someone to fight my battles for me, either my father, my mother or one of my brothers and now I had become convinced that the only way I was going to get back to Raby in time for my wedding was by using my own wits. The graunching scrunch of the key turning in the lock was a chilling reminder that there were daunting physical obstacles to be overcome even before confronting the twenty mile distance between Brancepeth and Raby. Seeing help from no other quarter, I threw myself on my knees beside the mean little cot that Lady Elizabeth had provided for me and began to pray.

The candle I had been left with had begun to gutter and I was steeling myself to contemplate the long darkness of the night when I heard that unnerving scrunch again.

'May I come in, Lady Cicely?' said the now-familiar voice of my knightly abductor. 'I would speak with you.'

I rose hastily to my feet, stumbling forward on stiffened limbs but preferring to converse on equal terms with my captor. 'Enter, Sir John,' I said, arranging my face into what I hoped was an implacable expression, while inside my stomach churned with apprehension.

He was carrying a lighted lantern and a tray containing a bowl and a jug. 'I noticed that you ate little at dinner, Lady Cicely. I have brought you curds and honey and some ale because I must warn you that we will be going on a journey. When the castle is sleeping I intend to take you on a ride which I hope will make you understand the injustice that has been done to my brother.'

It was as if my prayers had been answered. My chances of making a break for freedom were infinitely higher if I were taken out of the castle, but I did not want him to notice my surge of elation so I kept my expression blank.

'Thank you for the warning, Sir John. I am agog to learn how you think to change my perception.'

His grey eyes studied my face but their narrow gaze gave me no hint of his intentions. 'As I said, I plan to show you injustice, my lady. Now you should get some sleep. Be ready to ride before first light.' He said no more but he left me the tray and the lantern.

When I lay down sleep eluded me but a vivid memory rose to the surface of my mind like a waking dream. My father sat in his canopied chair, his bandaged leg propped up on cushions before him. Although only nine years old I knew there was an evil presence hidden under that thick dressing, which drew him daily nearer to death. Cuddy had told me that an old wound, received many years before, had resurfaced and now festered, sending rays of blackened flesh creeping up his thigh which emitted a putrid smell and warned us all that the great man had little time left.

For this important occasion maids had dressed me in my best pink gown; tiny white roses decorated the skirt and sleeves. I understood the meaning of betrothal and so did the boy beside me – Richard Plantagenet, dressed in the York colours of dark murrey-red and blue. He was thirteen and looked rather sulky, perhaps because although four years younger, I already stood nearly as tall as he.

My father's voice was mellow, despite the pain that etched deep furrows in his brow. 'Your vows to marry give me much pleasure, my children. I hope you will honour each other and share a mutual affection. We have done our best to teach you how.' He exchanged glances with my mother, who stood at his shoulder, beautiful in her sky-blue robe, her high, white forehead framed by a winged structure of pale gauze and gold filigree. She motioned us to kneel.

'We seek your blessing, my lord,' said Richard in a well-rehearsed sing-song tone, and took my hand in a moist clasp.

'May God in his infinite mercy bless you both,' pronounced

my father, his voice carrying to the crowd of retainers and servants assembled below the great hall dais. 'And when the time comes may he grant you the boon of children to unite the blood of York and Neville.'

I felt the betrothal ring bite into the sides of my fingers as Richard's grip tightened and we both flushed with embarrassment. The mention of children evoked the notion of coupling – anathema to our childish sensitivities even though we both knew it was part of the marriage contract. There would be have to be coupling – but not yet.

Minstrels struck up a lively tune and the Master of Revels took us off to lead the dancing. The great Raby Baron's Hall was decked with flowers and ribbons tied into love knots and above them rows of brightlycoloured ancestral banners hung from the rafters. I enjoyed dancing and smiled as I executed the intricate steps of the *estampie*, a new French dance which I had just learned, but my mind was still filled with concern for my father. When the music ended I went to pick up the jewelled hanap on the table beside him, kept exclusively for the earl to drink from. I lifted the cover and carefully held it beneath the vessel to catch any drips as my father drank. He returned the precious vessel to my hands with a smile.

'You play the cupbearer well, Cicely,' he said.

'You know I love to serve you, my lord father,' I told him in a whisper. 'I wish I could ease your pain.'

'I feel no pain when I look at you, sweeting. You are my solace and my hope. Look – what does it say up there, under the ship on the great pennant?' He pointed to the huge gold and crimson fretted battle standard which dominated the parade of banners in the rafters. In the centre, superimposed over the Neville saltire, was the black outline of a ship in sail, symbolizing the fleet commanded by Admiral Neuville which had brought the Conqueror's army to England. The motto read *Esperance me confort* – 'Hope comforts me.'

I spoke the words to him carefully, knowing them by heart.

'You are my hope, Cicely,' he said, his eyes holding mine. 'You are the one . . .'

The image was so vivid that when I opened my eyes I thought I could still see my father's grey gaze fixed on mine. Then I realized it was not memory but reality. Sir John was leaning over me with a lamp and his eyes were the re-incarnation of those that my mind had conjured up, even flecked with the same colours of chestnut and green as my father's had been.

He spoke in a hushed whisper, as if afraid to wake the rest of the castle inhabitants. 'We leave now, Lady Cicely, before it gets light. You must come.'

I threw off the covers and stood up, feeling suddenly dizzy so that I swayed on my feet. Sir John took my arm to steady me and for a few moments I found myself leaning against him with a rush of emotion that I could not put a name to. Then I realized we were not alone and hastily drew back. The stolid maid stood behind him and it was she who pulled my discarded riding huke over my head and laced up my boots. By the time I was ready the dizziness had passed and we crept quietly from the chamber and down the narrow stair. I cast a glance back at my prison and put up a silent prayer of thanks to St Agnes for my deliverance. I had no idea where I was going but surely anywhere had to be better than that cold, lonely cell?

A rear exit from Brancepeth opened onto a path leading directly down into the densely wooded dene on which the castle stood. My sturdy palfrey slipped and scrambled down the steep bank with remarkable agility while I clung to the saddle and left him to it. We then followed the course of a shallow but fast-flowing stream which our horses seemed to navigate more by feel than sight.

There were five of us mounted and one loaded pack pony; I recognized the two squires who had both been in the hall at dinner the previous night; Lady Westmorland's son Tam Clifford I knew from my spurious 'rescue' and the other I had gathered was Sir John's younger brother, Thomas. The fifth rider was the stolid maid who turned out to be called Marion, brought along I assumed because Sir John's sense of honour would not allow me to be in the company of three men without a female chaperone, for which, had she known it, my mother would certainly have been grateful.

For the first mile the only sound to be heard was the splashing of the horses' feet in the water and the occasional screech of a hoof slipping on rock, when we all held our breath. No one spoke, knowing that the Raby observers were camped within earshot above us on the flat land in front of the castle. For an instant I wondered if a cry for help would bring them running but then I realized there would likely be bloodshed and I did not want to be responsible for any death or injury. I was determined that this situation should be resolved peacefully and without bloodshed. The only thing I had not decided was how.

Once clear of the dene I ventured to speak. 'May I now ask where we are going?'

Dawnlight had begun to flush the eastern sky and the castle had disappeared into the forest gloom behind us. Sir John had carefully dropped back beside me leaving Tam in front and Thomas behind Marion, leading the sumpter. Even if I spotted a possible escape route, the knight's sleek charger would easily outrun my serviceable steed.

'As I told you, Lady Cicely, I am going to show you the true injustice of your father's legacy. We will ford the river you can see ahead and then we will cut across open country, avoiding several villages before we reach our destination. So there will be no opportunity for you to seek assistance, should you have it in mind.'

I made no response but kept a keen eye on our surroundings. I had enough local knowledge to guess that the river we crossed, wading hock-high through the spring-swelled flow, was once again the Wear and with the sun rising to our left we must be heading south. I guessed that Raby stood somewhere towards the west but how far and over what terrain? Although I harboured a spirit of adventure and believed I could elude recapture if the right circumstances arose, I felt daunted by the notion of making my way there alone across open country. In the anonymity of the surrounding moorland it would be easy to follow the wrong stream and become hopelessly lost.

At high noon in uncommonly bright spring sunshine we sighted our destination when a dark silhouette appeared on the horizon like a stump protruding from the earth. At that point we entered treacherous terrain where the going was flat and sinister, reeking with the stench of stagnant water and covered in a warning carpet of moss and myrtle. A moist humidity clung to it, producing swarms of biting flies which we swatted irritably as we followed a series of tall marker sticks sunk into the soggy morass to show where the ground was firm enough to take the weight of our horses. The stump gradually resolved into a grey stone edifice about thirty feet high, topped by uneven gap-toothed crenellations and standing square on a rocky mound attended by a huddle of low, straw-thatched hovels and a small stone chapel. A fearsome iron yett secured the ground floor and a random succession of tiny, deep-set windows pierced the thick stone walls of the tower, providing maximum defence but minimum light to the upper stories. It was what northerners called a peel, built to repel marauding reivers but offering nothing in the way of domestic comfort. I could barely suppress a shiver, imagining my next confinement in the grim twilight of an upper chamber, set in the middle of a stinking bog.

We had been riding slowly and carefully in single file, picking our way gingerly over the untrustworthy moss, but when we finally reached secure rock Sir John kicked his horse up to mine. 'This is what I wanted you to see, Lady Cicely. Thanks to your father, this dank place is where my brother Thomas will have to bring his bride, should we ever find him one willing to make it her home. Welcome to Aycliffe Tower.'

6

Aycliffe Tower

Cicely

The squat tower seemed to rise out of a deep tangle of briars, which at this early spring season were just beginning to hide their fierce thorns behind emerging green shoots. Someone had struck on the ingenious idea of planting wild roses in the sparse patches of soil that littered the rocky foundations and these now formed a dense, flesh-ripping defence against any enemy attempt to scale the walls. Only the entrance to the undercroft, guarded by its latticed yett and a pair of thick iron-bound oak gates, remained free of this thorny barricade so that both people and animals could speedily take refuge in an attack. Gazing at these impenetrable thickets of briars my first random thought was to wonder whether they bloomed red or white. The red rose was one of the symbols of the Royal House of Lancaster, loyally supported by all branches of the Neville family, ever since my father had changed his allegiance from King Richard to King Henry. Planted here in Lancastrian-held soil by a Lancastrian vassal, it occurred to me that it would be ironic if, when they flowered in June, these defensive English roses were not red but white.

After struggling with a gargantuan lock and key, Tam and Thomas managed to get the yett and the gates open, but in order to reach the narrow tower stair we were obliged to cross the lower chamber, where until very recently a herd of cows had wintered. As a result the earth floor was still mired with their excrement so that our boots and the hem of my skirt quickly became filthy. I shut my mind to the stench and the image of rats scuttling over my feet and headed for the stair.

The upper floor was divided into two chambers, the first furnished with a few rickety benches and a heap of grubby sleeping mats piled in one corner. There was a cold, ash-filled fireplace in one wall. The deep gloom was preserved by tightly closed shutters; these Tam hastened to throw open, allowing welcome light and air through the two small window holes, but the smell of cattle dung still clung with fierce pungence and I clamped my hand over my mouth to stop myself gagging. Bidding me to duck my head, Sir John ushered me through a low door in the rough stone dividing-wall which led into another room containing a settle placed opposite another dead hearth and a low bedstead which lacked any mattress.

Eying this, I asked coldly, 'Is it part of your plan, that I should sling myself on the bed-ropes to sleep, Sir John?'

'We have brought mattress bags,' he replied with a hint of a smile. 'I will have Thomas send villeins out to fill them with myrtle leaves. They make fragrant bedding.'

'I must take your word for that. Until I came to Brancepeth I had never slept on anything but feathers.'

'Perhaps then you will begin to understand the difference between a castle and a hovel.'

'I might, but I do not see how that will make me favour your cause.' I shot him a sceptical glance.

Ignoring this challenge, Sir John removed a large iron key from the lock in the heavy door to the chamber and held it aloft while he spoke crisply and concisely. 'You will sleep in here, the maid where you will. Tam and Thomas and I will sleep in the room above. There will be no keys but there will be a constant guard on the yett and a watch on the tower roof. Otherwise you are free to roam. The guard will not stop you but I do not advise trying to venture beyond the perimeter of the policies, due to the surrounding bog. Whole oxen have been swallowed by it in the past, when they strayed too close to the edge. The path is marked as you saw but the posts are removed at night. Only the reeve knows the safe route. Now I have arrangements to make. A meal will be served very soon. I hope you will join us.'

With a small bow he left the room, closing the door behind him. True to his word there was no dreaded sound of the key in the lock. I stared after him, trying to fathom his intentions in bringing me to this cheerless, dank little tower. To change my view of the Neville family feud?

The promised 'meal' was day-old bread, hard cheese and raw onion served on a trestle table. The men had removed their gambesons and boots and sat comfortably in tunic and hose, pointedly discussing Thomas' inheritance.

Tam Clifford was succinct in his assessment of Aycliffe. 'This place is a dump,' he said. 'What are you going to do about it, Thomas?'

Thomas pursed his lips. 'I really do not know. I will have to win some big prizes at tournaments when I am knighted, if I am to build new domestic quarters.'

With a sly glance at me, Sir John remarked, 'In any case it is no place to rear a family. Bogs may be a good defence against reivers but children do not thrive in them.'

'True,' Thomas drawled, downcast. Then, with a cheeky look at his brother, 'John, you do not seem to be in any hurry to marry. If you are not going to take possession of the constable's quarters at Barnard, perhaps I should move in there.'

It was news to me that Sir John was Constable of Barnard Castle, a royal stronghold not far from Raby. I supposed the post was connected to the earldom and had gone to the Brancepeth branch of the family.

He scowled. 'As you well know, commanding a garrison like the one at Barnard is no task for a squire. Besides, I have every intention of using those apartments myself in due course, other duties to our brother permitting.'

'Well I hope you take the young heir with you when you do. It is time young Jack escaped maternal rule,' remarked Tam Clifford. 'He is being mollycoddled.'

This criticism from Tam did not surprise me, even though it was of his own mother. I had already gleaned the impression that all the men of Brancepeth found the countess difficult to live with. I had only been under her roof for one night and found even the prospect of rat-infested Aycliffe Tower preferable.

I was uncomfortably aware that I needed a clean kirtle and the hem of my gownstill reeked of cattle dung, although Marion had brushed it, but I found myself enjoying the cut and thrust of male conversation again. Having shared my brothers' tutors for years, recently my mother had removed me from formal education and obliged me to acquire more feminine skills from her ladies. However, I now took care not to make any comment or contribution. Once or twice I felt Sir John's gaze lingering speculatively on my face and guessed he was assessing my frame of mind; whenever I caught his glance he turned away.

The meal was soon ended and I decided to test his assurance

that I could roam the tower's surroundings at will, even if it meant crossing the dung-covered floor of the undercroft once more. I was agreeably surprised to find the dung had been cleared and our horses installed there, with fresh straw spread around them. Some of the villagers had obviously been called from the fields to perform this task and I met one of them carrying a tinder-box into the tower, to set fires in the upper chambers, I hoped, for I assumed the evening would be cold, though the sun still shone brightly by day. The guard on the yett saluted as I passed but made no attempt to stop me.

The rocky island on which the tower was built was also home to the manor village and the workers' cotts. Buildings clustered around an area of land where there was enough soil, remarkably, to accommodate gardens and the burial ground of a small stone-built church. The cotts were roughly fashioned:wooden cruck-frames, walls of lath and mud-plaster and roofs covered with some sort of reed weathered in most cases to a dull dun colour, but streaked green with moss and lichen, and each leeward gable had a black-ringed hole in it where smoke escaped from within. Each cott had a small vegetable garden, fenced with woven briar hurdles against the lord's herds of pigs and goats which roamed the rocky demesne at will. A few chickens pecked listlessly in wattle coops, being reared no doubt as rent in kind to be paid at the next Halmote. I wondered if Sir John would preside at the Aycliffe manor court, at least until its putative lord reached his majority. It seemed unlikely that the earl, crippled as he was, would ever travel to this bog-bound manor.

Skirting the village and rounding the back of the tower, I discovered to my delight that Aycliffe possessed an unexpected pocket of natural beauty. On this south-facing side of the rocky outcrop the ground sloped gradually, a grassy meadow dipping gently to the shore of a small lake, the sort fell-dwellers called a tarn. Unlike the stagnant pools we had ridden past on our approach through the bog, this water gave evidence of being fresh and clean, spring fed and life-giving. Encouraged by the early-season sunshine, green shoots were sprouting from the tangle of brown reeds at its edge. Occasional flashes of silver beneath the breeze-rippled surface revealed the presence of small fishes offset by the background of the silt-covered bed of the lake in the transparent water. Water birds ducked in and out of little islands of vegetation, investigating potential nest sites.

In shadows cast by a stand of stunted willow a heron stood like a statue. I pondered the riches that this small lake brought to the manor folk; fish, roofing material, baskets, wildfowl, irrigation and, above all, fresh drinking water. As well as refreshing the spirit with its beauty, its products were the reason the manor was here at all.

I wandered down to stand on a lichen-covered rock that jutted out into the lake. The water tempted me to squat down and scoop up water to splash my face, and as I did so I became aware of footsteps behind me, then a flat stone skipped across the surface of the lake four times and sank, taking me and a busy pair of moorhens by surprise.

'I had a feeling I would find you here.'

I sprang up, my face dripping, to find Sir John not ten feet from me, bending to pick up another stone.

'The lake is Aycliffe's jewel. It is the only thing that makes it habitable.'

'It is beautiful,' I said, dashing the water from my eyes. 'And the peel could be also. Why does the earl not make it so? Drainage, a barmkin, some byres and stables, a church tower. These things are soon built.'

'The necessary funds, my lady, have gone to swell your mother's dower.'

I could not let that pass. 'Every widow must have a dower. That is enshrined in law.'

'Not three quarters of her husband's estate.' Sir John's face was stern. 'What widow needs so much?'

I fought down an urge to agree with him by reminding myself that it was my mother's closeness to the throne and the king's patronage which had brought such wealth to my father.

'My mother's dower is one third until her death. The rest is entailed for her sons. All widows have as much. That is why so many younger sons fight to win them in marriage, is it not? Even if they are ancient crones! You could do so yourself, Sir John. If funds are so urgently needed I wonder you do not.'

'I have no inclination to the wedded state,' he retorted. 'The earldom has its heir and due to my brother's infirmity I am its steward. No, it is Thomas whose future is threatened because his betrothal was made when your father was alive, before the terms of his will became known. His bride-to-be is Margaret Beaumont, a widow with a substantial dower. She was married as a child to Lord Deyning but he died before they were bedded and she was betrothed to Thomas soon afterwards. Her father says now that he will not allow that dower to be squandered on a penniless younger son, even one who is the brother of an earl, and he is taking legal steps to break the contract. His strongest argument is that Thomas cannot provide a home suitable for the daughter of a viscount and he is right. Thomas will lose a valuable marriage to a girl of whom he has unfortunately become fond, because your mother hoards all the best Westmorland lands, which she does not need as your father ensured that all *her* children made advantageous unions. That is why I brought you here, to see the effects of her avarice for yourself.'

This remark stirred my capricious temper and I felt the blood rush to my cheeks. But though greatly tempted to deny my mother's employment of the third deadly sin, I reminded myself that only one thing mattered, to escape back to Raby. Angrily confronting my abductor would not help achieve this and so I bit back the furious protest that sprang to my lips and took a deep, steadying breath.

'Thomas is young. There will be another marriage. But I still do not understand why you cannot solve your family's difficulties by making your own advantageous match. Whether inclined to matrimony or not, it is surely your duty, unless you are drawn to the religious life.'

It was his turn to exercise control. I could see his chiselled jaw clenching and unclenching as he turned away and let his gaze wander across the lake to where a pair of water birds were performing an elaborate ritual, shaking their crested heads to alternate sides, rearing up in the water and making each other gentle gifts of dripping weed. It was a charming sight but I was not prepared to let him retreat into ornithology. Leaning round to catch his eye, I shot him an encouraging smile and waited patiently for his response. When it came it took me completely by surprise.

He gestured towards the birds, busily involved in their courtship and unaware of the human passions building beside the lake. 'I have been told that grebes like these mate for life and rekindle their relationship every spring by performing this extraordinary dance. I have seen it many times and I believe it demonstrates God's intention that all creatures should make faithful partnerships. Did He not tell Noah to take only pairs of animals into his Arc? The Church teaches us that birds do not have souls and cannot experience human emotions like love and happiness but such behaviour indicates to me that they can only build their nest and lay their eggs if they have established some sort of bond. This ritual allows them to trust each other.' He turned to face me and his expression was one of extraordinary intensity, grey eyes boring into mine. 'I feel like that about marriage. Of course as noble men and women we must go through all the formal procedures of betrothals and contracts but I will only make a match with someone I can love and with whom I find a mutual understanding. So far I have not found such a one and I do not feel obliged to set my feelings aside to enter into a loveless marriage just because protocol declares it to be the right thing to do.' Once again he turned away. 'There, does that satisfy you? Or perhaps you now think me weak and hopelessly romantic?'

I was seventeen. Like most teenage girls I had cherished the notion of courtly love portrayed in the songs and lays of the minstrels who entertained us at feasts and celebrations, but ever since childhood I had been schooled to accept that such romances were fairytales; fairytales which were not for Nevilles. We were overlords, the rulers of the north; we had to make alliances with other noble families to perpetuate the power we had accumulated. Marriage was one way of achieving this. It secured treaties and preserved loyalties and I had to fulfil the role which God had given me by doing my duty and marrying the man my father and the king had chosen for me. Adolescent yearning for romantic love must be denied. I was, therefore, dumbstruck to encounter a man of power and position who not only cherished the concept of love and happiness but felt able to deny his obligation to God, king and family in order to do so.

I stared at Sir John wide-eyed and he, in his turn, wrinkled his brow in challenge.

I managed to hold his gaze but my heart lurched in a bewildering way. 'I understand the desire to break the rules,' I said faintly.

'But you will not?' His frown of disappointment forced me into a desperate attempt to make light of it.

'It would take a braver woman that I to defy the Church, the king *and* my mother!' I protested and when he did not react I stumbled on. 'Perhaps my parents had that kind of marriage. My mother certainly loved and trusted my father. Perhaps he repaid that trust in the way that he fashioned his will.'

It was not the response he wanted. With a sudden exclamation he stooped, picked up another stone and hurled it violently across the surface of the lake towards the grebes, causing them to break off their dance and dive underwater in panic.

His voice cracked with emotion. 'No! The old earl was much too shrewd ever to let his heart rule his head. When I was young my father served with him on the Northern March and we lived in his household for several years but when my father decided to follow the fifth King Henry into France they argued violently. The old earl thought Neville duty lay in the north, defending the border, but my father was lured by the prospect of wealth and honours to be won across the Narrow Sea. The rift between them never healed and by that time the sons your father had sired with your mother were growing to manhood. When your oldest brother Richard came of age, the earl made it clear that he wanted him as his heir, but for all his wily diplomatic skills, he could not change the laws of England to achieve that.'

'You did not like him then?' For some reason the thought of this distressed me.

'On the contrary, I loved him. He was always kind to us children, making us laugh and bringing us treats and presents. I was sad when he no longer came to see us but too young to understand why. Now I do, of course. My father had crossed him and the first Earl of Westmorland could never bear to be crossed, especially by his son and heir.' The knight cleared his throat as if struggling to continue. 'I was not with my father when he passed away in London but it was officially recorded that he died of the plague. I have never really believed that.'

There was something in the tone of his voice that drew from me an expression of horror. 'You surely do not believe that my father had anything to do with his death?'

Sir John shrugged. 'Not personally no, but these things can be arranged at a distance. And you have to admit that it served his purpose well, if he did not wish my father to inherit.'

'No, no!' I was incensed. My father had been a good man. I was certain of it. He was a powerful lord and a strong leader who demanded nothing less than complete loyalty from his vassals, but to arrange the death of his own son merely because he had defied him – I simply did not believe he could or would have done such a thing. Apart from any moral issue it would have condemned him to eternal hellfire.

'You are mad, Sir John! I swear before God that my father would never have killed his own son or even conspired in his death. I demand that you withdraw the accusation in the pres- ence of the Almighty. What good would it have done him anyway, while your father had a son to inherit the earldom?'

Sir John's lip curled at that. 'A son who was a cripple and a minor might possess no power against the might of an earl who stood high in the king's favour. My brother Ralph told me that after my father's death the old earl sent his lawyers to demand that he give up his right of succession. It was in the face of Ralph's flat refusal that your father spent the next four years until he died making sure my brother would inherit only a fraction of the Neville wealth. I will swear *that* is true on any holy relic you choose!'

Before I could prevent him, Sir John reached out and grabbed my hand and his eyes were so full of earnest zeal that I found myself powerless to pull it free. The touch of his fingers sent a shocking thrill up my arm which seemed to travel to my heart, causing it to race uncontrollably. Yet I continued to protest. 'No, no, no. My mother would never have allowed him to make such a demand of your brother. It is a wicked thing to do.'

Even as I spoke the words, I could hear the weakness in my own argument. I knew nothing of what plans and schemes my parents had made during my father's dying days. I had never spoken with him about the other half of his family. All his children by his first wife were strangers to me, as were their children. Apart from the man who now held my hand and his brothers, I hardly knew which of them still lived.

Sir John pursed his lips wryly and nodded. 'You are right, it is wicked. But you are not as familiar as I am with the wicked ways of the world. Even as we fight our family wars here in the north, in the south there are forces gathering around the young king of which he is also unaware. You and he are both too young yet to know how power corrupts people and causes them to act against God's commands and the laws of the land. But you must trust me, Cicely, because I do know and I can help you to understand. Justice is a fragile flower but if we treat each other fairly and deal reasonably together then justice can still be done.'

I tried to pull my hand away because the contact between us was confusing me. The messages passing up my arm were in conflict with the thoughts tumbling in my head. The first made me eager to believe the words of the man before me, while the second told me he was spinning a tale. Then his other hand rose to touch my cheek and my mind seemed to swim into a warm blue cloud and become lost to my rational self. I closed my eyes and let my starved senses relish the caress, then I felt his mouth close gently on mine and for what seemed like minutes I reveled in the first rush of fevered blood my body had experienced. The warmth of the spring sunshine was as nothing compared with the heat generated by the pressure of his lips on mine and the surge of pleasure it released. My bones seemed to turn liquid and I felt as if only our joined hands and lips were holding me upright. No carefully taught rules or command-ments remained to order my feelings or actions. I did not care if I was on the steps to heaven or the road to hell; whether it was the devil or my own intoxicating desires that were drawing me along this unmapped path.

7

Aycliffe Tower

Cicely

After what seemed an eternity while all my senses swirled in glorious commotion, my eyes flew open and reality flooded back, bringing confusion. Guilt, shame and elation fought for supremacy in my bewitched mind and the sunlight flashing off the lake dazzled me as I jerked away from him, blinking and gasping.

I pressed my fists together against my chest so that my nails dug into my palms and the pain of it mustered my scattered senses. I gazed at him, lips parted and eyes full of questions.

'You are beautiful, Cicely,' Sir John said quietly.

'No!' I tossed my head, as if to shake his words away. 'Do not say that. You do not have the right.'

His laugh was harsh with irony but his expression was tender. 'Hah! What has right to do with beauty? I find you beautiful. What is there to fear from that?'

'I fear where it may lead.'

'Now there you are right. Where do you think it may lead?'

My cheeks burned and I turned my face away. I wanted to

tell him that I, too, found him beautiful but the words froze on my tongue.

Instead I said, 'I do not know. That is why I fear it.'

He was not so tongue-tied. 'You felt the connection between us, though? I have never experienced such pleasure from another's touch. Tell me you felt it too, Cicely. I cannot believe you did not.'

My gaze was drawn back to his as if by some external force. His cheeks were flushed, as I knew mine were, and they blazed even hotter when he sank down onto one knee before me, his eyes locked with mine, fiercely questioning. I nodded slowly. 'Yes, I felt it,' I said. 'It burned like a brand. What does it mean? Why do you kneel?'

'Because it means you are my lady.' He reached for my hand and again I felt a jolt of recognition, as if our fingers ignited as they met. 'You are my lady and I am your true and faithful knight.' His words were solemn and fervent but after he pressed his forehead to the soft flesh above my knuckles, he raised his head to favour me with a sudden brilliant smile, which transformed his Nordic features with a curious blend of joy and mischief.

'Now, if I were a grebe I would bring you gifts of weed dripping with diamond drops. And I would build you a nest of rushes threaded with buttercups and yellow irises and you would float on lavender-scented waters and rule your besotted subjects with a green willow wand.' Ignoring my startled expression he rose and threaded my arm through his bent elbow to draw me to the water's edge. 'You would be queen of the lake. No predator would trouble you for I would slay them all and spike their heads on bulrushes so that the world would know that I am your consort and we two belong together forever in our peaceful, fragrant haven.'

I found myself laughing at this preposterous fantasy, delighted by its glorious sensuousness. 'And what would I do all day, lying among the buttercups and irises?' I wondered, tilting my head in enquiry and catching his eye.

The antipathy which had flared between us had evaporated as though it had never been and I felt reckless and light-hearted. Aycliffe Tower had suddenly become a wonderland rather than a place of conflict and confinement. Perhaps I was also light-headed from lack of sleep but I did not pause to consider this.

Sir John swept his free arm in a wide arc to indicate the pastoral scene. 'What do nymphs and naiads do in their watery idylls? Bathe in fresh springs and gossip in dappled shade.'

'Have you been reading a little too much poetry, Sir John?' I enquired with exaggerated concern. 'I would hardly call the breeze balmy and those fresh springs are probably freezing.'

He tossed back his heavy fringe of flaxen hair. 'That is no problem. To please his honoured lady a gallant knight would cause the breeze to blow warm and the springs to bubble hot from the earth.'

I pulled my hand from the crook of his arm and bent to dip it in the lake, splashing water up into his face. 'Brr! I do not think your spell worked.'

He raised one eyebrow sceptically and smiled as he brushed the drops from his cheek. 'We shall see. I think you may find it did.'

His air of smug male confidence suddenly annoyed me. I avoided his gaze and pretended to shiver. 'I am cold. I think I will go to the church. If I cannot hear Mass at least I can pray.'

'The priest is not of the kind you are used to,' Sir John said. 'He is only half literate and almost certainly not celibate. But the church will be peaceful. There will be a hot meal at dusk. I hope you will join us.'

I was already walking away and he raised his voice so that his invitation would reach me but I made no reply one way or the other. Instead I voiced what was suddenly uppermost in my mind again, my tone intentionally barbed. 'Perhaps you will have heard from Raby by then. I presume you have been in contact.'

My back was turned but I could feel Sir John's puzzlement at my abrupt change of mood. 'Any message will reach me here,' he said. 'But I get no sense of urgency from that quarter.'

His words echoed in my head . . . *No sense of urgency from that quarter* . . . and they troubled me greatly. Kneeling before the simple wooden cross above the altar of the little whitewashed church, I could not pray for delivery from my abductor because he had suddenly assumed the guise of my admirer. With only a slight sense of impiety, I found myself praying that there might be a way I could achieve my own freedom – since my family was making no great effort to free me – while also pursuing the emotional fulfilment of which I had so recently and entic- ingly had a taste.

I returned, disconsolate, to the tower, but my mood would not last. Either on her own initiative or on instructions from Sir John, the stolid Marion had packed a change of clothes for me in the sumpter's panniers, and my spirits rose as I discarded the mud-and-muck-stained garb I had been obliged to wear since leaving Raby. I presumed the fresh white linen kirtle and fur-trimmed green worsted gown I put on had been purloined from the Countess of Westmorland's wardrobe, but I did not quibble about their ownership. Marion further surprised me by showing a certain skill with comb and brush and managing to braid and style my hair into something more graceful than the wild curls I had hitherto been obliged to control under my battered riding hat. I had no mirror in which to check my appearance but the expressions on the faces of my male companions when I joined them for the evening meal were sufficient to tell me that there had been a substantial improvement.

Despite the restrictions of Lent, a simple but tasty meal had been prepared for us consisting of grilled perch and trout, accompanied by boiled crayfish and a mess of creamed leeks and onions. I ate hungrily for the first time since my abduction and noticed that the men did too and soon the level of tension had dropped as the food restored the equilibrium in each of us. Afterwards there was soft cheese and freshly griddled oatcakes which, preferring wafers, I had always considered peasant fodder, but which smelled so delicious that I could not resist trying one.

'I will never spurn an oatcake again,' I confessed as I reached for a second. 'Who has prepared this meal for us?'

Sir John cleared his throat and looked a little embarrassed. 'The fish and vegetables were cooked by the priest's, er, shall we say housekeeper? And the cakes come courtesy of our own expert campfire cook, Tam Clifford, Esquire.'

I looked across the table at Tam, gratified to see that the warm smile I gave him brought a blush to his cheeks. 'A man of many talents then,' I remarked. 'Groom, hat-finder and now oatcake-baker. Thank you, Tam.'

'He is also no mean swordsman,' put in Thomas, clapping his friend on the shoulder. 'Though no match for me, of course!'

'Ha! We will see about that at the next arms practice,' declared Tam. 'Meanwhile, I will challenge you at chess after dinner.'

'Done,' agreed Thomas. 'I will have you checked in three moves.'

'Braggart!' The young Clifford was indignant. 'You have never beaten me yet.'

Sir John broke into their banter. 'You can take the chessboard upstairs. Lady Cicely and I have business to discuss. And pour us more wine before you go.'

I frowned as Thomas refilled my cup but did not refuse. We were drinking a sweetish white wine which was stronger than I was used to and it had already made my head spin a little. I wondered what 'business' Sir John thought he had with me.

Soon we were alone and Sir John suggested we move across to a wooden settle that had been furnished with several threadbare but still serviceable cushions and set at an angle to the hearth where a fire was now glowing.

'I fear it may be too hot, Sir John,' I said, but I rose nevertheless.

'If so we can move the seat, but I have not noticed you shying from the heat, Lady Cicely.' I presumed his lop-sided smile indicated an intended double meaning, but I made no response.

Nevertheless I could feel my heart begin to beat faster as I took the proffered place on the settle and he sat down at the other end. Only a short distance lay between us. My hands were shaking as I took a sip from my cup, and I did not doubt that he could see this also. 'Have you news from Raby, Sir John?' I asked, unable to prevent myself spilling some wine as I placed my cup on a small table beside the settle. 'I presume that is the business you wish to discuss with me.'

He gulped down the entire contents of his own cup and leaned down to dump it on the floor where it rolled drunkenly away. His face was suddenly anguished and the distance between us vanished as he took both my hands in his. 'I have no news from Raby, Cicely, and of course that is not what I wish to discuss with you!'

All at once his lips were on my hands, he was kissing my fingers, turning them over to drop feathery kisses into my palms and onto my wrists. I felt the hairs lift on my arms and my belly clenching inside as his mouth began exploring the hollows of my throat and caressing the smoothness beneath my chin, then in between kisses he began murmuring softly, whispering words I had yearned for in my girlish dreams but never expected to hear in reality. 'Ah, Cicely, you are even more beautiful than I first thought. Your throat is like silk, your cheeks are like velvet, your eyes are the colour of the Virgin's robe and your lips are glowing coals that burn and burn and burn . . .'

As he mentioned each of these features he planted kisses on them, ending with another lingering, probing, searching of my lips, which mine instinctively opened to receive. The clenching sensation in my belly grew wilder and more demanding and without heed for my position on the settle, I arched my body into his in order to feel the beat of his heart and the response of his need to mine and then, as we clung feverishly to each other, the inevitable happened. The cushions slipped and pitched us both onto the floor. I found myself lying beneath him, slightly winded and breathless and he was staring down at me with a bemused expression, as if he could not quite understand what had happened. Then we both began to laugh.

However, with his body pressing down on me I could not breathe and had to push him off in order to give way to my mirth. When I could speak I spluttered, 'Do you woo all your ladies by throwing them on the floor?' By now I was sitting up and hugging my knees, feeling tears beginning to run down my cheeks. It had been funny but at this point I was not sure if they were tears of mirth or nervousness. I brushed them away. I had decided on my course of action and I was not going to change my mind now.

'I would ask the same of you,' he said with a grin, 'except that it would not be chivalrous to assume that you had experience in these matters.'

'Well now I have – and in future I'll avoid polished settles with cushions on.'

Rising to his feet, he then bent to help me up.

'Have you tried your myrtle-leaf bed yet?' he asked.

I gave him a surprised look. 'No I have not. Have you?'

'Of course not!'

'I am told they are fragrant.'

'Who told you that?'

I picked up my cup and took a long draught of wine, gazing at him over the rim. 'You did,' I said. 'Would you like to find out for yourself?'

John took the cup from my hand and put it back on the table. 'Oh yes I would, very much.' This time I took courage from the fact that his kiss was one of eager reassurance and encouragement.

'What if Marion comes back?' I murmured, my lips against his.

He opened the purse he wore on his belt and took out a key. I recognized it as the one he had removed from the door of my chamber earlier.

When the key turned, unlike the previous night, loneliness was not in my mind – and neither was regret. I was not afraid. I had chosen this course of action, fate had shown me what overwhelming feelings passion could release and it was somehow not in my nature to deny them. I had no thought for yesterday or tomorrow, only for the moment and what that moment might achieve. I was young and my senses were whirling almost out of control, except that, behind the powerful mutual attraction that had drawn me to the beautiful John and the joy I ardently desired to find in his arms, there was also a deep determination not to be used, either by him or by my own family. There was no doubt that my actions that night served my own needs as much as his but I was not to know that he would read them very differently. He was older and more idealistic and his feelings ran truer and deeper. I could not have asked for a more gentle and ardent lover to show me the delights of mutual passion. How could he have known that when he offered his love so sweetly, he chose the wrong woman?

Myrtle did indeed did make a wild and fragrant bed. After we had spent our passion John slept deeply and soundlessly but I lay awake, my mind in turmoil. I had barely noticed the pain of defloration and had subsequently wondered, after the thrilling throes of climax, what there was about it that the Church revered so highly and the virgin martyrs died for. My body ached from the unaccustomed activity of love-making but I nevertheless yearned to stay beside my lover, to feel again the pleasure of his caresses and the joy and fulfilment of union.

Nevertheless I forced myself to rise, softly and soundlessly, from the bed and reach for the dirty shift and kirtle that I had discarded before supper. The borrowed gown from which John had hurriedly unlaced me lay on the floor among the jumble of his doublet and hose and I almost stumbled over them as I searched for my riding boots. Carrying them I turned the key cautiously in the lock, holding my breath as it scrunched over the cogs and wheels, but I heard no stirring from the bed. As I had hoped, the outer chamber was empty and the door to the stairway open. I paused at the foot of the stair to slide my feet into my boots and thread the laces. I could hear rats scuttling about in the straw and I could not face crossing the byre barefoot. The horses snuffled and shifted on their feet, dozing like the guard propped up on a sheaf of straw against the wall. Everything now depended on what I found when I opened the heavy oaken gates; if the yett had been lowered, escape from the tower would be impossible.

8

To Aycliffe Tower

Cuthbert

In the trees behind Brancepeth church the ground dropped away into the same deep, narrow dene on which the castle stood. Feeling my way in the dappled moonlight, I led my horse to the edge where I found a useful thicket of bushes to tie him to while I ventured hand over foot down the steep side, clinging to roots and saplings. Within minutes I reached secure footing on a sloping gravel path dug into the dene wall. I climbed, guessing it would lead to the sally gate of the castle mentioned by my drinking companion. Where the ground levelled out, sure enough, I caught sight of the moon's glare reflected off a high expanse of the castle curtain, and at its base, flush with the stone wall, a small archway, defended by an overhead turret and sealed by a studded wooden door, just large enough to allow a mounted man to pass through.

Keeping within the shadow of the bushes, I turned and retraced my steps, for the path ended at the castle. The archway had been newly built, the door thick. Following the beck downstream towards the River Wear, I deduced that it would provide a discreet and direct route to the Bishop of Durham's hunting lodge at Auckland, on the edge of Spennymoor: this had lately been developed into a military fortification, with a large bailey to accommodate troops mustering for the defence of the Scottish marches. The bishop had appointed Sir John Neville as its constable, but I asked myself if Sir John would have taken Cicely to such a busy place.

As a young squire in my father's retinue, on the last of his annual tours of his northern manors, I remember hearing of a particularly poor and remote peel tower a few miles south of Auckland which struggled to wrest five pounds in annual revenue from woefully undernourished villeins. I wracked my brains for the name of the manor. The only thing I could remember of any relevance was that when the old earl's will was revealed, Hal Neville had remarked that 'the peel in the bog' was one manor he was more than happy for the new earl to keep. Instinct told me that this might be where Cicely had been taken and, after all, it was my instincts that Lady Joan had encouraged me to employ in her daughter's aid.

I collected my horse and followed the beck as far as the River Wear while the moon rose high in the sky, its bright light flooding over uneven moorland covered with large areas of gorse and dead bracken. Fast-moving shadows cast by scudding clouds did not hamper my progress south. I carefully avoided the small hamlets and fortified farms on the route, because on such moonlit nights lookouts would be posted for reivers, and I did not want to be sighted and apprehended as one of their ilk. But most of the country between Brancepeth and Richmond, thirty miles to the south, was Neville territory, and familiar to me; its manors were now distributed piecemeal between the two branches of the family. Lady Joan had, on occasion, detailed me to represent her in settling the feuds and disputes between tenants arising from this complicated division of property. So although I could not remember the name of the peel in the bog, I did have a rough idea of where it was located.

When I eventually spotted the tower, poking up like a lone tooth from a fetid maw of flat, moss-covered marsh, I faced the problem of approaching it without either being seen or swallowed in its mire. There was something truly ghastly about the way the moonlight glinted off the surrounding expanse of innocent-looking moss and reeds, concealing the lurking presence of a bottomless bog beneath; when I tried to urge him on, my horse snorted and danced on the spot, flatly refusing to take one step onto such unstable ground.

Common sense told me there had to be a safe path or else how did its inhabitants reach the tower? For nearly an hour I rode around the edge of the morass, trusting my horse's instinct not to venture onto dangerous terrain, but I could find no evidence of a marked route. I contemplated leaving my horse and trying to navigate the bog on foot but as the moon dropped in the heavens I realized I would be taking a foolish and possibly fatal risk, particularly in the dark. There was no option but to wait until sunrise.

As a squire I had spent months with the marcher scouts, a troop of hard-bitten, border-reared fighting men recruited for their intimate knowledge of the wild lands between Scotland and England and their ability to move secretly through them on their dale-trotter ponies. They could survive for weeks patrolling their section of the march, living off the land and avoiding human contact whilst observing all movement of men and animals without detection. I admired their skills and I would now apply all I had learned of them. I hobbled my horse in an overgrown spinney. My stomach made sharp protest at its lack of nourishment but I silenced it with a long swig from the wineskin slung from my saddle, rolled myself in my campaign blanket and lay down to gather what sleep I could in the undergrowth.

The unmistakable sound of a hue and cry roused me a couple of hours later. Shouting, the long wail of a hunting horn and the answering sounding of hounds ripped through the veil of sleep and jerked me to my feet, sleeve dagger at the ready. Dawn had mottled the eastern sky in shades of red, pink and grey and my horse's head was up, ears pricked. I crept to the edge of the spinney for a cautious search but could see no movement from the section of bog within my view. Nevertheless the sinister sounding of horn and hounds and the shouts of men in pursuit were loud to my left. I decided that being mounted would give me an advantage in a tight situation, and better visibility. In a matter of moments I had tacked up my horse and was heading out of the spinney.

The reason for all the noise quickly became evident: a mud-streaked figure was struggling at the edge of the bog, only yards from firm ground but caught thigh deep in wet mud and unable to reach safety. It was Cicely, almost unrecognizable, covered in mud, exhausted and clearly terrified, her face twisted into a desperate snarl as she rocked herself to free one foot or the other from the clinging ooze. The hue and cry was close by, any moment it would be here and what I assumed was a break for freedom would be brought to an end, or, more terribly, she would fall flat into the watery mud and disappear beneath its surface.

'Do not move!' I shouted, spurring my horse forward and galloping as near to her as the horse would go. 'It is me, Cuthbert. I will get you out. Wait.'

I jumped from the saddle, commanded my horse to stand and ripped my blanket from the restraint of its buckling.

'Oh, Cuddy, thank God it is you!' Cicely's eyes were enormous with fright in her mud-daubed face. 'Quick! The dogs are coming.'

'Yes, Cis, I can hear them.' Turning briefly, I caught sight of a man on the path pushing sticks into the ground as a companion behind him hauled on the taut leashes of two scent-hounds in full voice. I took aim and threw out the blanket. 'Here, catch this.'

One corner landed near her hand and she grabbed it like a drowning sailor might grab a life-line. 'Do not let go, Cis! Lie down, I'm going to pull you out,' I said urgently.

The Cicely I knew might have quibbled at falling face down in a bog but luckily she wasted no time in clutching two sides of the blanket in a white-knuckled grip and throwing herself horizontal, face down in the soggy blanket. Immediately there was less suction drag on the cloth and I managed to haul her swiftly towards me until I could hold her hands and heave her, drenched and panting, onto the firm ground.

I could see she was about to speak and I growled at her. 'Save your breath, Cis. I have a horse and we will ride away from this first.'

Although her weight was nothing to arms honed by years of sword-play and archery, her soaked skirts hampered my stride so that I stumbled rather than ran towards my stoical horse who fortunately obeyed orders and stood firm, even as I threw Cicely face down over his withers and leaped up behind her. 'Hang on for your life. I'll stop as soon as I can,' I yelled and dug in my spurs.

He exploded away just as the first pursuers stepped onto firm ground and began racing towards us, scent-hounds baying with excitement. Cicely's right hand closed on my leg like a vice as our hectic pace threatened to hurl her from the horse's neck. I am not certain we would have made it but instinctively the courser threw up his head, tossing her back towards me so that I could wrap one hand in the cloth of her skirt, while the other handled the reins. She must have been winded and in pain but she made no sound and we galloped away as if fleeing from a battlefield, the important difference being that we were victorious. The only glance I managed to make behind me showed a dozen mud-spattered men spilling from the bog-path yelling in frustration. One was noticeable for his red tunic emblazoned with a white saltire cross and his shock of fair hair. The tall figure of Sir John Neville was familiar to me from sharing duties with him on the Scottish march. White-faced and wide-eyed, he looked like a man in shock.

9

The Raby Bath House

Cicely

Cuddy rode away from that accursed bog as if the hounds of hell were at his heels while I pitched and bumped over his horse's neck, offering desperate but silent prayers to the Queen of Heaven. I had no breath even to murmur an Ave, every thud of the horse's hooves seemed to force out what little air I managed to drag into my lungs and every so often I had somehow to raise my head for a life-giving gulp. Fortunately, just as I had started to fear I could hold on no longer, the pace began slowing and we came to a halt. When I fell to the ground my legs would not support me and I crumpled in a muddy, sodden heap under the horse's feet, a safe landing place because he could not move another step. His head hung down and his sides heaved. We were both gasping like stranded fish.

It was several minutes before I found the strength to sit up. By then Cuddy had dismounted and satisfied himself that there was no sound of pursuit before pulling me out from under the horse and unhitching his wineskin from the saddle-bow. He put it to my lips and I spluttered as the sharp liquid hit my throat.

'How did . . . you know . . . where . . .?' I croaked, unable to go on.

Cuddy knew what I meant. 'Intuition. Instinct. Second sense. Your mother sent me on a wild goose chase and look – I found the goose.' He grinned. 'After all, I am your champion.'

I gave a weak smile and wheezed, 'My champion . . .' My voice cracked and failed once more.

He bowed. He did not seem breathless in the least. 'Glad to be of service. But you take the laurel wreath, Cis. How in God's name did you manage to break out of the tower?'

That was when reality hit me. Vivid memories came flooding back. I bit my lip to stop the tears and stifle the words threatening to spill off my tongue. I knew then that they would all ask the same question. How had I managed to get away from my captors? It was a question I decided there and then that I would not answer. Let them wonder. Except for Cuddy they had done nothing to help me. I did not owe an explanation. But had it not been for Cuddy, everything I had done to enable my escape would have been for nothing. I might as well have died.

I shook my head and decided it was easier to speak in short bursts. 'Not difficult. Bog was the problem. Frightening. Then I heard the horn. Tried to hurry. Fatal step – if not for you. Thank you, Cuddy.'

Gradually I felt strength returning to my legs. 'There is one more thing you can do for me, if you will,' I said, taking another gulp from the wineskin and handing it back. 'After you have helped me up, that is.'

I held out my hand and Cuddy pulled me gently to my feet. I swayed and staggered and he steadied me, regarding me appraisingly, his gaze travelling from my sodden skirts to my dripping locks. I had not found my hat in the dark and I daresay my cheeks were streaked, for I had not managed to hold back all my tears. 'I think I know what that one thing is,' he said.

'More intuition?' This time my smile was rueful.

'You do not want to return to Raby looking like a camp follower who has been caught in a thunderstorm.'

I nodded. 'Exactly.' For the first time I glanced around me, taking stock of our surroundings. We were in a small clearing among mature trees. It could have been almost any wood in England. 'Where are we?'

'Houghton Forest. About ten miles from Raby. It will take us an hour to get there once the horse is rested. There is a stream over yonder. You could wash off some of the mud while we wait. When we get to Raby you can hide somewhere safe and I will fetch Hilda. She will know what to bring to restore you to your customary splendour.'

He was teasing, his eyes twinkling, trying to lighten my mood, and I appreciated his restraint in not pressing me on my escape. Cuddy may have been conceived in a barn but his manners were castle-bred. 'And Hilda knows how to hold her tongue,' I said with a nod of approval. 'But where would I be safe?'

'There is an old bath house on a lake in the woods south of the castle. You can barricade yourself in there while I fetch Hilda. No one goes near it now but they say our father used to entertain there in days gone by.' Cuddy gave me a look, which told me not to enquire about who the old earl had invited to a bath house in the woods or what the entertainment had been. Of course there were plenty of rumours, but in deference to my mother nobody ever talked about other 'by-blows' her husband might have sired on pretty girls around the various Neville territories. No others had joined the household. For some reason, in our father's eyes, Cuthbert of Middleham had been special. Perhaps Cuddy himself did not know why.

The bath house was no woodland shack. It was a domed, stone-built grotto perched on the side of a glassy mere which reflected a stand of magnificent trees that must have been planted when our great-grandfather enclosed the Raby hunting park a hundred years earlier. Although the trees were still leafless, waiting for spring to spread its canopy of green, the castle itself was not visible, but I knew it was not far away because in order to reach the place unseen we had skirted the village of Staindrop and entered the park like poachers, avoiding all well-used tracks. Staindrop stood only a mile from Raby; my father lay in its glorious collegiate church, under a marble tomb, beside his first wife. Cuthbert forced his way into the bath house through a wooden door, not locked or barred but swollen from winter damp, and left me with the wineskin, telling me he would be back within an hour.

The bath house consisted of a single chamber. Stripped of any of the luxury or comforts it might once have contained, cobwebs festooned its walls, all hung about with insect carapaces; droppings of various small animals littered the floor and the curved steps that led up to the parapet of the round stone bath and, at the bottom of the bath, the remains of a deserted nest covered what I guessed must have been a drain for emptying the water into the lake. Outside, on the bank of the mere, I found a firepit where a cauldron would have been slung over the flames. My imagination conjured up a vivid image of servants fetching steaming bucket-loads from the cauldron, because surely nothing would have cooled the ardour of the 'bathers' more than icy water straight from the lake.

I could not wait in the bath house. It was full of echoes, the ribald shouts of men and the lusty laughter of women, the splash of water on naked flesh, and I did not like it. My father had always been my image of the perfect knight, lord and sire. In recent days that gleaming icon had become tarnished by the stories I had heard and the truths I had learned.

The silence and stillness of the mere drew me. I guarded against discovery by taking up a position a few yards from the bath house, hidden by the branches of a holly tree growing close to the edge of the lake. There I sat on a convenient log and I studied my reflection in the glassy surface of the lake. What I saw absorbed and disturbed me. It was not that my hair was tangled in Medusa-like curls and my face was still mud-streaked, despite my efforts to wash it: I was not the same person who had set out blithely from Raby with her falcon three days before. Then I had been thoughtless and carefree, a young girl on the brink of marriage but who had given little thought to what that marriage might mean. My life had been ordered for me and while I had occasionally rebelled against the restrictions placed on me, I had not seriously questioned my own feelings or considered my own future. I had scarcely known I had any of my own feelings. Now there was a new look in the wide blue eyes that stared back at me and a more determined set to the curved mouth which did not smile. There were secrets behind those eyes; thoughts and words which those lips had spoken but would never speak again. The child who had gone out hunting had come back an adult.

10

Raby Castle

Cicely

'**S**weet Mother of God, he brings a whole army! Does he intend to wed or make war?'

It was Will who spoke. I stood between him and Ned on the battlements of Clifford's Tower, the tallest at Raby, staring out through a crenel at the long procession snaking down from the Auckland road towards the castle gatehouse, the far end of which was not yet visible. Richard, Duke of York, was arriving at last and he rode at the head of an enormous retinue and baggage train.

'Does he think he is the king?' Ned cried. 'There must be three hundred retainers. Can we feed so many?'

'We will have to hunt more game, brother. That should be no hardship.'

'I am not sure the park contains enough deer.'

Viewing my betrothed's enormous train, I felt a mixture of awe and bewilderment. 'Why does he need such a vast retinue?' I asked. 'Has there been unrest in the realm?'

Will laughed. 'It is not a case of need, Cis. Richard is declaring to the world "I am the Duke of York. See how many follow me.

Behold my wealth and power." Brother Hal will be a little disconcerted. His Salisbury retinue numbers only two hundred.' Ned turned and headed for the tower stair, adding, 'He will be at the gatehouse soon and we are detailed to escort him in.'

They were both gone. It was Maundy Thursday. Tomorrow the whole castle would plunge into the solemn fasting and ritual of the Unveiling of the Cross before bursting into full celebration of the Resurrection on Easter Day with joyous feasting and minstrelsy. Two days after that would be my wedding to this rich and powerful new duke – the grandest nuptials ever to be celebrated within the walls of Raby castle. I lingered a little longer, mesmerized by the spectacle of the cavalcade approaching ever closer.

A trumpet blast sounded a fanfare of welcome. Next, Westmorland Herald recited the list of honours and titles in a high, penetrating voice that carried all around the outer bailey – 'Richard Plantagenet, Duke of York, Earl of Cambridge, Earl of March, Earl of Ulster, Baron Mortimer, Lord of Wigmore and Lord of Clare' – and my future husband. He rode in full armour and trappings, an upright, broad-shouldered man. Behind him rode his escort of retained barons and knights, all proudly in formation displaying the blue and murrey-red livery of York. White rose pennants fluttered at their lance-tips, fixed between their own individual pennants and the scarlet, gold and blue of the royal leopards and lilies, to which Richard was entitled as a royal prince and direct descendent of King Edward the Third. Behind each of three barons and twelve knight-captains, rode their troops of squires and men-at-arms and behind them the household officials, couriers, clerks and house-carls, huntsmen and falconers with their hounds and hawks and a procession of wagons containing clothing, furnishings, provender and presents.

Anyone would have marvelled at what I saw, but I was remembering the under-age lordling who had set out from Raby seven years previously to take service in the king's household. I could scarcely believe my eyes. Then he had been a scrawny lad of fourteen, spotty and insecure, an orphan who had fought hard to establish himself among the numerous squabbling henchmen and progeny of his Neville guardians. Now he was twenty-one, the wealthiest magnate in the kingdom, who carried his head so high it seemed to add inches to his stature. Immediately behind him rode a squire bearing his crested helmet and richly emblazoned shield. No wonder Ned had compared him to a king.

By the time the principal members of the procession had passed through the gatehouse, I had descended from the keep to the inner ward where my mother and brothers were already gathered to greet the new arrival. The clatter of hooves on the flagstones of the long Neville tunnel-gateway, built by my father to secure the castle's inner core, gave us warning of the duke's approach and, to the muttered reproof and intense relief of my mother, I slid into place beside her just in time. As the king's aunt, she was the only one who outranked Richard and as soon as he had swung down from his horse he strode up to bend his knee to her, a deference which gave me a chance to assess this bridegroom of mine before he scrutinized me. Seven years at court, three of them in France; how greatly altered was the boy to whom I had been betrothed at the age of nine.

Close to I saw that he was good-looking without being naturally handsome. His complexion was fair, his cheeks smooth-shaven and his hair, the colour of dark honey, was thick, curly and shining. Expert grooming, good posture and extreme fitness had given him a chiselled profile and the gleaming and costly silk of the crested jupon he wore over his armour was embellished with bold and intricate embroidery depicting the royal arms quartered with those of his Mortimer mother and his Castilian grandmother. My first impression was of an ambitious man who sought perfection in everything. I wondered if he would find it in me. The only feature that softened this image was that luxurious mane of burnished hair in which, suddenly and to my guilty surprise, my fingers itched to bury themselves.

Before I could banish this sinful thought to the dark recesses of my mind, my betrothed was moving to greet me, his eyes fastening so intently on mine that I felt sure he must be able to read it through their window. Consequently, to my chagrin, I blushed.

'My lady Cicely, my duchess,' he murmured and he squeezed my hand gently as he lifted it to his lips. His attitude was so charming and assured that I could find no similarity with the awkward, gawky youth who had slipped the betrothal ring on my finger and I quashed any comparison with Sir John Neville of Brancepeth. He was no longer to exist for me. The man who kissed my hand was my destiny, the future that was mapped out for me. Since my return to Raby I had prayed fervently for the strength and grace to embrace that future and fulfil the role expected of me. I lifted my head and felt the blush recede. To my relief I could see admiration in the flecked green eyes which studied me so intently.

My mother had insisted on an intimate talk with me on the day following my return. She had banished all family, companions and servants from her salon and settled us both in cushioned chairs near the hearth. I had expected this and after a much-needed bath, a hot meal and a good night's sleep, I felt confident that I could handle my mother's inevitable probing about my time as a hostage. I managed to avoid lying to her by concentrating on the fraught circumstances of my escape and Cuthbert's rescue and avoiding too much mention of my companions at Aycliffe Peel. Fortunately she was more interested in my encounters with Lord and Lady Westmorland, exclaiming indignantly over Lady Elizabeth's unkindness and Lord Ralph's unreasonable demands. I think she was so relieved that I had returned in time for Richard's imminent arrival and by so doing also avoided the necessity of her having to make any concessions over property that she neglected to ask any direct questions about Sir John Neville.

On the night of Richard's arrival, it being Maundy Thursday, there was a discreet and private meal in the Great Chamber behind the Baron's Hall, attended only by family members, visiting clergy and the principal York retainers. Only one course was served, consisting of fewer than twenty meatless dishes and accompanied by light Anjou wines and Spanish sack. When a single subtlety was paraded towards the end of the repast, Richard was delighted to recognize a gilded marchpane model of his own personal emblem, a falcon perched on a fetterlock, a special type of padlock used to secure valuable horses against theft.

'I compliment your cooks, my lady,' the duke said to his hostess. 'I only registered my personal badge with the Royal Heralds quite recently. I am surprised anyone so far north knew of it.'

My mother frowned. 'We are not completely out of touch at Raby, my lord duke, and my cooks have plans to conjure even more imaginative ways of celebrating your marriage feast on Tuesday, which I believe is also your saint's day.'

'Yes, the feast of Richard of Chichester – a truly English saint.

I shall look forward to those. But Raby has already conjured me a wondrous bride. What more could I ask?'

This gallant response had me blushing again, despite my desire to appear mature and controlled, and my mother made no secret of her delight at her future son-in-law's honeyed words. The frown disappeared and her sapphire eyes sparkled. Richard's time at court had certainly taught him how to charm the ladies and I could see that my brother Hal, not usually easily pleased, was more than a little impressed by the urbane and sophisticated nobleman that had developed from the diffident young squire who had left Raby soon after our father's death. By contrast I was beginning to feel gauche and insecure, not a sensation I enjoyed.

This sense of inadequacy was compounded by Hal's remarks to me later as we said goodnight. 'You will have a great responsibility as Duchess of York, Cicely. Richard gives every sign of becoming a force in the land and not only thanks to his birth. He is a man of fierce ambition which will need tempering and a good wife should be the one to put a curb on his pride. Otherwise what now appears to be admirable intent could end up looking like arrogance and he will make enemies. Your role will need great patience and subtlety. I hope you have these qualities.'

I frowned, surprised by his sensitivity. 'I thought that all a great lord wants from his wife is sons, Hal. And that is in God's hands surely.'

He shook his head. 'You are wrong. Believe me, my wife Alice has brought far more than three sons to our marriage. She has become my most valued confidante and adviser. Only she knows the true workings of my mind and gives me her sincere view of its direction. You can be of similar value to Richard if you cause him to respect your opinions.' He gave me one of his rare smiles. 'And a few sons would not go amiss as well, of course.'

I gazed at him with innocent enquiry. 'And I suppose the earldom of Salisbury which Alice brought you has nothing to do with the regard you have for her?'

Hal looked affronted. 'The earldom was not a foregone conclusion, Cis. We married just after Alice's father had re-married and it was assumed that his young second wife would bring him the son and heir he needed. Who could know he would be killed in action before this hope was realized? My wish is that Richard will find you as loyal and chaste a wife as Alice has been to me,' he said. 'I am sure he will expect no less.'

That set me back on my heels. Being only too grateful for my escape from my abductors, Hal had refrained from asking me how I had managed to achieve it and I wondered if this rather pompous delivery only days before my wedding contained a veiled warning that what I may have chosen not to vouchsafe to him should never be revealed to anyone, especially not to my bridegroom. I wished him a thoughtful good night.

During the long Passiontide vigil on the following day my prayers before the veiled crucifix in the castle chapel were intense and fervent. When, at the climax of the litany, I watched the priests lower the purple shroud to reveal once more the figure of the crucified Christ, I wanted to be the first to rush forward and kiss the Cross but I waited patiently for my mother to lead the way and wondered, as I took my turn, if there truly was redemption in the twisted and emaciated body we so reverently acknowledged. If there was not, then surely I was damned.

11

Raby Castle

Cicely

During the quiet, contemplative afternoon before Sunday's Feast of the Resurrection, Richard came to my mother's salon. I was sitting with Hilda, a little apart from the other ladies, pretending to embroider a chemise while we whispered girlishly together about what we would wear for the Easter celebrations, our first opportunity for dressing up since the Shrove Tuesday feast before the start of Lent. Despite the barrage of curious female glances, Richard entered the room with no sign of awkwardness. In fact he appeared the embodiment of self-assurance, attired in neat, sober apparel appropriate to the holy day but nevertheless displaying subtle touches of sartorial style. His deep-red Cordovan leather shoes were not excessively pointed but the laces were tipped with gold, anyone with an eye for style could tell that the rich chestnut fur trimming on his grey doublet was not mere lordly minerva but ducal sable and the brooch in his black draped hat contained a darkly-glowing garnet the size of a hen's egg, set all around with moonstones. I felt suddenly lacking in ornament in my rather demure if fashionable blue woollen houppelande, chosen in deference to the season, and wished that I had worn a more elaborate gown.

After greeting Richard warmly, my mother immediately apologized and declared that she was needed in the castle chancery to discuss arrangements for the wedding festivities, while her ladies were due to attend a dance class. 'We intend to make merry at your wedding,' she assured him, 'so I have commissioned a master from London to teach us the latest dance-steps. Cicely and I will be having our lesson later. For the present, I will leave you two together. Hilda will stay but she will not listen or interrupt. I am sure you and Cicely have much to talk about.'

I cringed at her lack of subtlety and rather gushing tone, but Hilda gave me a little wink and squeezed my hand before collecting up her needlework and slipping across the solar to a distant corner where a brazier had been set to ward off the chill so far from the fire. As Richard approached me I stood up, smiling a greeting and dropping into a slow curtsy. I daresay I should have modestly lowered my eyes but instead I kept my chin raised, re-affirming our childhood relationship which had always been candid and lively. 'I did not expect to see you before dinner, my lord,' I said. 'You must have a thousand matters to attend to with so great a train about you. I hope they are all adequately housed and fed?'

He bent down, took my hand and raised me to my feet. Our eyes met, green on blue. We were of almost equal height now but for a time as children I had stood taller than him, a situation which I had relished but which I knew had riled him. There was no sign of irritation in his eyes now though; rather he looked captivated by what he saw and I thanked St Cicelia that I had chosen to bundle my mass of russet hair into fine gold filigree netting on a pearl and gold fillet. If my simple blue gown lacked sophistication, at least my headdress supplied some evidence of elegance.

His response to my enquiry held a hint of amusement. 'My people have no complaints about the Raby hospitality, thank you, but I did not seek your company to discuss their wellbeing, Cicely. We have much more important things to talk about now that we are at last alone.' His glance swivelled to where Hilda sat, eyes cast down on her embroidery, and his smile widened. 'Well, almost alone.'

'Perhaps you remember Hilda?' I made a gesture in her direction. 'She has been with me since childhood. She is my closest friend and privy to all my secrets.'

He took my hand and led me to the window where my mother often sat to read. The salon was on the second floor of the eponymous tower my father had built especially for his second wife, with windows that looked over the curtain wall and the wide moat to afford a panoramic view of the surrounding countryside. The stone seat of this oriel was comfortably cushioned in bright-blue figured damask and within its deep embrasure we would be out of Hilda's line of sight.

'I hope that will not be quite so true after we are married. I believe that man and wife should hold certain matters secret between themselves,' he said, seating me gallantly before settling down himself at a carefully judged distance. This was my first indication that with Richard everything was carefully judged, that is until he lost his temper, but I was not to discover this important variation just yet.

'You were young when I left Raby but I remember your skill at horsemanship,' Richard added unexpectedly. 'Even at ten years old you would slip away to the stables to tack up your pony and ride out. Cuthbert was invariably with you, of course, but your fusspot of a governess would come scurrying around the outbuildings looking for you. It made us henchmen laugh.'

I shrugged. 'I tried not to stay within call. I suppose I was an unruly little girl.'

'Yes, you were.' Richard shifted about to make himself comfortable on the soft cushions. Afternoon sun shining through the leaded panes bathed us in soft, golden light. 'But I admired you even then,' he added – as an afterthought, it seemed.

'Admired me?' I echoed. 'I thought you considered me silly and annoying.' I had a sudden recall of a particularly disdainful look when I was in trouble following one of my illicit rides.

'No, I never thought you silly. Annoying perhaps but mostly because you were so confident you would be forgiven whatever you did. And of course you always were.'

I gave a little laugh. Had he known what I was thinking? But what he said was true. I said, 'I was spoiled; an occupational hazard of being the youngest child in a large family.'

'I envied you that privilege.' Richard leaned forward, suddenly earnest. Once again he took my hand in his, clasping it gently. His palm was callused from wielding his sword and I could feel the scratch of the raised skin against mine. 'I should like us to have a large family, Cicely.'

I felt myself blushing again and berated my lack of self-control. 'We must be content with whatever God sends I suppose,' I murmured. I stared down at our joined hands and had a sudden image of how our bodies would be joined after our marriage. It would be so soon after John – but perhaps that was just as well. A shiver ran down my spine but Richard seemed not to notice.

'I am the last of a line,' he was saying. 'The House of York needs sons. I intend to make the white rose flourish and there will be much to pass on to the next generation. Still, as you say, it is in the hands of God.'

He was fiddling with the betrothal ring on my middle finger. 'I remember when you put that ring on my finger,' I said. 'You did not look as if you admired me then. You are greatly changed from the boy that was my father's ward.'

'I hardly knew you. You were only eight or nine and I did not want to be betrothed to anyone. But on the contrary, Cicely, it is you who are most changed. You have become beautiful.'

His use of the word unnerved me. Emotion and memories rose like a tide and I could feel the same frisson running up my arm as I had when John had used it, only a few days ago. Was I so gullible, so vulnerable to flattery? I snatched my hand away but managed to hide the action as if assailed by a sudden sneeze, pulling my kerchief from my sleeve pocket.

'Please forgive me.' My words were muffled in the kerchief. 'It is not an ague – just dust I think. Or perhaps I am not used to flattery.' I managed another little laugh, turning back and tucking the kerchief away again. 'At least I hope my appearance coincides with what you consider appropriate in a duchess, although I am afraid you find me rather plainly attired today. It is Lent . . .'

He shook his head. 'You look just as I hope I may see you many times in the future, in private moments. But I do believe that greater display is needed for public appearances. People love a spectacle and it is important that we give our vassals reason to bend the knee. With you by my side they will have splendour and beauty. And to that end I have something for you which I hope you will wear at our wedding.'

He opened the gilded leather purse he wore on his belt and took out a silk pouch, tied at the neck. I gasped as he tipped it over his palm. Shards of brilliance began to dance around us when the object it contained caught the light from the window. It was a brooch, fashioned to represent the wild English rose from which the York emblem was derived. Five white diamonds set in gold were laid like petals around a large central stone of a much yellower colour, such as I had never seen before. The gems seemed to pulse with life in his hand.

'I had it made for you by a London goldsmith,' he said. 'The middle stone is a yellow diamond and very rare. May I pin it on your gown?'

We both stood up. My gown was fashioned with a central opening at the neck, through which the white linen and lace of my chemise showed. He pinned the brooch to my bodice, just above where the gown was cinched under my bust by a gold-braided girdle. I felt the pressure of his fingers on my breasts and was sure he could sense the nipples pucker. He smiled as if he knew my knees had gone weak and leaned in to kiss my mouth, raising his hand to caress the back of my neck. His lips left a warm, soft imprint on mine.

'It is the first of many jewels I shall give you, Cicely, for beauty demands beautiful things. I look forward greatly to our wedding on Tuesday but even more to our life together afterwards.'

Due to the season there were no fresh white roses at my wedding, which took place before a large assembly of guests in the Baron's Hall at Raby, but the white rose symbol featured liberally on the heraldic banners hanging from the rafters, on the badges of many of the guests and in the elaborate embroidery on the new ducal mantle draped on the shoulders of the bridegroom. As I stood before the Duke of York, waiting to confirm my betrothal commitment to him, I wondered if my father had envisaged this white rose challenge to the red rose of Lancaster, to which he had been so faithful. Up to the time of our marriage affinity badges had been small and inconspicuous; noble support for Lancaster had mainly been signified by the wearing of the double S collar and any rivalry between the red rose and the white had been restricted to the jousting lists. There was no reason to suppose that my union with Richard would be anything more than a peaceful one between two dynasties for the purposes of perpetuating their lines and establishing an accord between their families. However, looking back on the day I suppose we might have detected the first signs of discord, stirred by the flamboyance of Richard's retinue with their conspicuous white rose badges and the sly jokes this inspired among the other attendant peers, not least my own brothers.

At Richard's invitation, the nuptial mass in the castle chapel was presided over by the elderly bishop of Durham, Thomas Langley, a former Chancellor of England and an *eminence grise* of the Church. As he blessed our union I found the venerable Bishop's gnarled hand on my head a reassuring reminder of God's promise of forgiveness and in return I made a silent vow of marital faithfulness.

The wedding feast lasted well into the night, impressive for its ten ceremonial courses with their seemingly endless procession of dishes that were paraded shoulder-high around the hall before being removed to the carvers and divided into portions; for the ingenious table-fountains which flowed constantly with wine and hippocras and for the army of tumblers, mummers and minstrels that had travelled from far and wide to entertain us in the intervals while one course was cleared to make way for the next. From my seat of honour beside Richard at the high table I watched the guests grow drunker and the dancing become wilder and I laughed and smiled while my stomach churned with anxiety so that I ate little and drank less. I watched my mother nodding and laughing with Bishop Langley while on her other hand my brother Hal barely cracked a smile. Perhaps he was worrying about his absent wife Alice, who might at that moment be birthing their latest child.

I could not begin to imagine how much all this revelry had depleted the Neville coffers but Richard was well pleased by it. 'I confess I had wanted to hold our wedding at my castle of Fotheringhay,' he whispered during the feast, 'but your lady mother wrote that her husband had made a point of leaving special funds for our nuptials, providing they were held at Raby. It was a long way for my vassals to travel but this feast alone has made it worth their while. However, they are just having a feast, whereas I have gained a brilliant and beautiful duchess.'

My new husband raised the jewelled gold bridal cup we shared. On an impulse I leaned in close to hold the lid beneath it as I had used to do for my father and Richard's eyes lit up in delighted surprise. 'Thank you, my lady wife; no female has ever done that for me before. While we both live I shall never allow another to do so.'

This was no tipsy wedding promise. I understood his implied declaration of marital loyalty and when he had drunk, I gently took the cup from him and turned it, then pressed my own lips to where the rim was still warm from his and sipped at the rich red wine. Our eyes locked and I knew we had exchanged a solemn vow. 'I shall hold you to that, my lord,' I said softly. 'And while you live I shall never be cup-bearer to another man.'

This exchange and Richard's obvious sincerity did much to loosen the knot in my belly, as did the subsequent flow of wedding gifts presented to us. First and foremost a gloriously illuminated Book of Hours, ostensibly from King Henry but clearly acquired for him from France by his uncle Duke John of Bedford, judging by the skilful artistry displayed in its pages. My mother's gift was a set of tapestries from Arras depicting the miracles of Christ, including the wedding at Cana, while from Hal and Alice came a pair of jewelled hanaps, from the Bishop of Durham a portable altar and a beautiful chased silver flagon from Will and Jane Fauconberg.

The loving smile on the cherubic face of Will's childlike wife moved me deeply, especially when she laid her hands on her own swelling belly and asked in her piping voice, 'Baby for Cicely soon, too?' before embracing me enthusiastically. So she does understand what is happening to her, I thought, whatever people may think. I thanked my brother warmly for his gift and wished them both God's blessing for the impending birth.

In the midst of this a courier arrived, whose appearance stirred a noisy reaction on the floor of the hall. His tunic bore the Neville saltire differenced by a black bull's head and all present knew this indicated that he came from Brancepeth. He approached the dais and knelt, offering me a sealed letter.

I could feel my face drain of colour as he intoned clearly, 'I bring greetings to her grace the Duchess of York from Sir John Neville of Brancepeth.'

My hand shook as I broke the seal but I did not unfold the letter. Whatever it contained I did not want to be the one who read it first. Instead I turned and handed it to Richard, sensing that a demonstration of my new subjection to his will would gratify him. 'Read it, if it please you, my lord,' I said, my heart in my mouth.

To my relief, after scanning the page Richard smiled broadly. 'Sir John sends you a wedding gift, my lady. He describes it as "a gentle palfrey which will carry you faithfully into your new life". What a chivalrous gesture. Where is the palfrey, goodman?'

'In the stable, your grace.'

I heard my mother ask icily, 'Is there no present from the earl?' but there was no response. The courier merely studied the floor and shuffled his feet.

Richard appeared not to notice. 'We will inspect it tomorrow. Pray convey her grace's gratitude to Sir John.'

My lips smiled at the retiring courier but my heart and mind were still racing. For several minutes Richard stood and received more gifts and good wishes while I waited for my nerves to steady. Eventually, during the next lull in proceedings I stood up and walked down the table to address my mother.

'I would ask a wedding boon of you, my lady mother, if you will be generous enough to grant it.'

Alarm rose in her eyes but was quickly stifled. 'If I can, naturally I will,' she answered cautiously.

'Since Sir John Neville has been kind enough to send a wedding gift, I would like to return the compliment. His brother Thomas has recently lost a good marriage because he had no suitable home to offer his bride. I would count it a personal favour if our family was to grant him the manor of Slingsby as a place to establish a future family life.'

It was my mother's turn to blanch. She glanced furtively at Richard before biting her lip and frowning at me, clearly unable to comprehend my sudden desire to reward the very people who had endangered my own marriage. Yet she could not remonstrate because Richard was unaware of my abduction and she knew it to be imperative that he remain so. It was clear that my mother remained as unwilling as ever to relinquish an acre of the lands her late husband had left her, but it was my belief that the transfer of Slingsby into Thomas's ownership would ensure the silence of the Brancepeth Nevilles on the subject of her legacy and that of Sir John Neville in particular. My mother cast a beseeching glance at Hal, looking for assistance, but my gamble paid off. He was full of gratitude to me for escaping my captors without him needing to offer the palatial castle and substantial landholding of Sherriff Hutton as a ransom, and perfectly willing to surrender the comparatively unimportant manor of Slingsby at my request. 'I think that is a splendid notion, Cicely. I will make the necessary arrangements for the title to be transferred to Thomas Neville of Brancepeth. Once he is knighted and the lord of such a prosperous manor, he will have no trouble in attracting a well-endowed wife. We cannot have a family of Nevilles living in reduced circumstances.'

Confronted with a *fait accompli*, my mother had little option but to accept the situation. 'So be it,' she said and demonstrated her displeasure by turning her back on us.

At this point the minstrels struck up for dancing and after Richard and I had led a merry *estampie* and several prominent vassal-lords had raised toasts to our health and fertility, my new husband told the Master of the Feast to announce that we would retire, generating a chorus of whistles and catcalls from the body of the hall. The minstrels played a stately march but some scurrilously bawdy lyrics sung from the lower trestles marred our dignified exit. Fortunately it was only a short walk to the privy door, when I could hide my burning cheeks from general view.

'In the name of God, what is this?' Richard demanded, reaching down among the luxuriant covers of our nuptial bed.

Following Bishop Langley's fatherly blessing, when my mother and Hilda had drawn the curtains at my side and Richard's chosen lords had done the same on his, I could not have been more relieved. Amidst the lewd sniggers of the tipsy crowd of guests who had attended our formal bedding, I had made a silent vow that any children Richard and I might have would never be subject to such an indignity. A blessing on the wedding night was one thing but bawdy comments and suggestive remarks were another. I was not called 'Proud Cis' for nothing and I had not relished the ignominy of such a barrage of innu-endo. Nor, I suspected, had Richard, for in the dancing shadows of the night-lamp his expression was thunderous.

A wriggling movement among the fur covers in the great bed's nether regions revealed the cause of his new displeasure. He pounced and extricated a squirming brown and white animal which he held out to me with an expression of distaste. 'Is this yours?' he asked.

We were both still wearing the velvet chamber robes in which we had been put to bed but his had fallen open during his search and for a few seconds I found myself admiring the sculpted muscles of his torso as he held my pet dog at arm's length. I took the little creature from him.

'Caspar always sleeps on my bed,' I said. I could feel a volcano of nervous giggles threatening to erupt and I snuggled the terrier into my chest to muffle them in his wiry coat. 'He must have sneaked in. He has missed me all day.'

Richard reached over and firmly removed Caspar from my arms. As he did so one of the dog's claws inadvertently scratched me, drawing a bloody red line across the swell of my breast. Unceremoniously Richard dropped the terrier over the side of the bed and I heard Caspar scuttle away whimpering. My giggles instantly gave way to protest. 'He does no harm really. He just wants to be friends.'

'He has hurt you though. You are bleeding.' Richard was staring at my breast where beads of blood were oozing up in the red weal left by the little dog's claw. He pulled up the rumpled sheet and dabbed at them gently. 'Does it hurt?'

'No, not much; it does not matter.'

I was still worrying about Caspar and did not notice that Richard's expression had changed from frowning concern to narrow-eyed lust. 'It matters to me,' he said, bending to put his lips to the bloody weal. His voice sounded different – fervent and thickened and I felt his sexual tension as he licked at the blood. Tentatively I indulged my fantasy of plunging my fingers into his luxuriant curly bronze hair and he responded by lifting his head and pulling my robe fully open, taking my breasts in his hands and stroking the nipples with his thumbs. He was smiling now, a proud, possessive, sensuous curve of his moist lips. 'These are mine now. You are mine, Cicely. I want no harm to come them or to you.'

I was startled by my own rapid reaction to his ardour. I felt my breasts swell and my nipples stiffen under his caress and something like liquid fire trickled through the core of my belly and into the flesh between my legs. I was deliciously aroused and wanted it to go on but at the same time it frightened me. Surely this was wicked? Against everything I had been taught. Pleasure did not happen between man and wife. Ever since we were children I had expected to couple with Richard in order to get children; it was a duty to be performed, not an act to make me feel as I had felt with . . . no I would not name him even to myself. It was as if my mind and body were two different creatures; one crying out in protest, the other beginning to arch in ecstasy.

It was on the tip of my tongue to tell Richard to stop, that this was all wrong, when I felt a stab of pain and he was pushing fiercely inside me as I lay spread-eagled beneath him. As quickly as it had come, all my pleasure abated. I was his wife. I could not refuse him. I must ignore the pain and let him thrust his seed deep inside me so that God could make a child. That was my duty and after several thrusts and a groan of release, duty was done.

When we had rolled apart and arranged ourselves for sleep I realized that at least, thanks to Caspar, one of my worries was over. Richard had entered me and there was blood on the sheets. Our marriage was consummated and we were one body in the sight of God and the law of England. There was no going back.

PART TWO

France
1442–1444

12

Rouen, Normandy 1442

Cuthbert

Towards the end of the road to Rouen we broke free of the dangers of the forest and I ordered my troop to draw rein in order to walk the last mile. Armour and harness jangled less percussively as our horses slowed from their fast, working trot to a gentler pace while at the same time their necks stretched out and their nostrils flared as they caught their breath.

Ahead of us the city gradually came into sight. Once a jewel in the crown of France, it was now a battered shell, its pale stone walls displaying ugly gaps, like the smile of an ageing man. In the twenty-three years since the English had marched into the capital of Normandy after a long and bloody siege, repairs had been done to the cathedral and castle but the damage inflicted by Henry the Fifth's massive cannons on the city's outer defences still showed as gaping scars, testament to the fact that the tightly defended borders of the duchy now prohibited any French attempt to retrieve the city at its centre, making repairs unnecessary. In this Year of Our Lord 1442 the commander of those defences and the King's Deputy and Lieutenant General in France was Richard, Duke of York.

However, the sight that struck me most forcibly whenever I approached the city was not its crumbling walls but the extraordinary ghostly landscape surrounding them. In fields where crops had once grown, long strips of fabric in a hundred different shades of white now billowed in the breeze like the sails of some enormous land-locked armada. The famous linen weavers of Rouen had taken over farms abandoned as a result of the siege and employed them for cloth-crofting, the complicated business of employing the elements to turn their cloth the purest white. The process took months and involved successive soakings, first in urine and finally in buttermilk, with washing and extended periods of airing in between.

'This is a sight to see, is it not?' remarked the lady riding beside me. 'They used to send the raw linen to Holland for crofting.'

The lady was Anne, Countess of Stafford and I had been sent to Calais in command of a troop of men-at-arms to bring her safely to Rouen for her sister Cicely's lying-in. Strictly speaking, I was brother to both these noble ladies, although as a mere knight, the division between our ranks could scarcely have been wider and this hazardous journey across the plains and forests of Picardy and northern Normandy had been the first time the Lady Anne and I had ever met. I had expected to find the task of escort irksome but had now decided that a man of any rank could do worse than spend a few days in the company of this spirited female. Although she was nine years older than Cicely and already well into her thirties, she was far from being middle-aged in her attitude to life and her elegant red-leather trappings and fashionable fur-trimmed riding huke disguised a practical, down-to-earth disposition. Several times during our ride from Calais, where her husband was captain of the embattled English garrison, we had been forced to draw swords and engage with desperate gangs of bandits called *écorcheurs* who haunted the northern forests, preying on unwary travellers, and far from cowering behind her escort the countess had unsheathed a useful poignard concealed in her riding boot and wielded it in earnest.

'There is no trade with the Low Countries now, not since the Duke of Burgundy broke the alliance with England,' I replied, watching her shift her weight in her sideways saddle and tuck a stray strand of silvery temple-hair back under the scarf of her blue chaperon. 'So the weavers must bleach all their own cloth.'

'Well it is heartening to see the land put to some use,' she said. 'Even a wilderness of white linen is better than thistles and weeds, though it will not feed the people.'

'The duke has ruled that the weavers' guild should set up feeding stations for the poor and dispossessed. He has even endowed them generously himself,' I told her. 'There is less unrest in the city since he took up his post.'

She pursed her lips. 'I am glad to hear it. At least he puts his riches to good use.'

I made no comment. Richard of York was, as everyone knew, the richest man in the two kingdoms and there was much barely concealed envy among those of the landed nobility who were not so well endowed. Although the Earl of Stafford was almost as wealthy, it seemed that even his countess was not averse to passing the odd mildly caustic remark.

Our conversation was forced to cease because we had reached the city gate and became caught up in the crowds queuing to press through the narrow tunnel beneath the battered barbican. Encouraged by our trumpeters' noisy blasts they shifted reluctantly to let us pass but our royal banners and white rose badges were not greeted with any enthusiasm by the sour-faced citizens of Normandy. Indeed, despite the fact that many of their leaders now apparently worked willingly alongside their English conquerors, the common people of Rouen still tended the graves of their siege-starved forebears and went about their daily tasks in silent resentment, taking the money their goods could earn but hating the hands they took it from. It was pointless to tell these stiff-necked Frenchmen that the men they called 'conquerors' were Normans like themselves, back in their own duchy two hundred years after the French had stolen it from them. In their eyes the invaders were '*cochons Anglais*', English pigs, who hid tails under their doublets and murdered their kings. Rouen may be peaceful but it was not content.

I led the troop across the busy market square towards the castle where extensive patches of new stonework indicated the level of damage the siege artillery had inflicted. It was a sprawling warren of towers and courtyards centered on an imposing buttressed hall with a steep sloping roof of green slates which housed the law courts and meetings of the Normandy Estates. It was the seat of English government and therefore the official residence of the Duke of York. I was pleased to see the lily and lion standard flying from the hall tower, indicating that the Royal Council was in session. The duke would be entertaining his fellow councillors and my rumbling stomach welcomed the fact that there would be plentiful feasting at dusk.

Elbowing a squire out of the way, I made a point of assisting Lady Anne to dismount myself. She smiled as I set her lightly down on the cobblestones of the central courtyard. 'Thank you, Sir Cuthbert, although after all the hours we have spent and alarms we have experienced together I think I may truly call you brother. I envy Cicely her good fortune in having you to rely on.'

I returned her smile and added an admiring bow. 'I am

honoured to be related to two such great ladies but I will not yet say farewell. Cicely instructed me to deliver you to her side and that is exactly what I shall do. Her chamberlain will show your female companion to your lodging where your baggage will be sent and, with your permission, I will personally escort you directly to the privy apartments.'

The splendid civic clock, recently installed in the marketplace, was sounding four when, having adjourned his council meeting, Richard, Duke of York, surrounded by his entourage, came striding out of the great hall and intercepted us at the foot of the grand stairway which led up to the ducal lodging. 'My lady of Stafford, good sister, you are safely arrived! May God be thanked,' he said enthusiastically, bending over the countess's hand. 'How kind it is of you to make such an arduous journey to support Cicely at this crucial time. She will be overjoyed to see you.'

'It was not so arduous with Sir Cuthbert beside me,' responded the countess. 'He is the kind of companion who clears the road and lightens the load, to say nothing of seeing off bandits with a flick of his sword. I have never felt safer outside the walls of Calais.'

The duke raised his eyebrows at me. 'Praise indeed, Cuthbert! I can see Cicely chose the right escort for her sister.'

I grinned back at him. 'Allow me to tell you, brother, that whenever swords were out, Lady Anne was doing her fair share by a masterly use of the small blade. I cannot believe it was not I who trained her.'

Anne laughed and bent swiftly to demonstrate her sleight of hand with the poignard. It appeared in her hand without a visible movement of her skirt and Richard took an involuntary step back, as surprised as I had been the first time I saw her do it. 'I pride myself on giving no quarter,' she said proudly. 'It has proved useful in the past but on this journey I drew the blade for show only, I was protected from all danger.' With equal skill she re-sheathed the knife and took the duke's proffered arm. 'But tell me, Richard, how is my sister? I am sorry I was unable to attend her previous lying-ins. Has she recovered from her grave disappointment . . .?'

They began to climb the stair together and I followed a step behind. The rest of the entourage had dropped well back. 'In truth I think she has not,' the duke replied. 'She tries to hide it from me but there is her lassitude, I have never seen that in her before, and she spends much time with our confessor. I know Cicely is deeply melancholy. But I cannot discover if there is a reason, other than the death of our son, of course. Perhaps you might have more success.'

'Is not the death of a longed-for son enough reason to be melancholy?' demanded Anne. 'It is only a year ago. And before that our mother died. Cicely was closer to her than any of us. Perhaps she has not recovered from either death and now she must face another birth and with it the possibility of another death. It is not easy, my lord. You must be patient.'

Richard frowned, his head uncharacteristically lowered. 'I hope she does not find me impatient. I never blamed her for the death of Henry. I, too, was devastated, but it was God's will.'

The countess patted his arm. 'These things happen, but you are both young. There is plenty of time. I will try and cheer her up. Does she have any other ladies to help her? When will she take to her chamber?'

'Next week. There is to be a service in the cathedral and then she will retire.'

'So the babe will be born in May then?'

'Do not ask me! That is women's talk. Perhaps tonight will cheer us all. We have a banquet and entertainment planned for the members of the council and their wives. I am sorry your lord could not attend but I hear the pirates in the Straits of Dover have been trounced. Two ships captured and ten scoundrels hanged. It was worth him missing the meeting.'

'He will think so,' said Anne grimly. 'It is hoped their confederates might be deterred, for the present.'

When we reached the arched doorway that led to the great solar the guards threw back the double doors. Servants and chamberlains waiting in the ante-chamber scrambled to their feet as we entered. One of the chamberlains bowed and knocked on a door with his staff for entrance to the solar. The door was opened from within.

The young ladies stood and curtsied but Cicely remained reclined on a cushioned couch, one hand on her swollen belly, the other extended in welcome. 'My dearest lord, you are finished early in council. And Cuthbert and my sister are here at last! You are so very welcome, Anne.'

The two women embraced warmly, seats were brought and the young lady companions trooped from the chamber in response to Cicely's wave of dismissal. I stood to one side and studied my pregnant sister's face. It looked puffy and her belly seemed to pin her down like a barrel. Sensing my gaze, she turned and I caught a glimpse of the old Cicely in the smile she gave me.

'Thank you, Cuthbert, for bringing Anne to me. I have been counting the hours.' She turned back to the countess. 'You are so good to come – and through such hostile territory, too. Did you have any trouble?'

Lady Anne brushed the enquiry aside. 'Never mind all that. How are you, Cicely? You look very pale.'

Although they both now lived in France, to my knowledge the two sisters had not seen each other since their mother's funeral nearly two years before, when the whole Neville clan had suspended hostilities to gather at Raby castle. The cortège journeyed from there down to Lincoln where Lady Joan was to be buried in the cathedral beside her beloved mother Katherine, Duchess of Lancaster. Being great with her second child, Cicely had opted not to follow; instead her own procession, and I with it, embarked on a cautious fifteen-miles-a-day progress south to Fotheringhay Castle. Riding beside her cushioned litter, I had listened to her sustained sobbing.

'I should not have endangered my baby by travelling to Raby, but how could I not attend my mother's funeral?' she had cried in despair during one unscheduled stop at a crowded roadside inn when she had complained of dizziness and agonizing cramps. 'I do not have good feelings about this baby, Cuthbert.'

Those fears had proved well founded. Her little boy, baptized Henry after the king, had died a week after his birth in early February. It seemed to me that she had not regained any of her spirit since.

In response to Lady Anne's enquiry, Cicely's brow furrowed. 'Is there any wonder I look pale? It has done nothing but rain lately, I have barely left these apartments for weeks, and Richard has been absent during all of Lent inspecting the border garrisons.' She glanced at the duke enquiringly. 'Did the council agree your plans for strengthening them, my lord?'

Richard of York was rarely defeated in council: he was a man in his prime, thirty years old and toned in body and mind. It seemed that today had been no exception, the ruling Normandy barons and captains of the council had agreed. 'And wisely so,' remarked Richard, 'for they knew I would deploy reinforcements anyway, whether funds are forthcoming from the royal exchequer or not.'

'Has there been any word from the king?' Cicely's question was laced with concern, as well it might be, I thought. While the duke ruled his own council with a rod of iron, he was constantly frustrated in his attempts to garner financial support from the king's council in England.

His face clouded but an initial scowl was hastily replaced by a look of resignation. Richard did not like to be seen to lose his temper. 'The king sends copious letters but no gold. As usual it is all promises with Henry but no delivery. No matter, 'twas ever thus, as you know, sweetheart. Humphrey suffers from this as well, does he not, Anne?'

Lady Anne hesitated for a split second before replying. 'Reinforcements were sent to Calais in order to tackle the pirates but no funds to pay them,' she admitted. 'My lord was obliged to open his own purse, and it was an expensive campaign, but well worth it.'

'No doubt of that.' Richard nodded. 'But like Humphrey, I find defending Normandy a constant drain on my own exchequer, when it should be royally funded. I hold the Earl of Somerset responsible. I suspect that the king wishes to compensate Somerset for the thirteen years he spent as a French prisoner and all available funds are being diverted to his campaign in Aquitaine. I confess I look forward to discussing ways to tackle this situation when Humphrey manages to get here.'

'But meanwhile we neglect our duty as hosts, my lord,' Cicely said reproachfully. 'My dear sister has not come to Rouen to talk tactics and finance. Cuthbert, since I have sent my chamberlains away would you be kind enough to pour some wine and serve the wafers? We dine at sunset but you must both be hungry and thirsty and I am sure my lord is too, after all that talking in council.'

I had been eyeing the platter of delicious-looking cakes laid out on the buffet and so I was more than willing to oblige. Lady Anne partook readily before remarking, 'Cicely is right, my lord duke, I have not come here to discuss our mutual grievances with King Henry. I have come to help her bring a strong child into the world.'

'A strong *boy*-child,' emphasized Richard, carefully wiping crumbs from his fingers with a kerchief. 'And I hope you can allay your sister's fears about his chances of survival, my lady. I see no reason why God should deny us a healthy son when we have founded churches, endowed chantries, supported monasteries and furnished chapels to His glory, all in the hope and expectation of His mercy. Cicely must have faith.'

Cicely smiled wearily at her sister. 'Richard and I do not agree on this, Anne. I cannot believe that faith is some divine business arrangement, where we have merely to purchase enough indulgences or endow the right shrine to sway the celestial scales in our favour. God deals with us as He sees fit and since I have not produced an heir in eight years of marriage it is obvious that I must have grievously offended the Almighty. I pray constantly that He will reveal to me how I should atone for my sins so that my lord may be granted the son he so richly deserves.'

For the duration of this confession Lady Anne was shaking her head. 'No, Cicely, that cannot be right. You have a healthy daughter – my namesake Anne, who I hope to see very soon – and there is no reason why you should not have a healthy son. Besides, if children were only granted to those without sin then there would be no bastards born since they are, by definition, conceived in sin. Sin is no barrier to bringing new life. We have our magnificent brother Cuthbert here to prove it.'

Although her comment was made with an apologetic smile in my direction, I could have wished the countess had used another example for her sister's encouragement. I had not found bastardy an easy burden to bear and her remark, though kindly meant, brought back memories still painful to me of events at Cicely's mother's funeral. An encounter redolent with ugly prejudice and a woeful misuse of seigniorial power that would live with me for ever . . .

13

Raby Castle November 1440

Cuthbert

Lady Joan Beaufort, dowager Countess of Westmorland, had not died in her eponymous tower at Raby as perhaps she might have wished but at Howden on Yorkshire's border with Lincolnshire. Her son Robert was bishop of Durham and possessed of a splendid episcopal palace on the River Ouse at Howden, the southern capital of his sprawling diocese. She had been visiting him there when, at the age of sixty-one, she died suddenly of a seizure.

As soon as word of her death reached him, the Earl of Westmorland sent his brother, Sir John Neville, galloping from Brancepeth to take seisin of the Raby castle and lands in accordance with the will of the old earl. Such haste might have been thought to show a lack respect for the deceased dowager but from Lord Westmorland's point of view it had been a wise precaution because Sir John and his troop of Brancepeth retainers had arrived only hours ahead of the Earl of Salisbury, who had led his personal army in a forced march over the high moors from his castle at Penrith with exactly the same aim. Had the order of arrival been reversed it might well have resulted in a siege, but as it was, Hal had been obliged to recognize the rule of law and back away, achieving only permission to send in servants to pack up Lady Joan's personal belongings and make arrangements for her body to rest in the castle chapel after it arrived from Howden. Denied a welcome in his childhood home, he was obliged to seek accommodation down the road at the college of priests his father had established alongside the church of St Gregory in Staindrop.

I too had been refused entry. I was escorting Cicely's closed and cushioned litter, but when we reached Raby I was told by the captain of the guard: 'Only blood relatives of the late countess are to be admitted to the castle. One personal servant is allowed; all other relatives and retainers must find their own accommodation.'

When I relayed this news to Cicely she demanded that the captain approach her litter. 'Who is responsible for this lamentable state of affairs?' she enquired in her most ducal tone.

'The c-constable, if it please your grace,' he replied, visibly quaking.

'My mother's constable would never have given such an order.' Cicely was fixing the captain with such a basilisk stare that I began to feel quite sorry for him. 'Her instructions were that all weary travellers should be admitted and in view of her reverence for the Virgin Mary she would especially be hospitable to expectant mothers and their company.'

'The Earl of Westmorland's constable is in charge now, your grace – Sir John Neville. It was he who gave the order.'

The change in Cicely's expression was extraordinary. Her face drained of colour and all sign of belligerence seemed to vanish. There was a tense pause and when she spoke again her voice had lost its stridence.

'Convey my greetings to Sir John and tell him I will enter the castle with my companion Hilda Copley. I will require accommodation in Lady Joan's Tower and access to the chapel where I wish to keep vigil over my mother's coffin. My brother Sir Cuthbert of Middleham will accompany me with a small guard for our personal security. We will not stay longer than necessary and will not interfere in any way with his command of the castle. He has my solemn oath on that.'

Having digested this message the captain disappeared back through the sally port in the main gate. Hilda stepped down from the litter and I dismounted to speak to her. 'We cannot wait long, Cuddy,' she warned. 'For her baby's sake we must have warmth and shelter tonight. What shall we do if her ultimatum is refused?'

The expression in Hilda's troubled brown eyes stirred in me the deep feelings I consistently held for her. I yearned to draw my sword and fight my way into the castle to save her from anxiety, but all I could do was try to reassure her. 'We will wait until we hear the chapel bell ring for the next Office but I have sent harbingers out to find alternative accommodation, just in case. Even though he held her hostage once, I do not believe Sir John will risk public censure by turning Cicely away now.'

Hilda shrugged. 'She seems confident of that too but she is still praying to Our Lady for her intervention.'

I gave her a lopsided smile. 'Well, it must be owned that she knows Sir John rather better than we do,' I said.

On the first clangs of the bell for the afternoon Office, the heavy portcullis juddered off the ground and the gates behind it began to grind back on their runners. The luxurious York litter was waved through the gatehouse arch with Cicely and Hilda inside. Most of the escort trotted off in the direction of the village while I followed the litter on horseback with a contingent of six men-at-arms. The knot of tension in my stomach eased but, even as I put up a prayer of thanks to the Virgin for her intercession, I did not know that I was riding into a personal nightmare.

Cicely appeared calm when Sir John Neville stepped forward in the inner courtyard of the castle and greeted her with a bend of the knee. They had not met in the seven years since she had escaped his clutches at Aycliffe Tower and their conversation was brief and stiff. As I stood a good few yards away I could not hear what passed between them but when Cicely turned to make her way to her accommodation in Lady Joan's Tower, I kept a close eye on Sir John's expression. I had expected it to be hard and soldierly but instead, to my surprise, he looked benign, almost protective.

Having left a guard on the entrance to Cicely's chambers, I made my own way to the Baron's Hall by passages and stairways still familiar from my days as a Neville henchman. As I expected, the long room was busy with servants attending small knots of barons, knights and squires, all soberly garbed and recognizable as relatives, tenants and vassals of the Neville affinity. Black hangings covered the brightly coloured tapestries which normally enlivened the walls and only Lady Joan's personal banner with its royal lions and Beaufort portcullises hung from the rafters, festooned with black rosettes. Food and drink were laid out on trestles at either end of the room, each the focus of a distinctly separate group, and the atmosphere was charged with tension rather than the quiet sadness of a house in mourning. There was a noticeable gap between the groups, as if two sides were gathering for a game of camp-ball, a sport I had never seen played without it degenerating into violence and injury.

In the gap a table had been placed for two clerks who were to register the funeral attendees. Seated between them, in a high-backed chair that signified authority, was the man I least desired to encounter under any circumstance, Sir Gerald Copley.

When he saw me approach the table, his lips stretched in a mirthless smile and his voice rang out in the hushed chamber. 'Ah, the Bastard of Middleham has arrived.' He turned to one of the clerks, keeping his voice at the same volume. 'He is neither Neville-born nor blood of the deceased. You can list him under "others".'

With an effort I ignored the insult and smiled at the flustered clerk, whose quill hovered over a vellum scroll held open by weighted rulers. 'I am known as Sir Cuthbert of Middleham, Master Clerk. That is how I am listed by the King of Arms.'

Sir Gerald pushed back his heavy chair and stood up. 'But still a bastard, whatever gloss you put on it, *Sir* Cuthbert.' He laid mocking emphasis on the knightly title.

Still I kept my anger in check. 'And I am proud to carry that baton on my Neville coat of arms, Sir Gerald. Some men are born bastards and others are born brutes,' I said, looking straight at him. 'I know which I would rather be.'

Copley's face contused with a rage he could not contain but there was a table between us and, unable to launch himself across it to reach me, he shoved it so hard that the clerks' inkhorns tipped and spilled, spattering their scrolls with blots. Their yelps of dismay and scrabbling movements to right the horns destroyed the calm of the chamber and the grouped guests erupted into surprised oaths, making a general movement towards the source of the alarm. It might have been enough to kick off a ruckus if a loud shout had not risen above the general hubbub.

'My lords and gentlemen, order please! Let us remember why we are here.' The tall figure of Sir John Neville had emerged through the privy door onto the hall dais and his voice carried clearly over the heads of the gathering. 'As I am sure you are all aware, Raby Castle is now in the stewardship of the Earl of Westmoreland and he has appointed me his constable.' Sir John's choice of apparel was carefully neutral; brown doublet and hose rather than black as he was not related to the deceased by blood, and he wore no evidence of affinity other than a small hat-badge showing a red enamel and silver saltire, the ubiquitous Neville device. He stepped down into the body of the hall and pushed his way through the crowd to the table where Sir Gerald was still huffing and puffing and glaring at me murderously.

Sir John addressed me directly. 'Sir Cuthbert, I trust my deputy constable has explained the rules and procedures for the dowager countess's funeral,' he said pleasantly. 'Sir Gerald Copley is known to you, I am sure. I have made him responsible for assisting the steward with seating and accommodation arrangements. There is much strain on the castle's resources but for a few days we must all make an effort to rub along together out of respect for the deceased.'

I made him a bow of acknowledgement. 'I understand completely, Sir John. Lady Joan was an important influence on my life and I will do all in my power to honour her obsequies. If Sir Gerald should need any assistance . . .' I let the offer hang in the air as a derisive snort was forthcoming from the said knight.

Sir John frowned at his deputy then raised his head to once more address the gathering, whose loud exclamations had subsided into low murmurings. 'Cool tempers and clear heads will be of most assistance at this time. Lady Joan's immediate family will keep a vigil beside the coffin in the castle chapel but they would welcome prayer and support from those who wish to pay their last respects. Please enter the chapel in small groups; it is not large, as you know. The funeral procession to the church will begin at dawn the day after tomorrow, the feast of Saint Katherine of Alexandria, an appropriate day since Lady Joan desired and arranged to be buried beside her beloved mother Katherine, Duchess of Lancaster, in Lincoln Cathedral. The cortège will leave immediately after the funeral mass and make its first stop at Durham Cathedral where his grace Bishop Neville will lead another requiem mass for his mother. All those who wish to follow the catafalque should make their intentions known to the clerks.'

Having delivered his announcements, Sir John made a point of speaking to several of the senior knights at the Brancepeth end of the Baron's Hall. I made for the exit nearest to the chapel but before I reached it Sir Gerald had swept past me and accosted me at the door. With him was a grey-bearded man wearing a furred merchant's gown and a large guild-master's chain around his shoulders.

'Before you leave, allow me to make an introduction, Sir Cuthbert.' There was something spine-chilling in the dulcet tone of his voice, a sudden contrast with the intense anger he had displayed only minutes ago. 'This is Master Simon Exeley, a prominent member of the York Guild of Mercers, who is a very good friend to the Nevilles and a very good friend to me. Master Exeley, may I present Sir Cuthbert of Middleham – as he likes to be known.'

In the interests of peace-keeping I let pass the quip and bowed politely to the merchant. I knew little of the wool market, only that many of its merchants were extremely wealthy due to the flow of fleeces through the English ports to Calais, and the high quality of the woollen cloth returning from the looms of Europe. Everyone in the north above the rank of peasant wore clothes fashioned from the product of the York Mercers. Master Exeley was clearly a prominent member of his guild, judging by the breadth of the fur trimmings on his gown and the weight of the medallion on his chest.

'God's greeting to you, Master Exeley,' I said, wondering why Hilda's brother was making this introduction. I was not left long in ignorance.

'Master Exeley is to be my brother-in-law,' declared Sir Gerald with a triumphant grin, peering intently at me as if determined to relish the emotional turmoil his words would cause. 'A contract of marriage has been agreed between him and my sister Hilda. The marriage will take place in a few days.'

I felt as if my heart would explode out of my chest and I think my eyes must have popped from their sockets as I stared, appalled, at the desiccated face of the merchant, who was showing what teeth he had left in a nightmarish vision of a smile. Clearly he expected me to congratulate him but my tongue simply would not form the words.

'My first wife died last year, leaving my four children motherless,' he cackled, as if that explained everything. 'Sir Gerald and I have come to a very satisfactory arrangement.'

By which Hilda warms your bed, satisfies your goatish lust and mothers your ugly children while you pay off the vast debts her villain of a brother has accumulated! Those were the words I wanted to say but somehow, with Lady Joan in mind, I blurted out some bland phrase of felicitation and blundered away, clasping my right hand firmly in my left to stop it drawing the secret dagger from my sleeve and telling myself that a display of bad manners was better than the bloody murder I was contemplating.

In my distress, and not really knowing what my intentions were, I made my way to Lady Joan's Tower. I was certain that Hilda must be unaware of the heinous pact between her brother and Master Exeley and as I felt my way along the dark connecting passages I formed a plan in my head that would save her from the dreadful future that her brother's announcement had conjured in my mind. But when I reached the chambers where she and Cicely were lodged, the guards told me that they had eaten a meal and gone straight to the chapel to keep vigil beside the late countess's bier. Temporarily defeated, I returned to the Baron's Hall to make my own meal and endeavor to avoid all contact with Sir Gerald Copley or Master Simon Exeley.

Inevitably this proved impossible and within minutes a smug-faced Sir Gerald had accosted me, though thankfully he was no longer in the company of the York merchant. 'Hilda has given her consent to the marriage, you know,' he told me in a voice full of suppressed glee. 'It is time she was married and it will be a comfortable billet. Exeley is the richest merchant in York and his house is one of the largest and most luxurious in the city. She will not miss the plush furnishings of the York palaces at all.'

'I do not believe she has given her consent to marry a man old enough to be her grandfather,' I responded, gritting my teeth to prevent my knuckles connecting with his jaw.

Gerald laughed. 'Perhaps you do not know her as well as you think, Cuthbert. There is a mercenary streak in my little sister – and a touch of pride. She wishes to preserve the family honour. She would rather marry money than allow our lands to be sold and she would rather marry a true-born older man than the bastard son of a peasant.'

I had noticed that under his short black cutaway doublet Sir Gerald was wearing hose of the new style, with a codpiece flap at the fork. I moved in close, as if to embrace him warmly and instead grabbed at the flap and connected hard, squeezing the soft flesh of his private parts. 'Now I know you are lying!' I growled in his ear. 'And I will prove it.' Then I stepped back, mild-mannered, as if nothing untoward had happened.

Gerald's face slowly returned from puce back to its usual pink. He was not smiling now. 'You filthy, misbegotten prick-feeler – you will find no proof, if you even live long enough to try.'

When I leaned in close again I was gratified to see him back off hastily. People around us were beginning to notice trouble brewing and I once more resisted the urge to punch him on the nose. 'I believe that constitutes a threat to my life,' I hissed through smiling lips. 'Your liege lord of Westmorland might be interested to hear of that, but I owe a debt of gratitude to the woman we are gathered here to honour so I will refrain from throwing down the gauntlet. I will ask Hilda myself, and if she confirms her consent to marry Master Exeley then I will have to accept her word but if she does not I give you notice that I will match the merchant's bride price and marry her myself.'

'Ha! You will never be able to match Exeley's bride price and Hilda will never marry a baseborn nobody – not while I live.'

So confident did he sound of this that I began to question my own belief in Hilda's opinions about my birth. The subject of marriage had never been broached between us. I did not even know whether she had ever given any thought to the possibility, although it had been my unspoken aim ever since I had taught her to shoot an arrow as a girl of thirteen. If the truth were known, I had never considered marriage to any other woman and the thought of her marrying anyone else, let alone an old greybeard however rich, was anathema.

Yet when Lady Joan's funeral was over and we set out on the first leg of our journey to Fotheringhay, Cicely was without Hilda and so, to my everlasting distress, was I. I had asked her directly if she was willing to marry Master Exeley: she had locked her deep-brown eyes with mine and said yes.

'He may be an older man than I expected to have, Cuddy, but he is not a bad man,' she insisted. 'Our ancestors have been lords of Copley for three hundred years and before he died, my father told me that he relied on me to marry well enough to protect the manor from Gerald's spendthrift ways. Master Exeley will keep my wastrel brother under control. I am only doing what my father bade me do.'

I longed to tell her that her brother was more than just a wastrel – he was also a scoundrel who maltreated women and did not fight fair – but I suspected she probably knew her brother as well as I did and so there would have been no point. Bonny, practical Hilda had always been a woman of her word and once she had given it there would be no changing her mind. I could not believe that she would have considered the stain of bastardy a bar to her marriage but I did not dare to ask her that question. As I marshalled Cicely's escort for departure, I was forced to watch Hilda ride north beside her cruel and lecherous brother to what I considered an unbearable future. I felt the loss of hope for my own happiness like a missing limb. It was a pain which I feared would endure for the rest of my life.

14

Cicely

R ichard always insisted on formality and show at his official
banquets. He firmly believed that authority was vested in
those who demonstrated their worthiness in wealth and power
and this was best done through feasts and largesse. Guests were
expected to wear their richest finery and were placed strictly in
order of rank, lesser knights and their ladies at the lower trestles,
senior magnates and captains at the high tables, centered on the
garlanded ducal board, where the great York silver salt cellar was
prominently placed. Etiquette was rigid and there was little
opportunity for casual conversation during the elaborate rituals
of parading, carving, tasting and serving the scores of dishes
placed during each course. The pantlers cut the trenchers of
bread, the ewerers held the bowls for hand-washing and the
naperers offered the napkin for drying them; each pair of high-
table guests had a cup-bearer who held the shared hanap
throughout the meal, retrieving it after his lord or lady had drunk
and taking it to the butler for refilling. Between each course,
consisting of up to a score of dishes, subtleties were paraded and
there were entertainments in the centre of the hall; minstrelsy

and mumming, tumbling and fooling, sometimes even a masque or dance in glorious costumes. Everyone was encouraged to eat and drink as much as they wished but it was to be orderly excess; any argument or rowdiness was fiercely controlled by the stewards and culprits were made well aware of Richard's grave displeasure.

On the day Anne arrived from Calais, the flambeaux in their high wall sconces had been replaced three times before I was able to bear her away from the feast to my solar to enjoy some relaxed female gossip and exchange of news, and even then I was obliged to invite several other wives of senior barons and captains to join us. Unfortunately one of them was Lady Talbot, wife of the veteran Royal Marshall, Lord Talbot, upon whom Richard relied heavily for military advice.

'You must be tired, your grace,' this lady said, giving me a pungent whiff of her wine-sour breath as she bent to place an extra cushion at my back. 'It is only a week until your lying-in is it not?'

Lady Talbot had been born Margaret Beauchamp, the eldest daughter of King Henry V's famous general the late Richard Beauchamp, Earl of Warwick. Her much younger half-brother Henry, the present Earl of Warwick, had been educated beside his namesake King Henry VI and was one of his closest friends, consequently all the Beauchamps had to be carefully handled.

I smiled my thanks and eased the unnecessary cushion away as soon as her back was turned. 'Thank you, Lady Talbot. Yes, I will take to my lying-in chamber in a week's time, which is why my sister has kindly come to be with me.' In accordance with Richard's strict instructions I tended to restrict my remarks to the banal and casual in this lady's presence, knowing her to be an inveterate gossip.

'And on my journey I collected an expert nurse to care for

Cicely's baby when it comes,' said Anne cheerfully. 'She is a wonderful Frenchwoman with a great reputation for bringing children successfully through their vulnerable early months.' By talking babies my sister thought she was avoiding contentious subjects but found she was wrong.

Lady Talbot was astounded. 'A Frenchwoman! Is that wise?'

The other ladies had taken up their embroidery but I felt too weary to thread a needle and wondered how soon I could suggest retiring. However, I could not resist challenging the Talbot woman's implied criticism.

'What could be considered unwise about it?' I asked. 'We have to live alongside the French and so surely it is sensible to expose our children to the language at an early age. Besides, this woman is a skilled maternity nurse who has proved her worth.'

Lady Talbot sniffed, rather offensively I thought. 'I see little evidence of the French living harmoniously alongside the English. We are their masters and conquerors but few of them show any sign of accepting that situation. How many of them take the trouble to learn English, for example? In my opinion we would all sleep easier in our beds if we kept the French outside the castle walls.'

Anne took up the cudgel for me. 'This nurse came highly recommended by our sister-in-law Lady Isabel, the Duke of York's sister.'

As well as being Richard's elder sister, Isabel was also married to Anne's husband's half-brother Henry Bourchier, Comte de Eu, presently proving a very effective Captain in Picardy, the most volatile of Normandy's borders. He was also half-French, a fact which seemed to have escaped Lady Talbot's attention.

'Isabel's five healthy sons must surely be held to demonstrate the woman's nursery skills,' I suggested.

'And, of course, your grace is naturally hoping for an heir yourself this time,' gushed Lady Talbot, pursuing her theme regardless. 'But I am sure any English nurse could rear him just as well. I have a pensioner in my own household whom I would have been delighted to recommend.'

'Thank you, Lady Talbot, I will bear that in mind,' I said, adding firmly, 'but meanwhile Isabel's French nurse is already settling in.'

The conversation turned to other topics and I forced myself to take up my needle in order to stay alert. The diplomatic world was so small and gossip travelled surprisingly quickly between Rouen and London. Margaret Talbot's sister Eleanor was married to Edmund Beaufort, Earl of Mortain, another close confidant of the king, and I knew that any incautious remark of mine would be relayed back to the royal court as fast as a courier could cross the Channel. Although Richard relished his lieutenancy in France, especially the military success he had achieved with Lord Talbot's skilful generalship, he worried constantly about what was going on during his absence from the English court, where the king was now twenty years of age but showing little sign of exerting his authority in the council. The Beaufort faction irritated Richard most because it encouraged the king's peace-loving attitude towards both the war and his uncle Charles de Valois, who also called himself King of France. On occasions like this I found myself treading a hazardous path, trying to demonstrate loyalty to my husband whilst attempting to keep the door open for reconciliation between Richard and the my mother's Beaufort relatives. It did not help that the head of that family, John Beaufort, Earl of Somerset, was at present busy squandering vast amounts of Treasury funds on a futile campaign to oust the French from

Aquitaine while Richard had received no royal finance to defend Normandy.

I succeeded in steering away from that topic for the next half hour, after which I ostentatiously stifled a yawn and gratefully accepted Anne's speedy suggestion that I should be encouraged to seek my bed. The captains' wives dutifully packed away their needlework and took their leave. Anne then unceremoniously shooed my young lady companions out of the room and told them to wait until I called them to help me to bed.

'Now, Cicely,' she said, putting on a mother-hen face and bringing a cushioned stool up to my chair, 'I have been waiting to talk to you about this ever since the subject was raised earlier in the day. You cannot really believe that God will not grant you a son because you have sinned in some way that He has not revealed to you. I think that either you have another reason or else your sin is so heinous that you do not dare to tell us, and of the two alternatives I favour the first.'

When Anne decided to tackle a subject she went straight to the point and took me completely by surprise. For an incautious instant I considered taking her into my confidence about John Neville, but the years of carefully guarded discretion had become ingrained habit and I took a deep breath before responding. 'My belief that God will not grant me a son is based on more than wild surmise, Anne,' I said.

'Well I know that you lost the last one but . . .'

'He was not the first son I lost, Anne. There was another, years ago, at the beginning . . .' I found my voice catching and tears sprang unbidden to my eyes so that I had to stop. 'Richard knows – he was there – I do not know how he still has faith in me.'

'He has faith in God, which you clearly do not,' Anne said gently. 'Tell me what happened?'

Once I had started, the whole sad story came pouring out and Anne, God bless her, just listened without interrupting.

'After our marriage Richard wanted to show me all his estates and introduce me to his people so we travelled the length and breadth of England and into the Welsh marches. And then there were the Irish lordships in Ulster. The crossing to Ireland was rough and I was pregnant, six months or more into my time. I was sick, so sick. Have you ever suffered from mal de mer, Anne? It is like plunging into Purgatory. My stomach heaved so much I thought I would bring the child up through my throat.'

I could feel big, slow tears begin to slide down my face as the memory of that dreadful voyage surfaced in my mind.

'The retching came in spasms, violent paroxysms which held me in a deadly grip, they were unrelenting and gradually dislodged the baby in my womb. We prayed so hard, Anne, while the ship tossed and creaked like a living thing. Well, Richard prayed while I vomited but it was all to no avail. My retching gave way to violent cramps and you can imagine the rest. It was a boy. The baby gasped a few breaths but there was no priest to baptize him and he never had a name. They buried him at sea – a little lost son of York. And last year, poor Henry – my beautiful, fated Henry. When he arrived he was perfect, even though he had been rattled and bumped all the way up to Raby for my mother's funeral and all the way back. I thanked God. Richard was ecstatic, the bells rang for days at Fotheringhay. Within a week though, the bells had changed to a death knell. I do not know why he died. Why does a baby fail to suckle, go all limp and simply stop breathing? That was when I recognized the wrath of God.'

Seeing that I was becoming very distressed, Anne took my hands in hers. 'But you had little Annie between those two lost boys, Cicely, the healthy, bonny child I saw in the nursery this afternoon. And look at you now!' She gestured at my very round belly. 'You can hardly consider yourself barren!'

'I know, I know. I was so happy when I discovered I was with child. I did not expect it because Richard only came back from campaigning on a flying visit last August. It was baking hot in the castle and he could see I was wilting so he ordered tents to be erected in the river meadow at the Abbey of Saint Catherine. We dined in the open air, the two of us on the bank of the river, and when it got dark the sky was full of falling stars. We lay on cushions gazing up at it. I had never seen this miracle before but Richard said it happened every year and called them celestial embers. It was beautiful. This baby was conceived under a shower of Heavenly brilliance and so at first I was full of optimism, but as the birth draws nearer I have become terrified again. Perhaps it was not celestial embers but God's wrath descending.' I stumbled to a halt and gazed at Anne, blinking away the tears that continued to brim in my eyes.

'You think I cannot I understand your fear, Cicely, but you are wrong. You were just a baby when I was betrothed to Humphrey at the age of nine and went to live at Stafford, and the years since have set us apart. Listen: I was fourteen and Humphrey was sixteen when we were bedded and told that our duty was to get children, but no one told us how they were conceived. For two years we thought that kissing was enough and when we discovered the truth we were too embarrassed to actually perform what was required of us. Two more years passed before we stopped being just friends, which we had been from the start. After that, like you, I had a slipped pregnancy, then a beautiful little boy that died and then another. But we did not despair. Finally, after nine years of marriage we produced little

Humphrey and then Henry and John – three healthy boys in quick succession, followed by Annette, as we call her. Then our troubles started again – Margaret only lived a few months and George and William barely breathed at all, one after another. I thought I would have to be content with four healthy children until, as you know, Joan arrived two years ago and then Catherine last year. So now we have three boys and three girls who, God willing, will all grow and prosper. We can never be sure, of course. But you are not alone, Cicely! God works his wonders for some of us and for others there are no miracles of birth at all. You already have a healthy child and you must believe that the one you are carrying now will be another – perhaps the son you crave, perhaps not, but you should remember that we Nevilles are prolific breeders. Look at our mother – fifteen children in twenty years and only two of them did not live to adulthood. You may think now that you have failed but, in truth, you have probably hardly begun.'

She reached out and gave me a clumsy hug, laughing as she did so. 'See, you are so near your time that I can hardly reach around you! This will be a healthy baby, whether male or female, and you will go on to have many more, I am certain. Until one day you will be only too glad to say "No more! I have done my share of producing sons and daughters for the dynasty of York." Mark my words and have faith.'

I felt my spirits rise as they had not done in months, comforted by her laughter and positivity. 'Oh, Anne! I am so glad you have come. You will stay to see me through this, won't you?'

'I am not going anywhere, little sister. After the midwife, I want to be the first to set eyes on the next Duke of York!'

15

Cuthbert

When he was not campaigning, Richard practiced his arms skills daily. These fights and jousts were nominally friendly, but they were always ruthlessly competitive. Sometimes he challenged one of his retainers, a young knight or squire whose mettle he wished to test, but most frequently he chose me to cross swords with or ride against in the lists, I think because we were well matched. On occasion these practice bouts between us had lasted up to two hours, even in full armour. Then, at the St George's Day tournament, I had been hailed the champion and I was fiercely proud of this recognition of my knightly prowess and, importantly, much boosted financially by the prize purse that went with it. However, I was not surprised when, only five days later, Richard chose to challenge me at the practice ground.

'I become the champion if I beat the champion I think, Cuthbert. Let us see if your grey hair will stand a second trial in a week.'

'I will let you know when I find one, your grace,' I said. I was all of a year older than Richard and he liked to draw attention to the discrepancy.

It was not hard to guess why he was challenging me. Since daybreak the whole castle knew that the duchess had gone into labour in the early hours; the duke was seeking distraction from the matter that was uppermost in his mind.

'What shall we wager on the outcome?' I asked.

'Which outcome?' he asked. 'Whether I win or whether you find a grey hair?'

'As you will not win and I will not find a grey hair, that would be betting against a certainty in either case. Instead I will wager my champion's purse that before one of us yields your wife will be delivered of a lusty boy.'

'I will certainly not bet against that!' he protested. 'And do not imagine that you have the advantage because my mind is elsewhere.' He strode out into the middle of the arena and his squire hastily ran after him with his helmet, earning a cuff round the ear for his pains. 'I had not forgotten the helmet, Yves! You were too slow in bringing it.'

That told me all I needed to know about Richard's state of mind. I had no fear for my champion's crown. If this fight ever came to a result, as far as I was concerned, it was a foregone conclusion. We were of similar height and physique, we both had stamina, but a knight who fought with half his attention focused on the outcome of a dynastic birth-struggle playing out in a closed room high above him in the castle keep could not hope to prevail. In less than the time it took for a priest to say high mass, I had Richard backed up against the perimeter fence with the blunt tip of his sword buried in the sand.

'I yield,' he panted, spreading his hands wide. 'Sir Cuthbert of Middleham remains the champion knight.'

I raised my sword high and bowed and as I did so I noticed Richard's Chamberlain, Sir Andrew Ogard, hurrying across the bailey, a wide smile on his face. He fell to his knees heedless of the dusty ground and announced jubilantly 'The duchess has safely delivered a son, your grace, not ten minutes ago.'

Richard made the sign of the cross. 'God be thanked,' he breathed. 'A son you say – and all is well? Does he wail lustily and how fares her grace?' Sir Andrew gave his assurances on both counts but Richard did not really listen. He threw his arms around me and clasped me in a fierce bear-hug. 'Heaven be praised, it is a boy, Cuthbert! May God bless my son and make him strong and fearless. Come, brother, let us storm the keep and get a glimpse of him!'

With his arm around my shoulder, he hauled me along with him whether I would or no. All around us news of the birth spread like flames in a breeze, causing sudden bursts of noise in celebration. On the practice ground sweating foot-soldiers dropped their weapons and raised their fists and voices in triumph for their lord, on the topmost tower of the castle the white rose emblem rattled up the flagpole and in the forge the smiths and armourers hammered out a crescendo on their anvils to salute the newborn son of York.

'Tell them to ring the chapel bell!' Richard yelled over his shoulder at his Chamberlain. 'And send word to all the churches. I want to hear every bell in Rouen chime. The House of York has an heir!'

We took the successive keep stairways two steps at a time and arrived breathless at the lying-in chamber but Lady Anne would not grant us entry. 'This is not a place for men,' she declared firmly and gestured at our armour and sheathed swords, 'especially not for men who clank and reek of combat. Cicely is being tended by the midwives and presently will be ready to receive you. But if you wish to celebrate with your lady wife, my lord, I suggest a clean doublet and soft shoes.'

I glanced sideways to gauge Richard's reaction; he looked angry and crestfallen but I could see that he acknowledged the justice of her advice.

'Very well, but I demand that you bring the baby out to me now, Lady Anne,' he insisted. 'I must see my son and heir.'

Several officials of the York household were gathered in the ante-room. I knew Richard would not wish to lose face in front of his servants but when I caught Lady Anne's eye I saw there an unmistakable twinkle. She dropped a curtsy and opened the door wide. 'Indeed you must, your grace, and acknowledge him as your son for all to see.'

A nurse stood behind her with a bundle of warmly wrapped baby in her arms. The small newborn features of his face were framed by the folds of white shawl. I am no expert but he looked peaceful, pink and healthy. Richard bent to peer closely at the crumpled face and as he did so the child's eyes opened. One of the few scraps of information I had about tiny infants up to that time was that their focus is blurry, but this one seemed to gaze steadily and deeply into his father's eyes as if he saw into his soul.

Richard was captivated. 'Tell Cicely we shall call him Edward,' he announced without looking up.

Lady Anne gave a satisfied nod. 'After your uncle, the last Duke of York. It is a good Plantagenet name.'

'Yes, my lady, after my Uncle Edward, Duke of York, but also after his grandfather King Edward the Third and *his* father King Edward the Second and *his* father King Edward the First. This child is a prince. I would have everyone recognize that the blood of England's kings runs in my son's veins.'

Richard's gaze was still riveted on his boy's face and so he did not see Lady Anne and I raise our eyebrows at each other. Neither of us spoke but it was clear that we were both somewhat taken aback by the messianic tone in the duke's voice.

Lady Anne shrugged. 'I will tell Cicely what you have said my lord. As you can imagine she is tired but utterly delighted to have given birth to a boy. She immediately gave praise and thanks to God and made fervent prayers for the child's future health, as did we all. We will have her washed and radiant for your return. Oh, and she said to tell you that the baby is very long. He is going to be tall.'

Any further words were drowned out by the sudden clamour of bells. The peal started in the nearby cathedral belfry and was gradually echoed from every church tower in every corner of the town – a glorious, dissonant, joyous sound – as Rouen rang out a deafening welcome to young Edward of York.

Later, after Richard had donned a gown of truly triumphant crimson figured damask with long, trailing sleeves, dagged and lined with blue satin, he visited Cicely alone and then came to the great hall of the castle to lead the toasts to the baby's health and receive the congratulations of his household and vassals. In the castle cellars a tun of wine from the Garonne was broached and orders were given to the cooks to prepare a great feast for the following day. I was among those who approached the duke to offer a personal toast.

'I cannot find the words to say how pleased I am for you and my sister, your grace,' I said formally, raising my cup. 'I drink to the future of England and France and your son's undoubted role in it.'

Euphoria still suffused his countenance, or else it was the wine that coloured his cheeks. Suffice it to say that Richard received my toast with visible glee – and an audible slur. 'Oh you are right there, Cuthbert. He will be a prince among princes! I saw it the moment I laid eyes on him.'

For the second time that day he put his arm around my shoulders, this time his whispered words borne on wine-charged breath.

'I will let you into a secret, brother-in-law. This evening I made a decision. I intended to set off this new gown of mine with the gold Lancastrian collar King Henry presented to me before I departed for France, but when I put it on it made me feel like a dog. Dogs wear collars and work for scraps, do they not? I will not be the king's dog. So, to celebrate my son's birth I am going to have my own collar made, one that shouts to the world "This is the House of York!".' He drew back and briefly laid his finger to his lips. 'Don't tell Cicely, will you?'

I kept my voice low to match his. 'You have my word on it, Richard. Where will you have it made though? The best gold-smiths are in Paris but I do not think even you can wrest that city back from the French without the support of parliament and the king. As things are, that does not seem very likely.'

He gave an airy wave of his hand. 'We have contacts, Cuthbert. Believe me, it will not be made in London where spies would spread word of it around Westminster before the gold is cold. I am only sorry it will not be made in time for Edward's baptism.'

'And when is that to be, my lord?'

The duke's brow furrowed. 'Ah, now there Cicely and I differ. I want my son to be baptised in Rouen Cathedral with full pomp and ceremony but Cicely cannot forget the death of little Henry. She thinks Edward's health will be at risk among a great crowd of people in the cathedral and wants him baptised in the castle chapel. I have decided to bow to her maternal fears. The baptism will take place in the chapel tomorrow.'

'Cicely is right, Richard,' I said making the sign of the cross. 'The devil must be driven out as soon as possible and there is no point in taking risks. There will be plenty of occasions for pomp and ceremony when the boy is a little older.'

Richard stepped back and took another gulp of wine, beckoning a passing servant to refill his cup. He nodded solemnly. 'There will indeed, brother. I assure you he will be brought up to understand the importance of such things in the exercise of power.'

16

Rouen Castle, 1443

Cicely

Anne had been right. My belief in the unforgiving wrath of God was unfounded and, a little over a year after Edward's birth, Richard and I were blessed with another healthy baby boy. This time I was confident enough to allow him to be carried to the cathedral for a full ceremonial baptism. We called him Edmund after the first Duke of York, Richard's grandfather and also after his mother's brother, Edmund Mortimer, Earl of March, whose untimely death had almost doubled Richard's inheritance.

I did not attend the baptism, but afterwards Richard proudly related that he had carried Edward into the cathedral and revelled in the gasps of surprise from the guests when he set his son down and they watched him walk unaided to his nurse.

'You should have seen their faces, Cicely – only three weeks after his first birthday! There he was in his red velvet gown and little jewelled slippers, his head held high as he toddled across the floor. He grinned at them all, so proud and pleased. He already knows how to charm his public.'

I smiled indulgently, enjoying Richard's immense pride in his elder son. Nevertheless I could not resist reminding him whose baptism it had been. 'And Edmund – how did he behave?' I asked.

The Duke of York had the grace to look a little guilty. 'Edmund? Well, how do newborn babies behave when they are dunked in water, even if it be warmed and holy? He yelled his head off – and the devil was successfully dealt with, thanks be to God.'

'Good. I hope he will learn to accept being second to Edward in everything, as you clearly intend him to be.'

'I do not!' Richard was indignant. 'I am already acquiring as much territory in Normandy as possible so that Edmund will have his own revenues and a good motive for keeping the French at bay. It will not do for him and Edward to fight over my York estates.'

I frowned. 'Cuthbert tells me our household servants are already calling Edward "The Rose of Rouen". That could prove an awkward name if you intend to set Edmund up over here.'

Richard appeared pleased by this piece of news, ignoring my warning. 'The Rose of Rouen? Do they really? People love an alliterative epithet, do they not? You were called "The Rose of Raby", as I remember.'

'I still am in the northland I believe. You see no harm in it then?'

'Harm? What harm could there be? York is the house of the White Rose and now there are two heirs to ensure its future. That can be nothing but good.'

Of course the fortunes of the house of York did not rely entirely on the flourishing of our children. A good deal depended on what went on in the halls and chambers of Westminster Palace, where the young king seemed incapable of resisting the overtures of those with the smoothest tongues. To Richard's exasperation, slick operators like Cardinal Beaufort and his nephews, the Earls of Somerset and Mortain, pushed their preferences through the council while the king's personal attention seemed focused not on the parlous situation in France but on the endowment of new schools and colleges in England.

'Education is all very worthy,' Richard fumed when he learned of the astronomical sums parliament had voted for King Henry's pet projects at Eton and Cambridge, 'but it does not pay the soldiers who defend the borders of his French kingdom. Does he not realize that ranks of scholars will not win back the towns and castles which the French seize because our garrisons lack reinforcements and supplies?'

I knew he was thinking of Pontoise, the important eastern gateway to Paris, overrun by the French the previous year, since when several less important but no less strategic towns had fallen as a result. Despite the thousands of crowns Richard had spent from his own coffers, Normandy was becoming more and more vulnerable. Then instead of the expected attack on Normandy, the French made a surprise assault on Gascony; England had held it for centuries; most of the wine that flowed down English throats came from there.

To add insult to injury, the Earl of Somerset had been appointed Captain General of Aquitaine over Richard's head and given a force of twenty thousand men to chase the French out.

His wrath at this news had exploded through the door into my solar, sending my young ladies scurrying for the door. 'By St George and St Michael, Cicely, this time I have had enough! I have petitioned the king time and again to send money and reinforcements and he never does. Now he writes that he has been obliged to divert all funds and forces to Somerset for his expedition to Gascony. A king is never *obliged*! Henry is not obliged, he is cozened!'

I could think of nothing to say that might calm his anger. But Richard's tone had moderated slightly when he continued, 'We can only pray that Somerset keeps the French so busy in Gascony that they will leave Normandy alone. Meanwhile I shall begin my own negotiations to secure a truce with Burgundy so that at least the merchants of Rouen can begin to trade with the Low Countries again.'

For myself, I felt thoroughly let down because I had always considered the Beauforts to be allies. Now I thought back, however, since my mother's death it had become more than obvious that they no longer felt any loyalty to her family. It seemed that Neville links to the Lancastrian throne were disintegrating.

On the twenty-first day of September there was a tournament to celebrate Richard's birthday. His sister Isabel came from Picardy with her husband Henry Bourchier, Count of Eu, and my sister Anne and her husband Humphrey made the risky ride from Calais. Scores of lesser knights and nobles rode in to compete in a variety of jousts, which offered tempting purses to the victors, but none succeeded in unseating my brother Sir Cuthbert of Middleham, who added another pot of gold to his winnings from the St George's Day tourney.

At the banquet which followed, Richard chose to reveal another deal he had done while negotiating his new trade treaty with the Low Countries. A recent merchants' train had delivered a fabulous new collar made to his design by goldsmiths in Antwerp and as we made our grand entry down the centre of the Hall of Estates a wave of astonishment accompanied our progress. Displayed prominently around his throat, a dazzling river of gems and gold brought gasps of awe from the guests. It consisted of a chain of twenty white-enamelled gold roses, each set with an enormous yellow diamond at its centre, similar to the rare and beautiful stone that had so struck me on the brooch he gave me before our wedding. Other smaller gemstones – sapphires, emeralds and rubies – gleamed along the filigree gold links, while from the front hung a single magnificent colourless diamond, intricately cut across its surface so that the light from the candles and flambeaux was fractured into brilliant multiple rays that appeared to dance around the hall, reflected off walls and ceiling, clothes and faces. This unique jewel, called the White Rose, flashed a glittering message of possession, wealth and exalted rank. There was no mistaking its purpose was to declare York's pre-eminence in the peerage and proclaim Richard's royal lineage.

As we took our places at the high table, I marked the star-tling contrast between Richard's sparkling York White Rose and the plain gold gleam of the Lancastrian SS link collar set on the shoulders of the newly created Duke of Buckingham, my sister Anne's husband, Humphrey. Nor was I the only one to do so.

'The goldsmiths must have scoured the gem markets of Europe for that white diamond.' Humphrey kept his voice low so it would not carry past me to Richard. 'Even Croesus cannot have spent so much on one bauble.'

Happy though I was to have my sister join the ducal ranks, I raised my chin and challenged her lord's sardonic gaze. 'Great princes should not pretend to be paupers,' I said. 'The House of York is a royal house; it should have its regalia.'

'There can only be one royal house in England,' said Humphrey, fingering the links of his own chain. 'The throne belongs to Lancaster, as do the crown and sceptre. Regalia are for kings, not princes.'

'You wear a Lancaster collar, my lord, yet you are not a son of Lancaster. That is your choice. The Duke of York chooses to wear the symbol of his own house.'

'I am loyal to the king and wish to display my loyalty.'

'My lord is also loyal but the king should not be surprised if one of his loyal subjects sometimes wishes to wear his own "bauble" as you call it.'

'No,' said Humphrey, his voice thin and flat. 'The king will not be surprised.'

Troubled by this conversation, I reported its content to Richard as we lay beneath the covers that night, thinking that he would share my concern, but he gave a crow of delight.

'Humphrey is jealous. He wishes he had thought of it himself but now he is bound to wear the SS collar forever, like a fawning hound. There will be no renown for the House of Buckingham. It is a house of followers, not leaders.'

The wearing of the Rose had also caused my sister Anne to whisper a warning to me during the evening's entertainment. 'You must be careful, Cicely. You and Richard have been away from England for a long time and the king is impressionable. He will be told of this new collar and there is an affinity at court which will lead him to conclude from it that York is a threat to his throne.'

I had thought to repeat her words to Richard too but now decided against it. It was his birthday. He was entitled to celebrate his achievements and revel in the stir he had created with his precious collar. So I leaned over and ran my hand down his chest, threading my fingers through the familiar growth of dark hair and feeling his stomach clench as I reached his navel. 'It is a beautiful White Rose, my lordly love, fit for a magnificent prince.'

Richard smiled and rolled over to take me in his arms. 'You cannot deceive me, Cicely,' he said running his own hand over my slightly rounded belly. 'I suspect you are already carrying our child again but let us pretend you are not. It is these children we make that will blaze the honour of the White Rose into history.'

Elizabeth of York was born the following April but during my pregnancy Richard had watched with deep concern as major moves were made from London towards a truce with France, to be fortified by a marriage between King Henry and the Duke of Anjou's daughter Margaret. The Earl of Suffolk and his wife led an English mission to the proposed bride's home in Nancy but it was noticeable that they made no courtesy visit to Rouen on the way. Negotiations were protracted and even after Suffolk had stood in for Henry at a proxy marriage, King Charles of France insisted that the young bride come to Paris for a series of celebrations and processions to demonstrate the strength of French support for her. He also took the opportunity to instigate further negotiations before the truce was finally concluded.

'No one in England has had sight of this treaty yet,' Richard fretted as he waited for a summons to Paris to collect the new queen and bring her to Rouen. 'Only Suffolk knows what it contains, just as only he and his entourage have laid eyes on young Margaret of Anjou. She may be hare-lipped or lame-brained for all we know.'

'Gossip among the ladies of my salon would indicate the opposite,' I countered, taking advantage of his private visit to my chamber to kick off my shoes and raise my swollen ankles onto a cushioned stool. I was only weeks away from my lying-in. 'They say she is uncommonly beautiful and descended from a line of strong-minded women.'

'Strong-minded?' Richard echoed. 'The opposite of Henry then; how will he cope?'

I laughed. 'As most men do I imagine – by getting her with child and then ignoring her.'

He glared at me from under knitted brows. 'It is not something to jest about, Cicely. This Frenchwoman is now our queen. You will have to dance attendance on her.'

I returned his glare with a submissive smile. 'I know, my lord. I pride myself on being able to do that with grace and patience. I get plenty of practice.'

From the change in his expression Richard was uncertain how to take the last remark but, predictably, he chose to ignore it. He brooded instead on the treaty, wondering out loud, 'What exactly has Suffolk promised in order to obtain this marriage?'

We were not to get a full answer to this question for several years. In mid-March Richard set off for Paris, no doubt much changed since his last visit which had been for King Henry's French coronation, at a time when it was still under our control. Expecting to participate in one of the impressive processions that had been arranged for Queen Margaret's farewell, he took an escort of six hundred archers in English royal livery, only to disover on arrival that these were over. King Charles had left Paris for his favourite residence at Chinon, a departure which

Richard construed as a snub to his office as King Henry's Lieutenant in France. Instead he was joined by the Duke of Orleans to escort the young queen to Poissy, an abbey town to the west of Paris where a flotilla of barges, freshly painted, was assembled to convey her and her entourage down the Seine to Rouen.

Margaret of Anjou was, as rumour had suggested, very beautiful. Not blonde and pearly complexioned, which the English considered the essence of feminine loveliness, but dark-haired and olive-skinned like her redoubtable Spanish grand-mother, Yolande of Aragon. She was also well-mannered and mature beyond the sum of her years. I was charmed on first acquaintance when she caught my hand as I began to sink into my courtesy.

'Non, non, Madame la Duchesse,' she began solicitously, then attempting her rudimentary English. 'Do not incline yourself. You are *enceinte*. You must sit.'

In deference to my advanced pregnancy, we had met in the middle of the Hall of the Estates and not at the foot of the exterior stairway, as was customary, and she broke away from her entourage to take my arm as if I was a delicate pottery figurine and escort me up the steps of the dais, chattering away in French as she did so.

'*Vous devez rester, Madame de York. Vraiment je crois que c'est présque le jour de vôtre accouchement. C'est aimable de tous, vous me bien acquéillir à Rouen.*'

I nodded and smiled at her, thinking that I must ensure my own children were taught such kindness and consideration. Within moments we were seated together at the high table and involved in a conversation about her journey, how well she had been looked after by the Earl and Countess of Suffolk and how much she was looking forward to reaching England, but not to crossing the Channel.

'*J'ai peur du mal de mer*,' she confided, making a little French mou with her lips, which I found quite endearing, '*mais il faut passer sur La Manche n'est-ce pas, si je veux me rencontrer mon marié?*'

I was about to reply that it was indeed necessary for her to cross the Channel if she wished to meet her bridegroom when a good-looking, bearded man of middle age stepped between us, bowing punctiliously to the queen. 'Forgive me, your grace; I am happy to see that you are making the acquaintance of her grace of York. Have I your permission to let the trumpets sound for the start of the banquet?' He tugged a little nervously at his beard and lowered his voice to murmur, daringly close to the queen's ear I thought, 'And the stewards have arranged the order of seating with your grace in the centre of the table, rather than here at the end. May we assume your graces will move into the assigned places, where your canopies have been erected?'

I frowned, piqued that the Lord Suffolk appeared to have usurped the function of our own steward but unprepared for Queen Margaret's unyielding reaction to his intervention. She apparently had no difficulty understanding his English and frowned fiercely. 'But no, my lord of Suffolk, the duchesse does not wish to move now that she is er – *confortable. Les baldaquins doivent être ajustés.*'

My lips twitched as I watched Suffolk's obsequious submission to this order but I also made a mental note that not far beneath the surface charm of my young companion there lurked a very strong will. Later, when the dancing started, I also noticed that Richard, who had been prejudiced against Queen Margaret before he met her, was now more than willing to lead her out in a quadrille.

His attitude to the Lord Suffolk had not changed, however, and their body language was unmistakably hostile whenever they met. Since we kept separate bedchambers while I was so big with child, I was surprised to receive a visit from him soon after I had retired.

'Suffolk is up to his tricks,' he said, seating himself on a stool beside my bed. 'The sly fox thought to cause us embarrassment by not telling us that it is Queen Margaret's birthday the day after tomorrow. That is when she turns fourteen.'

I shifted on my mattress, trying to find a comfortable position. 'She is remarkably mature for that age,' I remarked. 'More like sixteen than fourteen.'

'She is still quite small, though. I think it may be a year or two before she conceives, always supposing Henry is capable of procreation.'

I was shocked at the casual way he said this. 'Why should he not be? He is twenty-two.'

Richard shrugged. 'Never reveal that I said this but I have always wondered if he is attracted to women. Oh, I do not mean he is inclined to sodomy. His steadfast faith would not allow him to commit such a carnal sin but he is simply . . .' he paused, seeking the right word. '. . . disinterested. I think he finds the whole notion of coupling distasteful and his confessor, Bishop Aiscough, does not discourage that attitude. In fact, he positively encourages it.'

'Perhaps Henry will change when he sees Margaret, she is a pretty and spirited little thing. Considering her age a tentative approach might be wise after the marriage, but as I judge it, in the long term she will not be averse to her conjugal duties. Are not men stirred by a little coquetry?'

It was his turn to look a little shocked. 'I do not like the idea of you knowing that, my lady.'

I met his accusing gaze with an innocent one of my own. 'It is what I have been told,' I said with a pretence at primness. 'But what about this birthday? How did you find out?'

'Suffolk's wife let it slip. I wager he will chastise her for that tonight.'

'What do you have in mind to do about it?'

'Some sort of surprise present. She likes hunting apparently.'

'A horse or a hound? You have plenty of each.'

Richard shook his head. 'No. The king sent her a very fine palfrey as a wedding present. I would not want to appear to be competing.'

'Perhaps a hawk then?'

'That is a good idea. Something fit for a queen. A Gyrfalcon.'

'It would need to be a Tercel, would it not? Surely Henry hunts a male Gyr.'

'Of course. I will have the falconer seek out a female Gyrfalcon though it will need to be trained and it may be impossible to find one at such short notice. Do you have any other ideas?'

'Margaret seems very well read – perhaps a book to be going on with. Many young ladies like the poems of Boccaccio. I have a French translation of his *Decameron*. I would want it replaced, of course.'

He bent over to plant a kiss on my cheek. 'You are my savior, Cicely. Have it wrapped in a beautiful length of cloth. Lady Suffolk tells me our new queen is sadly short of sumptuous apparel. Worst of all, she has no dowry! Henry was so desperate

171

to make a peace with France he accepted a penniless queen. Let us hope she is not a spendthrift for it is certain that the coffers of the Royal Exchequer are sadly depleted.'

I shifted about, trying to arrange my swollen belly so that I might get some sleep. 'I like her though, Richard. That is something.'

He gave a sigh of uncertainty. 'I hope it is enough,' he said.

PART THREE

Fotheringhay Castle
Northamptonshire, Coldharbour
Inn & Westminster Palace, London
1448

17

Fotheringhay, Early June

Cuthbert

'Come on, Edmund! Jump!'

The imperious treble voice of young Edward of York reached me through the barred windows of the armoury at Fotheringhay castle where my squire was assisting me to remove my hauberk.

'No. It is too far. I cannot. Help me, Edward!' That was unmistakably the voice of a somewhat distressed Edmund.

I took little notice. More often than not in their games around the castle bailey Edward would challenge his brother to a feat that Edmund, a year younger and good deal shorter, found beyond his abilities.

'I cannot reach you. You will have to jump. Oh, Edmund, you are such a gowk!'

Cicely ensured that a squire or a tutor was always on duty to watch out for the boys when they were playing so I did not respond, but Tom Neville, the squire who was hauling the heavy chainmail hauberk off over my head, reacted to the note of panic in Edmund's voice.

'Shall I go and see what is up, sir?' he asked. He threaded the sleeves of the fine-meshed steel tunic onto a pole and slung it between two wall brackets to join the rows of similar war-vests hanging there.

I shrugged and nodded, thinking that Tom was probably over-reacting but aware that he was particularly fond of his two young York cousins. He was the second son of my half-brother Hal, Earl of Salisbury, and approaching the age of knighthood, a time when squires tended to take the chivalric code very seriously. I called after him, 'Make sure you check the horses though, Tom, and clean yourself up before you serve at dinner.'

In Tom's case these orders were probably unnecessary and I caught his irritated scowl as he hurried off. We had trotted into Fotheringhay soon after noon at the end of our journey from the north, whence I had led a contingent of York retainers to boost Hal's forces in his ongoing campaign against the Earl of Westmorland's affinity, which still regularly raided the scattered manors attached to the honours of Middleham and Sheriff Hutton. Despite his own troubles the Duke of York felt bound to give occasional help of this kind to his wife's family. As York's Master of Henchmen, I considered the intermittent clashes with bands of ruffians operating under the bull banner of the Brancepeth Nevilles to be good field training for the young squires of the household, of whom Tom was one. They learned tactics and gained invaluable experience of real combat before they might be launched into a pitched battle. The way things were going in the kingdom of England at present, I believed it to be only a matter of time before these lawless skirmishes between affinities turned into something more serious.

The screams of fright from the bailey ceased soon after Tom departed. However, when I left the armoury a minute later I was vexed to see that Tom was up to his knees in the horse pond, coaxing five-year-old Edmund down from the branches of an overhanging alder.

'If you get help I have won, Edmund!' shouted Edward from his perch on the shingled roof of the building beside the pond. 'From the stable to the kennel without touching the ground, that is what we said.'

'That is probably what *you* said, Edward,' Tom shouted back, easing Edmund's chubby thighs around his neck and settling him on his shoulders. 'I do not suppose you gave Edmund much choice in the matter. You should make allowances. He is younger and shorter than you.'

'Ha!' Edward shinned down the wooden drainpipe which fed a water butt at the end of the kennel to sit on the lid of the butt curling his lip. 'Edmund is a little weed. He screeched before he even tried to jump.'

Tom waded out of the pond, knelt and deposited the smaller boy on dry ground. Edmund sniffed loudly and turned to confront his brother. 'You nearly fell in the pond yourself, Edward,' he shouted, hands on hips. 'I saw.'

Edward grinned broadly and bit his thumb at Edmund. 'But I did not fall, did I? I dared and I succeeded. That is the difference between you and me.'

'Enough!' I strode across the ten yards of hard earth between us. 'Tom is right, Edward. You have a duty to protect those younger and weaker than yourself. That is the mark of a chivalrous gentleman. In future you will invent games that give you both an even chance. Remember that. Now you should apologize to Edmund for calling him names and for putting him in danger.'

For a moment I thought Edward would refuse; his grey eyes narrowed, his grin disappeared, his lips formed a thin, stubborn line, but then he shrugged and made his brother an exaggerated bow. 'I am sorry for calling you a gowk, Edmund,' he said. With a mischievous glance in my direction, he added, 'But I still think you are a weed!' and scampered off. 'Race you to the stables!' he yelled over his shoulder.

Edmund made as if to run after him, then checked and looked up at Tom who shook his head. 'Let him go,' said the squire. 'Come with me to the kennel instead. I'm told my deerhound Mab gave birth to seven puppies while I was away. Would you like to see them?'

'Do not be long, Tom,' I warned with a mitigating smile. 'Lady Maud will not be too impressed if you serve her at dinner with the perfume of horse pond and kennel on your clothes.'

I had learned from his companions' taunts during our sortie to Yorkshire that Tom Neville had developed a crush on one of Cicely's companions. Unfortunately, Lady Maud Willoughby was married to a feoffee of York, albeit a man old enough to be her grandfather. Marriages arranged among the high-ranking nobility were often incongruous in this way, but it did not make the vows any less sacred and, as far as I knew, Tom's adoration remained of the courtly variety. A faint flush stained the squire's cheeks, confirming that his infatuation with the beautiful Maud Willoughby remained acute.

As they walked towards the kennel entrance I called after them, 'Where is your minder, Edmund?'

The boy gestured back towards the far end of the long timber stable range which leaned against the high wall of the bailey. 'Somewhere over there, I think.'

I decided to investigate and, peering around the corner of the building, spied a small group of house-carls concealed from general view and gathered around an upturned barrel. A man I did not recognize was busy separating his audience from their meagre earnings by means of a clandestine game of Chase the Knave. On the Duke of York's instructions, all gambling was strictly forbidden within the confines of Fotheringhay castle but from the look of the bulging pack placed prudently beneath his backside, this stranger was a peddler who had developed a lucrative sideline as a card sharp. I had a shrewd idea which of the young men attracted by the activities of this villain was the one who should have been watching Edward and Edmund.

I stepped into full view and cleared my throat loudly. The cards instantly disappeared and the men all tried to look innocent. 'Any of you seen Lord Edward and Lord Edmund?' I asked casually, 'they seem to be missing.'

The face of my chief suspect flushed scarlet, confirming my instinct. 'I am sorry to see you wasting your time and money here, Harry,' I said directly to him. 'I take it, since I could fry an egg on your face, it was your duty to guard the duke's sons today. Tell me, how would you explain to the duchess that Edmund had drowned in the horse pond while in your care?'

The lad in question was Harry Holland, another of the duke's young henchmen, a truculent lad of nearly eighteen who was sulky at the best of times. Now his smoldering flush turned to a raging fire. 'He cannot have drowned. That pond is only a foot deep.'

'A child can drown in a puddle, sirrah. You have neglected your duty and could have caused a disaster. As it is you only have to apologize to the duchess for abandoning your charges and letting young Edmund get himself stuck up a tree. Luckily for you, Tom Neville happened to hear his shouts. I expect to see you kneel before the duchess at dinner in the great hall tonight. She will not know why but you will tell her in front of the entire household.'

It did not surprise me that the prospect of such humiliation turned Harry's cheeks from flame-red to puce. 'I will do no such thing,' he spluttered. 'You cannot make me!'

In a few years he would be right, for when he turned twenty-one this spotty-faced youth would be the Duke of Exeter and achieve his inheritance of extensive manors and properties throughout the south of England. After York, Exeter held the most lucrative estates in the realm, and Richard had paid an eye-watering four thousand crowns to the king for the honour of taking the young heir in ward when Harry's father had died the previous year. The exorbitant sum gave the world a clear idea of just how depleted the royal exchequer was. The fact that he could afford such a sum had not endeared Richard any further to the king's council: already, since his return from France, a wide gulf had opened between the duke's York affinity and that of the king and his Lancastrian household. In this climate, Harry constantly chafed against York's authority, being like his dead father a dedicated supporter of the Lancastrian cause.

Now I shrugged off his defiance. 'Oh, I could make you do it, Harry, I assure you, but as it happens I expect you to do it of your own accord. The duchess is bound to hear of the drama from the boys, and she will ask why it was Tom Neville who had to rescue Edmund from a ducking in the horse pond.'

I had thought it impossible but Harry's scowl deepened and he made a one-fingered gesture showing his opinion of his fellow-squire. 'Tom Neville is an arse-licking crawler,' he snarled. 'And you are both Yorkist scum!'

This last jibe caused a flurry of oppositional mutterings among his fellow gamblers and I noticed that whilst all attention had been on my altercation with Harry, the card sharp pedlar had hefted his pack and slunk out of sight.

'As you are living in York's household I do not think it is in your best interests to insult Yorkists, Harry. And, by the way, if you thought your stake money was safe you were wrong. I think you will find the man who holds it has scarpered.'

Harry suddenly found himself at one with the rest of the house-carls who had left a considerable stack of coin on the barrel and now suddenly realized that the whole lot, along with the sleight-of-hand pedlar, had disappeared. While they all scattered in search of him and their money, I turned on my heel and strode off towards my quarters in the castle gatehouse, thinking to refresh myself and my attire before seeking admittance to Cicely's chamber to hear the latest news. However, passing by the kennel I encountered an excited Edmund emerging into the sunshine with Tom Neville, a wide grin splitting his childish face.

'Look, Uncle Cuthbert! Tom says I can have this puppy for my very own.'

Curled up in the curve of his two small hands lay a tiny rust-coloured puppy, its twitching pink nose and tightly closed eyes showing little resemblance to the long-snouted, keen-eyed deer-hound it would become.

'That is very generous of him, Edmund,' I said. 'A well-bred puppy like that can fetch a pretty price.' I glanced enquiringly up at Tom, who was close behind the little boy, keeping a wary eye on the safety of the fragile pup.

The squire shrugged. 'Edmund has promised to train him carefully. They should both be ready to go hunting by the time he is a full-grown dog.'

'And Edward has not got a dog to hunt with,' Edmund added triumphantly.

'What has Edward not got?' The older boy had wandered up behind me, returning from the stables.

Edmund's grin faded and I hoped Edward would not spoil his delight by making a negative remark. It was a hope quickly confounded.

'Is that one of Tom's deerhound pups?' the older boy asked indignantly. 'There is no point in you having one of those, Edmund, when you will not be allowed to hunt for years, but I will train it for you if you like. Our lord father says I may go hunting now that I can ride a bigger pony.'

This was news to me but it was quite likely that Edward's exceptionally long legs made it possible for him to graduate to a mount large enough to keep up with the deer hunt.

'No!' Edmund nearly dropped the pup in his distress. 'Do not let Edward train my dog, Tom. He will make it *his!*'

Tom quickly supported the lad's little hands with their precious burden in his own callused palms. 'Of course Edward is not going to train your pup, Edmund. Perhaps he will get a hound of his own if he is going to be allowed to hunt. Now let us put the pup back with his dam while you decide what name you will give him.'

Edward watched his brother and cousin go back into the kennel. 'I wonder if Tom would let me have one of Mab's pups as well,' he mused aloud. 'The hunt master says the sire is the best hound in the pack.'

Despite knowing how it annoyed him, I ruffled his hair. 'Well you can ask him, Edward, but prepare to be disappointed,' I said, grinning as he jerked his head away crossly. 'It sounds as if you will soon be having a new pony so it is only fair if Edmund gets a puppy.'

To his credit Edward accepted this notion and looked excited, as if the prospect of a new pony had not occurred to him. 'Do you really think I will be given a new pony, Uncle Cuthbert?'

'I would say it is inevitable since you grow at such a pace nephew. You already come up to my elbow and how old are you?'

'I am six and a quarter,' he replied proudly. 'My lady mother says I take after my grandsire, her father. He was very tall.'

'He was indeed. The Earl of Westmorland was my father too but I did not grow as tall as him. You have his grey eyes as well.'

Edward stared at me hard. 'Your eyes are not grey, Uncle, they are pale blue.'

'Are they?' I gave a harsh laugh. 'Well, I am a Neville and yet not a Neville, so to speak. But you are all Neville.'

A flush of indignation seemed to make Edward look even taller. 'No, I am a Plantagenet. My father told me so. Plantagenet is a royal name.'

I was about to tell him that he should not forget his Neville heritage when Edmund skipped out of the kennel, announcing, 'I am going to call my puppy Orion, Edward.' He looked pleased with himself. 'Orion the hunter.'

Edward's lip curled. 'How original!' he said.

18

Fotheringhay Castle, June 1448

Cicely

Maud Willoughby had been staying with me at Fotheringhay for more than a month and I dreaded the day she would be obliged to return to her own life. She reminded me greatly of my childhood friend and companion Hilda Copley. How I wished I had taken the precaution of arranging a suitable marriage for Hilda to a member of my household whilst I had the power to do so. But I had scarcely had the chance, she had been so abruptly removed from my company by her objectionable brother when he took affinity with the Westmoreland Nevilles after my mother's death and obliged her to marry a rich merchant from York, far from young, to whom he owed money. The few letters Hilda had sent to me over the years gave the impression of a loveless union and I feared that running his household and children was a burden that even she, with her almost boundless energy and spirit, found hard to bear. I bitterly regretted her situation. Maud bore no physical resemblance to Hilda, being fair and slender rather than dark and curvy, but she was a good friend, lively and amusing with her storytelling and ability to invent games all the children wanted to play.

Edward and Edmund excitedly recounted their adventures at the horse pond to Maud and me as we gathered in the ante chamber before dinner. I would have scolded but Maud teased them both while managing to make it clear which she thought right and which wrong, and I was grateful, as often before, for her light-hearted touch with them. 'I would congratulate the bold leader,' she said, aiming a smile at Edward, then pausing halfway through a bow and a flourish, 'but one that leaves his follower behind rather ceases to be a leader, does he not?' She winked at Edward and turned to Edmund. 'And a follower who keeps climbing when he cannot see how to get down is brave but rather foolish I would say. It sounds like Tom Neville was the hero of the hour.'

The young man in question had just arrived, late and looking flustered. His flush deepened noticeably as Maud spoke his name. It seemed his feelings had not changed in his absence. My nephew Tom had sought every opportunity to be in Maud's company since she arrived but I was not perturbed; beautiful though she was, Maud was a level-headed young lady. A year ago she had become the second wife of one of Richard's oldest vassals and most experienced advisers, Robert Willoughby, Baron of Eresby, who was presently in London with Richard, giving him much-needed support in his battles with the king and council. On their return I knew she would be obliged to leave with him for his Lincolnshire estates. He had only one daughter, whose mother had died, and had married a much younger second wife so that she might bear a son to inherit his barony. I was certain Maud would be careful to allow no shred of doubt to be cast over its siring. She had confessed to me that she found the physical side of her marriage an unpleasant duty, but at the same time she was only too aware that the birth of such an heir would greatly enhance her own position. Yearn though he might to engage Maud's affections, Tom's youthful ardour would be better focused on another. I made a mental note to discuss a possible candidate with his father, my brother Hal, at a suitable moment.

Meanwhile I had another matter on my mind. 'Why was it Tom Neville who had to help you down from the tree, Edmund?' I asked. 'Who should have been looking out for you?'

My son shuffled his feet awkwardly and would not meet my gaze. 'I – I am not sure . . .'

Edward shot him a scornful look and said outright, 'It was Cousin Harry, lady mother. He was on guard duty.'

My heart sank. When it came to dealing with young Harry Holland, I preferred to let Richard handle it. The lad had no respect for women and could be unbearably coarse and rude, even in front of others. Valuable though the wardship was, offsetting at least some of the debt owed to him by the royal exchequer, I fervently wished Richard had left it alone. The question of Harry's marriage was one of the matters he had gone to Westminster to settle with the king, with what result I dared hardly think about.

I could see no sign of the rebellious squire when the steward gave the signal that the hall was ready for our entrance, but while people were scrambling for seats he appeared on the dais before me and bent his knee. Little notice was taken from below the salt because it was part of a squire's training for knighthood to learn and perform all the hosting duties of a great household and they were always bobbing up and down at the high table with bowls and napkins, flagons and cups.

'Have you something you wish to say to me, Harry?' I enquired.

Harry Holland's hazel eyes flashed up to meet mine, laced with an alarming measure of dislike. 'I have nothing to say to you, my lady, but I am told I must beg your forgiveness for letting your sons do what all boys will do, given the chance.'

'Indeed? I find it difficult to forgive a misdeed I am unaware of, apparently perpetrated by someone who has nothing to say to me. Cast a little more light on the matter, if you please.' I found it well nigh impossible to keep my voice neutral and feared my antipathy was as obvious as his.

'No.' Harry rose to his feet abruptly. 'I have done what was ordered and now I will take my leave.'

I compressed my lips as he made a cursory bow and marched stiffly away. I saw him deliver a sideways glare at Cuthbert at the reward table where he and other senior household officials sat to one side of the dais. On his long walk down the centre of the hall Harry spoke to no one and cut a lonely figure as he made his way out through the screen arch. He would be in for censure and probably further punishment from the steward for abandoning his serving duties at the high table. I raised an eyebrow at Cuthbert, who responded with a shrug. We both knew that young Harry Holland was his own worst enemy.

At that moment the outer door in the side wall of the great hall was thrown open and Richard strode in unannounced. Judging by the fact that he was wearing his hauberk and spurs, he had just leaped from his horse. Behind him followed several of his knights and lords, including the venerable Lord Willoughby, Maud's husband. Their unexpected arrival plunged the hall into silence so that their booted footsteps on the flagstones were loud as they made their way between the trestles, stirring the rushes. Then there was a sudden loud graunching of bench and chair-legs as I and everyone rose to greet them. The duty squires rushed to collect the washing bowls and napkins which would be required by the dusty travellers before they ate. I signalled to the steward to re-arrange the high-table seating and several occupants were hastily hustled down into the body of the hall.

'Welcome home, my lord,' I said with a bend of the knee as he rounded the high-table and advanced towards me. 'Pray forgive the lack of preparation. We had no warning of your coming.' I was shocked by his drawn expression and the haunted look on his face. He had only been gone a month but he seemed to have aged by a year or more.

Richard raised me ceremoniously and placed a kiss of greeting on my lips. 'I did not send a harbinger because we galloped nearly all the way. None of us could wait to get back to Fotheringhay,' he declared. 'We wanted to be among loyal friends, did we not, my lords and sirs?'

His companions murmured their agreement and made their own greetings while squires bustled about removing items of armour and weaponry and servants offered wine. Down in the body of the hall the whispers and shuffling slowly died down as diners readjusted their positions at the trestles. I gestured to Tom Neville who was standing nearby and he hastily hauled the ducal chair from the back wall into position at the table.

'Sit, my lord,' I said, indicating his place. 'You look exhausted.'

Richard sank back against the cushions, his expression relaxing as he gazed up at the York symbols embroidered on the canopy. 'Ah, it is good to see the white rose above my head. There has been too much of the red in evidence lately. The queen has taken a liking to it and has it sewn on liveries and canopies and flown from every turret. Berkhamstead Castle was littered with them.'

'You have come from Berkhamstead?'

'Yes. The court is there because the queen does not like to be in London. She knows that the Londoners blame her for Gloucester's death. They loved him and believe she and Suffolk conspired to murder him.'

Owing to Richard's disfavour at court and the demands of motherhood I had not been in Queen Margaret's company since she had passed through Rouen on her way to England to become King Henry's wife more than three years previously. Then she had been only fourteen but I had found her already a forceful young lady, very much encouraged in this attitude by her proxy bridegroom, William de la Pole, then Marquis and now further elevated to Duke of Suffolk, who had negotiated the marriage and since become the king's Chamberlain and favourite courtier. Suffolk had long been allied to the Beaufort cause, in favour of preserving peace with France and opposed to Richard's policy of expanding and consolidating the territory conquered there by King Henry the Fifth. In this aim Richard had enjoyed the support of the conqueror's brother, Humphrey, Duke of Gloucester, but Gloucester had died suddenly early last year, in mysterious circumstances, while attending a special session of Parliament in Bury St Edmunds.

I counted in my head. 'But the queen was only sixteen at the time of Gloucester's death, Richard. Even under the influence of Suffolk, I am sure she was not of an age or inclination to do anything so vile as to procure a murder? Besides, we do not know exactly how Gloucester died. It was most likely a seizure. He was well into his fifties.'

'I know that and you know that but try telling the Londoners. Margaret is French and a woman, that is enough to make her the embodiment of evil in their eyes.' Richard reached for his cup and waited while a hovering Tom Neville re-filled it for him. The squire seemed to have taken over the job of his uncle's cup-bearer, perhaps because it kept him near to Maud Willoughby at the high-table. Richard leaned in Willoughby's direction and raised the brimming vessel. 'Here's to the comfort and security of home, eh, Robert? It is nice not to have to watch our backs.'

The old warrior grinned wearily through his grey beard and nodded before returning the toast. 'I will drink to that, my lord duke,' he said, 'and to soft, warm company!' This last was offered to Maud, who now sat beside him. She blushed prettily and lowered her gaze while Tom suddenly became uncharacteristically clumsy and splashed wine over the cloth.

When the meal was over we retired to the ducal solar where Richard and his senior knights were served with more wine whilst I and my ladies nibbled sweetmeats and listened to accounts of their experiences. Recently Richard had taken to using Coldharbour Inn as his base in London, a large house on the Thames near the Bridge which had belonged to the Duke of Exeter and would revert to Harry Holland when he came of age. It was a sprawling residence which lacked much luxury but provided enough accommodation for the four-hundred-strong retinue he felt it necessary to maintain while sharing the city with Suffolk and his Beaufort cronies.

Predictably Richard had nothing favourable to say about them. 'Since he was created Duke of Somerset in March, Edmund Beaufort prowls the streets like a wolf surrounded by his pack.' As he spoke I frowned at a new and very obvious tic in Richard's left eyelid, worrying that it might be a symptom of some developing ailment. 'He lords it over hundreds of retainers at his inn and always has a mass of them around him every time he ventures out. The streets between his inn and Suffolk's are worn hollow by their horses' feet.'

'Perhaps it is vainglory,' I remarked. 'He must have come into a considerable inheritance since the deaths of his brother and his uncle, the cardinal, and so he can now afford to make a grand impression.'

Richard shook his head. 'I wish it were mere vainglory but he did not inherit. Mindful of his transgressions on earth, wily old Cardinal Beaufort willed most of his vast wealth to good causes and the Somerset estates went to the late duke's daughter, Margaret. She must be the richest five-year-old in England and the king has predictably granted her marriage to Suffolk, who of course instantly betrothed her to his infant son. The new Duke of Somerset would be virtually penniless if he had not wormed his way into the king's favour and set about milking the royal coffers. While the queen keeps the king out of London, only Somerset and Suffolk attend council meetings, along with the Chancellor and Treasurer who are both their men and you will be appalled to hear, my lady, that this cabal has now appointed Somerset the king's lieutenant in France and paid him twenty thousand crowns in advance. Twenty thousand! I, on the other hand, am appointed Henry's royal lieutenant in Ireland without any advance; an office which, if I do not die of plague like my uncle of March, they doubtless hope will beggar me whilst keeping me well away from power and influence.'

I could see now why Richard looked so angry and stressed. This was the accumulation of all his worst nightmares. Ireland! My heart sank. My last venture across the Irish Sea had resulted in a miscarriage on the storm-tossed ship, followed by a miserable tour of Richard's estates which had been undertaken in what had seemed like a constant deluge. I had never been back and had no wish to, but any discussion of this would have to wait until we were away from listening ears. Fortunately the duty chamberlain announced some new arrivals, which instantly put a smile on Richard's face.

'Edward, Earl of March, Lord Edmund, and the Ladies Anne, Elizabeth and Margaret, your graces.'

Wearing clean tunics and hose and with brushed hair and scrubbed faces, Edward and Edmund marched into the solar together, followed by their solemn elder sister Anne, holding the hand of three-year-old Elizabeth who had been born in Rouen soon after Queen Margaret's visit, while little Meg, only just two and born at Fotheringhay, was carried in by their motherly head nurse Anicia. Ten months ago, within weeks of his birth, we had tragically lost another son, baptized William, and I had not yet told Richard that I was once again expecting a child, due in the autumn. After a shaky start, fertility was proving the least of our problems and the thought now struck me that this next expectation would at least give me an excuse not to travel to Ireland this year.

As always Edward managed to be just a step ahead of Edmund in kneeling for his father's acknowledgement. 'I give you good evening and welcome, my lord father,' he said looking up with the dazzling smile that always made my heart lurch. Surely there was no more promising son than this tall six-year-old who seemed so quickly to master every new skill he tried.

'Thank you, Edward,' Richard said, bending to lay his hand on the gleaming head of his son and heir. 'May God bless you – and you also, Edmund,' he added, moving his hand across to his younger son's wiry mouse-brown mop. 'It gives me great joy to see you both so bright and healthy.' He turned to greet Anne and Elizabeth, who made careful curtsies, and to stroke little Meg's rosy cheek. 'And my beautiful brood of girls – you are all the pride of York.' He smiled across at me. 'Are they not, Cicely?'

'Indeed, my lord.' I nodded agreement but could not help knitting my brows disapprovingly at Anne, who had sauce stains on the front of her blue kirtle; at nearly nine, I considered her old enough to take more care of her appearance. 'I am glad you think they do you credit.' With Richard being so tired and burdened with his political setbacks, I did not consider it necessary to mention the boys' escapade in the bailey and I had forbidden anyone to make any mention outside the nursery of Anne's recent relapse into bed-wetting. Anicia had told me there was gossip among the maids that she would marry Harry Holland and it was this that had tipped her back into infantile incontinence.

Being a man and unaware of Anne's sensitivity, Richard baldly launched into an announcement which soon had her eyes widening in alarm. 'This would seem a good moment to tell you, my friends and family, that I did not stay long in London but travelled to visit the king and queen at Berkhamstead Castle. You would like it there, Cicely. The rose gardens are beautiful and Queen Margaret likes to hunt in the nearby Forest of Ashridge. It is not unlike Fotheringhay.

'But my main purpose in going was to approach the king regarding the marriage of the Duke of Exeter. Ah, there you are, Harry.' Richard had been scanning the room and spotted the sulky squire who, having missed his dinner was lurking in a shadowy corner consuming the contents of a dish of comfits. 'I am sure you will be pleased to hear that King Henry has agreed to a union between you and our daughter Anne. It is an excellent match, one that will join two great and noble houses and has been approved by the Vatican without objection.'

I could have shaken Richard for not letting me prepare Anne for this momentous news. Did he not realize that the arrangement of her marriage was the most important matter in a young girl's life? Not something to be announced in front of a score of people, some of whom were relative strangers. However, before I could reach out to her, Harry scurried between us to launch a violent protest.

'No, no, no! I do not give a tinker's fart for the Vatican but *I* have objections. I have no wish to live in the House of York, let alone marry into it. I shall inform the king that I refuse the match. What man would want to marry this snivelling brat?' He almost, but not quite, poked his extended forefinger into Anne's gravy-stained chest. 'She dribbles when she eats and pees the bed. I refuse to marry a moron, particularly a York moron!'

I was scandalized. How dared he call Anne a moron? And how did Harry know about Anne's night-time lapses? I leaped up to put an arm around her and lead her away from him. I could feel her violent trembling.

'Silence, knave!' Richard's voice thundered into the vaulted ceiling of the solar making everyone jump. 'How dare you defy the king and disparage the House of York?' He shouted an order at the chamberlain who stood goggle-eyed at the door. 'Summon the guard! I want this braggart locked away.'

Two guards who had been on duty at the entrance to the privy apartments quickly arrived and the sight of their sharp-edged halberds aimed at his throat drained the blood from Harry's hitherto flushed face. 'Jesu, do not kill me!' he cried, turning terrified eyes to Richard. 'I am your ward.'

Richard gestured impatiently to the over-eager guards to back off a little. 'A fact you would do well to remember, Harry,' he said grimly. 'The king has placed you in my care and I am responsible for your future, which I have arranged with the king's consent. Your betrothal to Anne will take place tomorrow.'

'No!' Harry's fierce anger boiled up again, despite the proximity of the guards. 'I told you, I do not agree to this union. It is unsuitable. My father would never have consented to it and I will not be forced into it.'

It was with obvious difficulty that Richard maintained a level tone. 'It is not a matter of force and your agreement is unnecessary. The king has agreed, the pope has agreed and as your guardian I have agreed; so it will be accomplished whatever adolescent objections you think you may have.'

Harry had not finished, however. 'I am of the blood royal,' he hissed, glaring around the room as if to challenge anyone to deny this. 'My father was a grandson of the great John of Gaunt, Duke of Lancaster. He would never have permitted me to ally myself to York!'

'Harry, Harry!' Richard assumed a benign expression and approached me where I stood comforting Anne, lifting my free hand and kissing it in a courtly fashion, smiling at me briefly. 'Surely you are aware that York is already allied to Lancaster. My wife is also a grandchild of John of Gaunt. Your marriage will reinforce that bond. Now calm down, my fiery young lord, and have done with this madness.' He released me and moved to place a fatherly hand on his ward's shoulder.

Harry was still not finished, however. He shrugged off Richard's conciliatory gesture with an oath and pointed a juddering finger at me. 'Christ's blood! Her mother was a Beaufort. Beaufort is not true-born Lancaster. Only King Henry and I are of the true royal line, descended from Edmund the Crusader, bringer of the red rose. We are pledged to trample the white rose into the dust! We shall not rest until it is wiped from the heraldry of England.'

Now he was spitting venom, apparently heedless of the

consequences of his words. Alarmed at his spiralling aggression, Cuthbert had moved silently up behind him, unobserved. I pulled Anne further away. Richard also stepped back, signalling to the guards. 'Lock him up,' he ordered bluntly. 'Let him cool off.'

The squire's hand went for the dagger he wore at his belt but Cuthbert was too quick for him and had the weapon out of its sheath before Harry could touch it. Alerted by the duty chamberlain, more guards arrived at the solar door and within seconds the squire was surrounded. 'You cannot do this!' he screamed, fear and fury sending his voice soaring high. 'I am the king's cousin. No man may lay hands on me except by his order.'

'It is by the king's order that you are in my care, Harry,' Richard said, pushing through the guards, anger glinting from narrowed eyes. Advancing his fist to within inches of his ward's face, he raised his thumb and two fingers one after another and spoke slowly and clearly, as if to an idiot. 'Soon you will be eighteen . . . nineteen, twenty, twenty-one . . . three years. Three more years before you come of age and in the meantime I am master of all that you do and all that you own. Mark me well, Harry Holland. Three more years!'

The duke lowered his hand and stepped back. Harry was being held by two sturdy men. 'I have decided there will now be no betrothal. Rather, you will be guarded night and day until the time of your wedding, which *will* take place and which *will* be soon.'

Harry yelled as the guards manhandled him through the door. 'York will regret this. The red rose will prevail!' Then the door closed and his voice was muffled by thick stone walls.

I wanted to give Anne reassurance, but in view of Richard's emphatic assertion that the marriage would take place I could find no words to soothe her shuddering sobs; meanwhile he was reaffirming his intention, while apologizing to the occupants of the solar.

'I regret that this unpleasant scene should have taken place before you all. I particularly regret that Anne has witnessed such uncontrolled behaviour on the part of her future husband and trust that he will find some way to redeem himself in her eyes.'

'Jesu, I fear the boy is mad,' I muttered under my breath, desperately wondering how I might manage to talk Richard out of pursuing this dreadful marriage.

At that moment, however, he appeared adamant. 'Harry will calm down and meanwhile he is still the Duke of Exeter and, as he so vehemently points out, one of the last full-blooded Lancastrians. We cannot afford to allow that connection to be exploited by others. We need to keep him in the family. The marriage must take place.'

Clinging to my neck, little Anne burst into a new paroxysm of weeping. Edward approached us and stood gazing at her, puzzled. 'There is no need to cry, Anne,' he said. 'It is only a marriage.'

19

Fotheringhay, June 1448

Cicely

Situated a short distance from the castle, the Collegiate Church and Chantry of St Mary and All Saints at Fotheringhay was the most spectacular evidence of Richard's firm belief that his own personal faith in Christ, together with divine mercy reinforced by a generous financial outlay, would minimize his soul's sojourn in purgatory. A dozen masons still worked on the magnificent vaulting of the choir, while in the cloistered hall alongside the church lived thirteen canons and thirteen choristers dedicated to chanting near-continuous masses and prayers of intercession for the souls of the Lancastrian kings and the dukes of York. In the windows, instead of the usual stained-glass images of saints and bible stories, coloured glass medallions showed the arms and emblems of the House of York and the families which had married into it. The tragic little bodies of our two dead baby sons, Henry and William, occupied a corner of the Lady Chapel, in the sanctuary were the tombs of Richard's uncle and grandfather, the first two Dukes of York, and he intended that we would lie there ourselves when the time came.

The morning after Richard's return and Harry Holland's outburst and detention, I had gone to the church to pray at the tomb of my sons. Richard and I had argued about the marriage the previous night after retiring to our chamber. I knew it could mean nothing but a life of misery for Anne, but Richard did not see this mattered in the least. 'Marriage is not about happiness, Cicely,' he had insisted. 'I am doing the very best I can do for her. You are looking at the short term, while we should both be considering the future of our dynasty. In a few years Harry will not be the foolish, insecure hothead he is now.'

I could not contain my anger. 'No, he might be even more dangerous, considering his antipathy now. Anne carries your blood, Richard, just like Edward. How can you throw her away on a lunatic like Harry Holland?'

Predictably Richard exploded. 'Throw her away? This marriage has cost me six thousand marks! As for blood, it is for blood ties that I made it, so that the Exeter line to the throne will be joined to ours. That is the reason it is important and that is why I will listen to no more of your objections. I expect you to defer to my wishes, Cicely. The marriage will take place.'

At least when we had simmered down, the news that I was once more safely into a new pregnancy gave Richard hope that our departure for Ireland might be postponed. In fact I received the distinct impression that, angry though he was at me for defying him over the marriage, he was grateful to be provided with an excuse for delay over the Irish appointment.

I returned from the chapel for a meeting with Richard and the Master of the College to discuss the marriage of Anne and Harry. When a lay brother arrived to say that the nurse Anicia urgently wished to see me I was, to be frank, relieved to excuse myself. Anicia was waiting for me, her plump round face a mask of anxiety framed in a blue wimple. 'The Lady Anne is not to be found, your grace. She would not eat her breakfast and asked to be permitted to go the chapel. I thought prayer and a talk with the chaplain would be a good thing, so I sent one of the nursery servants with her and he left her in the charge of the priest but when Lord Willoughby came seeking confession Lady Anne must have slipped out of the chapel. Now she has disappeared and I do not know where she can be. She is not normally disobedient, as you know, but she is very upset about the marriage.'

Being only too aware of Anne's fragile state of mind, I felt a pang of guilt that I had not paid a visit to the nursery that morning but I had an inkling as to where she might be so I tried to reassure the nurse. 'I am sure Anne will not have gone far and I will find her, Anicia. Instruct the rest of your staff to say nothing about this. I do not want the news reaching the duke's ears and adding to his worries unnecessarily. Now go back to the nursery – I will bring Anne back there shortly.'

During the fine summer weather I made it my habit to walk daily in the garden I had caused to be planted in the castle's outer ward, among the orchards which grew along the river. When I visited all the York castles during the course of my wedding trip fifteen years before, I listed Fotheringhay as my favourite. It lay in a beautiful setting beside the River Nene as it flowed from Northampton to Peterborough on its way to the great drains and fleets of the fens. It was also located in the centre of England and convenient for Richard both in attending his vast and scattered estates and keeping well informed about court business through the spies he kept in the king's nearby residences and London. During our years away in Rouen, Richard had spent a considerable sum having the ducal apartments made more comfortable and spacious but it remained a reassuringly impregnable fortress, defended by a deep moat, three solid towers, a gatehouse and a massive keep perched high on a steep motte much like the one at the royal stronghold of Windsor. Perhaps coincidentally or perhaps by design, the keep was built in the shape of the York fetterlock symbol, with a stout barbican defending the entrance to an unusual oblong tower where I knew I would always be safe with the children when Richard and his entourage were away.

I had had a 'mount' built, a man-made hill like those I had noticed in many French seigneurial gardens. It formed a view-point lifted above the noise and bustle of castle life, offering a panorama of the river and surrounding countryside and boasted a turf seat within a leafy arbour where I knew little Anne loved to play her games of knights and ladies.

In the rose-garden at the base of the mount, Richard had expressed a wish that all the blooms should be white but when I planted one deep-red damask rose in the middle in memory of my mother, he could hardly object. It was just coming into flower, poignantly reminding me of the girl I had once been – the young and vivacious red 'Rose of Raby'. The path up to the arbour wound through a planted 'wilderness', where honeysuckle and wild roses clambered over rustic trellises, and ever-greens and foxgloves and wild campion flourished. Perched on the turf seat, under a cascade of flowering elder, was Anne, hugging not a doll as might have been expected of a girl of her age, but a pair of golden slippers. She must have heard me coming for she was sitting bolt upright, her face a picture of misery.

She flinched as I sat down beside her. 'I have not come to scold you, Anne,' I said gently. 'Poor Anicia thinks you are lost but I knew where you would be. It is quiet and peaceful up here at this time of year.'

Anne said nothing but it was my turn to flinch as she sniffed loudly and lifted her arm to wipe her nose on the sleeve of her kirtle. It was blue like the one she had worn the previous evening, but it must have been clean that morning because there was no sign of the gravy stains on the bodice which Harry had mocked so cruelly. However both sleeves already bore evidence of the fact that she carried no kerchief and had used them as a substitute several times. I sighed inwardly. As so often in her company I felt irritation when I should have felt love and compassion. It irked me that Anne showed little sign of growing into an elegant and graceful lady. Having inherited my father's height and my mother's poise I freely admit that I found it hard having a daughter who was short, plump and gauche. I comforted myself with the thought that she was all Plantagenet and Richard, too, had been shy and sturdy when he first came to Raby as a boy. Somehow, however, I could not penetrate Anne's timid, mousey shell to find the sweet, sensitive girl beneath. Worse, I knew that Harry Holland would never do so either.

'You are nearly nine, Anne. It is not too young to be married, you know. Your father and I were pledged when I was more or less your age.' I tried to speak with encouraging cheerfulness. 'You will not have to live with Harry for years yet.'

'I do not want to live with him ever!' Anne's voice was shrill and full of panic. 'He is mad. You said so yourself, my lady mother.'

I chastised myself for making my muttered comment the previous evening, even in a whisper. 'He is still a boy,' I said gently, 'but he thinks he is already a man. He is confused. He will not stay angry. By the time you are fourteen or fifteen he will be mature and in control of himself and meanwhile you can look forward to being a duchess and having beautiful clothes. You like beautiful things do you not, Anne? Those shoes for instance.'

She stopped hugging the gold shoes and held them out to admire them. They were fashionably but not exaggeratedly pointed at the toes, with red laces tipped with gold aiglets, and the soft leather uppers were stamped under their covering of gold leaf with a pattern of wheatears. They were costly items which Richard had ordered in London for her and they had arrived in his baggage the previous day. They must have been delivered to the nursery that morning and she obviously treasured them or why would she have brought them up the mount? I had not the heart to tell her that the wheatear was Harry Holland's personal device, the badge his retinue would wear once he came into his Exeter inheritance. With the marriage already arranged when he ordered them, Richard must have specified that the symbol should be used on the shoes to mark Anne's new status.

'They are beautiful,' she agreed. 'I will wear them this evening and thank my lord father when I see him after dinner. But I cannot thank him for the marriage. Harry is not nice and he hates us. I have heard him talking to his horse when he grooms him in the stables. You should hear what he says, Mother; then you would know he is mad.'

I shook my head sorrowfully. 'People do talk nonsense to animals sometimes. They do not necessarily mean what they say. Your father has your best interests at heart, Anne. As well as thanking him for the shoes, I expect you to also thank him for arranging a great marriage for you. There are only five dukes in the kingdom and the other four are married. You are a very lucky young lady. You must prepare yourself for the wedding. There is no more to be said.'

A shutter seemed to close in my daughter's red-rimmed eyes and, knew I had not succeeded in giving her any reassurance. 'Yes, my lady mother,' she said dully.

A week later, Anne stood in the nave of the collegiate church stiff and immobile, like a wooden doll, albeit one dressed like a duchess in a gown of gold tissue and a mantle trimmed with ermine, her tawny hair hanging limply from a bridal coronet. No matter how hard Anicia tried, it could not be made to curl or look lustrous. Given the fabric and colour of her wedding gown, there had been no objection to her wearing the treasured gold slippers and so she was able to stare down at them throughout the ceremony, taking comfort from the gleaming tooled leather. This kept her eyes modestly downcast and led to whispered comments among the congregation about the dignified deportment of so young a girl. For once I felt proud of my little daughter, particularly after she showed no reaction when, after the joining of hands, Harry flung hers away as if it had scorched him.

The bridegroom had refused to don the new red quilted satin doublet which had been provided for him and appeared in the plain brown woollen jacket and hose he had been wearing when he was marched off to his tower chamber a fortnight before, garments which showed all the stains of sweat and wear inflicted on them since. It was clear to all in the church that the putative Duke of Exeter was making no concessions to a union which, despite concerted efforts to persuade him otherwise, he steadfastly continued to repudiate.

The ceremony was performed by the Master of the College who doggedly pursued the necessary declarations and vows, accepting the bridegroom's wild protests and mutterings as if they were the appropriate responses and ignoring the fact that two armed guards stood at the young man's shoulders with a hand on each elbow in case he should try to make a bolt for it. In consideration of the bride's youth, the nuptial kiss was declared inappropriate but in any case it was unlikely that the bridegroom could have been prevailed upon to cooperate. When the wedding group processed under the screen into the choir for the mass, a soaring anthem sung by the college choristers covered the sound of Harry's strident objections to being frog-marched along with it. Behind the unhappy couple and their two armed attendants, Richard and I walked stony-faced, decked out in full ducal regalia, our gold coronets sparkling with rubies and sapphires and the trains of our crimson velvet mantles carried by pages in liveries of murrey and blue. Above us rows of banners hid the scaffolding which allowed the masons access to work on the intricate stone vaulting of the ceiling and, I held my breath as I realized that, as well as displaying the York emblems of the White Rose and the Falcon and Fetterlock, some of the banners also showed the Red Rose of Lancaster and, revealingly, should Anne have glanced up, the Exeter Wheatear. However, her eyes remained firmly fixed on her golden shoes.

At the wedding feast a flower-decked canopy did much to disguise the presence of the burly guards standing behind the bridal couple but even so the two youngsters hardly looked like newlyweds. Jaw jutting defiantly and submitting the assembled guests to a baleful stare, Harry deliberately ignored Anne, who pretended not to notice because on her other side Edward kept her entertained playing a spying game based on the animals to be spotted woven into the brightly coloured hunting tapestries that covered the walls of the great hall, a favourite pastime among the children whenever they were allowed in there. The customary formality of York feasts had been suspended for what should have been a joyous family occasion and guests were free to talk and laugh and move about as they wished, enjoying the continuous flow of food and wine, constant music from minstrels in the gallery and riotous interruptions supplied by fools, tumblers and mummers. The only person who failed to take any pleasure in this entertainment was the bridegroom, who remained isolated and largely ignored except when toasts were made to his health, gestures he refused to acknowledge. On a day when he should have been enjoying centre stage, receiving the congratulations and good wishes of his friends, young Harry, Duke of Exeter, sat ignored and excluded, a sad and brooding figure smouldering with resentment.

I was seated alongside my brother Hal of Salisbury, who had travelled down from Yorkshire for the event. He would doubtless also use it as an opportunity to confer with Richard over the situation at court. Never a man of social vitality, Hal made a cheerless dinner companion. 'I hope you can win him round, Cis,' he murmured, indicating the slouched figure of the bridegroom. 'He is a danger to himself and others in this frame of mind.'

I rolled my eyes in despair. 'I fear he may be a lost cause,' I said, keeping my voice low. 'We seem to have no lines of communication. Richard thinks he will get over his resentment but I believe he grows daily more vindictive against York. I believe we have done Anne a dreadful turn in making this marriage.'

Hal shrugged and took a thoughtful gulp of his wine before producing a predictably male reaction to my misgivings. 'There is no denying that it is a brilliant match though, Cicely. Richard has endowed her well no doubt and young Harry will need funds when he comes of age because his estates are woefully tied up in trusts and obligations. His mother commands a substantial portion and could live for many years yet and she has quite a young daughter – another Anne I believe – who must also command a dowry. There is talk of her marrying our kinsman Lord John Neville, Westmorland's heir.'

I visualized the curious little boy I had encountered at Brancepeth all those years ago and realized with a jolt that he must be a man by now. 'Harry's sister to marry Jack Neville? Are you sure?'

'No.' Hal regarded me quizzically. 'As I said, there is merely talk. Why, does it matter?'

I hesitated. Any mention of that branch of my family always stirred the murky waters of my memory. My bitter dispute with Richard still rankled and, unbidden, I had a sudden recall of Sir John's very different attitude towards love and marriage. 'I suppose not,' I said, turning away to break off a corner from a manchet loaf in order to hide the tears that sprang to my eyes; a rush of yearning for a different life, a different love. But these were futile thoughts. I took a deep breath and cleared my throat. 'Do they still plague you, the Westmorland Nevilles?'

Hal gave a cynical laugh. 'Plague is the right word. Their thugs descend without warning on any corner of my estates. They raid grain stores, rustle cattle, trample crops – anything to prevent my tenants leading a peaceful, profitable existence. And every time they attack they leave a proclamation nailed to a tree or a door denouncing my right to Middleham and Sheriff Hutton. I must tell you that I bitterly regret our mother signing Slingsby over to Sir Thomas Neville. Remember your wedding boon? It provided Westmorland's two bandit brothers with a base right in the heart of my territory from which to orchestrate their campaign of attrition.'

'Sir John Neville is involved?' I hardly dared to ask the question lest I give myself away but the sudden urge for news of my erstwhile lover was irresistible.

'Involved? He is the brains behind it all. His hothead nephew – Jack you called him? – is a wild young man but Sir John is the strategist who pulls his strings. And he keeps my lawyers permanently snarled up in litigation. He sues over everything from a lost cow to a park license. He even disputes my right to be Justice of the Forest beyond Trent, a hereditary post the king granted me four years ago. Sir John maintains that it should have gone to Westmorland as the senior earl. You can imagine what the king said to that.'

I gave a grunt of laughter and adopted a regal voice, grateful to lighten the tone. '"*I can grant whatever I like to whomever I like!*" Only I expect he put it more gracefully and in Latin.' I laid a conciliatory hand on Hal's tastefully dagged sleeve. 'It is vexing though, is it not, this continuous battle over the inheritance? It casts a shadow over our father's great achievements.'

He shrugged. 'Yes, to a degree, but at least it gives the knights in my retinue something to do. Now that there is little fighting in France the young bloods need action elsewhere to test their mettle. When I leave here I have decided to take a force north into Scotland. The Scots have attacked Alnwick and they need to be taught a lesson. As usual I have had no directive from the council so I will be acting on my own initiative.'

I was shocked. 'But that is anarchy surely? Does the king not punish such arbitrary action?'

Hal snorted derisively. 'He does not notice it, Cicely. With his nose in his books and his attention focused on his college foundations, he is blind to what goes on. Henry should have been a monk rather than a king. I swear he sees more of his confessor than his queen. Even though she has beauty enough to dazzle any man, there is no sign of an heir and that is what England most needs.'

'Richard says Queen Margaret is acquiring great power because of the king's indifference to it.'

Hal scowled furiously. 'That is true, much too much power – especially for a Frenchwoman. Sometimes I am sure she does not even consult the king before expressing what she calls his "will" to the council. We are not well served from the throne.'

His voice had dropped on this last remark and I caught my breath. I had never known my cautious brother to lower his guard enough to utter what, to all intent, amounted to treason. Hal was a staunch Lancastrian, just as our father had been, but it was clear he was rapidly losing faith in the present incumbents. 'Why do you not voice your misgivings in the Royal Council, brother, instead of taking unilateral action?' I asked.

He gave me an exasperated look. 'Like Richard, I have no access to the council, Sister. Somerset and Suffolk have complete control and we are not invited to participate. So I simply do the job I was appointed to do, which is police the border with Scotland. If the borders of the kingdom are not defended, the king would have no kingdom to rule.'

'Have you and Richard discussed this?'

'Of course we have. While the king allows two rogue dukes to rule his roost, all we can do is bide our time and protect our own interests. That is why I remain up in the north and Richard will be sailing for Ireland.' His gaze went to Harry, who was playing some strategy game with little balls of bread on the table cloth, seemingly lost in his own unfathomable world. 'And he would do well to take his loose cannon of a son-in-law with him. The insurgencies of the wild Irish clans will give the lad some action on which to vent his very obvious frustrations.'

One of Harry's bread balls rolled off the trestle and he dived beneath the cloth to retrieve it, emerging with a loud grunt and a sudden burst of scornful laughter. 'Ha! Ha, ha ha!' He pointed an accusing finger at Anne, who cowered back towards Edward. 'Look at her – she is a fraud. She says she does not want to be Duchess of Exeter any more than I want her to be but she is already wearing my livery!' He disappeared under the trestle once more and returned with one of Anne's golden shoes in his fist. 'Here, look! See the pattern?' Harry waved the shoe under Anne's nose, almost hitting her with it. 'Those are wheatears, you ignorant cow! When I am duke every one of my retainers will wear the wheatear badge and people will tremble at the sight of them. The wheatear will trample the fields of York and burn the crops and I shall laugh as the flames rise.'

Anne flushed bright red and retaliated as only a furious eight-year-old girl could do, without thought for dignity or decorum. She jumped down from her seat, struggling to move the heavy throne-like chair and took Harry completely by surprise as she snatched the shoe from his hand and waved it in his face. 'No!' she shouted shrilly. 'My lord father will not let you! You are horrible, Harry, horrible! And I hate you and your beastly wheatear!' Swiftly she crouched down, pulled the other shoe off her foot and threw both of them, one after another, over the high-table where they tumbled down the dais steps. 'Hateful, hideous shoes! I shall never wear them again.'

20

**Coldharbour Inn, London
& Westminster Palace
Early October 1448**

Cicely

H arry started shouting the minute we rode into the great
courtyard of Coldharbour Inn. Our baggage train had
preceded us and our chamberlain had already allocated accommodation, allowing the servants to unload the carts so that all
should be ready for our arrival.

'I do not see why the snivelling sons of York should be housed
in the apartments where I always stayed when my father was
alive! Those chambers are meant for the Exeter heir. They are
my rooms, not Edward's or Edmund's!'

'You are housed with the rest of the young squires and
henchmen in the south wing, Harry.' Richard swung down from
his horse and made a determined effort to remain even-
tempered in the face of this outburst from his troublesome
ward. 'My sons are young and housed close to their parents, as
is proper. Of course if you wish to share Edward and Edmund's
quarters, you are very welcome to do so but I am sure you will
find the activities of the henchmen more to your taste than the

lessons of two young boys struggling with Latin declensions and Greek poetry.'

'Ugh!' Harry shuddered. 'The boys can learn Latin and Greek in any dark corner. Those are my chambers!' He confronted the chamberlain belligerently and pointed at the tower which flanked one gable-end of the sprawling mansion, near to where the ducal apartments were located. 'Have my baggage taken there.'

The chamberlain remained stony-faced and waited for his lord to make pronouncement.

'No, they will remain in the south wing, Harry,' said Richard mildly. 'Where you choose to sleep is your affair; in the stable straw if you wish, but your belongings will be where the chamberlain has ordered, as will those of Edward and Edmund.'

All this took place before I had even dismounted and I watched as Harry stamped off in high dudgeon, leaving his horse untended. In due course a stable-lad would take care of it but I wondered what kind of disorganized household there would be at Coldharbour Inn when it reverted to Harry's ownership. Once again I felt pity for Anne, who would be its chatelaine. Would she manage to introduce some sanity and order into their life? Personally, I would not be sad to seek alternative London accommodation for I found this inn draughty, damp and smelly; its walls seemed to suck up the stench of decay and detritus off the River Thames beside which it stood. Wearily I accepted the help of a groom to dismount from my palfrey. I was now over six months' pregnant and resented Richard's insistence that I make the four-day trip to London. He had been summoned back to court by the king to receive his official credentials as Royal Lieutenant of Ireland and wanted us to make it a family appearance. He did not say so but I presumed his aim was for the court and council to receive the full impact of the thriving York dynasty, compared with the barren marriage of the king and queen.

From Queen Margaret's visit to Rouen on her way to take ship for England, I remembered a self-confident and darkly beautiful fourteen-year-old girl. I also recalled her unexpected concern for me, only a few weeks from the birth of Elizabeth, and the warmth I had felt towards her as a result. For these reasons, after two days to recover from our journey, I approached our visit to Westminster Palace with interest.

Fortunately, all the children were in good health and I looked on with pride as my two sons and three daughters lined up to make their entrance into the presence chamber. Edward and Edmund led the way, smartly dressed in new murrey-red doublets and blue hose, each with an enamelled white rose brooch pinned on his draped velvet hat. Edward seemed to have grown enormously in the last few months so that he now could have been taken for three years older than Edmund instead of just one. I knew I should be equally proud of all my children but on such an occasion I found my heart swelling just a fraction more at the sight of Edward, straight as a young birch, his grey eyes alight with the excitement of being at court, while his brother's, speckled green like his father's, darted about as he hunched his shoulders and fiddled nervously with his belt buckle. Behind them I had to admit that for once Anne looked quite calm, even motherly, in her dark-green velvet gown and jewelled girdle, clutching the hands of her two little sisters, four-year-old Elizabeth, fair and classically pretty in pale blue, and little Meg, auburn-haired and wearing bright green, at only two and a half already holding her chin high like a duchess.

'We should be very proud of our family,' Richard whispered

in my ear as the doors opened to admit us. 'The future of York is assured.'

I smiled, took a deep breath and threw back my shoulders, hoping he was right but not convinced that this display of York dynastic strength was a good idea. Following the usher, Edward stepped confidently into the room and the crowd of courtiers fell away to let our little procession through to where the king and queen sat on their crimson-canopied thrones, ermine-trimmed mantles draped carefully over the velvet-covered steps of their dais. Our boys moved to the right and the girls to the left and we all bent our knees as Richard kissed King Henry's hand and then the queen's. I was not surprised to find that Margaret of Anjou had matured into a strikingly handsome woman of eighteen. She still had her pretty marguerite emblem liberally embroidered on her gown but compared to the sweet, smiling girl I had liked so much, she now looked formidable, regarding us with hooded brown eyes, her lips forming a thin, straight line.

'I am your graces' loyal and obedient subject,' Richard said in greeting, punctiliously keeping his head lower than theirs. 'The Duchess of York and I beg permission to introduce our children: Edward, Earl of March, Edmund, Anne, Elizabeth and Margaret Plantagenet.'

King Henry nodded and smiled at each child individually and said, 'You are welcome to our court – all of you – welcome indeed.'

Queen Margaret, however, now had her eyes fixed on Richard, or more particularly on his right knee which, although bent, was not actually in contact with the dais step. When she spoke it was in slightly accented English, sharp and clear and audible all around the room. 'Your knee is not on the floor, my lord duke. Do you not kneel to your sovereign lord?'

I held my breath, heard the sudden murmur of voices behind me raised in comment and prayed that Richard would contain his temper. He did, although his knee seemed to take an age to touch the red velvet and he bowed his head further to hide the anger in his eyes. It was obvious that there was history behind this incident and I wondered what could have caused bad feeling between the queen and my husband.

'That is better.' Queen Margaret smiled, showing perfect teeth, brilliant white against the deep red of her lips and the smooth, olive sheen of her complexion; but the curve of her lips did not soften her gaze, which now travelled over the children. 'You have a fine family, my lord, although some of them are perhaps a little young to bring to court; one of them I see is not yet even born.' She stared at my obviously rounded belly and her smile vanished. 'You have been busy since we last met, Duchess.'

On this occasion she made no effort to take me to a chair or even bid me to rise and I realized with a sinking heart that it had been a mistake to bring the children; so much fecundity displayed before a woman who had nothing to show for three and a half years of marriage had caused offence. I searched desperately for some safe response. Should I blandly agree that yes, I had been busy, or should I mention that I had waited for nine years to produce a son and heir?

'God has been good to us, your grace,' I said softly, hoping she saw the sympathy in my eyes; saw that I knew what it was to wait and hope and pray for the missed courses, the quickening womb.

If she did see it, her face remained expressionless. 'He has indeed,' she said flatly. 'And will you travel to Dublin in your present condition, Lady Cicely?'

I was sure she could see the horror with which I greeted this idea. 'Oh no, Madam, I could not undertake a sea journey.' My back was beginning to ache and I shifted uncomfortably but still no gesture was made for me to rise.

Richard broke in, addressing his remarks to King Henry. 'While I am here to accept your grace's appointment, I also humbly request a postponement until my wife and family are able to accompany me to Ireland next year.'

Without appearing to give the matter any thought, the king nodded agreeably. 'Of course, of course. As soon as you are able to travel please let our council know. Ireland is something of a thorn in our flesh. We will be grateful for your skilful govern-ance there.'

Richard made no further response and the queen frowned. There was an awkward pause. Looking along our family line, I noticed that Anne was beginning to have trouble keeping little Margaret in position; there was much to attract the interest of a curious two-year-old. She whispered something to Anne about the queen's gown which I could not catch but Queen Margaret obviously had sharper ears.

'Yes, little girl,' she said, 'they are daisies. The daisy is my personal flower. Do you like them?'

Meg stared up at the queen with wide green eyes but she was struck dumb at being addressed directly and Elizabeth came to her rescue. 'We sometimes make daisy chains in the garden but we like roses best – white roses.'

My heart was in my mouth and I glanced at Richard, who had inevitably worn his brilliant White Rose collar on this formal court occasion.

Queen Margaret gave a harsh little laugh. 'Yes, we can see that but you have to be very careful with roses, do you not? They have sharp thorns.'

At this moment the Duke of Suffolk stepped forward from where he had been standing behind the thrones, bowing low. Doubtless William de la Pole had once been handsome but now, advanced in age and affluence, he was jowled and paunched, his profile blurred and his chins doubled. He handed the king a scroll, heavily laden with impressive seals. 'Perhaps if you were to make the presentation, your grace, the duke and his family might be invited to rise?'

Although he was still a young man, at that moment King Henry gave the impression of a man on the cusp of his dotage, who had lost track of his own thoughts, for he gave a visible start, as if surprised to find that we all remained kneeling before him. 'Oh yes, indeed, of course. Thank you, my lord of Suffolk. Here is your deed of office, Richard. I hope you are able to make good use of it. Please do stand up – and the rest of your family.' He made urgent rising motions with his free hand. 'We are happy to see you at court. We have much news to give you.'

As Richard got to his feet the scroll was abruptly and unceremoniously thrust into his hands and the king also rose from his throne and took his elbow to lead him down to join the Duke of Suffolk on the floor of the chamber, eagerly engaging them both in conversation. King Henry's sudden lapse from the stiff formality of monarchy into the casual address of his youthful friendship with Richard was surprising and not a little disturbing. One minute he had seemed like an absent-minded old man and the next he had reverted to childhood ways. As I lumbered to my feet I noticed that Queen Margaret was frowning at the king's display of friendly intimacy with his two nobles. Perhaps to her they made a disquieting trio. When she caught me watching her she rose from her throne and glanced around for her ladies-in-waiting. An attractive, middle-aged woman in a jewelled headdress stepped out from the courtier crowd, ushering a pair of young ladies forward to pick up the train of the queen's mantle.

'Ah, Alice, do you remember Cicely, Duchess of York?' Queen Margaret said, waiting until her mantle was lifted before she descended the steps of the throne. 'As you see, she has brought her children to meet us.'

Alice de la Pole was Suffolk's wife and had been companion and adviser to Queen Margaret from the moment she left Nancy to travel to England for her marriage to King Henry. Alice and I had met a number of times, initially when my brother Hal married her stepdaughter, Alice of Salisbury, then again when I first came to court as Richard's wife, which was shortly after she had taken the Earl of Suffolk as her third husband in rather romantic circumstances in France following the fall of Orleans. He had been taken prisoner soon after their wedding and she had returned to England to raise his ransom. Although she was ten years older than me, I think if we had ever been able to spend any time together, Alice and I could have been good friends, but our husbands' circumstances had kept us largely apart and now their leadership of opposing affinities was set to make any fruitful relationship even less likely. Nevertheless, I was happy to reacquaint myself with this intelligent and lovely granddaughter of the famous poet Geoffrey Chaucer.

'I was so happy to hear that since our last meeting you have had a son and heir yourself,' I said to her, when we had exchanged formal greetings and all my children had gathered around us to be introduced. 'He would be about the same age as Edward here, I think.'

I laid a hand on Edward's shoulder and he gave Alice a characteristically winning smile. 'I am almost exactly six and a half,' he informed her politely. 'My birthday is in April. When is your son's birthday, my lady?'

The Duchess of Suffolk returned his smile with a delighted one of her own. 'John is not quite as old as you,' she replied. 'He was six only last month. Nor is he as tall as you, Edward.'

'I am lucky,' my loquacious son declared. 'I take after my grandsire who was six feet and four inches tall. He was the Earl of Westmorland.'

'Yes, I know. I met him once. My stepdaughter is your Uncle Salisbury's wife and I met him at their wedding. It is a small world, Edward, is it not?'

During this exchange I had followed Queen Margaret's gaze which had wandered back to the king, who was still in earnest discussion with Richard and the Duke of Suffolk. They had withdrawn to a window embrasure and, judging by Richard's guarded expression, were involved in a conversation which he did not find at all palatable. As we both watched, Richard exploded into furious speech at which the king recoiled and Suffolk shrugged.

Without a word or a glance in my direction, the queen walked off towards the window, catching her train-bearers by surprise so that they had to scurry after her to prevent her mantle becoming snagged. Alice broke off her conversation with Edward. 'What has happened?' she asked me anxiously, seeing the queen move so swiftly across the chamber. 'Is something wrong?'

I shook my head. 'Something has been said that has caused Richard to become angry. The queen appears to think the king needs her.'

'Then shortly the queen will need me,' said Alice with a sigh. 'I had better follow her. I would like to speak more with you, Cicely. I will look for you as soon as I can get away.'

If it had not been for the children, I would have been left standing alone and isolated in the midst of the crowd of courtiers, not one of whom appeared to wish to speak to the Duchess of York. It was a moment that made it painfully clear how extremely Lancastrian the court had become. For present members even to be seen talking to a member of the York family was clearly considered unwise and so, for a few fraught minutes, I stood holding Meg's hand while the other four children, brows creased in bewilderment, simply stared back at the people who were staring at them. Accustomed as they were to appearing at York gatherings where most were known to them and everyone was a family friend, they must have felt, as I did, like freaks in a fairground exhibit.

I was contemplating taking the children home when Richard came striding over to us, his arm raised, clutching the seal-hung scroll of office which condemned us to Irish exile. 'Come,' he said, 'we have got what we came for and the kingdom has lost more than it bargained for. It is time to leave this sorry court.'

Our exit was a good deal less formal than our entrance had been and it took place amid a chorus of tuttings, made I presumed because we had not sought royal permission to leave. It was not until we were standing in the vast palace courtyard, waiting for grooms to bring our horses from the stables, that Richard explained the cause of his outburst to the king and our unceremonious departure.

'The truce with France is a shambles,' he revealed. 'I knew there was more to that treaty than met the eye. Apparently Suffolk not only agreed that the queen would be acceptable without a dowry but also that King Henry would hand Anjou and Maine back to French sovereignty. King Charles has threatened to invade Maine if it is not ceded to him by next month and Henry intends to let him have it. That accursed Frenchwoman has not only bewitched our king but she has beggared his kingdom. And Suffolk can say what he likes about Henry having approved the deal but he was the one who signed the treaty. Wait until the people learn of this. They will demand Suffolk's head!'

Given Richard's violent antipathy towards the Earl of Suffolk, it was fortunate that he was not at Coldharbour the following day, when I was surprised by a visit from Alice de la Pole. As a favour to my brother, Will Fauconberg, I had taken his two older daughters into my household to supervise their education and was teaching my fifteen-year-old niece, Joan, the proper way to address letters to the various ranks of the nobility when a page announced her. After greeting Alice warmly, I told him to arrange refreshments and shooed Joan from my solar, telling her I would continue our lesson later.

'Joan's mother is sweet but simple-minded,' I explained to Alice as I joined her at the hearth where a coal fire glowed. 'Her father is my brother Lord Fauconberg, who is Captain of Rochester Castle, and she and her sisters would not receive the care they deserve and need if I did not supervise it. Fortunately, none of them suffer their mother's affliction. They are bright and intelligent girls and no trouble.'

'You Nevilles are a large family, I know,' said Alice. 'Let me just say how sorry I am that your visit to court was cut short, Cicely. I had hoped to have more conversation with you but when I am serving the queen she tends to demand my close attention. However, I will say now what I could not say in front of the queen. You have a lovely family and such a promising son and heir.'

'Well thank you, Alice. We are proud of all our children,' I

221

said, thinking that she surely could not have come simply to say that.

This quickly proved to be the case. Her next remarks were clearly intended to be the advice of an older woman who was more familiar than I with the ways of King Henry's court. 'We tend to keep our John away from court,' she added. 'Children are a subject that distresses Queen Margaret, as perhaps you can imagine. She is not deaf to the whispers about her barrenness and now that the news is out about the king agreeing to return Maine and Anjou to the French, she knows that her popularity will plummet.'

I noted Alice's careful omission of her husband's part in the fateful marriage treaty and I wondered how much it troubled her. She would know as well as anyone of the people's love for the king's hero-father, the fifth Henry, and the national sense of triumph that his conquests in France had engendered. Future prospects did not look good for Queen Margaret, especially if she could not provide the people with an heir to the throne, but nor were they rosy for Alice's husband, the Earl of Suffolk, who had negotiated the dreadful treaty and brought the penniless bride to England. No matter how much he was a favourite of the king, he would need all his political skill to avoid taking responsibility for the whole French fiasco.

Meanwhile Alice revealed a further reason for her visit. 'I imagine you will soon be travelling back to Fotheringhay, before riding becomes too uncomfortable for you and I wanted to ask you to keep in touch. Even if we are unable to meet again soon, we can exchange letters and, in case you think I have an ulterior motive in asking you this, I promise not to show your letters to the queen, or to my husband. Let us keep them strictly between us.'

The fact that she felt she had to say this showed how shaky was the ground beneath us and how shadowy the future. I shivered and took her hands in mine. 'I promise to write and to think kindly of you, Alice,' I said, 'whatever happens.'

Her lips twitched and she nodded, then she squeezed my hands in return. I realized more clearly than ever that our family visit to court had achieved nothing and may even have made a bad situation worse.

PART FOUR

Ireland & Northern England
1449–1450

21

Dublin Castle & Carrickfergus Castle
The Dublin Pale & The County of Ulster

Cuthbert

I did not know precisely when things started to go wrong between Cicely and Richard but she certainly became very depressed during Advent, when another baby son died soon after birth. The tiny body of John was laid to rest beside his brothers Henry and William in the Lady Chapel of the church at Fotheringhay. I am not saying that Cicely did not love her three daughters but I can imagine that the loss of three infant sons must cause a woman much heartache and Richard cannot have relieved her misery when he insisted that rather than taking them to Ireland, a new and independent household should be set up for Edward and Edmund at Ludlow in order for them to learn the process of lordship by administering, nominally at least, the extensive Mortimer holdings of the Earldom of March. He never said so, but I wondered if in fact he had been ordered to leave his sons in England as hostages, to deter him from conspiring against the crown while he was in Ireland. I would not have put it past the wily Earl of Suffolk to persuade the king of a necessity for this.

The whole York family travelled to the Welsh border and I am sure Cicely yearned to remain with the boys at Ludlow but she and her daughters were to travel with Richard to the west coast of Wales to take ship to Ireland. Leaving her sons, especially Edward, caused her immense distress and the tedious journey cannot have done anything to raise her spirits, for although it was June the mountains of Gwynedd and the steep valleys around the high peak which the Welsh called the Great Throne were shrouded in mist. Nor did the Yorks travel light; the baggage train was nearly a mile long and escorted by an armed retinue of five hundred men, for protection in territory that was historically hostile. Inevitably progress was slow and stops were frequent but although the harbingers usually managed to find shelter for the ducal family, it was often modest and, to put it bluntly, frequently infested. I did not hear Cicely complain but nor did I see her smile and each day it seemed that her shoulders drooped further and she did not sit her horse with her usual air of command. When we reached the port of Penrhyn we could see the high walls of Beaumaris Castle across the narrow strait on the Island of Anglesey but our ships were waiting at the mainland dock and we spent only one night in a fortified manor house belonging to a knight of Richard's Welsh affinity before boarding for our voyage to Dublin.

For once the Irish Sea was calm and so I was surprised to see Cicely rush to the ship's rail towards the end of our passage. 'I am afraid there is another child on the way,' she confessed ruefully when I went to her aid with fresh water and a clean napkin. 'Thank you for playing nursemaid, Cuthbert. You are always there when I need you.'

'Is that not what our father intended?' I said with a smile.

Her voice was muffled as she dried her face. 'I think it was for your fighting skills that he selected you as my champion and I fear they may be needed before too long.' She stared morosely ahead at the misty outline of mountains on the horizon, drawing ever nearer. 'God took my baby the last time I sailed these waters. Perhaps he will be merciful and send another storm. I do not care to think of bringing a child into the world in that benighted island.'

This evidence of the depth of Cicely's melancholy took me aback and words of comfort did not instantly spring to mind. Nor did I notice Richard rushing to offer consolation. In fact I hardly saw them speak to each other during the entire crossing. I thought it sad if there was a serious rift between them because I had always considered their union an example of how dynastic marriages could prove successful.

Inevitably Richard was unhappy too but outwardly at least his dejection centred on his political status. 'I am contracted to rule this godforsaken place for ten years but Ireland is an ungovernable bog,' he complained as we rode together from the port of Howth to Dublin Castle. 'Nor have my ancestors fared well here. Fifty years ago it proved the downfall of poor King Richard, my Mortimer grandfather was killed by an Irish mob, and my uncle of March died here of the plague. In this damp and miserable place the white rose will never flourish and that is why they sent me here. May the devil take Suffolk and Somerset!'

In the end Cicely stayed in Ireland less than a year. In Dublin Castle in October she delivered another son whom they called George and, contrary to her worst fears, he proved a healthy boy with a lusty cry and a dimple in his chin, confirming for me that there was no logic to the wheel of fortune; it simply turned as and when it would and babies, like all God's creatures, lived and died according to His will. Cicely doted so much on this new son that I began to feel rather sorry for her clutch of rather neglected girls, Anne, Elizabeth and Meg, especially Anne who, instead of starting to blossom as she passed her tenth birthday, seemed to become more introspective and was plagued with ugly eruptions on her face. She went to great lengths to avoid contact with Harry who, for his part, used every possible opportunity to pass comment on her complexion, calling her a 'spotty dog' and yowling at her like a hound on the scent whenever they crossed paths. If I caught him at it I put him on punishment duty but despite being regularly confined to the castle and therefore unable to visit the Dublin stews like most of the young henchmen, he still persisted in tormenting his unfortunate bride. For some unfathomable reason it seemed to give him perverted pleasure. I mentioned it once or twice to Cicely, to see if she could protect her daughter from him in some way but she merely suggested that I speak to Richard.

'He was the one who insisted on the marriage, let him deal with the consequences,' she said with a lack of maternal concern which I found shocking but interpreted as another symptom of the rift in their marriage and her general malaise.

Anne must have breathed a huge sigh of relief when Harry joined the force of a thousand men which Richard and I took north to Carrickfergus Castle in his county of Ulster for a gathering of the northern Irish lords. During the month he spent meeting with the warlike and rumbustious clan chiefs who had succeeded in keeping the English out of so much Irish territory, I became more and more impressed with Richard's powers of diplomacy. When he was the king's lieutenant in

France he had shown considerable skill in preserving relations between the natives of Normandy and their English conquerors and in Ireland he displayed a similar charismatic ability to bring to heel many Gaelic clan chiefs who had originally come to his table with intentions that were far from friendly. It helped that he had a rudimentary grasp of the local language, acquired during a summer spent as a young man on his Ulster estates, and that his mother had been sister to Roger Mortimer, the sixth Earl of Ulster, until now the most popular Englishman to attempt to rule Ireland. Richard was justifiably proud of what he had achieved by the time we trotted back through the Irish march lands and into the area known as the Dublin Pale. Treaties had been made in that month with men whose ancestors had repulsed their English overlords by sword and fire for generations. In the north at least he was confident that several of the chieftains would start to administer their estates according to English law and in return receive protection from the Dublin administration. It was a small start but a significant one.

Important news was waiting from England when we reached Dublin Castle. Richard and Cicely did not dine with the household in the great hall but after the meal he sent for me to join him in his official chamber. Cicely was there already, seated at a large table covered in letters and scrolls and the remains of a hurried meal. As soon as I stepped through the door I felt an atmosphere of contention. Her face was set like stone and her hands were clenched together in her lap.

'There is news of some moment, Cuthbert,' Richard said, handing me a paper covered in closely written script. 'A meeting of Parliament has been called and has accused Suffolk of selling England to France. He is in the Tower.'

This was indeed a momentous development and one which Richard clearly welcomed, to judge by his expression. The letter I took from him came from a member of the parliament who was one of Richard's supporters. A Bill of Complaint had been tabled which listed so many charges of neglect and embezzlement against the Earl of Suffolk in his capacity as steward of the royal household that the king had been obliged to agree to his detention in the Tower, albeit in the palace rather than the prison.

'What about the Earl of Somerset?' I asked. 'Has he been recalled from France?'

Since Richard's other arch enemy Edmund Beaufort, Duke of Somerset, had been chosen to replace him officially as lieutenant of France, the city of Rouen, which Richard had spent so much money and effort to defend, had fallen to the French, followed one after another by its surrounding satellite towns. There was now very little of Normandy left under English rule. What is more, while Somerset had been paid in hard coin for his services, the king still owed York tens of thousands of crowns.

'All the Normandy lands I acquired for Edmund have been overrun. Somerset made pathetic efforts to save his own estates and I believe he is still over there, but with Rouen gone he will be forced to return to England pretty soon. That is if he dares to show his face. But first King Henry has to deal with parliament's accusations against Suffolk. As you can imagine I am eager to offer him my advice and am minded to return to England straight away. Of course it would be against the council's orders but the chief villains of the council are not in a position to complain.' Richard indicated Cicely, who had so far said nothing. 'However, Cicely does not feel able to handle affairs here.'

'That is not entirely accurate,' said Cicely coldly. 'I do not wish to be left here with our children when a rebellion is brewing in the south of Ireland. Until his return today, my lord was not aware that while he was sweet-talking the chieftains in the north, those in the south have been preparing an attack on the Dublin Pale. It seems there is not much love lost between the chiefs of the two ends of this benighted island. I have told my lord that for the children's safety I wish to return to England with them and I believe it is his responsibility to remain here and deal with any insurrection.'

The look of gleeful pleasure generated by the news about Suffolk had vanished from Richard's face. 'It is unnecessary to burden Cuthbert with our personal differences, my lady,' he snapped.

'Cuddy is my brother,' she retorted. 'He understands the necessity of securing the safety of our children even if you do not and I am sure he will agree to command a suitable escort for us to return to Ludlow as soon as it can be arranged. That is why you asked him to attend you, is it not, my lord?'

Richard rustled the papers on the table impatiently. 'There is certainly plenty of evidence here that there is unrest in Galway and Tipperary and the trouble is spreading. However, I am sure it can be quickly nipped in the bud.'

'But not by me, or by any deputy you might appoint,' observed Cicely swiftly. 'Your success in the north can be repeated in the south. You have said so yourself. How better to demonstrate your ability to govern than by bringing Ireland fully under the English crown? Something no one has yet managed to achieve.'

Richard gave me an exasperated look. 'Now you can appreciate how I am hen-pecked, Cuthbert. But Cicely is right about one thing – I believe I can unite Ireland under English rule and in return for doing so I will demand that King Henry acknowledges me publicly as his heir. For that reason and for that reason alone . . .' – he cast a fierce glance at Cicely – 'I have agreed to your sister's request to return to Ludlow. She can check on the boys' health and education and I would appreciate your assessment of their military training. I know I can trust you to make any changes you think necessary.'

I made Richard a brief bow of acquiescence and caught Cicely's fleeting smile of satisfaction as I lowered my head.

The duke nodded and made a polite gesture of dismissal, then added an afterthought, 'Oh, and Cuthbert, I will send a hundred fighting men as an escort for my family but I would like you to recruit and train another five hundred loyal men for my personal retinue, ready for my return before the end of the year. I do not anticipate staying in Ireland longer than that.'

I was grateful not to have to organize a larger party for the journey. With our escort, baggage, horses, Cicely's women and the York children and servants, we just managed to squeeze into two ships for the Irish Sea crossing, but the winds turned against us and it was not until the first week of May that we finally made landfall, not as expected at Penrhyn but having been blown further east to Conwy on the border with England. By that time sea sickness had affected almost everyone and conditions on board were torrid but nevertheless every day that brought us nearer to the mainland had lifted Cicely's spirits higher.

'I had not realized how sad I had become,' she confided to me when we were finally on dry land again and riding south down the Welsh march, along the Conwy River. It was a safer route than the one we had taken to Penrhyn and we felt less threatened. Under a clear sky, spring lambs were gambolling in the lush valley pastures as only young creatures can and the sight was enough to gladden the saddest heart.

Cicely was entranced by them. 'Do you know, Cuddy, there have been times recently when I thought I would never smile again,' she said, pulling out of the procession and stopping to admire their antics. 'Those lambs remind me of Edward with their long legs. Like them, he is never still.'

I eased my horse out to join her. 'Well, you are not far from Edward now,' I observed. 'He has had a birthday recently has he not? How old is he now – eight?'

'Eight – and aching to be eighteen. I have never known anyone grasp at life the way he does. Come on, Cuddy, let us scatter a few sheep!'

'Mind the lambs!' I called after her, clapping my heels to my horse's sides. 'Do not forget you have six of your own.'

Cicely did not keep up the hectic pace for long but the speed brought a becoming flush to her cheeks. We slowed up some distance ahead of the column of our cavalcade and she pulled off the turban hat she always wore when riding and let her long hair fly in the breeze. It was still the same deep auburn it had been when she was a girl. I counted the years – she was thirty-four – and I could discern no trace of grey, despite the worries and responsibilities she had carried since her marriage.

'I can never forget my six lambs, or the four I have lost, any more than I can forget that England is being beggared by a bunch of incompetent fraudsters and the father of my lambs is on what amounts to a one-man crusade to stop them. But just for a few minutes I would like to banish all of that from my mind!'

'Before you do just tell me – do you think Richard has any chance of succeeding?'

She ran her hands through her springy hair as if she would slough off the question. 'I have no idea, Cuddy, but one thing I do know, he will have to make a lot more friends and allies than he has at present if he wants to get back to the king's council table. It is strange that he seems able to charm the Irish, because he gets on the wrong side of people at home. His lands and titles provoke jealousy and his grandiose attitude may impress the masses but not his peers. I have told him but he will not listen.' She wheeled her horse and headed off towards the river which dissected the pasture. 'Enough of that, I want to ride in the water!'

We rode splashing into the peaty stream at a trot through a rainbow spray of droplets. Cicely shouted with delighted laughter. It was a sound I had not heard for at least two years.

At Ludlow Castle her two boys were waiting to greet her in the inner bailey, at the foot of the stair to the great hall. They were dressed smartly in velvet doublets and draped hats and Edmund was trying not to jig up and down with excitement at seeing his mother again. Edward, however, was straight-faced and serious, which I thought surprising until I recognized the good-looking man at his side. It was young Richard Neville, known to the family as Dick, Hal's eldest son. No doubt Edward was in awe of his twenty-one-year-old cousin and wanted to make a good impression on him. As an an example of precocious worldly advancement, this new Earl of Warwick was surely it.

'What is *he* doing here?' Cicely had not sounded particularly pleased to see this visitor as we entered the inner defences of the castle.

Ludlow was a stoutly protected stronghold. Its vast outer bailey, ringed by battlemented walls, covered a wide area and contained kennels, mews and stables, a forge and workshops, butts, jousting lists and arms-training grounds. The great hall, food-stores, kitchen, dairy and bakery, chapel and privy quarters were tightly ranged around a small, irregular-shaped inner bailey fortified by numerous outer towers and a solid four-square keep, linked by a ten-foot-high secondary curtain and accessed via a drawbridge over a dry moat. No wonder Richard had considered it the safest place to leave his two eldest sons during his absence in Ireland.

I watched the young Earl of Warwick as he chivalrously handed Cicely down from her palfrey and bent his knee to her. With his fighting-man's build, dark hair and features, he was a handsome creature and Cicely responded to his deep, clear voice with a practised smile. 'God's greeting to your grace,' he said. 'My cousin Edward has kindly permitted me to stay here and break my journey south to my estates in Glamorgan. I hope this meets with my lady aunt's approval.'

A carpet had been laid over the bailey flagstones and Edward and Edmund dutifully knelt on it to receive their mother's blessing. Then she bent down eagerly to hug them. 'It is so good to see you both – and looking so well and strong. Of course I approve of you welcoming your cousin Dick. I hope you have given him an opportunity to gauge your knightly skills while he is here.'

'Indeed they have,' said the young earl, offering his arm to his aunt to ascend the steps to the great hall. 'I am greatly impressed by their achievements.'

'That is praise indeed, coming from someone whose own skills are considered unmatched. Dubbed knight at sixteen, confirmed as Earl of Warwick in your wife's right and still only twenty-one. That is unparalleled achievement I would say.' Cicely's words expressed enthusiasm but her face did not.

Her nephew shrugged. 'I would call it good fortune, Aunt,' he declared without apparent guile. 'With God's help I will prove that it was fortune well deserved.'

'My cousin pierced the quintain ring ten times in succession yesterday, lady mother!' Edward spoke with the fervour of hero-worship. 'I have done it twice running but Edmund cannot even do it once.'

'Edmund does not have quite your reach yet, young Ned.' I was pleased to hear Dick point this out. 'Nor such a big pony, but he will catch you up like my young brother Tom caught me.'

'How is Tom?' asked Cicely. 'We have all missed him since he left us after Anne's wedding.'

'He is fighting with our father on the northern march. They lead the Scots a merry dance I can tell you.' Dick grinned at her and then back at me where I followed behind. 'It is a while since you did duty on the border, is it not, Sir Cuthbert? My father says you are still considered cock o' the north though.'

I could not help feeling a little gratified. 'I proved my worth more than once,' I admitted. 'But others must have eclipsed my efforts since.'

'No, I think your reputation still stands. You are from those parts, are you not? Sir Cuthbert of Middleham. It is where I was mostly brought up and I am my father's constable there now. Is it long since you were there?'

We had entered the great hall now and I glanced at Cicely, who was looking impatient. 'I will gladly burn the candles down talking about Middleham with you later, Dick, but now we are all in need of rest and refreshment. It is the end of a very long journey.'

Warwick was suddenly all contrition. 'Forgive me, your grace – my lady aunt – I am discourteous. As you see, the steward has prepared a meal and I believe hot water has been carried to the great solar. Will you dine in hall or in private?'

'I will give the orders in my lord's castle, thank you, nephew.' Cicely was suddenly on her high horse. 'Edward, Edmund, come to my chamber in an hour, when you can greet your sisters and your new brother. We will dine together as a family.'

She swept out of the hall and up the inner stair like the duchess she was, trailing the procession of little girls and nurses behind her. I exchanged glances with Dick of Warwick, who gave me a slow wink, waiting until Cicely was out of earshot. 'My father told me he used to call her Proud Cis,' he remarked. 'Now I can see why.'

I was not prepared to let that pass without comment. 'I think a certain impatient weariness is allowable in a great lady who has been travelling in some discomfort for several weeks,' I said, approaching the two boys who were staring after their mother a little disconsolately. 'I am looking forward to seeing this new skill at the quintain, Edward, and I hope you have trained that puppy of yours well, young Edmund. Tomorrow I would appreciate a demonstration of your progress in these matters.'

To the older boy's obvious delight, Dick immediately slung his arm around Edward's shoulder. 'I have been giving this young man some coaching, Sir Cuthbert, and I think you will be surprised by his improvement. He is becoming quite a prodigy at the jousting rail.'

I looked at the pair of them bunched so close together. The

top of Edward's head was almost level with his cousin's chin. However, it could not be many years before they would be standing eye to eye and I wondered if their relationship would remain the same then, or if the youngster might prove a rival to the young Earl of Warwick's obvious ambition.

'Well, tomorrow will tell.' I turned to the younger boy. 'And what of Orion's progress, Edmund—?'

A cloud seemed to pass over Edmund's face. 'He is a lovely dog but Edward says he will never lead the pack.'

I cocked my head enquiringly. 'And since when did Edward become an expert in that field?'

'Since he took him out hunting without my permission!' Edmund's voice climbed high with indignation and I could see his lower lip trembling but he managed to keep the tears in check. Clearly the unequal competition between the two brothers continued unabated. Dick pushed Edward firmly forward to encourage him to respond to his brother's accusation.

He blustered a little. 'I only took Orion out on a training hunt with some of the pages. He did not respond to the horn or to my call and he was a bit of a babbler, that is all. Edmund gets upset about nothing.'

I patted Edmund's shoulder consolingly. 'I am sure you can get advice from the huntsmen about reaction to the horn and babbling is probably just because he is young and keen. He will grow out of it.' Huntsmen used the term 'babbling' if a hound sounded on a scent when there was none. Sometimes they learned better and sometimes it put an end to the hound's career. I crossed my fingers that with Orion it was the former.

Dick could not refrain from offering his penny-worth. 'But, Ned, you should not have taken Edmund's hound out without his permission. A hound answers like a vassal to his lord or a subject to his king – his loyalty does not shift lightly to another.'

Edward lifted his chin and showed that he was not completely overcome by hero worship. 'You expect the vassals of Warwick to change their loyalty from the Beauchamp swan to your bear-with-the-ragged-staff – and they do.'

Richard of Warwick shot his cousin an impish grin. 'So they do, young Ned, so they do. But men understand an offer they cannot refuse, whereas hounds do not.'

Edmund had the last word. 'And you do not have my permission to take Orion out again, Edward, not ever!'

22

Ludlow Castle & the city of York, June 1450

Cuthbert

A letter reached me at Ludlow which had been several months in a courier's bag, following the York household from Fotheringhay to Ludlow, Ireland and back again. It was probably the last letter I could have wished to be so delayed and as soon as I had read it, I brought it straight to Cicely's notice.

—§§—

From Mistress Hilda Exeley, widow of York, to Sir Cuthbert of Middleham, greetings.

It is with regret that I write to inform you of the death of my husband. As you know he was a wealthy and successful wool merchant and my widow's dower that the law requires, viz one third of my husband's estate, would provide for me but the truth is I have been deceived and defrauded by my eldest stepson, Simon, who insists that when his father died he was owed more than the value of the dower by my brother Sir Gerald Copley and therefore the estate is under no obligation to me. My brother declares himself unable to pay the debt and to make things worse he refuses to allow me to return to our family manor of Copley.

I write to tell you this because you have always shown yourself to be my friend. I am still at present living in my husband's house but I cannot tell how long that will be possible. I have certain funds put aside but these will not last long if I am forced to move out. Although I left her grace your sister at an unfortunate time, as you know this was beyond my control and I am wondering if you may be able to persuade her to accept me back into her household. It is my only hope.

I am your loving friend,
Hilda Exeley

Written at Exeley House, York on the Feast of St Chad in the year of our Lord fourteen hundred and fifty.

—§§—

Having read the letter, Cicely immediately went to her breviary and consulted the list of saints' days. 'I should remember the feast of St Chad because he is a northern saint but – ah, it is the second day of March.' She gave me a stricken look. 'That is more than three months ago, Cuddy! Whatever can have happened to Hilda since?'

We were alone and so we could talk freely. 'I desire nothing more than to travel to York to find out, Cis, with your permission of course.' I retrieved the letter and tucked it carefully into the front of my doublet. 'I will write reports for Richard on the boys' military training before I go in case he returns before I do.'

'Be sure to bring Hilda with you when you do,' said Cicely, an expression of deep anxiety clouding her face. 'How can she think for one moment that I might not have her back?'

'Her perilous position may have caused her to doubt everything and everyone. I only hope she is still in York and has not thrown herself on the mercy of her appalling brother. If she is back at Copley I may have to fight Gerald to get to her.'

Cicely sucked air through her teeth, then issued a stern warning. 'She says he has cast her out! But I think Hilda will never forgive you if you kill her brother, Cuddy, under any circumstances. Remember that and keep your hand off your sword.'

Her words stayed with me on the long journey to York which, undertaken in good weather, took only a little over a week. I knew she was right. Hilda had begged me for help but that would not include killing her brother, even in a fair fight. Yet that is the thing I yearned most to do, in revenge for his disparagement of me, and because I hated him for selling his sister to the merchant and ruining the life of the only one I had ever loved. I was forty and I knew I could never again allow any man to keep me away from Hilda. Especially I could not allow her brother to do so. As I rode, I prayed that it would not come to that.

I had not been to York for many years and had almost forgotten what a large and bustling town it was. I fought my way through crowds entering through the Walmgate, thankful that there were no traitors' heads displayed on its barbican, and made my way up the Fossgate, where I recalled that I would find the Merchant Adventurer's Hall and therefore someone who might direct me to Master Exeley's house. It was mid afternoon and both I and my horse were tired from our journey but rest and refreshment would have to wait. There was no time to be lost in discovering whether Hilda was still in the city.

Approaching the Merchant's Hall, I collared a passing urchin to guard my horse while pondering which entrance to use. People going in and out of the door on the ground floor were poor and shabby with the humble look of alms-seekers, whereas those climbing the outer stair had the sleek, prosperous appearance of wealthy merchants. Choosing to follow the latter, I found myself in an enormous high-beamed hall where twenty or thirty men were gathered in small groups, involved in earnest conversations. I paused, unwilling to interrupt, but my need was urgent and so I approached two middle-aged men in long gowns who stood near the entrance.

'God give you good day, good sirs. Pray forgive the interruption but perhaps you can help me. I am seeking the house of Master Simon Exeley. I believe he was a member of your honourable guild.'

They may have been on the verge of sealing a deal, for the younger man frowned and tapped his foot but the older of the two crossed himself and addressed me solemnly. 'He was our Grand Master, sir, and a man of great worth. But since you speak of him in the past tense you are obviously aware that he died some months ago. His son of the same name is now running his business.'

'I have come from the south and am not familiar with your city. Could you kindly direct me to the Exeley house?'

'It is in Merchantgate, down by the Fosse Bridge but there is no need to go there. Master Simon Exeley the younger is here in the hall. May I introduce you to him?'

This offer put me in a quandary. I really had no wish to confront young Master Exeley in public, owing to the impression Hilda had given me of his inexcusable obduracy over her dower and yet I was tempted to take the opportunity to give him a piece of my mind. But I also wanted to find Hilda as quickly as possible and so I backed off.

'That is kind of you, sir, but my business is private. I will wait at his house.'

It was not difficult to find. Quite the largest and most imposing house on a street full of merchant houses, it commanded a bend in the River Fosse where it flowed into its confluence with the Ouse and a view over nearby rooftops of the great round keep of York Castle on its steep motte. At its rear was a dock where the contents of a barge were being unloaded. Porters and stevedores laboured in the late afternoon light, manoeuvering barrels and crates from barge to warehouse with the help of cranes and cradles. It was a scene which suggested that the Exley business was one of the richest and busiest merchant-traders in York. I decided to stable my horse at a nearby inn and, slinging my saddle-bags over my shoulder, returned to the house on foot. To my intense delight, Hilda answered my knock in person.

She was wearing a shapeless black gown and within the frame of her widow's wimple her once fetchingly-plump face had become thin and hollow-cheeked but the expression on it told me all I needed to know about her feelings on seeing me. 'By all God's Holy Angels – Cuddy! I thought you were not coming.'

There were tears of relief in her eyes but I did not want her to succumb to them in full view of the street and made what I hoped was an amusingly exaggerated bow. 'How relieved I am that you recognized me, Mistress! Will you allow an old friend to enter?'

At least she had not lost any of her spirit for she summoned a wicked little smile and cast a swift glance up and down the street. 'And set the neighbours gossiping even more than they already do? Certainly not.'

Then, in direct opposition to her words, she threw the door open and stepped back into the shadows beyond. In two strides I was inside and she was in my arms. As her lips met mine, I heard the door thud into its frame. I could have wished for much more but she gave me only the chaste kiss of friend greeting friend.

She stepped back decorously and, with a sigh, the spirited Hilda vanished before my eyes. Her haunted look returned. 'You are so well come, Cuthbert. You cannot know how much.'

I dropped my saddlebags and looked around the conspicuously grand hall, noting its dark polished wooden tables and benches, carved stone chimneypiece and single spectacular tapestry hung behind the dais which ran along one wall, depicting a battle at sea between pirate galleys and big-bellied merchant ships. Predictably, and against all likelihood, the latter seemed to be winning. Gently I took Hilda's hands, feeling the roughened skin and ragged nails of hard physical work even through the tips of my own combat-scarred fingers.

'I have come to take you back to Cicely,' I said. 'She cannot wait to have your company again.'

The tears which had been brimming before now flowed freely and she snatched her hands back to reach into the sleeve of her unbecoming black gown for a kerchief. Through its snowy folds came murmured words of relief and gratitude. 'Oh Saint Hilda be praised – and Saint Jude too! I have prayed for months to hear those words.'

'You are prepared to leave with me then?' I asked.

As I posed the question we heard the sound of shouts from

the open inner door which apparently led to the domestic quarters. The flow of tears dried and Hilda suddenly became all businesslike and practical. 'I would like to leave right here and now but it is growing late; Simon will be back soon and we would never get far enough away in daylight to be safe from pursuit. It will have to be tomorrow.'

'Safe from pursuit?' I echoed. 'I thought your stepson could not wait to be rid of you, minus your dower of course.'

Hilda darted to where my saddle bags lay and picked them up. 'Come with me, Cuthbert. Things have changed since I wrote that letter. You must leave in case Simon comes home and finds you here. I will take you out the back way.'

She scurried down a dim corridor and ducked out of a door which led onto an outside passage and I followed in her wake, listening to her gabbled explanation as we went. 'My canny husband had left a copy of his will with his lawyer and so young Simon was not able to deny me my widow's dower after all. However, he decided instead to make an arrangement with my unprincipled brother whereby I worked as his unpaid housekeeper, while the money he might have paid someone to do that job was set against the unimaginable sum of money Gerald owes to the Exley business. That way Simon could keep all the coin in his coffers.'

She stopped for a moment in the passage and I gently took the saddlebags from her. 'But you did not have to agree to that, surely?' I asked, puzzled. 'With the lawyer involved, you could have taken Simon to court.'

Deep creases appeared between her brows and she shook her head. 'Court cases take years, Cuddy! Meanwhile I would have nowhere to live and nothing to live on. Simon said the only way he would release the dower money was to a convent, if I would take the veil, but that is the last place I want to go. He fears I will remarry and take my dower and the secrets of the business to a rival merchant. But I am not cut out to be a nun, as you know.'

I smiled at that. 'No – much too shrewd! You would never obey all those rules.'

'So I will come with you and forget the whole nightmare. But it will not be easy. Simon likes to control people. He controls my brother financially and he is determined to control me. Besides, he will not be happy to lose his unpaid housekeeper. We have to be careful, Cuddy. He is a violent man.'

I felt sure there was more to these remarks that she was revealing and the final one caused the hair to rise on the back of my neck. I made a snap decision. 'In that case you must not remain here one more night. We will go now. Anything you need we can buy. My horse is at the inn around the corner, we can leave town before curfew and the road is dry. You can sample the freedom of life on the road with your own knight-champion to protect you. What do you say?'

It was a test of how desperate she felt her plight to be and I soon had the answer. For a few seconds she regarded me like a bright-eyed blackbird, head on one side; then she nodded briefly. 'So be it. Let us go now.'

Suiting the action to the word she marched to the end of the passage which led into the warehouse yard. It was crammed with carts and bustling with sweating men struggling to load them with goods to be dispatched the following day. The Exleys obviously drove their workers hard for it was already the hour leading up to Vespers, when shops were putting up their shutters and most other working folk were wending their way home to a hot meal. We slipped between the carts, receiving curious glances on the way and finally escaped the noisy confusion through the wide open doors of the warehouse, dodging two porters staggering out under seemingly impossible burdens. Inside, as our eyes adjusted to the dim light Hilda suddenly froze and muttered one word under her breath.

'Beelzebub!'

I followed the direction of her gaze to where a stocky man in a short, fur-trimmed robe and a dark draped hat stood with his back to us, talking to a tally-man in a loose tunic and coif, with a writing table slung from his neck. Hilda pushed me unceremoniously behind a pile of canvas-wrapped bales, mouthing the word 'Simon' as she did so.

Automatically my hand went to my sword hilt; then I thought better of it and quietly slid my dagger from its leather sheath instead. The two men were talking together but were far enough away to be inaudible to us. From what I had seen it was obvious that Simon was checking progress with the warehouse foreman and, with any luck, when he had satisfied himself of that he would make his way to the main house. If we managed to remain hidden, we could slip out of the door at the far end as planned. I placed my hand gently on Hilda's shoulder and beckoned her further round the pile of bales so that we were out of sight both of the two men inside the warehouse and those working in the yard outside.

'Will the other door be unlocked?' I breathed the question at the place on her wimple where her ear would be, fleetingly relishing the faint scent of lavender from the linen cloth.

Hilda lifted her shoulders, opened her eyes wide and raised both her hands, indicating that she did not know. We would have to wait and hope. Simon wore pattens to keep the bottom of his robe free of street detritus and the sound of his iron-shod footsteps on the wooden floor prompted us to slip further round the bales as he walked past and out into the yard. To my relief the foreman was at his heels. Neither of them saw us but we caught a snatch of their conversation as they passed.

'Shut the yard gates now, Seth. The men can leave by the warehouse door when they have finished loading – and not before. Make sure you secure it well after them and you can leave through the house.' I had not yet seen the man's face but Simon's voice had a whiplash tone which I instinctively did not like and the cringing note in his foreman's whine told me all I needed to know about the young merchant's relationship with his men.

'I will do as you say, Master. Yes indeed. Exactly as you say. You can rely on me.'

My fingers itched on the handle of my dagger. I hated to think how a man who caused his workers to grovel in such a way had treated Hilda in her subordinate position as housekeeper. There was one thing I knew for certain; she would never have grovelled.

I re-sheathed my dagger and took her hand. Together we moved up the aisle between the piles of stores, creeping slowly so that my spurs should not clink. Knights do not dress to slink in alleyways but to stride or ride purposefully forward in confrontation. The door was fitted with brackets to take a heavy securing bar but I muttered an oath when I saw that it also had two heavy iron bolts which were both rammed home. As I reached for the top one I hoped it had been oiled and would not squeak. The first one slid back easily.

'I will do the bottom one,' Hilda suggested. 'You move one of those crates up here if you can and we'll push it through and leave it against the door in case they follow us.'

The crate was heavy and as I manhandled it I had to admit that it would seriously delay any attempt at a hasty exit if it was rammed against the outside of the door. It confirmed what I already knew, that as a travelling companion Hilda would be a help, rather than a hindrance.

At the inn I managed to arrange the hire of another horse, albeit a somewhat flea-bitten mare with a cast in her left eye. I told the innkeeper that I would leave the nag at the inn in Tadcaster, the next posting town on our route south. We decided it was too risky to leave the city by the Walmgate and headed instead across town in the direction of the Micklegate Bar but as we passed the top of the Fossgate I heard Hilda exclaim in alarm.

'Oh no! Simon is coming at the run. He was shouting at another man so I do not think he saw us but he is not far behind.'

With difficulty I controlled an oath. Inevitably one of the porters had told him about the stranger who had entered the warehouse with Hilda. Now it was clear that he had questioned the innkeeper who had hired us the mare and learned that we were swapping horses at Tadcaster. Even if Simon did not manage to stop us at Micklegate, he would have plenty of time to assemble a search party. Sandal Magna was a long, hard day's ride away and I realized that if I wanted to protect Hilda from Simon Exley I would have to get her to a closer place of safety, and quickly. It was only ten miles to the Earl of Salisbury's castle of Sheriff Hutton. It would mean riding through the dusk over wild moorland, running the risk of footpads, but we would not have Simon Exley on our heels because we would be heading in the opposite direction to the one he would believe we had taken.

I turned my horse about. 'Change of plan; we must go east,' I said to a surprised Hilda. 'We can cut through the Shambles. Simon will not set foot there, even in pattens!'

She did not argue. Explanations could come later. I made Hilda go first, keeping close on her horse's heels in case of trouble and we plunged into the dark, stinking lanes of the Shambles where butchers gutted carcasses in the street, leaving entrails clogging the gutters and bloody hides hanging out for collection by the tanners. The stench and the flies were appalling and I almost wished I had a veil I could pull over my nose like Hilda did but I shut my mind to them and concentrated on finding the right alley that would lead us to the eastern side of the city. As we left the Shambles behind, we passed close to the magnificent twin towers of St Peter's Cathedral and the bells began to ring for Vespers, indicating that the sun had set. There was only an hour or so of gathering twilight by which to find our way.

At Monkgate Bar people were streaming into York from outside the walls; farmers, friars, pedlars, merchants, all manner of folk hurrying to beat the curfew and reach their homes or locate some lodging for the night. We seemed to be the only ones travelling the other way and as we passed the gatekeeper's lodge under the archway he called out to us, 'I hope you are not planning to cross Heworth Moor, friend. Percy bandits hunt there. It is not safe unless you wear the blue lion badge.'

I called my thanks but we did not stop. We needed to shed the stench of the Shambles and made speed to the Monk's Bridge over the River Fosse. Wading the horses under its arches, we were free to talk for the first time.

'Where exactly are we going, Cuddy?' Hilda asked, loosening her reins to allow her mare to drop her head and drink. Although the sun had set, it had still been hot and stuffy in the narrow streets of the town. It was pleasant to feel the breeze on our faces.

Heeding the gatekeeper's warning, I removed my hat and set about unpinning my York white-rose badge from its crown and tucking it away in my purse. 'To Sheriff Hutton,' I said. 'We might get there by dark if we set a good pace.'

'If Percy thugs do not accost us on the way.' Hilda had heard the warning as clearly as I.

'I would rather run my sword through a Percy out on the moor than through Master Simon Exley in the streets of York,' I said ruefully. 'That justified act of retribution might attract too much attention. I suppose you do not have a weapon hidden about your person?'

She gave me a dark look. 'I am not in the habit of carrying a knife up my sleeve, no. Especially not when I am in the midst of making soap, as I was when you knocked on the door.'

I grinned and bent to grasp the hilt of the small dagger I always wore in the top of my boot. 'Well nasty Master Exley will have to find someone else to wash his linen now, won't he?' I handed her the dagger. 'Can you handle this without cutting yourself?'

She returned my grin with one of her special sideways glances, which had always set my blood racing. 'I should be able to, since it was you who taught me,' she said, taking the sheathed blade and tucking it away carefully in the sleeve pocket most ladies' gowns seemed to contain.

'I am glad you remember.' It pained me to think that it was nigh on twenty years since I had instructed Hilda and Cicely in archery and self-defence at Raby. How many opportunities had I wasted during those years to tell this lady of my heart

254

how I felt about her? And this would be another one, I thought grimly, as I hauled on my reins to bring my horse's head up from the stream. Getting her to safety was more important at this moment. 'And now we must ride, fast and with caution. Our route takes us straight across Heworth Moor so you keep your eyes peeled for trouble on the right and I will spy out the left.'

'Who will watch our backs?' she asked pertinently as she pulled on her mare's bridle.

'Did I not also teach you the rules of scouting? How remiss of me. If they come up behind us it means we have missed their hiding place. Look back every time you see a copse or a cove where they might lie in wait. If they come from both sides, flight is the only hope and you must follow me.'

She made a face. 'I will not have much choice on this old girl,' she said, giving the mare an encouraging pat on the neck. 'Please do not leave me behind!'

My eyes met hers. 'I will never do that again,' I said, giving the words a depth of meaning she could not have failed to understand. 'Never.'

23

Heworth Moor & Sheriff Hutton Castle, Yorkshire

Cuthbert

Heworth Moor was ideal bandit territory. It was a stretch of undulating landscape rising from the valley of the River Fosse towards the steep fells further north. Pockets of dense woodland thrived in the moor's sheltered spots, while its high ground consisted of wild tracts of sun-bleached grassland and rock, dotted with thickets of gorse. It was a place to approach with caution even in daylight with armed men at your back, as I had done in the past when commanding patrols for the Earl of Salisbury; tackling it at dusk with only a woman for company – albeit a feisty one – was a daunting prospect. However, I did not wish to alarm Hilda so I hummed a little tune as we left the water mills and workshops of the city suburbs behind us and followed the river through strip fields and common grazing until they ended and the wilderness began.

'Your humming does not fool me, Cuddy,' remarked Hilda. 'I know you are nervous but I never could stand that tune.'

I stopped humming. 'I am not nervous,' I lied, 'merely cautious. Anyway we should step up the pace because we no longer run the risk of trampling a child or a stray fowl. The only hazards now are loose stones and potholes.'

'And Percys,' added Hilda.

'Yes, so keep your eyes open,' I ordered and kicked my horse into a slow canter. It was a pace I knew he could keep up for many miles but I was not confident about the stamina of the flea-bitten grey mare.

At first the going was good; there was no roadway but a clear path had been worn by the spring migration of livestock up to the common grazings and where that became too stony we could take to the grass alongside. To right and left, brakes of gorse formed threatening clusters of cover for possible assailants, dark and menacing in the deepening gloom, but as the horses settled into their easy pace I became less anxious. If we managed to keep up this speed the chances of being waylaid receded and the likelihood of getting to Sheriff Hutton before dark increased. We rode side by side in companionable silence, broken only by occasional glances that passed between us and sparked the exchange of satisfied smiles. I had always admired Hilda for her unquenchable vitality and on that twilight ride I realized that despite the black gown, the widow's coif and her shrunken frame, that energetic spirit was still in ample evidence.

However, I knew that neither she nor her horse would be able to maintain the speed of pace I had imposed without occasional stops to draw breath and on the first of these I took the opportunity to dismount and put my ear to the ground. To my disappointment I heard the distinct reverberation of hoof-beats in the hard earth, which told me we were not alone on the moor. Before rising I gave myself time to consider whether or not to tell Hilda and had decided not to when she posed the direct question, 'Well, did you hear anything?' and I realized that we were in this situation together and it would be foolish to try and protect her from the truth.

'Horses hooves,' I said, 'but they are some distance away.'

She did not seem surprised or particularly alarmed. 'Can you tell which direction?'

'They're definitely behind us but it is impossible to say how far or how many. More than two though, I think.'

'Could it be Simon?' Alarm had crept into her voice.

I shook my head. 'I do not think he could have learned which way we went and rounded up a search party in so short a time. But it is unlikely to be innocent travellers at this hour.' I scrambled back into the saddle. 'Let us keep going and in a mile or so I will look out for a likely place to hide, where I hope we can safely watch them ride on by.'

There was no exchanging of smiles as we continued our journey. The mood between us had changed from optimistic to apprehensive and the dark, brooding moor ate away at our confidence as the light dwindled to a pinkish smudge on the western horizon and the comforting sounds of roosting birds vanished. In my growing anxiety I found my breathing falling into the rhythm of the horses' gait, too fast for comfort. Making use of the little light remaining I began to look for a suitable retreat.

The terrain was rising towards the summit of the moor and suddenly, ahead to our right, a silver sliver of twilight reflected briefly off the pale walls of a cove. I raised my arm and pointed in its direction, steering us off the track and into a gap in the gorse. Neither of us spoke, realizing instinctively that although the sound of our horses' hooves would be disguised under those of the followers, our voices might carry above it. Behind the gorse brake we were forced to slow to a walk because the ground was scattered with broken shards of stone, the remains of a fall of rock from the horseshoe of cliff into which we had ridden. In the gloom it was hard to see the whole cove but I had noticed such features of the moorland landscape on previous visits to these wild northern parts and been told that they were useful hideouts for raiders and reivers, places where they could rendezvous for attacks on farms or villages, or temporarily corral the rustled livestock which were the usual plunder from such raids. I hoped this particular cove was not the intended destination of the riders heading towards us. More by feel than sight, I led Hilda behind a bushy stand of broom which hid an indentation in the rock wall, giving room for us to halt side by side and listen to the menacing sound of horses at the trot, approaching ever nearer.

'What if they stop?' Hilda asked in a whisper.

'Just what I was thinking,' I whispered back. 'Let us pray they do not.'

The jangling of harness grew louder and louder, but through the broom and the gloom and the gorse we could see no sign of who or how many they were. Of course this also meant they could not see us, which was our only crumb of comfort and at this point I decided to dismount, mainly to lay precautionary hands over both our mounts' noses. Nothing alerted troops to the presence of others quicker than the sound of a horse's whinny, however slight.

To our horror the pace of the invisible riders slackened gradually then stopped and a voice reached us. 'A short halt, men, if you want to relieve yourselves. I am going to check the cove.'

I froze, my mind whirling. This must be an armed posse but the only clue to its identity was the fact that our hiding place was known to the leader. I therefore doubted it could be Simon

Exley. I moved round to whisper to Hilda, 'Is it Simon?' and at the shake of her head I added, 'I am going to take a look at them. Stay here.'

Moving cautiously over the stony ground I edged my way around the broom bushes. I could just make out the silhouette of a man weaving his way through the rocks at the foot of the cove and cautiously unsheathed my dagger as a precaution. There was no badge on his back and I did not want him to turn and see me before I had discovered if these men were supporters of Percy or Neville. I crept nearer to the gorse bushes beside the track to try and get a glimpse of the rest of his troop and spied one of them who had dismounted and was busy relieving himself only yards to my left. As he turned, adjusting his clothing, I ducked out of sight but not before I had just managed to make out the badge on his padded gambeson – a bird with wings outspread. It was Salisbury's Vert Eagle, meaning these men must be from Sheriff Hutton. I breathed normally for what seemed like the first time in minutes.

Suddenly I felt my neck clamped in an arm lock and a voice growled in my ear. 'Announce yourself, knave!' My head was forced back and I felt the prick of a knife at my throat as I surreptitiously slipped my dagger into my boot. Being caught was bad enough but being caught with blade in hand might prove fatal.

'Friend of Neville,' I said as clearly as a man could who was being half strangled. 'Friend of Sheriff Hutton.'

'Name!' demanded the voice.

'Sir Cuthbert of Middleham.' Giving my real name was a risk but I had to hope that it would be remembered among Salisbury's retainers.

'Drop the knife, soldier, or your blood flows too!'

Both of us were so surprised by the female voice which gave this order that we jumped and turned and I heard the man's blade clatter as he dropped it. Hilda held the dagger I had given her so close to my assailant's gambeson that it must have made a slit in the padding as he swung round. He raised his hands and his teeth showed white in the darkness when he saw her.

'Blessed St Michael, a nun!'

I stepped up to Hilda and gently took the dagger from her because I could see it shaking in her hand. 'Not a nun but a lady and a very brave lady at that,' I said. 'Thank you, Mistress Exley. You could very well have saved my life but actually I think we are amongst friends. Is that not so, soldier?'

He eyed me suspiciously, still wary of the knife. 'Sir Cuthbert of Middleham is a name I have heard mentioned around Sheriff Hutton but I have never laid eyes on the man and you wear no livery that I can see.'

'A precaution,' I told him. 'We are on our way to claim hospitality from the Earl of Salisbury, being in the service of his sister the Duchess of York.'

'Well you are in luck. My lord of Salisbury is in residence and so you can ride with us to Sheriff Hutton, sir knight, but only if you put up that knife.'

I handed the dagger back to Hilda, who returned it to her sleeve pocket. 'You know my name but I do not know yours, soldier. I cannot commend your actions to the earl unless I have it.'

'Troop Captain Sam Natland, sir. I come from Kendal and I know Middleham. If that is your home you will know the dale in which it lies.'

He was testing me and I obliged. 'I was born in Coverdale,

Captain Sam. In a bastle above Coverham called Carlsthorpe. Do you know it?'

The soldier cleared his throat. 'I know Coverdale, sir, but not the place you mention. If you come from there, sir, you are a man of steel, for I have never set foot in a wilder, more wind-blasted place.'

I grinned at him. 'It certainly produces stalwart men. You should make a point of recruiting there.'

This exchange seemed to settle his mind for he saluted me and made a rough bow in Hilda's direction. 'There are ten men in my troop. You are welcome to join us for your better protection but we must leave straight away. This cove is clear but there is no telling what ruffians lurk about this moor.'

'Thank you. We will fetch our horses,' I said taking Hilda's arm.

'You trust him then?' she murmured as we carefully picked our way over the stony ground, back to where the horses stood patiently, tied by Hilda to the broom bush. By now night had fully fallen and although the sky was clear and stars were beginning to appear, the moon was in its final quarter and shed little light.

'We have no choice. We would never outrun them and they will not leave without us. They wear Hal's badge. We must assume they are genuinely his retainers.'

'You did not tell them you are the Earl of Salisbury's brother.'

'No, I think it is not always wise to claim kinship with great lords, especially in these parts where Nevilles fight with Nevilles and everyone suspects everyone else. But I have told them nothing but the truth. We are in the service of a great landholder, just as they are. That makes us fellow travellers.'

I was holding her elbow in support and felt her squeeze my

hand against her in an instinctive move which sent a thrill of pleasure through my body. 'You are a clever man, Cuthbert of Middleham,' she said, 'clever and good.'

In less than an hour we sighted the great square silhouette of Sheriff Hutton castle, standing proudly on its hillock above us as our cavalcade trotted through its attendant village and up to the gatehouse. Once news filtered through to his private apartments who the visitors were that had arrived with the regular scouting party, Hal received us himself. He was in company with several of his knights and squires in his richly furnished solar above the dais end of the magnificent great hall which, as we were ushered through, was already filling with soldiers and servants seeking a warm place to lay their bed-rolls. Sadly for our rumbling stomachs, all evidence of the evening meal had been removed and the trestles were stacked against the wall.

Having greeted us in his familiar solemn way, Hal made a point of apologizing to Hilda. 'I fear you have come to a fortress presently lacking in female company, Mistress Exley. My wife prefers to stay at Bisham in Berkshire for most of the year. She says it is warmer and the manor house is not constantly full of knights and soldiers as my northern castles tend to be.' He gestured around at his companions, all military men who were indulging in the usual evening pursuits of drinking wine, talking tactics, throwing dice and making wagers.

'My late husband had three sons when I married him so I am used to male company, my lord,' Hilda responded. 'But I confess that I look forward to re-joining the ladies of her grace, your sister's household.'

Hal smiled at her amiably. 'We must bring that about as soon as possible then, must we not, Cuthbert? I owe our brother of

York a favour since he has supplied me with frequent support in my constant feud with my nephew of Westmorland and his pesky Percy friends. So I will get one of my captains to select a suitable escort to accompany you to Ludlow. I take it you will return with her, Cuthbert?'

'Those are my orders and as you know, Hal, we do not argue with orders from Proud Cis!' This teasing pleasantry received no glimmer of mirth in return. Having not seen him for a while I had forgotten my half-brother's poor sense of humour. 'If it is not asking too much, we would like to set out as soon as possible. Our detour here was entirely due to the circumstances of our departure from York and we need to put some distance between Hilda and her stepson as soon as possible.'

I could see that Hal was curious about this necessity for haste but thankfully he put hospitality first. 'We will discuss logistics later,' he said briskly. 'First you need refreshment. My squire will show you to a separate chamber and have a meal provided there immediately.'

Remains of the meal which had been served for supper in the great hall were brought to the small ante chamber which Hal's young squire prepared for us, setting out a table and chairs and pouring wine into fine silver hanaps with engraved lids. I ate hungrily at first, until I noticed Hilda merely toying with a slice of mutton pie. 'You should eat,' I urged. 'You have become too thin and you will need strength for the coming journey.'

She looked up from her trencher and I saw that her eyes were brimming with tears. When she spoke her voice cracked. 'I have no appetite. Now that I am safe, suddenly I feel very vulnerable. I suppose it is because a woman alone *is* very vulnerable.' She dabbed at her eyes with her napkin. 'Take no notice. I am being foolish.'

With a swift glance around to see that the squire had left the room, I abandoned my place at the opposite side of the table and went down on my knees beside her. 'You are not alone!' I declared. 'And as far as I am concerned, I would like to make sure you are never alone again – if you will let me.'

Her doleful expression changed to one of surprise. 'Cuddy, what are you saying?'

'Hilda, you must know how I feel about you – how I have felt about you for many years. When you told me you had agreed to marry Master Exley I thought my heart would break. Now it definitely will break if you do not agree to marry me.' I took her bony hands, still clenched on the napkin, and kissed her work-worn knuckles. 'You can have no idea how much I want to put flesh on these fingers; I long to put rings on them too and buy bright colours and furs to adorn the bonny lady that you truly are. Please do not condemn me to another ten years of misery by saying no!'

Hilda regarded me with an expression that I could not readily interpret. It could have been amusement or it could have been chagrin. Her face was hard to read in its restrictive linen frame and I wanted to tear the ugly widow's coif from her head and plunge my fingers into the mane of dark hair that I so vividly remembered as her crowning glory. It did not occur to me that it might not still be exactly the same, thick and wavy and tumbling down her back as it had when, as a young man, I had stood behind her and steadied her girlish hand on the taut string of her bow.

'I never allowed myself to imagine that you were still thinking of me in that way.' Her voice was constricted with emotion. 'That is why, when you did not immediately answer my letter, I lost all hope that you would come. And now you have come and you are my savior. Yes, Cuddy, I will marry you – but only if we receive the permission and blessing of Cicely.'

I felt as if a tight band had snapped somewhere in my chest and for a moment I could not breathe and then words tumbled out of me as I crushed her fingers between my hands. 'But of course Cicely will give us her blessing. There is absolutely no doubt about that. We will be married at Ludlow as soon as the banns have been called and I am certain that not only will she give us her blessing but she will provide us with accommodation befitting her senior knight and her first lady of the chamber. You will see. She will be almost as happy about our marriage as I am.'

That elicited the kind of smile a man might dream of. 'You are such an optimist, Cuddy,' she said. 'I have always liked that about you. Very well, we will travel to Ludlow and ask Cicely but I cannot consider us betrothed until I hear her say the word.'

Impatiently I stood up and pulled Hilda to her feet so that I could put my arms around her. She was tiny and thin and through the fabric of her hateful black gown I could feel the sharp bones of her shoulder blades but I could also feel the excited beat of her heart and it brought joy to my soul. 'Perhaps we are not yet betrothed, my love, but I think we are now what might be called "intended", so does that not warrant at least one kiss?'

She lowered her eyes from my intense gaze and I could not tell if it was from shyness or submission. 'Not only an optimist but also a strategist,' she murmured, then lifted her head so that our lips were only inches apart. 'How can I refuse?'

Our kiss began gently because she was, after all, a widow and I was hesitant about offending her sense of propriety but within seconds the growing pressure of our lips had stirred passions that must have lain dormant for years. Hilda's arms twined around my neck and I was almost lifting her off the ground as my heated blood seemed to set my whole body on fire. I thought my sudden arousal might dismay her but instead she pulled me closer as if she would merge her limbs with mine. I closed my eyes and relished the eagerness of her.

When I opened them I saw that her usually bright, teasing brown eyes were dark and smouldering with the passions that our amazingly unchaste kiss had inflamed. Slowly, and with obvious reluctance, she withdrew her arms from around my neck and I felt her breath fan my cheek as she released a soft, prolonged sigh.

'Oh dear, Cuddy,' she said with a rueful smile. 'How long will it take us to get to Ludlow?'

24

Ludlow Castle, July – September 1450

Cuthbert

Hilda and I were married in the beautiful round Chapel of St Mary Magdelene at Ludlow Castle. As I had predicted, Cicely was so delighted by the prospect of a union between us that she ordered a wedding feast to be held in the Great Hall and arranged accommodation for us in one of the privy towers in the inner court. Our chamber was close to the great ducal solar and had its own garderobe and latrine, a privilege granted only to the highest-ranking officials and guests. Previously, when she had been one of Cicely's damsels, Hilda had always shared a bed and chamber with other lady companions so this new arrangement pleased her enormously. However, when I revealed that soon after our wedding I would have to spend some weeks touring Richard's Mortimer estates recruiting men for his new army of retainers, Cicely made a suggestion.

'You could move in with me while Cuthbert is away, Hilda. I always have one of my women sleep in my chamber when Richard is not there. It would be like it was when we were girls at Raby but we do not need to share a bed as we did then. There is a truckle which slides out from under the great bed which I am assured is very comfortable. If it is not you can tell me and we will order a new mattress.'

I guessed that this offer was indicative not only of how glad Cicely was to have her childhood companion back at her side, but also how nervous she felt sleeping alone in the great ducal chamber, a room of daunting size and height, even though there were trusted guards placed at the only entrance all through the night. There was a small wainscoted room off this large chamber, which Cicely used as an oratory, for prayer and confession and for private conversations away from the listening ears of her staff. After mass we three had seated ourselves there in the window alcove, overlooking a bend of the River Teme where it flowed through the steep gorge which defended the castle walls to the west and north. On the opposite bank wooded slopes rose sharply into the foothills of the Welsh mountains, demonstrating Ludlow's crucial position as one of a line of strongholds built and used for centuries by the marcher lords to quash any attempt at rebellion by the unruly natives of Wales. Having settled the question of Hilda's sleeping arrangements, we soon discovered that was not the only reason Cicely had called us to her private closet.

During our journey from York we had found the north country abuzz with news of the violent and mysterious death of the Duke of Suffolk, whose trial by parliament on charges of defrauding the royal exchequer had resulted in a death sentence for treason. Using his royal prerogative the king had commuted his favourite's sentence to one of exile for five years but the duke's ship had hardly left the shores of England before it was boarded by unknown criminals who had pirated a royal vessel from the port of Sandwich in Kent expressly for the purpose. Within minutes, and without ceremony, the sentence of execution from which the king had reprieved the duke was crudely carried out with a rusty sword by the unidentified leader of these 'pirates' and a few days later Suffolk's bloodied body had been found on the beach at Dover with his severed head impaled on a pikestaff beside it. Royal revenge for this murder had been swift and aimed at the county of Kent where a number of men had been summarily hanged for their supposed involvement. In response Kent had risen in revolt, led by a man named Jack Cade, who also called himself John Mortimer. It was the use of this name, that of Richard's mother's family, which had sparked a rumour that even though he was known to be in Ireland, the Duke of York was responsible both for the murder of Suffolk and for the Kentish rising.

Cicely unfolded a letter she had been holding in her hand. 'Richard is furious about the use of his mother's name by this Jack Cade, especially as the scoundrel is now marching on London at the head of an army of five thousand men and has issued a list of complaints and demands, one of which is that the Duke of York must be brought back from Ireland to replace Suffolk on the Royal Council. Now we hear that a mob of rioters in Wiltshire have turned on Bishop Aiscough of Salisbury, who as you know is the king's confessor, and murdered him in cold blood outside a church where he was taking mass. Then they nailed a proclamation to the church door blaming the bishop for persuading King Henry to make peace with France, encouraging him in monkish ways and discouraging him from lying with the queen. They want Richard to come back from Ireland to show the king how to rule and to urge him to perform his marital duty and provide the heir to the throne that the people require.'

Cicely lowered the letter and smiled wryly at us. 'The

proclamation might be comical if it were not so serious but everyone knows that Richard and Bishop Aiscough have been at loggerheads for years over French policy and now the king has fled to Kenilworth in the Lancastrian heartland, convinced that he will be attacked next.'

I was incredulous. 'Not by Richard surely! After all, he is in Ireland.'

Cicely shrugged. 'The king fears sorcery and is very influenced by the queen, who seems to believe that Richard has conspired to commit murder from a distance. The upshot of all this is that when Richard has dealt with the trouble in Galway, he intends to return to England. Although he has had nothing to do with the uprisings here, he believes that they demonstrate significant popular support for him. He wants to make sure that the next parliament is not biased against York like the last one.' She handed me the letter. 'Read it, Cuddy. He wants you to make a tour of his Mortimer manors not only to recruit fighting men but also to assess the loyalty of his people. As you will see, he believes that in the absence of an heir of the king's body there would be more stability in England if the line of succession were made clear.'

'And who does he think should be first in line?' I asked, tongue in cheek, scanning the clerk's cramped script.

'Well Richard *is* the clear heir,' Cicely replied with conviction. 'He is directly descended from Edward the Third through the male line.'

'So are the Beauforts, are they not? And by a senior line. He will clash head on with Somerset over this and it is more than obvious whom the king favours.'

My logic was met with a fierce frown. 'The House of York has always considered the Beaufort claim spurious. Richard maintains that John of Gaunt did the country no favours when he married his mistress and legitimized their children. In the past I looked on it rather differently, being the daughter of one of those children, but now I am Duchess of York my allegiance is to my husband's cause. Besides it is undeniable that the kingdom needs strong leadership and the Beauforts have never shown much of that. When a man has been single-handedly responsible for losing most of Normandy, it makes no sense to make him heir to the throne of England. You have seen at first-hand how much success Richard had in Normandy and how much progress he has made in Ireland, whereas under Edmund Beaufort's lieutenancy France has routed England. You will undertake this important task for Richard, will you not, Cuthbert?'

Her use of my baptismal name indicated that she expected a swift and formal confirmation but I hesitated. I was not a landed knight. I had no stake in the fabric of the kingdom and my allegiance was not to Richard but to Cicely. Strictly speaking I was not bound by oath to York and if the duke was coming back to England to exert his claim as heir to the throne, I could see his conflict with Somerset swiftly escalating from a war of words into violent confrontation. If I were to recruit what amounted to an army to fuel that conflict and spy for Richard at the same time, at worst I could be accused of treason and at best find myself embroiled in a campaign that might result in a battle for the throne of England. I glanced at Hilda. She and I had only just discovered the joy of a happy marriage and I was loath to jeopardize that happiness by involving myself deeply in a quarrel which might plunge me into treason and bloodshed.

Hilda surprised me by returning my enquiring glance with

a fierce glare. 'Why do you hesitate, Cuddy? You are Cicely's liegeman. Where she goes, you go and I go too. We have been committed since childhood.'

I had no wish to offend Cicely. I could tell from her expression that she was puzzled by my wavering and Hilda's vehemence tipped me into compliance. 'Until now I have always thought of myself as a Lancastrian who was lending my loyalty to York,' I said, 'but now I see that it has come to the point where I cannot support the red rose while I serve the white.' The letter dropped from my grasp as I slipped from my seat to my knees and held out my hands to Cicely as if in prayer. 'My lady of York, as proxy for your lord Richard I declare to you that in future I will be faithful to him and to you and serve York against all persons as your liegeman of life and limb. May God smite me if I fail in this my vow.'

For a moment Cicely looked rather stunned and then she took both my hands in hers in the legal and traditional way. 'Sir Cuthbert of Middleham, I accept your vow in good faith both for myself and for my liege-lord, Richard, Duke of York. In return I give you York's faithful promise before God to protect and defend you and yours against your enemies.'

A solemn silence fell between us and then beside me I felt Hilda drop to her knees and offer her own vow. 'I bring no sword to your service but I, too, declare my love and loyalty to you, Cicely, Duchess of York and call on God and his Holy Mother to witness my oath.'

It was done. There was no going back to Neville now; no going back to the fealty I had sworn to my father, the old Earl of Westmorland, or the oath I had made to Countess Joan. We had made ourselves vassals of York, sworn to support the actions of the duke, whether or not we considered them wise. I turned to help Hilda to her feet and squeezed her hand as I did so. The looks we exchanged were fleeting and rueful.

'Thank you, Hilda, thank you, Cuthbert,' Cicely said graciously, inclining her head in the heart-shaped padded head-dress she had taken to wearing, which I thought made her look unmistakably grand but dauntingly severe. 'I shall be sure to inform Richard of your fealty and willingness to serve him. He will need all the support we can give him in these very uncertain times.'

I pondered these words later, wondering if the rift I had detected in their marriage when we left Ireland had closed during their time apart. She had found Dublin a frightening place, full of hostile forces and far removed from friends and family. Being back with her older sons had certainly reduced Cicely's level of anxiety and the security offered by Ludlow's stout defences, coupled with reassuring visits from the loyal barons, knights and ladies of the surrounding Mortimer lands, had noticeably lightened her mood.

Having Hilda back at her side must also have had a great deal to do with it. During the weeks that followed, my own travels around the numerous honours, recruiting men for Richard's new force, took me away from Ludlow a good deal but the two women seemed to have slipped easily back into their girlhood friendship and the atmosphere in Cicely's great chamber whenever I attended one of her salons was noticeably more light-hearted than it had been for years. There was music and laughter and sometimes dancing and Hilda believed that part of it was also down to an improvement in Cicely's health.

'I have been counting, Cuthbert,' she told me as we lay in our chamber one night discussing recent events, a luxury which I greatly appreciated having spent so many years as a knight

274

bachelor. 'Cicely has carried nine children in ten years and suffered the loss of three of them soon after birth. She thanks the Virgin and St Margaret for her own survival but it must have taken a great toll on her mind and body.' She sat up and looked quizzically down at me. 'I hope you are not going to put me through that kind of schedule.' It took several seconds for me to fully grasp the meaning of her remark but then I reared up on one elbow and the expression on my face made her break into delighted laughter. 'Oh, Cuddy, you look like a goggle-eyed frog!'

With difficulty I straightened my face. 'Hilda, are you telling me that you are with child?'

'Yes my dear husband; God willing, you are going to be a father.'

It was no wonder my eyes had popped. Before I married, fatherhood had not been high on my agenda. Being illegitimate myself, I had not wished to inflict that state upon another and earnestly hoped I had avoided doing so. As there had been no offspring from her marriage to Master Exley, I had assumed that Hilda was not able to have children but had given little thought to it. I had married her for herself and not for any dynastic purpose. Now suddenly, and to my surprise, I found myself absurdly thrilled at the notion of becoming a father.

Hilda must have taken my stunned silence as disapproval for her face fell. 'It is quite a common result of an active marriage bed you know,' she said. 'And I would like to point out that ours has been particularly active.'

I felt the blood rush to my cheeks and pulled her into my arms. 'Oh no, Hilda, you misunderstand. I am completely and utterly delighted. It is just that I had given no thought to the possibility. Please believe me that the prospect of you carrying my child gives me great joy but I admit also to some trepidation. I am forty – a little old for fatherhood perhaps.'

She snuggled into my embrace with a contented sigh. 'It is rather too late to worry about that I think. Anyway, when it comes to giving birth I am no spring chicken myself but we shall have to leave the outcome in the hands of the Almighty. Let us just enjoy the idea of a new life growing which is all our own work.'

Through the thin fabric of her chemise I cupped her breast in my hand and registered with astonishment its new fullness and weight. With my lips to her ear I murmured, 'If that is work then I regret having to down tools but I believe the Church considers it a sin in these circumstances.'

My intentions were good but my body betrayed me and I would have rolled over to hide the fact but shamelessly she placed her hand on the offending organ and whispered, 'Is that not what confession is for, my love? We can sin and receive absolution. I spent ten years failing to inspire such desire in Master Exley; please do not make me reject it now.'

Towards the end of August Cicely received a letter informing her of the duke's intention to return to England via Wales and containing an order for me to meet him near Chester with my newly recruited army. Perhaps wisely he did not specify his movements and made no mention of coming to Ludlow. The unrest in Kent had subsided, largely due to the capture, mortal injury and death of Jack Cade and a purging of the other ring-leaders, which inevitably resulted in another rash of hangings. By now the king's advisers seemed even more convinced that the Duke of York was in some way responsible, to the extent that troops were ordered out from the royal castle at Chester to intercept and arrest him. However his scouts brought a warning so he managed to avoid them and the following day I and my new army made rendezvous with Richard at Shrewsbury. This brought the size of his force to over seven hundred, large enough to deter any further interceptions as we set off to gather more armed support from his estates in the Midlands and Gloucestershire. It was during this march that I began seriously to question his intentions and wonder even more seriously whether I had done the right thing throwing in my lot with York.

Richard had always maintained that the common people were impressed by conspicuous splendour and he had not abandoned any of his propensity for grandeur. Each member of his army of retainers wore a York livery jacket or jupon in parti-coloured murrey and blue and from every pike and lance fluttered a pennant depicting the duke's falcon-and-fetterlock. His horse's trappings were of heavy gold-trimmed azure silk, the bridle studded with gold medallions and the saddle hung with gilded stirrups. When he rode in armour it had to be polished so that the sun glinted off every joint and plate, his spurs were of silver-gilt and his helmet was ringed with a gold ducal coronet; if he did not need to wear it a squire carried it behind him on a velvet cushion. Harbingers preceded each day's march, arranging camp sites and organizing suitable lodgings for the duke and his knights, if these were available. If they were not, the duke's tent was erected, a canvas palace painted in bright colours, hung with heraldic pennants and fully equipped: trestles and chairs for meals and meetings, a curtained tester bed and a screened side tent with close stool and wash basin. All this pomp and show did not sit easy with me and every time my squire handed me the York jupon I pulled it over my head with a knot in my stomach. It had been bad enough finding myself cast on one side of a family quarrel at Lady Joan's funeral ten years before but joining this pageant of York appeared dangerously like becoming part of a spectacular and treasonous bid for the throne of England.

25

Ludlow Castle, September – October 1450

Cicely

I cannot deny that I had left Ireland agitated, fearful and exhausted, desperate to return to England and to check on the health and wellbeing of my two elder sons. Having Hilda back at my side restored my equilibrium and allowed me to admit that the relationship between myself and Richard had been on the verge of disintegrating. We had been in urgent need of a break from each other. Looking back I am guilt-struck by my marital disloyalty but the fact remains that one day at the end of September, while out riding with Hilda and my four oldest children I admired the sun shining on the golden stubble fields along the valley of the River Teme and suddenly realized that I had not felt so alive and energetic for years. When I remarked on this, Hilda made an observation which gave me pause for thought.

'Little George will be one year old next month and you are not yet expecting again, Cicely,' she said. 'Perhaps that is why you feel so well. I do not believe you have had more than three or four months' break from pregnancy since Edward was born.'

I gazed ahead at the four children. Edward had cantered along the river, followed by Anne, Edmund and Elizabeth, to a place where cattle had trodden a slope down the bank for drinking and there they had waded in, their ponies hock deep so that they could bend down from the saddle and splash each other, shrieking with laughter as they did so. Two grooms stood sentinel in case of accidents but were content to let the youngsters frolic in the warm autumn sunshine while the patient ponies dropped their heads and took the opportunity to drink. I recalled when baby Henry had died and I had come to believe that I would never carry a living son. Now, God be praised, I had my two strapping lads and little George, as well as three healthy girls; enough for any noble dynasty. But I could never forget the sons I had lost and the bitter heartache endured in grieving over their tiny corpses. The recent break from childbearing had been a break as well from the dread of another such tragedy. And there was no escaping the fact that it had only been achieved by putting the Irish Sea between Richard and me.

'I hope that by starting late I will not be quite so fecund,' added Hilda with a wry smile.

I halted my horse and stared at her. 'You are pregnant?'

'I am,' declared Hilda gaily, not drawing rein but adding over her shoulder, 'You are not the only one who can achieve it, my lady!'

I spurred my horse to catch her up. 'Congratulations!' I cried. 'Please feel at liberty to take over the birthing role entirely. When is the baby due?'

'I assure you we did not anticipate the wedding, so I should think sometime in April. I shall need all your expert advice.'

'Get a good midwife is my advice. I have not given birth at Ludlow so I do not know of one but Lady Croft will know the best.'

Lady Croft was the wife of Edward and Edmund's governor

and mentor, Sir Richard Croft, whose family were long-term tenants of Mortimer lands and whose castle lay only a few miles away. She was a little younger than me and rather bossy but kind-hearted and often attended my salons. Hilda did not look impressed. 'I am a knight-retainer's wife, not a hereditary land-holder's. Lady Croft is rather grand but I imagine there are several perfectly good midwives who tend the burgher's wives in the town.'

I was tempted to remind Hilda that she was now Lady Middleham and perfectly entitled to seek the services of the most eminent midwife, but I took the hint and did not pursue the subject further at that time. Hilda could be touchy about such things. However, her remarks sowed the seeds of an idea in my mind, which I resolved to raise with Richard whenever he did actually rejoin his family.

Meanwhile I was exchanging letters with Alice de la Pole, a process begun after I sent her my condolences on the terrible death of her husband. I was perturbed and intrigued by her reply, penned at Kenilworth, where she was in attendance on the queen.

—§§—

To the most gracious and honorable Lady Cicely, Duchess of York, greetings from her friend, Alice, Countess of Suffolk.

I am in receipt of your very kind letter expressing sympathy for the death of my beloved lord and husband and thank you most earnestly for remembering both him and me and marking his dreadful and undeserved demise.

As you may imagine, the news of it came as the most appalling shock, received as it was less than a week after he had set sail in obedience to his sentence of exile. Who is responsible for the crime of William's capture and murder I do not know, it remains a mystery, but I want you to know Cicely that I totally reject the suggestion that the perpetrators were in the pay of the Duke of York or in any way connected with his affinity, despite persistent rumours to that end. I know that allies of the duke, your husband, spoke out against my lord in the session of Parliament which ultimately led to his arraignment for treason but I am sure you will understand that the crimes with which William was charged only arose as a result of his diligent pursuit of the king's wishes with regard to his marriage and his fervent desire no longer to cross swords with his uncle in France. It was because the king was so conscious that William was being held responsible for something that he, King Henry, had asked him to do that he used his royal prerogative to commute the death sentence handed out by the Lords and reduce it to one of five years in exile. When he learned of his murder he immediately transferred all the Suffolk estates to me in tenure for my son.

So distressed was Queen Margaret by William's death and the way in which it occurred that she became prostrate with grief and the irony is that I had to be called to Windsor in order to tend her grace's prostration! I am happy to say that she is recovered now but I truly do not think that I shall ever recover from losing my dear lord and especially from the manner of his death. I believe the image of his head impaled on a spike beside his butchered corpse will haunt my days and nights forever.

Our son John is a quiet and peace-loving boy who suffers from losing his father at such a tender age. We have lost the dukedom and he will only be Earl of Suffolk when he comes of age. However, his grace King Henry has tried to make *recompense by confirming his marriage to the Somerset heiress Margaret Beaufort. We are awaiting the papal dispensation.*

Meanwhile I am still attending Queen Margaret and therefore acquainted with the activities of court and council. In the absence of my dear lord she has become very reliant on the Duke of Somerset for advice and it was he who instigated the court's move here to Kenilworth. It is a very comfortable and well-situated castle set in the middle of a large lake where the queen feels safe. After the murder of my husband and also that of the king's Confessor, Bishop Aiscough, she fears the violent displeasure of the people and envies York's apparently growing popularity.

I tell you this out of friendship and because I think you should warn your husband to tread carefully when he returns to England. Envy creates enemies I fear and there are many interpretations of treason.

I keep you in high regard, Cicely, and remain your discreet and faithful friend,

Alice, Countess of Suffolk

—§§—

As Richard travelled through the York estates in the Midlands and Lincolnshire, gathering a larger and larger force of men, I began to worry about his intentions and almost wish I were with him. It was becoming more and more obvious that he was heading to London for a confrontation with the council in order to express his grievances and to defend himself against the false accusations made about his part in the recent uprisings. His letters to me were silent on the subject however and in the end it was Cuthbert who wrote to tell me that Richard had joined forces with the Duke of Norfolk and the Earl of Devon and arrived in London at the head of four thousand men, an intimidating army even when faced with opposition from a force of similar size mustered by barons allied to the Duke of Somerset. Cuthbert told of chains being hung across the streets of the city to keep the opposing factions apart.

Correspondence from Richard himself perturbed me further because it appeared that Harry Holland, who had marched to London among the York army of retainers, had immediately been called before the council and invested with livery of his father's estates and title. This contravened the agreement concluded when Harry had been made Richard's ward, it being nine months before the young man's twenty-first birthday, the legally recognized age of majority. With some justification, Richard saw this as another slight engineered by the Duke of Somerset to defraud him of due revenue. It did not surprise me that Harry had immediately severed all ties to York and allied with Somerset, officially pledging himself to the Lancastrian cause and demanding that Richard's household and bodyguard quit Coldharbour Inn.

Reading all this sent cold shivers down my spine and the next time I saw Anne I was obliged to take her to one side and gently tell her of her husband's desertion of the House of York and adherence to the cause of her father's arch enemy. 'Of course it need not affect you at present and by the time you go to Harry he may have had second thoughts,' I added but she was not deceived.

'If it were not a mortal sin I would kill myself before setting one foot under Harry's roof, Mother,' Anne said with quiet conviction. 'I pray daily for God to smite him before my life sentence can begin.' I longed to be able to give her a hug but in the two years since her marriage she had acquired a brittle shell which I found hard to penetrate. Now a gaping chasm existed between me and my eldest daughter. I blamed Richard for this.

When the king finally agreed to grant Richard an audience, it turned out to be far from private or peaceful.

Richard wrote: 'I went to the king's Great Chamber at Westminster Palace hoping to be able to re-establish our childhood friendship and found myself confronted by the Earl of Somerset and all his cronies who consistently harangued me, construing every word I uttered as criticism of themselves or the king. Henry just sat there on his crimson and gold throne looking as if he wished he could be anywhere else; every time I tried to address him directly one of his councillors interrupted to answer for him. I could see regret and contrition in his eyes but he seemed unable to exert himself to stop them. It is no wonder the country suffers from such inept government when people like Somerset have for so long been allowed to steer the ship of state as it pleases them and cream off the richest posts and grants for themselves. Tomorrow I intend to draft a Bill, to be placed before the new parliament when it opens in November, urging the arrest of those responsible for the false execution of the king's justice and prerogatives and presenting myself as his honest and loyal vassal who is willing and able to redress the situation. My agents have ensured that this time the Commons membership will consist of a high percentage of York supporters and that the Speaker will therefore be a candidate chosen by me, so my Bill will be presented early. Until then, for my own *safety and contentment, I intend to leave London and hurry to your side at Ludlow.*

In haste and great joy at the prospect of our imminent reunion,

I am your faithful husband
Richard, Duke of York.'

He was as good as his word, leaving London before Somerset's men could discover the existence and content of his bill. I awaited his arrival with some trepidation, wondering if he would bring with him all the anger and frustration that he had communicated in his letters.

In the event it proved to be the joyful reunion he had anticipated. It had been a good summer in the Welsh Marches; there had been little unrest and a plentiful harvest and game was abundant. Richard took great pleasure in taking his older sons hunting while Hilda and I planned feasts and entertainments to enliven the lengthening October evenings. It was after one of these lively evenings, when Richard was mellow with wine and laughter, that I broached the subject I had been mulling over since Hilda had told me of her coming child.

'What is your opinion of Hilda and Cuthbert's marriage?' I asked Richard when the curtains were drawn around the bed. 'Were you surprised when Cuthbert told you?'

'Yes, I was a little surprised,' he admitted. He had removed his chamber robe and was comfortable under the covers, lying back propped up on his pillows. 'I had always considered Cuthbert to be one of those knights bachelor who are dedicated to keeping their skills and weapons honed to perfection; the ideal champion for a great lady such as yourself.'

'Oh I think he is still that,' I responded. 'Cuthbert will always be a perfectionist when it comes to being a knight but he is to be a father now. Did he tell you that?'

'No, he did not.' He looked surprised. 'That was quick work. Dame Fortune has smiled on them, considering their ages. When will the babe be born?'

'In spring – April, by Hilda's reckoning. She says Cuthbert was amazed when he told her.'

'Amazed or horrified?' Richard grinned a little impishly. 'She was married for a long time previously without any sign of children. Perhaps he had counted on having all the fun and none of the responsibility.'

I was seated on the bed but not yet in it, still wearing the bed gown my women had wrapped me in. I chastised him with a light-hearted nudge. 'Do not mock, Richard! Cuthbert is delighted at the prospect of becoming a family man but we should provide them with a more secure future, do you not agree?'

Richard pursed his lips doubtfully. 'We already pay them well and provide comfortable accommodation. What more do you suggest?'

I took a deep breath. I was determined on my course of action but I did not want to provoke an argument. 'It was something Hilda said when she told me she was with child. I realized that she lost a great deal when her brother disowned her. Her family had long been Neville tenants. They were landed, not just retained knights and I would like to restore her to her proper status. My dowry was paid in coin not manors so I cannot make the grant myself but I wondered if, for my sake, you would consent to settle some York land on my faithful knight champion and his wife?'

When Richard's brow creased in a frown I thought he was going to refuse my request point blank but it seemed he was giving it serious consideration. 'It is not a bad idea but I cannot immediately think which of my manors might be suitable. Cuthbert would no doubt prefer to have a foothold in Yorkshire but your brother of Salisbury has seigneurial rights over the lion's share of that, however hard the Percys try to take it from him. I will think on it.'

I stared at him, nonplussed. I had been diffident about raising the topic because I thought Richard's mind would be focused on what might be going on in London but suddenly I realized that Richard had always taken his responsibilities of patronage and reward seriously and he had not changed. I felt a sudden rush of love and relief.

'Thank you, my dear lord. I should tell you that before your return from Ireland, Cuthbert and Hilda both swore their oath of allegiance to York. Until then they had considered themselves bound to Neville so it was not a decision taken lightly. Their loyalty really does deserve reward.'

Richard's expression changed from one of pensive consideration to something more intense. Impatiently he reached out and pulled my gown off my shoulders. 'Enough of thinking about the future of others – let us consider the here and now of ourselves.' He stroked the line of my jaw with his finger and drew it down my throat to the swell of my breast. 'I desire evidence of the love and fidelity of my wife.'

I arched my body towards him in response and threw off the robe. 'And you have it, my liege, ever and always.'

But as I surrendered willingly to his familiar caresses and possession, I could not help crossing my fingers. Perhaps I could give him love and fidelity but, a little wickedly, I prayed that I would not once again give evidence of fertility.

PART FIVE

Lincolnshire & Yorkshire
Summer 1453

26

Tattershall Castle

Cicely

'You honour my house with your noble presence, your grace.' Lord Cromwell's words flowed smooth and honeyed on a bed of gravel. He was magnificently gowned in belted black fur-trimmed damask copiously figured with his personal emblem, which was a gold, tasselled purse, signifying a lifelong intimacy with high finance.

I edged a sincerity I did not feel into my response. 'Such a house is worthy of an emperor, my lord, and I am honoured to enter it.' Marie! I thought, I do not like this sharp-faced, egregious baron. Nor do I like this ugly red and white castle of his.

Ralph Cromwell had grown rich in the service of the crown, having served as Lord Treasurer during King Henry's minority and being at present Lord Chamberlain of the royal household. As a result he had built several new and glorious residences on his estates but I had been told that he considered Tattershall Castle to be the jewel among them. It was constructed of red brick, a new and favoured building material in the low-lying landscape of Lincolnshire where stone was hard to come by, and so the small amount of white stone he had imported was restricted to the merlons and machiolations, which on this massive square tower looked more like sugar decorations than defensive necessities. There was no denying its menacing domin-ance over the surrounding countryside, however. On our approach to it I had not been able to suppress the thought that it resembled a huge erect phallus, disproportionate and threatening.

Richard firmly believed Cromwell had amassed his fortune at the expense of the crown but that the embezzlement had been too subtle to be prosecuted, all of which proved to me that this lubricious old man was uncommonly clever, for in my experience prising money out of the royal coffers was like squeezing blood out of a stone. Nevertheless, as one who was still owed a vast debt by the exchequer, my husband had felt an antipathy strong enough to excuse himself from attending the wedding of Cromwell's niece Maud to my nephew Tom Neville, even though Tom had been one of Richard's personal squires for several years. But I had accepted the invitation, in support of my brother Hal's family, of course, and because Maud, during her marriage to Richard's staunch ally, the elderly Baron Willoughby, had been my dear friend. I had admired the spirited and gracious way she had handled Tom's youthful passion for her without cruelty to him or compromise to her union with the now-deceased Lord Willoughby and liked to think that this marriage was a reward for them both.

Standing beside Lord Cromwell on the sweeping steps of the castle fore-building was his wife, a tall, solid woman wearing a purple and gold headdress wired in a way which gave her a rather ox-like appearance. Lady Margaret was a distant cousin of mine on my father's side and beneath this alarming headpiece there flashed a pair of shrewd grey Neville eyes. Her smile did not reach them when she added a conventional greeting to that of her husband.

There was nothing cool about the welcome of the beautiful woman beside her, however. 'I am so very happy that you have come,' said Maud Willoughby, taking my hands and offering her peach-skinned cheek for a kiss.

'I could not have failed to respond to such a warm invitation,' I told her. 'It is a union I hope will bring joy to you both and friendship between our families.'

I was sincere in my wish for I knew that while affection might be involved to some extent, this was nevertheless a match of political expedience, arranged by Hal and Lord Cromwell in order to seal an alliance of their considerable forces at a time of great insecurity in the kingdom.

'I see you have brought the Duchess of Exeter with you, your grace,' said Lady Cromwell, fixing her gaze over my shoulder. My fourteen-year-old daughter's name had not been included in the invitation but she remembered Maud's visits to Fotheringhay and Tom's kindness to Edmund and she had begged to attend their wedding. I think it was a sense of guilt at my own lamentable lack of maternal affection for Anne that had prompted me to agree to bring her.

'Yes, Lady Cromwell. My daughter was eager to attend and I was sure there could be no objection. Weddings amuse the young, do they not?'

The baron sniffed loudly through the pinched nostrils of his long, pointed nose. 'That may be so, your grace, but as you have been travelling you cannot have heard that the Duke of Exeter unlawfully seized my manor and castle of Ampthill a little over a week ago. If this wedding had not been scheduled I should even now be journeying to court to petition the king for restitution. You will understand I am sure that being obliged to welcome his duchess under my roof is – how shall I put it – undesirable.'

I tried not to let it show but I was furious to find myself in such an awkward situation. I turned to look at Anne whose face, already inflamed, suffused even further, causing ugly blotches to appear on her neck and throat. She stared helplessly at me in mute appeal, too mortified to speak.

'As yet my daughter is Duchess of Exeter in name only, my lord,' I said. 'I appreciate your understandable objection but since Lady Anne still lives under her father's protection I hope you will find it possible to welcome her for his sake. I am sure the Duke of York will do all he can to help you get your manor and castle restored to you.'

Lord Cromwell pursed his lips and then nodded briefly. 'She is welcome as your daughter then, your grace. Though not, I feel bound to stipulate, as Exeter's wife.'

Maud stepped forward, anxious to dispel the atmosphere of contention. 'May I be allowed to show her grace to her apartments, uncle?' she asked with one of her winning smiles. 'We can catch up on family news as we do so.'

The West Tower of Tattershall, where we were to be lodged, was the only surviving part of the old limestone fortress which had once stood on the site, built with footings in the waters of a wide inner moat and linked to the new red-brick keep by a wooden bridge. Maud and I led the way, followed by Anne and her cousin Alys, my brother Will's youngest daughter, who had come to the York household two years ago to be prepared for her marriage to Sir John Conyers, Hal's new constable at Middleham Castle. Alys, a little older than Anne, had proved a great boon for the two had become good friends, which had improved Anne's outlook on life enormously. They hung back behind us, whispering earnestly together, no doubt discussing the embarrassing scene they had just witnessed.

'Here we are,' said Maud, opening a carved oak door which led into a hexagonal chamber hung with fine pastoral tapestries. A lancet window with cushioned seats in its embrasure was fitted with a leaded casement which stood open to the warm August air, giving a framed glimpse of the inner court and the distant variegated green of the Lincolnshire Wolds. 'There are two other chambers through there and an attic for your servants. I hope you will be comfortable.' She pointed to a connecting door and the two girls immediately passed through it to investigate.

'I was sorry to hear about the death of your brother, Maud,' I said, fingering the tapestries and noting their weighty quality. 'Were you very close?'

Maud laughed. 'No. We hardly spoke. He was a slothful lay-about who boasted to anyone who would listen that he was my uncle's heir and would be as rich as Croesus one day. I consider it nothing but justice that death has intervened. Lord Cromwell is not best pleased to have no male heir but he has acknowledged me and my sister now and my portion more than satisfies your brother, Lord Salisbury's expectations for Tom. Is that not fortuitous?'

'I confess I was surprised that your uncle sought an alliance with Salisbury,' I said. 'Is he very frightened of Exeter?'

'Terrified,' Maud confirmed. 'He believes Harry might murder him in his bed. That is why he lives so tightly immured in Tattershall's moated keep. What is the matter with young Harry Holland? He rampages around England like a madman.'

'Yes, it seems there is no stopping him since he came into his estates,' I agreed. 'His retinue grows by the year – he must have at least a thousand wearing the Wheatear badge by now. Most of them are hardened campaigners, newly returned from France and of course they need paying, so I imagine that is why he seized Ampthill – for its revenue.'

Maud threw up her hands in exasperation. 'He simply overran the place without warning, claiming it to be part of his inheritance, although my uncle has full royal tenure and legal proof that he purchased it years ago from Harry's father. The king should exert his authority.'

I stepped forward and closed the chamber door against being overheard. 'King Henry tends to leave authority to the queen I believe. On the rare occasion that he exerts any, it is only to advance the House of Lancaster. Even the Suffolk cause, once so close to his heart, has now felt the loss of his favour. I received a letter from the Dowager Countess a few months ago bewailing the fact that the king had acquired a papal annulment of her son's marriage to the Somerset heiress and given her instead to his half-brother Edmund Tudor, the new Earl of Richmond. The Tudor boys are the new royal favourites and of course any son of Margaret Beaufort would carry the Lancaster line. However, that all happened before King Henry knew that Queen Margaret herself was pregnant.'

'Yes, that was a surprise to everyone. They must be wearing their knees out praying for a boy. But tell me, what news of his grace of York? I am sorry he is not here with you.'

I thought it politic not to mention Richard's antipathy towards the origins of Lord Cromwell's wealth and so I took a different track. 'Well, Richard is away lending support to my nephew, the Earl of Warwick, potentially another young firebrand like Harry Holland, who is in dispute with Somerset over the lordship of

Glamorgan in Wales. And you will know all about the feuds in Yorkshire between Tom's family and the Westmorland Nevilles. Armed conflict erupts everywhere. I am surprised Lord Salisbury is coming to his son's wedding at all. Is he here yet?'

Maud went to the window and looked down into the inner bailey. 'There is no sign of his arrival, although fore-runners came in this morning saying he was on the road.' She turned back towards the door. 'I will go and check that your servants are bringing your baggage. When Lord Salisbury arrives we will dine *en famille* in the keep hall. Lord Cromwell fears crowds which is why our wedding will be small. I will send word. Until then I bid you good day, your grace.'

Cheerfully she proffered me a low curtsy and a wide smile and disappeared through the stair door, closing it behind her. The room fell quiet except for the low murmur of the girls' voices from the next chamber. I crossed to the window and sank gratefully onto the cushioned seat, my muscles aching from three days' riding and I was not yet fully recovered from a difficult confinement ten months before. All my hopes for an end to child-bearing had been in vain and I had laboured long and hard to bring our latest boy into the world. My prayers now were all for the new baby who was small and curiously formed, not crippled but slightly shortened in the trunk and weakened by it in some way. He had not yet sat up without support but his eyes were bright and his smiles were wide and charming in dimpled cheeks. In looks he was the most like his father of all our living sons, which was providential because we had called him Richard, with a nursery name of Dickon. I prayed that he would be blessed with his father's drive and determination because God had not granted him an easy start.

Persistent post-natal discomfort and a dread of further

childbearing had caused me to withdraw from my husband both emotionally and physically. For the last eighteen months he had based himself at Ludlow with Edward and Edmund while I remained with the rest of our children at Fotheringhay. Sometimes I reflected that our differences were symptomatic of the disintegration of the kingdom. The breakdown of Richard's relationship with the king had tested his allegiance almost beyond endurance, just as childbirth had tested mine.

Lulled by the warm sunshine streaming in through the window, I closed my eyes. I did not sleep but my mind drifted, recalling our last conversation six months previously, before Richard had set off on another quest for justice from the king. I had only recently been churched after the birth of Dickon and I was still damaged and weak. I had barely been able to walk up the long nave at Fotheringhay for the churching, yet when Richard came to acknowledge his son and bid me farewell he offered no words of comfort or encouragement but instead launched into a long rant against the Duke of Somerset and his blatant acquisition of all the most lucrative royal appointments.

'He has made himself Captain of Calais, Chamberlain of the Royal Household and Steward of the Duchy of Lancaster. Why does he not simply make himself Archbishop of Canterbury, Treasurer and Lord Chancellor as well and occupy every seat at the council table? He, who abandoned Rouen and slipped out of Normandy with his wife and children, leaving poor Shrewsbury to handle the ignominy of surrender to the French! He should be impeached for that treachery alone.'

Feeble of body and mind though I was, I could not help but remonstrate with him. 'You say you will march your army of retainers to London only in order to obtain justice and force the king to dismiss Somerset but the world will see it as an attempt to usurp the throne, Richard. You risk being accused of treason. You could end up like your father, a convicted traitor with your head on a spike and your sons attainted and penniless. I beg you not to do this!'

Perhaps I should not have made mention of his father's fate but I was desperate. Richard had been only three years old when his father, Richard, Earl of Cambridge, had been beheaded for conspiring against the Lancastrian throne, and the present York claim to the succession was based on the very same principles used in that conspiracy. He knew he was on dangerous ground but he proved oblivious to my plea for caution.

'It is in order to assure our sons' future that I do as I do,' he said, his anger visibly growing. 'Somerset is steering the realm into disintegration and the king must be made to see that, otherwise there will be no future for York or any other family which does not kiss Beaufort's hand. It is not I who conspire against the throne but Somerset who seeks to enforce his own illegal claim to the succession. He must be curbed or the kingdom is doomed and York with it.'

I sighed wearily. 'Everything you say is true, Richard. But violent confrontation is not the way to handle it. I beg you to heed my brother Hal if you will not listen to me. He has written to say that you will get no help from him, or from any other peer of the realm, if you persist in following this course. You will stand alone and isolated, while Somerset will have the support of the king and queen and half the nobility. It is madness to place yourself in that position.'

Richard's face was now contused but he kept control. 'On the contrary, it is the only honourable course to follow. I do not deny the danger but I believe that I have the support of the people. They will back my stand and the Commons will make the king see that with no heir of his own body, justice demands that I be acknowledged as heir presumptive. He has only to dismiss Somerset and reinstate me in my rightful position beside the throne. The king is a peace-loving man and I am his cousin. There will be no clash of arms, of that I am sure. He will recognize the justice of my demands without recourse to violence but I must show strength, Cicely, in order to convince him I mean business.'

I had known it was hopeless to argue. It only made things worse between us. Richard had swallowed as much pride as he could stomach. His dignity had been systematically undermined and he could no longer bear to stand idly by and suffer it and to a certain extent I understood. I was his wife and must perforce support him but I was also mother to a promising son and heir in Edward, whom I could not bear to see consigned to the scrap-heap of history because of his father's mistakes.

'Go then,' I said with resignation. 'But always consider this – you have four sons who do not deserve to be tainted as you were with the stain of treachery. You have been blessed by God in the way the wheel of fortune has turned for you but the same may not be true for your sons, or indeed your daughters. If their future is blighted by your actions do not imagine that you will ever have my forgiveness, in life or in death.'

I was jerked out of my reverie by a scratching at the door. I returned to the present feeling a rush of gratitude to God and his Saints that although Richard's action in marching on London had not achieved the outcome he wished, neither had the king agreed to Somerset's demands for his arrest and impeachment.

'Enter,' I called and Hilda's familiar face appeared around the door. 'The baggage is here, your grace,' she said, making a bobbed curtsey and opening the door wide to permit a succession of chests to be carried in. 'Now we can prepare you for the first of Lord Cromwell's feasts. Some of your most glittering finery, I think. Oh, and the Earl of Salisbury has arrived.' Sensing my melancholy she asked softly so that the servants should not hear, 'Are you well, Cicely?'

I nodded as briskly as I could to dispel the mood. 'Yes, thank you, Hilda. I am quite well.'

The wedding took place not in the Tattershall Collegiate Church of the Holy Trinity, Lord Cromwell's costly investment in the passage of his soul heavenward, but in the modest stained-glass jewel of a chapel situated in the castle's Inner Ward, and the guest-list was small. My brother Hal had ridden in with an escort two hundred strong and the stables and Outer Wards were crammed with men and horses.

'I would have brought more men, Cis,' he confided during a quiet moment at the marriage feast, 'but I had to send reinforcements to strengthen the garrison at Sheriff Hutton. Believe it or not, Egremont and Westmorland have made a new alliance and have sent out sergeants to muster recruits in York.'

The mention of Lord Westmorland triggered sudden bitter-sweet memories of my abductor John and our stolen night of love at Aycliffe Tower. As the rift between Richard and me grew wider those memories seemed more frequent and to have become more sweet than bitter.

I forced my attention back to Hal, who was looking at me quizzically. 'That is alarming news,' I said hurriedly, banishing nostalgia. Lord Egremont was the Earl of Northumberland's heir and there had been bad blood between our branch of the Neville family and the Percys since the turn of the century.

'Westmorland steps further outside the law every year,' said Hal. 'Both he and Northumberland bear dangerous grudges.'

'Like young Harry of Exeter. I suppose you know he has occupied Lord Cromwell's manor of Ampthill.'

'Yes and this latest feud concerns Cromwell, too. It is over Wressle Castle in Yorkshire, which was granted to Lord Cromwell after the Percys were attainted years ago. It will form part of Maud's inheritance and it sticks in Egremont's craw that a member of our family will become lord of what he still regards as a Percy honour.'

I eyed my brother speculatively, ticking off on my fingers the names of all the substantial lands and castles which he and his sons had acquired through marriage and inheritance. 'Middleham, Sheriff Hutton, Salisbury, Bisham, Warwick, now Wressle – your family has certainly drawn fortune's long straws, Hal. If you and your son Dick were to join forces with Richard, the king might truly feel threatened.'

Hal did not often laugh but now he did, although quietly and with a swift glance around for eavesdroppers. 'Anyone would think your husband had recruited you into his spy network, Cis,' he muttered, speaking behind his hand. 'However, Richard and I are brothers-in-law, not in brothers-in-war. We have no secret alliance.'

'I am not one of Richard's agents,' I assured him, 'but I do pray that, should it ever come to war, you and he would not be fighting on opposite sides.'

The smile disappeared from Hal's face. 'A few skirmishes over a castle or two may be one thing but God forbid that these petty feuds should escalate to full-scale war,' he said, making the sign of the cross. 'It does not bear thinking on.'

'Perhaps if the queen has a son and the succession is settled, the crown will have more authority and things will calm down,' I suggested, although not with any great conviction.

Hal snorted. 'Ha! There is already so much speculation about the royal child's paternity that I, for one, rather hope it is a girl.'

It was my turn to show astonishment. 'I never thought to hear a man say those words!'

'Well if it is Somerset's brat at least there is no question of a female succeeding to the throne,' he retorted, 'and no heir is better than one with a doubtful bloodline. Anyway, Cis, be honest, do you not harbour a sneaking desire to be queen?'

I dodged the question. 'I certainly think Richard has a better claim to the throne than any Beaufort and at least he has plenty of sons to allay your fear of a female succession, Hal.'

My brother raised his cup to me. 'Yes, there is no denying you have done your duty there, Cis.'

At this point our conversation was interrupted by Lady Cromwell who sat on Hal's other side at the high-table. She had been occupied with the bride and groom while we held our muttered conversation but now she turned and leaned over, gesturing at Anne, who had been duly demoted from the rank of duchess to sit among the young ladies at a lower trestle and was silently chewing her way through some morsel, her jaw moving ponderously in her plump cheeks. 'Does your daughter's marriage not trouble you, your grace?' the lady enquired. 'She must be nearing the age of maturity and the Duke of Exeter is such an unstable character. Or do you think she will be able to effect some miraculous change in her husband?'

I resented the sarcasm in her voice but chose to answer in a measured tone. 'I am sure you agree, Lady Cromwell, that no young girl adjusts easily to married life. Look at the queen for example; only fourteen when she arrived from France as a bride and denounced as barren for the first seven years of her marriage. It must be a great joy to her that she has now confounded the critics and, God willing, will give birth to the heir we all crave.'

Lady Cromwell gave an incredulous laugh. 'I am surprised to hear that you would welcome a royal heir, duchess. Was it not York's desire to be acknowledged as the king's successor that earned him such opprobrium last year?'

'The duke seeks only the stability of the kingdom, my lady,' I replied stiffly. 'The birth of a prince would ensure that.'

'Well, perhaps the birth of an heir might stabilize Exeter. That is about all your daughter can hope for I think.'

27

Cicely

I stayed at Tattershall only as long as good manners dictated and my excuse for leaving the day after the wedding was that I needed to travel ahead to make preparations for Tom and Maud's honeymoon stay at the York stronghold of Conisburgh on their way to Sheriff Hutton. The going was good on the summer-dry road but the passage of many hooves stirred up clouds of choking dust so I made a point of riding at the front of the procession. Cuthbert patrolled the column of armed men, carts and servants, keeping an eye out for any trouble.

I made a point of riding beside Anne, contriving to edge Alys back to Hilda's side so that I could speak privately with my daughter.

'Did you enjoy the wedding, Anne?' I asked, biting back the urge to tell her not to slouch in the saddle.

I had expected a noncommittal response but she smiled shyly at me, straightening her back as if she read my mind. 'Yes, I did, my lady mother. It was the first time I had seen a couple look happy to be getting married.'

'I think there have been feelings between Tom and Maud for

some time now, so they are lucky to be able to carry them into their union. That does not happen often but when it does it is pleasant.'

'Well it will not happen for me,' Anne declared. 'Harry will never look at me the way Tom looks at Maud.'

'What makes you say that?'

'Because Maud is beautiful and I am not.'

'God does not always favour the beautiful,' I protested, wishing I could contradict her.

Her retort was undeniable. 'But men do, do they not?' Her face assumed an expression of anguish. 'What will happen to me, lady mother, when I have to go to Harry?'

I gazed across at her; she had celebrated her fourteenth birthday a week before we left Fotheringhay for Tattershall. Legally she was old enough to be bedded but it was my intention to delay the process until she had at least grown out of her disfiguring pimples, about which I knew Harry would taunt her cruelly, despite being no portrait himself.

'You will perform your role as you have been taught,' I said gently, 'and pray for patience. Perhaps it will not be as bad as you fear. That is often the way.'

I felt guilty that I could find nothing more comforting to say and a flash of Anne's moist blue eyes confirmed the inadequacy of my reply. 'Or perhaps he will completely ignore me. That is what I pray for.'

'You will be lonely if he does,' I said helplessly.

'I would rather be lonely than humiliated. That is what I fear most. Being held up to ridicule as the wife he was forced to marry.'

I stretched over and stroked a tear from her cheek. 'Do not torture yourself, Anne. All noble marriages are forced in that sense. None of us freely chooses our partner. There is no shame in being married for reasons of finance or politic; even Harry knows that.'

'Do you really believe Harry thinks as others do?' she asked. 'I think that if we are to live together with any kind of success I must realize that he is not as other men are.'

In that moment I felt a sudden respect for my daughter. Perhaps I should not have been regarding her as a timorous mouse waiting to become a victim but as a spirited girl who had analysed her future and decided how to approach it. Was it possible that Anne might become a figure of some distinction, with a shrewd head on her shoulders?

I smiled at her approvingly. 'I have great faith that you will be a match for young Harry, Anne,' I told her. 'God does not favour the beautiful, as I said. He favours those who use what they have been given and you have been given good sense. If you believe in yourself He will show you how to use it.'

Anne lifted her chin and turned eyes on me that were shining not with tears but with bashful joy. 'Oh, my lady mother – God is good I know, but if *you* have faith in me I can do anything!'

'Then you can, sweetheart, you can!' I felt as if a lead weight had lifted from me. Never since Anne had been an infant had I involuntarily addressed her with an endearment and yet that 'sweetheart' had leaped off my tongue without bidding. The effect was almost miraculous. Anne began to laugh, a bright, delighted sound which I had only previously heard when she was in the company of girls her own age. It transformed her plump, round face from dullness to radiance, her wariness vanished and she became shyly confiding.

'I know that I will have to go to Harry soon,' she said, blushing. 'And I know what is expected of me as a wife but to tell the truth I do not yet feel ready to become a duchess.' She gazed at me with wide eyes. 'You are so . . . so . . . dignified, my lady. Nothing ever seems to upset or disturb you. You are always calm and serene and I do not think I could ever be like that. Is it something I could learn? Could you teach me?'

I thought back to the emotional scene between Richard and me before he had embarked on his fruitless campaign against Somerset; I remembered the miserable depression I had suffered before the birth of Edward; there came to me the dreadful, secret guilt I had felt on my return from Aycliffe Tower: the impression Anne had acquired of me was a false one. Yet it was true that the image I tried to present to the world was that of a restrained, gracious noblewoman, in command, in control and never rattled.

Impulsively I edged my horse nearer to hers and lowered my voice to murmur discretely in her ear. 'Shall I tell you a secret, little daughter? I am not really like that at all. I am really a wild, reckless, giddy girl who would like to tear off her coif and gallop across the stubble with the wind in her hair. I put on a show to convince people that I am responsible and careful, able to run a household, rear my children and behave like a duchess, and if I can learn to do that, so can you. Actually you already have a head start because you are more level-headed at fourteen than I was at twenty.'

Anne's mouth dropped open, hearing this revelation from her normally reticent mother. Then she cocked her head on one side like a curious robin and smiled. 'So did you laugh and gossip when you were a girl, just like I do with Alys? It seems so strange to think that you were young once too.'

'Marie! Am I so old now?' I cried with mock dismay. 'I am thirty-eight. I suppose to you that seems like Methuselah's mother?'

Anne was immediately contrite. 'No, you will never be old – not even when you are a hundred. There is no grey in your hair and you are not fat and flabby like Lady Cromwell. I wish I was as trim as you.'

I nodded, knowing Anne did worry about her plumpness. 'You are like your father. He visits the tiltyard every day to keep his body hard and muscular. It is not a natural thing for him.'

Anne giggled. 'I can hardly start exercising with the squires, can I? I have never seen a duchess do that!'

'No. I am afraid fasting and self-control are the only answer for a lady, Anne. I am sure you will learn that, just as you will learn the other disciplines you think are beyond you. It is not so hard.' As I spoke my attention was suddenly caught by a flash of reflected sunlight and I looked up to see a large cloud of dust on the horizon to our left. 'St Christopher! What is this?'

A dust-cloud of such dimensions could only be formed by a cavalcade of similar size to our own approaching at a considerable pace. The flat, treeless fens made ambush impossible for there was no cover but nonetheless there was something threatening about the swift advance of this second column of horses. The thunder of their hooves intruded on the oppressive heat like the rumbling of a rock-fall in a quiet valley.

Cuthbert cantered up beside me. 'I do not like the look of this,' he warned.

'Who are they? Can you identify them?' I asked.

'Not yet. I have sent out scouts.' Two horsemen could be seen galloping away across the stubble of a recently harvested bean-field.

'Where are we?' I glanced around. The landscape was deserted, a wide expanse of field and furrow on either side of the road. Only the occasional windmill relieved the flat line of the horizon, sails idle in the still air.

'On Willoughby land,' replied Cuthbert. 'They call this county Kyme, I believe.'

I frowned at him. 'Are the men ready for trouble, Cuddy?'

He grinned reassuringly at Anne who was looking scared. 'Have no fear. This is why we travel with such a large force. We are ready.'

Pikemen had already formed protective flanks to either side of us and our archers had unslung their bows and drawn arrows from their quivers. White rose pennants hung limply from the lances of their captains and tense faces were turned to the south-west. The scouts galloped back and drew rein.

'They fly the wheatear, my lady – the badge of Exeter – but I could not make out whether the duke is with them.'

Anne gave a small cry, swiftly stifled behind her hand. Cuthbert and I exchanged glances but no one spoke. As the cloud of dust grew closer we could see many fluttering pennants of Lancastrian blue and white but on the main standard carried behind the leading horseman was the wheatear, gold on green. The column did not skirt the field of rippling barley in its path but galloped straight across it, trampling the ripe crop. It was an act of wanton destruction which instantly confirmed to me the identity of the leader, his helmet crested with a fox's tail. This was the man who had once been Richard's ward and now liked to be called The Fox – Harry Holland, Duke of Exeter.

The cavalcade halted. 'Greetings, mother-in-law!' he shouted above the noise of stamping hooves and jingling harness. He was wearing half-armour; a padded gambeson, a burnished breastplate and greaves strapped to his mailed thighs. His booted feet were furnished with huge gilded spurs. A short blue and white mantle hung from his shoulders and his great warhorse was caparisoned in the same heraldic colours, blue and white plumes nodding from the steel chamfron which covered its face. The red rose featured on the badge of each of his retainers.

Cuthbert rode up beside us, signalling to several squires to follow him. 'God give you good day, your grace,' he called, bowing punctiliously and preserving a careful distance between him and the young duke. 'Is there urgent news that you ride so fast and trample the crops?'

'Crops?' Harry glanced vaguely around him. 'No news but my quest is urgent. I come to collect my wife.'

'Your wife?' echoed Cuthbert, astounded. 'Here? Now? In the middle of a field?'

'Why not? I heard she was at Tattershall and have ridden from Ampthill to carry her home.'

I heard Anne's gasp of alarm behind me and I turned to speak to her. 'Come forward, Anne, and greet your husband.'

Reluctantly she urged her palfrey a few steps forward and whispered words of greeting which Harry ignored.

'This is a strange meeting place, my lord duke,' I said. 'We lodge in Lincoln tonight. I wonder you did not meet us there.'

Harry gestured impatiently. 'Too far. I cannot be away from Ampthill for so long.' For the first time his attention swivelled briefly to Anne and he grimaced. 'She does not get any better looking, does she? Pity she does not favour you, duchess. Only in looks of course; I would not want a wife with a brain.'

I saw the blood rush to Anne's cheeks and tears brim in her eyes. 'Do not weep,' I hissed fiercely. 'That is what he wants!' More loudly I called, 'I am surprised you confess to preferring brainless company, my lord of Exeter. You know the maxim – birds of a feather flock together.'

Harry's voice in reply was sharp with suppressed anger. 'I do not call a wife company, Mother-in-law. Any more than I would call a brood mare company.' He kicked his horse forward until it was alongside Anne's. 'She comes of good breeding stock and her dower is good so I will take her.'

He would have laid his hand on Anne's rein but Cuthbert forestalled him, clamping his gauntleted fist around the young man's wrist. 'Her grace has not granted permission,' he growled. His horse jostled Harry's, which was mettlesome and nervous and rose in a half-rear, nearly unseating its rider.

With his free hand Harry jagged down on the bit, swearing at his mount and then at Cuthbert. 'Saint Michael's bones! Remove your hand, bastard!' he yelled. 'I do not need to ask permission for my wife to accompany me. She is mine and I will have her.' He wrenched his arm from Cuthbert's grip and waved it in a signal to his men who began to fan out, confronting the two flanks of the York force. Harry yanked on the reins to back his stallion off and it flicked its tail and tossed its head, trying to escape the cruel bite of the bit. 'I will retire a few yards to give you time to consider.' He sneered at Anne. 'Say your farewells, madam, for make no mistake, you are coming with me.'

Cuthbert and I closed our horses protectively around Anne's but I knew there was really little point. Harry's methods may be violent and his manners uncouth but he was indisputably in the right. He had married Anne, she was of legal age and by law she was his property. Short of a miracle endowing her graceless husband with sudden compassion, she would have to go with him.

'I do not want to go, Mother,' she whispered in panic. 'I am not ready. I will die of misery.' Her eyes were wide with fear.

I gazed at her sorrowfully and shook my head. 'I am sorry, Anne; there is no help for it. It is scandalous but it is not a situation we can dispute without putting these men's lives at risk.' I gestured towards the alert archers and pikemen in their murrey and blue livery with the white rose badges. They were all sweating profusely in the turgid heat but their weapons were at the ready, their muscles taut.

'We can fight them off,' Cuthbert said, surveying the opposition. 'Exeter's men may wear the red rose but they are mercenaries. They will not fight if it comes to a real battle. Our men are loyal retainers. We can trust them to make a strong stand.'

'Please, Mother, you must protect me,' Anne begged in a terrified moan. 'I cannot go with him.'

I yearned to do as she asked but I would not risk the lives of men when I knew the law to be on Harry's side. 'Behave sensibly, Anne, as I know you can,' I urged her. 'You are Harry's wife. You cannot allow these men to risk injury or worse protecting you from the very man to whom you legally belong. The circumstances may not be ideal and you may not be ready but it is your duty to obey your husband. He orders you to come. You have no choice.'

'If my lord father were here he would prevent it,' declared Anne in desperation. 'He would not be dictated to by Harry of Exeter!'

I could have said that it was her father's fault she was in this position in the first place but I did not. 'Perhaps if your lord father were here Harry would not have dared to make his move,' I said with all the patience I could muster. 'But he is not and you must be brave.'

I instinctively felt that only my strong will was keeping Anne from breaking down. Any sympathy on my part would tip her into an exhibition of wailing weakness which I knew Harry would make her live to regret. Much though I hated this marriage, there was no denying it now. Whatever the future held for Anne it was inextricably bound up with that of her turbulent husband. Sooner or later she would have to accept that.

I handed her the kerchief from my sleeve and as I did so an idea occurred to me. 'You will have to go, Anne, but perhaps you will not have to go alone.' As she dabbed at her eyes and blew her nose I beckoned to Alys, who sat her palfrey quietly nearby. 'It is not an easy task I am about to ask of you, Alys,' I said, 'but I feel certain you are equal to it. If you go with Anne it will be easier for her. I will inform your father of your whereabouts and when Anne is more settled we will arrange for you to travel back to Fotheringhay. After all it is not so far from Ampthill.'

The light of adventure kindled in Alys's eyes. She was a tall, spirited girl of sixteen with a sweet oval face and a strong sense of fun; yet she was not easily brow-beaten and would make a formidable ally for Anne. I knew Harry would not dare to mistreat Alys because if he did he would have to answer to her father, my redoubtable brother Will, who in these days of factions and affinities somehow managed to stay friendly both with Richard and the king. Widely liked and held in high esteem by friend and foe, Lord Fauconberg was not a man to cross and Harry of Exeter would know this.

'Of course I will go with you, Anne,' she said, kneeing her mount close to her friend's. 'If we are together we can pretend it is a game. Come – it will not be so bad.'

'It may seem like a game to you,' said Anne bitterly, 'but you have only to go to his board, not to his bed. Oh but I do thank you, Alys. If I must go, your company might just make it bearable.'

I saw Anne's expression change as she turned to me and it was immediately clear that any warmth that might have

314

blossomed between us in the last half hour had now completely vanished. Her old wariness had deepened into open hostility and she almost spat her next words at me. 'For a minute back there I stupidly thought that you cared for me, lady mother, but I see now that I was wrong. Like all the rest of your children I know only too well that you care only for Edward. Edmund, Elizabeth, Meg, George and now little Dickon too, I suppose – we all ask in vain for your affection but you think only of Edward. And the worst of it is that Edward does not care.'

Hearing this, my face must have twitched with pain for she drove her point mercilessly home. 'You did not know that, did you? It is true though. He does not seek love because he knows he can charm whoever he wishes. The only person he will ever love is the one who denies him and that will never be you, for you can deny him nothing.'

Having spat her poison, Anne fell silent; only occasional gasps and hiccoughs escaped her as she fought for self-control. Sadly I leaned forward, took back the kerchief and wiped the traces of tears from her cheeks. Then I gently kissed where I had wiped. 'There, keep hold of that anger, Anne, and let those be the last tears you shed, or you might find that Harry can be even more unkind to you than you have just been to me. I am sorry we do not part friends but at least for a time you will have Alys.' I turned to the other girl and forced a smile. 'I am very grateful to you, Niece, for agreeing to stand by Anne. I know you will be a great comfort to her. And now I think the time has come.'

I turned my horse and rode towards the Exeter lines; behind me I felt rather than saw Cuthbert trotting at my horse's tail. Harry had removed his helmet and was refreshing himself with wine from a jewelled cup poured for him by a hovering squire.

Having drained the cup he tossed it away, forcing the squire to grovel dangerously among the horses' hooves to retrieve it.

'I trust you recognize my right, Duchess,' Harry called. His wiry red hair was sweat-soaked and clung to his head, giving him an imp-like appearance.

'The lady Anne is preparing to accompany you, my lord,' I responded coolly. 'But it is not fitting that a lady of rank should travel unsupported by someone of her own sex, so my niece Lady Alys Fauconberg will bear her company until other arrangements can be made.'

I could see that Harry was giving careful thought to the implications of this. He glowered and chewed his lip for a while but eventually nodded. 'So be it. I hope both ladies are prepared to ride hard. We have much ground to cover today.'

'They are not mercenaries,' I reminded him icily. 'The qualities you might prize in a wife surely do not include an aptitude for marathons in the saddle.'

Harry gave a loud shout of laughter. 'Duchess, I prize nothing about my wife save her dowry and her fertility. For the sake of the latter, I will not push her until she drops.'

'Good,' I said tersely. 'You will have to negotiate with the duke over the dowry. I will have the ladies' baggage sent to Ampthill, if that is where you will be?'

He shrugged. 'I will remain at Ampthill until I am satisfied that it is secure. After that you will have to look for your daughter where you can find her. I have not yet decided which of my castles to make my main home.'

'Perhaps Anne might help you with that,' I suggested in a last-minute effort on her behalf. 'Talk to her, ask her opinion. You will find her a sweet and pliant wife if you are kind to her.'

Harry made a juvenile face and a rude noise. 'Pah! She can

do what she likes as long as she breeds me a son. Otherwise she is merely a nuisance and will be treated as such.' At this he drove his spurs into his stallion's sides, making it snort and leap forward, bearing down on the two girls, rounding them up like a pair of heifers. 'Come! We leave now. Captain, we have what we came for. Let us march!'

Anne rode past me without a word. Her round face looked like a squashed cushion and she sat her palfrey like a sack of meal, her head drooping and her hands gripping the reins as if they were her last hold on reality. 'God be with you, Anne,' I whispered, tears stinging my eyelids. I felt as if I had failed my daughter, failed my husband and, if what Anne had told me was true, failed to inspire love in my eldest son. The wheatear standard began to stream out as the Exeter cavalcade wheeled past our stationary column and back across the field, trampling the remainder of the crop.

28

Conisbrough Castle & Nostell Priory, August

Cicely

As soon as we arrived I wished I had not agreed to host my brother and his newly married son and daughter-in-law at Conisbrough. The castle represented a bitter legacy for Richard as the place where he had been born and where his mother had died shortly afterwards of childbed fever and I had disliked the musty old pile the first time I visited it shortly after our wedding. The more comfortable and splendidly sited York stronghold of Sandal Magna, only twenty miles away near Wakefield, was greatly to be preferred.

My wretched parting from Anne haunted me and my heart still ached from watching her ride away surrounded by Harry's mercenaries. I brooded over whether I could have stopped him, whether I had let her go too easily and if I should have agreed to an attack on his men as Cuthbert had suggested. I longed for some word from her or from Alys but nothing came and instead I tried to distract myself arranging feasting and enter-tainments for the imminent wedding party. I was busy discussing menus with the steward and cook who had ridden over from Sandal Magna to oversee the ill-trained and inadequate staff available at Conisbrough when a servant hurried in with a letter. It was addressed to me in handwriting I recognized immediately, despite the passage of twenty years since I had last seen it on the note which had accompanied the unexpected gift of a palfrey during my wedding at Raby. It was from Sir John Neville.

'Where is the courier who brought this?' I asked the bearer, my heart suddenly hammering at my ribs.

'Gone, your grace,' the man responded, wringing his hands at the sharp tone of my enquiry. 'I happened to be near the gatehouse and he threw the letter at me, said it was for you and galloped back under the portcullis as if he thought it might come hurtling down and prevent him leaving.'

Noting the Brancepeth horned-bull impression on the wax seal, I thought it no wonder the man had fled. With a wave of dismissal to the servant and a muttered excuse to the steward and cook, I hurried to the privacy of the solar to read the letter.

Your grace, it began without any pretence of further courtesy.

> *Since you are in the vicinity I write to request a meeting with you as soon as possible. Forces are ranged against us so it will not be easy but there is a matter I must confide to you face to face concerning your nephew Sir Thomas Neville and his new wife. Come with your brother, Sir Cuthbert, to Nostell Priory as soon and as discretely as possible. I will await you there.*

It was signed as tersely as it had begun, *John, Baron Neville.*

Receiving the letter at all was surprising but the signature intrigued me. Baron Neville was the title associated with the heir to the Westmorland earldom, which could only mean that young

Jack, whom I remembered as a sturdy, over-mothered little boy and who should by now have been all of twenty-five, must have died before his time. Why had I not heard of this?

It meant it was John and not Jack who had recently sworn an alliance with the Percy heir and was mustering a thousand-strong force with him at Spofforth Castle, only twenty miles from York. What could have disturbed John so much that he contemplated betraying that alliance by seeking a meeting with me, of all people? I read and re-read the letter but it revealed nothing of the man behind the words. What was he like now, I wondered? I remembered him vividly – could see his lean, sunburned face clearly in my mind. He must be over forty by now. Had that chiselled jaw blurred into soft jowls and broken veins and had those steely grey eyes sunk into wrinkled pouches? Could his long, lithe figure have become paunched and padded with advancing years? Did any spark remain of the passion that had ignited so wildly and irresistibly while the grebes danced and the myrtle cast it fragrant spell. There was only one way to find out. I sent a page to bring Cuthbert to my chamber.

He scanned the letter swiftly and silently then stared at me solemnly for a few moments before suddenly grinning broadly. 'When do we go?' he asked.

'You think I should, Cuddy?' I was surprised, expecting him to offer some opposition.

He laughed. 'No, I do not, but I cannot think you will refuse. It is more likely that snow will fall tomorrow, when it is August.'

'What makes you say that?' I was half offended and half amused.

'Dear Cis, as far as I know you have never revealed to anyone how you managed to escape from Aycliffe Tower but one thing I am sure of, you did not fight your way out with a sword. No, sharp wits and womanly charms are your weapons and I do not believe you will resist the temptation to find out if they still work on Sir John.'

His analysis of the long-kept secret of my escape from Aycliffe was too close to the truth for comfort so I decided to ignore it. 'Did you know he was now Baron Neville Cuddy? I wonder what happened to the heir they called Jack.'

Cuthbert shrugged. 'He had a reputation as a young hothead. He probably got himself killed in some scrap somewhere. I believe he was knighted though.'

'Yes, and married too, if rumour is right, to Harry Holland's half-sister Anne.'

'Perhaps that is what Sir John wants to talk to you about.'

'How far is it to Nostell Priory?' I asked abruptly. 'Could we get there and back in a day?'

'Easily, if we leave at dawn.'

'We will go tomorrow then, just you and me. Dress very plainly, Cuddy – no armour and no white rose livery.'

He nodded. 'And you leave off the jewels, Cis, and borrow some plain clothes from one of your maids. I will organize the horses.'

The ride to Nostell lifted my spirits. The stifling humidity which had made the journey from Tattershall so taxing had cleared, blown away by a brisk easterly wind gusting down the valley of the Don off the cool mudflats of the Humber estuary. Even the horses responded to the tug of the breeze in their manes and we made swift progress. It was many months since I ridden out so freely, without the restriction of a large escort, or a pack of hounds, a posse of hunt servants and a bevy of noble companions. Cuthbert and I set our horses' heads north east and rode across country, skirting fields where the harvest was well underway and plunging through forest where deer leaped nervously from our path. I wore boots and a moss-green kirtle and hid my distinctive auburn hair under a wimple and a good-wife's hood, all borrowed from Hilda, and Cuthbert had found a plain grey hooded tunic and hose and travelled hatless in the mild temperature. For the first time I noticed grey hairs in his thick dark thatch but made no mention of them, nor did I ask if he had a dagger concealed in one of his buskin boots, assuming he did. Well before noon we spied lay-monks wielding scythes in open fields and picking fruit in the grey-walled orchard beyond. Nostell was a remote religious community nestled in a fold of wooded hills above the River Went, its monks living according to the rule and writings of St Augustine of Canterbury. Although it was not ten miles from our castle of Sandal Magna in one direction and the royal castle of Pontefract in the other, it was a good choice for a clandestine meeting-place.

Cuthbert approached the gatehouse, calling for the porter. 'Has a pilgrim called Neville passed here, I pray you?' he asked of the grizzled lay-monk who responded.

'You will have to see the sub-prior,' the monk replied. 'I do not keep a record of visitors and, anyway, all females have to report to him.'

I kept my head bowed modestly under my hood but managed to peer through the gate arch to the paved courtyard beyond where an ox-cart was being relieved of its load of barrels, perhaps the winter supply of salted herring or the prior's store of fine wine. The place had an air of busy prosperity overlaid by the sound of bells, which began to call the monks to their noon office.

'You can wait in the prior's parlour until he is free to see you,' muttered the porter, crossing himself as the bells sounded. A file of cowled brethren crossed the court towards the church, hurrying from their work in cloister and scriptorium. We consigned our horses to another lay brother and were guided to a fine stone-built house and a panelled room within containing several cushionless benches, a table and a large crucifix hanging over an elaborate stone fireplace, carved with figures of saints. After a few minutes the door opened to admit a tall, thin man in a short rust-coloured gown and a dark-hued chaperon hat. For the first time in thirteen years I found myself face to face with John Neville and it was like being struck by lightning.

I had to bite my lip to prevent myself crying out. One glimpse of that sensitive face with its piercing grey eyes released a whirling surge of emotions and every ounce of guilt and remorse I had felt since creeping away from the myrtle bed seemed to resurface. I heard myself whisper 'Holy Mary!' and put a hand to the wall for support.

A sudden pallor beneath John's weathered complexion revealed the jolt he too experienced. 'It has been a long time since we met, your grace,' he said with a punctilious bow. 'And, Sir Cuthbert, I believe we served together as very young men on the Western March.'

Cuthbert was staring at me, concerned and curious about my state of shock but he dragged his gaze away to respond with a brief bow of acknowledgement.

Meanwhile I had struggled to regain my composure. 'God's greetings, my lord,' I said, my voice sounding high and strange, even to myself. 'It is Baron Neville now, is it not?'

John nodded. 'My nephew was killed a year ago, in an incident at Middleham.'

My eyes rounded in alarm. 'At Middleham?' I echoed. 'How did that come about?'

John made an angry gesture, strode to a table which stood under the parlour window and pulled up a straight wooden chair. 'Will it please you to sit? The prior promised that we would not be disturbed.'

Having regained control of my legs, I walked slowly to the proffered chair and sat down, easing the homespun hood down to my shoulders with both hands. I could see him eyeing the white coif I wore beneath it distastefully, as if he wanted to pull it off to see what lay beneath, then he sat down opposite me leaning his elbows on the table, his chin on his fists. The polished surface stretched between us. Tactfully Cuthbert took a seat on one of the settles, at a distance but within earshot.

I found myself feasting my eyes on John's face with nothing to say. After a pause he spoke. 'You came very quickly. I wondered if you would come at all.'

I frowned. 'You said there was danger to my nephew and his bride. Of course I came.'

'The danger is very real.'

I noticed that his hair was still exceedingly fair and straight, falling over his forehead. There was no sign of grey among the flax, just a dulling of the glossy sheen of youth. Prominent lines ran between his nose and his mouth and deep creases lined his brow but otherwise he showed little sign of ageing.

'Did you know that Egremont and I have exchanged oaths?' he continued.

'Yes. My brother told me. I found it hard to believe.'

He lifted his chin, releasing his hands in order to indicate no help for it. 'Egremont is a useful ally. He is aggressive and daring and I need such friends now that I have lost Jack.'

'Can a Percy ever really be trusted by a Neville?' I asked.

'Not by your brother Salisbury and his ilk, that is certain,' declared John, casting a glance at Cuthbert. 'But Jack was always on good terms with his Percy cousins. They were very alike in many ways, proud, ambitious, foolhardy perhaps at times but intensely averse to your brother's encroachment in Yorkshire and united in their hatred of his braggart son Warwick. When he was Constable of Middleham his Bear and Ragged Staff standard flew everywhere and his men behaved like bears – violent and dangerous. He claimed to be loved but he was feared.'

'How was your nephew killed?' I thought of my recent conversation with Hal at Tattershall and wondered why he had made no mention of the death of the young Lord Neville. Middleham remained his honour, despite Dick of Warwick's recent command of the garrison; he must have known about it.

Pain snatched at the muscles of John's face. 'Jack wanted to avenge a brawl his men had with Warwick's bears. He decided to break up Saint Alkeda's Fair. You probably remember that it is held at Middleham on the feast day of the town's patron saint. I advised against the raid, fearing that blood would be spilled but Jack said he only wanted to show the folk of the dale that the strutting Earl of Warwick could not protect their property. His plan was to creep secretly into the market and release all the pigs in the swine pens. He thought it would be a fine sight to see them run amok through the town.' John grimaced. 'That was his sense of humour I am afraid. He only took a handful of followers and they all dressed as dalesmen, no badges or armour. But the bears were waiting for them; they must have known they were coming. It was a lynch-mob.' His face suffused with anger. 'That devil Warwick sent Jack's bloodied body out of the town naked and tied to a mule. It was ignoble treatment of one knight by another. For all he is your nephew, the man is a scorpion!'

I did not say, as I could have done, that if a knight dressed as a peasant he could expect to be treated as one because in my opinion no unarmed peasant should be treated thus and I had been no great admirer of Warwick before I heard John's story anyway. I merely said, 'So now you want revenge on Warwick.'

John gave a fierce nod. 'That is no secret. And I want your brother out of Yorkshire; that too is no secret. But Egremont plans to ambush Tom Neville and his bride on their way to Sheriff Hutton and I do not consider a newly married couple a legitimate target.' He flicked the hair off his forehead. 'After much deliberation I have decided to warn you of the ambush. You should be able to get them to change the route, or delay the journey. Do you understand?'

'Of course I understand!' I snapped. 'But why do you not simply refuse to support Egremont's scheme?'

'Because it is the first test of our alliance and I cannot renege on the oath so soon. Surely Tom Neville could find urgent business elsewhere – at Middleham for instance. Then he need not take the road over Heworth Moor, which is where the ambush is planned.'

I narrowed my eyes at him, carefully considering his words before I spoke. 'Why should I believe you? The route to Middleham would take them very close to Spofforth, which I am informed is where you and Lord Egremont are mustering an army. I could suspect that you are trying to lure my nephew and his bride right into the spider's web.'

John slapped the table with his hand. 'No,' he almost shouted. 'Why should I lie?' He stood up and began to pace the room. 'This ambush is not an action of which I approve. You can prevent it. It is in both our interests.'

I rose also and moved to sit on the settle beside Cuthbert.

'What is your opinion, Cuddy? Should we trust this man? Or is he diverting us into a trap?'

Cuthbert's gaze slid from me to John and back again. 'Is there any particular reason why you should not trust him?' he asked.

I darted a swift look at John who now stood on the other side of the room, drawn up to his considerable height, his face stern and impassive, studying us both. 'Perhaps there is,' I murmured, my mind racing. John's side of the family and mine had been adversaries ever since my father's will had been made known. The passion that had flared at Aycliffe Tower had surely been but one aberrant instant in a history of family enmity, a mad, youthful kick at the traces which constantly reined us in. Was it logical to base trust on such a fleeting moment? Or had it been something more? John had told me that day that he believed that true love bred trust between a man and a woman. Did he cling to the memory of that one night of love we had shared and still feel the heat of the flame it had kindled? Or did he plan revenge for what he saw as an unforgiveable betrayal on my part? I could not find an answer in his face.

I rose and walked over to him. We stood close together, eye to eye as we had at Aycliffe Tower. 'Why have you never married?' I asked.

I saw indignation blaze. 'I do not think it any of your business! However, as Westmorland needs heirs I intend to remedy that imminently.'

I felt my heart beat a little faster. Had he now found his one true love? And could I trust him if he had. 'Who will you marry?'

He favoured me with a sly smile, as if he knew that what he was about to say would shock me. 'I am going to marry my nephew's widow.'

327

I gave an involuntary gasp. 'Surely you cannot! Legally she is your niece.'

He shook his head. 'She is still only thirteen. Their marriage was never consummated, therefore it can be annulled. She is my ward and she is willing. We will do well together. Besides she is related to the king and it would be a pity to lose that connection.'

'She is Exeter's half-sister, is she not? Anne Holland.'

'The same,' John agreed. 'But happily she resembles her mother; more Montague than Holland. Your son-in-law is uncontrollable they tell me, whereas his half-sister is sweet and biddable.'

I held his gaze, my expression stern, thinking of my Anne. 'I hope you will not seek to sire the necessary heirs too soon, my lord. She is very young.'

He laughed at that and his face lit up in a way that tugged sharply at my memory. 'I can wait,' he said. 'I am a patient man.' Fleetingly I felt absurdly glad that his new bride would be too young to share his bed, then he drew me resolutely back to the matter in hand. 'Do we have a bargain?'

I lifted the old-fashioned hood back onto my head, giving myself time to form a reply. 'I will ask Tom to consider altering his route but I do not have much hope he will agree. I doubt he will want to appear a coward.'

'Then our journeys have been wasted,' John said with a shrug. 'It seems a pity.'

'Not entirely wasted,' I responded, holding his gaze and smiling into his eyes for the first time. 'It has been good to see you.' I held out my right hand, ringless except for the gold York signet.

He took my fingers in his, studied the engraved symbol of

the falcon and fetterlock then bent and kissed the knuckle directly above it. The touch of his lips burned me like a flying cinder. 'I trust it will not be another twenty years before we meet again,' he whispered. As he raised his eyes to mine I caught a glimpse of the softness beneath the steel. Twenty years since our last meeting? He had forgotten our brief encounter at my mother's funeral and remembered only the night of love. But did he also remember the betrayal that followed? I would not know until Tom and Maud crossed Heworth Moor.

Before Cuthbert and I left the priory, I emptied all the coin in my purse into the prior's grateful hands. It was more than I would normally have donated but I did not care. In his stark parlour, feelings had re-ignited in me that I thought had shrivelled and died long ago. As we rode slowly through the gatehouse arch I turned hesitantly to my brother. 'Would you undertake a secret mission for me, Cuddy?'

The formality he had used in the priory persisted. 'You know I am always at your grace's command.'

I sucked my teeth impatiently. 'I do not mean for her grace, the Duchess of York, I mean for Cicely Neville, your sister.'

'I thought they were one and the same,' he remarked dryly, dropping his official pose. 'Why are they suddenly separate?'

I could feel the blood rise in my cheeks. 'I want to send a letter to John.' My gaze slid sideways to gauge his reaction.

He raised an enquiring eyebrow. 'John?'

'Lord Neville!' I cried in exasperation. 'You are not blind or stupid, Cuddy. You must realize there was more between us than a failed abduction.'

'Yes, but what am I to conclude from it? If you want me to carry correspondence between you and our brother's arch-enemy there will have to be truth between us.'

I took a deep breath and stared between my palfrey's ears for a long minute. 'We were lovers,' I said at length but my words came out in a whisper.

Cuthbert leaned nearer, his brow knitted. 'What? I did not hear what you said, Cis.'

Vexed, I turned and shouted the words at him, loud enough to flush a charm of goldfinches from a nearby bush. 'We were lovers!'

The birds flew over our heads, twittering in alarm. 'I know you were, I just wanted to hear you admit it.' He out-stared my astonished glare. 'I am not stupid, Cis. There was no other way you could have given him the slip.'

I gasped. 'Ah! You never said.'

'If I had you would have had to trust me not to reveal the secret and as there was no need for you to worry about that I did not tell you.' He shrugged. 'So now you know you can trust me, as I have kept it for twenty years.'

'I always knew that, Cuddy, and always will trust you.' We rode along silently for a few minutes before I plucked up courage to ask him again. 'Will you take a letter to John, then?'

29

Heworth Moor, 24th August

Cuthbert

'Will you take a letter to John, then?' Cicely asked.
It had not taken much imagination to deduce how
matters had progressed between Cicely and John when they
were thrown together in such tense circumstances at Aycliffe
Peel. She had been a giddy girl of seventeen, inexperienced and
headstrong but she had preserved the secret of exactly who had
seduced who and how she had contrived to make her escape as
a result and I considered she had a right to keep it. However,
having witnessed their meeting at Nostell Priory I understood
without asking that the spark which had lit the original flame
was still alive, despite the subsequent passage of years. I had
seen the way they looked at each other and felt the fiery undercurrents flowing in that stark priory parlour.

'I never told anyone,' she stressed, 'not even my mother, even
though she quizzed me with grim determination before my
wedding. But I have been a good wife to Richard, have I not? I
have borne his children, kept his household, been his counsellor
– and I swear before God that since we took our marriage vows
I have never been unfaithful.'

I was bound to agree that she had been all of the first and I presumed she had not been the last. Then I added, 'But I detect a change in the wind. Am I right?'

Tears welled in her eyes. 'I have been dutiful and obedient to God and my husband but now I have discovered that something still lives which I thought had died and I cannot bear to let it lie unexplored. I cannot contemplate the rest of my life spent solely on church and children when I know that a spark of lost love lies waiting to be fanned into life. Is that so wicked?'

I could almost see the devil's imp clinging to her shoulder and said what was in my mind, despite the risk of stirring her anger. 'You have spent twenty years building a successful marriage. I spent most of those years believing I would never have the chance of similar fulfilment but now that I have Hilda and Aiden and hold land to call ours, I set great store by faith and loyalty . . .'

She cut me short. 'And you think I do not?'

I thought of my two-year-old boy Aiden – the son I had believed I would never sire – and Hilda, the wife I thought I had lost for ever, and the manor in Coverdale, near Middleham, which Richard had purchased from Hal in order to grant me land near the place of my birth. I owed so much to York. However, my deepest debt would always be to Cicely herself, the little girl to whom I had reluctantly committed myself as a favour to her proud and beautiful mother, who had ignored the fact that my very birth was evidence of her husband's infidelity and taken me into her household. A debt of honour such as that could never be superseded.

'Yes I think you *do*, Cis, but you also have unfinished business with Lord Neville; business which will plague your heart until it is settled.'

'So you will help me?'

I reached over and gripped her hand as it loosely held her palfrey's rein. 'God help me sister, I will take your letter,' I said, 'but if it is adultery you plan then I do not know if I can help you commit it.'

She took her reins in one hand and turned the other in mine, clasping my fingers and lifting our arms into a pointed arch between our horses in unspoken salutation. Our eyes met and I saw indecision in hers. 'God help *me*, Cuddy, I do not know what I plan. Let us see what happens on Heworth Moor.'

I delivered Cicely's letter to Spofforth Castle but they would not let me enter. I never knew what was in the letter or whether it was put into John Neville's hand.

Cicely insisted on accompanying the wedding party to Sheriff Hutton. As she had predicted, Tom's pride would not allow him to contemplate changing his route or his destination and his father backed him up.

'I do not know how you learned that Egremont plans an ambush, Cicely,' Hal remarked with a frown, 'but from what I hear of the rabble he has recruited to his banner they will be no match for our disciplined men and now that we can add your escort too, I expect we shall outnumber them. My guess is they will take one look and melt away into the moor, if they even put in an appearance. Tom is right; we should ignore this unreliable information.'

And so after a one night stop in York the wedding party trotted over the Monk's Bridge towards Heworth Moor. The bright streamers and ribbons which had first been unfurled at Tattershall were now faded and ragged but continued to give a festive air to the cavalcade. Tom Neville's white-on-red saltire standard flew at the head beside Maud's Stanhope lozenge, while

Salisbury's green spread-eagles flew at the rear and the pennons of the supporting knights fluttered throughout the column like bunting. In the midst of it, under the white rose, rode Cicely and her escort, a pocket of murrey and blue liveries among the majority of Neville red and white. In all we were nearly four hundred and the bridal nature of the party could not be mistaken owing to the fresh flower-garlands decorating carts and harness and the gaily dressed minstrels playing tabors, pipes and hurdy-gurdys in wagons at the front and rear.

Even Cicely's warnings of possible ambush did not dampen the exuberance of the cavalcade. As we passed through Heworth Green Market the tinkling of the silver bells hung on Maud's bridle brought marriageable girls flocking to touch her skirt for luck. 'Heaven bless you, hinny!' called the goodwives, blowing kisses. One little girl ran forward with a posy of wild-flowers – bright-blue scabious, red poppies and creamy lady's bedstraw – and Maud, already decked in flowers, leaned down with a smile to take the nosegay while Tom tossed the lass a silver penny.

I smiled, enjoying the incident, before returning my anxious gaze to the road ahead. The common land stretched away uphill towards the gorse-strewn moorland which I remembered from my twilight journey with Hilda fleeing her wicked stepson Simon Exley. Even on this bright sunny day Heworth Moor did not look any less hostile than it had then and, scanning the horizon, I caught my breath as a line of horsemen suddenly appeared in sinister silhouette against the cloudless blue sky. The scene unfolded. Below them on the sun-scorched slopes, scrambling foot-soldiers emerged from the head-high bracken to form flanking wings on either side of the track, while between them two armoured knights on prancing chargers took centre stage, their standards streaming out behind them on the frisky breeze, borne aloft by mounted bearers. Prominent among these flags, beside the cross of St George and the Lancastrian red rose, rippled the blue lion of Percy and the black bull of Brancepeth; Lord Egremont to the left, Lord Neville to the right. John had honoured his alliance oath and brought his men to the ambush.

To our rear the market erupted into action as speedily and wisely the people made themselves scarce, scurrying back along the road to the Monk's Bridge carrying what they could manage, fleeing for the safety of the city wall. Within the last few years the citizens of York had seen brawls aplenty between Percys and Nevilles and suffered cracked heads and broken limbs if they failed to get out of the way in time.

Meanwhile our procession faltered as all eyes turned to the threatening ranks ranging on the hillside ahead. Hal cantered up to the front of the column and consulted quickly with Tom, who raised his arm in a pre-arranged signal. Thanks to Cicely's warning it had been decided that in case of trouble the procession would close up and move forward at the trot, keeping a tight formation and leaving the onus of attack on the provocateurs. To turn back was pointless; by the time the clumsy ox-carts had lumbered around they would all be in disarray and the ambushers would be upon them.

Meanwhile the lion and the bull were splitting apart, moving in opposite directions across the hillside. 'They intend to surround us!' I yelled, cantering up to Tom. 'If they cut us off before and behind we will not stand a chance.'

Tom had discarded his wedding garland and donned his helmet and Maud rode close at his charger's heel, pride and excitement lighting her pretty face. I guessed that, being in love, she believed her hero-husband would outwit the enemy, protect her from harm and carry her triumphantly to Sheriff Hutton. Neither he nor I were so confident. Nevertheless the column trotted on, the ox-carts lumbering along in ungainly fashion, threatening to overturn if they encountered rough ground. A trumpet blast was the signal for the men of the Percy blue lion to stream noisily down the slope towards the carts where they obviously expected to find the richest pickings; wedding gifts of plate, rich cloth and household goods.

'Gold! Cromwell gold!' the attackers yelled, waving a motley assortment of scythes, pitchforks and hatchets, terrifying to see but useless against the long lances of the mounted knights. Only few foot-soldiers made it through to the carts, intending to cut the traces or disable the drivers but most of them ended up under the wheels as the procession kept on moving.

Despite Cicely's urgings that I should join Hal's defending forces at the back, I stuck determinedly by her and Hilda and the handful of York household knights who cantered along beside them. It was hard to see what was happening ahead but at least the continued movement of the column indicated that nothing was hindering the advance. I strained my eyes to peer through the dust-clouds sent up by hundreds of hooves and thought I could just spy the black bull standard still flying high on the crest of the hill. If John Neville intended to attack the van of the cavalcade surely he would have done so by now but instead he seemed to be shadowing our progress, cantering along the skyline so that through the dust I caught irregular glimpses of him at the front of his horsemen. When we reached the cove at the rock wall where Hilda and I had hidden on our previous visit to the moor it had been my intention to swerve Cicely and her train away from the column to take refuge behind the gorse. Had we been discovered I believed that the cove would have been relatively easy to defend with only a score or so of men, but as there was no attack from the front there seemed no need for this last-ditch action and the rock wall fell behind us as we cantered on. At this point I glanced across at Cicely and was intrigued to catch her smiling broadly, as if the failed ambush was the highlight of her year.

'He is not going to attack, Cuthbert!' she shouted across to me in jubilation. 'He fulfilled his agreement to be here but he did not attack. I think honour is satisfied on all sides.'

As Heworth Moor petered out, giving way to cultivated fields and small hamlets, the shadowing column of horsemen drew rein and we followed suit, slowing more gradually so as not to cause a pile-up further back. To my surprise the black bull standard dipped deeply in salute. Immediately Cicely signalled to the bearer of the white rose standard, stationed at her horse's hindquarters, to dip it in reply. 'We have reason to be grateful to the black bull of Brancepeth today,' she told him, easing her bay palfrey down to a walk.

All around us the mounted men were doing the same. Instead of dust, clouds of steam rose from the sweating horses' flanks and their riders breathed sighs of relief. Shouts of identification could be heard down the line as the captains established if there were any absentees, while scouts were sent back to look for wounded men. Tom Neville cantered past on his great black stallion, calling his thanks and pausing by each of the anxious drivers who had leaped off their carts to check on their distressed oxen.

Maud rode up to Cicely, concerned for her wellbeing. Her eyes were sparkling in her dust-streaked face. 'Was that not marvellous, your grace?' she cried after Cicely had reassured her. 'Lord Neville did not attack after all.' I rolled my eyes skywards as Cicely smiled warmly back at the elated bride. 'No he did not,' she agreed, her eyes equally bright. 'Lord Neville is an honourable man.'

30

Coverdale, West Yorkshire, September

Cicely

Cuthbert shot me a proud smile and made an expansive gesture. 'Welcome to my manor,' he said.

We were on Cuddy's land: the manor Richard had bought from Hal to grant to Cuthbert and Hilda, as I had requested. From Middleham Castle we had ridden in driving rain through a maze of treeless, stone-walled sheep pastures and forded the Cover Beck with the water up to our horses' hocks but I could not complain because it was I who had insisted that we travel by the back route in order to be unobserved. I blinked the moisture from my eyelashes and peered out from under the hood of my dripping cloak. I had been expecting a manor house but what I saw before me looked more like some kind of stone-built animal shelter, albeit a large one.

'It is a barn, Cuddy.' I tried to keep my tone light but my disappointment must have been clear.

Cuthbert threw back his head, showering water off the brim of the beaver hat he wore and to my indignation he laughed. 'Oh, what a duchess you truly are, Cis!' he spluttered. 'Have you never seen a bastle before? These dales are full of them. It is the

339

only way the farmers have of protecting themselves and their stock from raiders; animals on the ground floor, people living above. We have approached it from the back, as you requested, but at the front you will see there are windows; not very big windows it is true but at least they let in the light. A bastle is a cross between a barn and a castle. Come, let us ride round to the front and get some shelter from this accursed rain.'

Red Gill Bastle had been built on the banks of the fellside stream for which it was named and down which, as a result of the downpour, cascades of white water were gushing and thundering over a steep fall, tumbling down towards the Cover Beck. Like the walls of the surrounding fields, it was built of pale limestone cut from the hills behind. From the front it looked a little more welcoming. As well as a row of small, square, shuttered windows, it had a sturdy ladder-stair leading up to an arched doorway protected by an even sturdier iron yett. There was another well-defended entrance at ground-level. I had shuddered at the thought of having to cross the floor of a filthy byre as I had at Aycliffe Tower, but here people and animals were kept quite separate.

As if he read my mind, Cuthbert said, 'All the sheep and cattle are out on the moor until next month. It will smell as sweet as a summer field in there at this time of year. Wait one minute and I will open the door.' He swung down from his horse and flung the reins over a rail, set for the purpose. 'Believe it or not there is a key so that it can be left locked if there is no one here.'

I dismounted and hitched my horse as he had, then tucked the skirt of my kirtle into my belt so that I could climb the ladder-stair. There were noises of locks turning and the creak of hinges as the yett swung outward, back against the wall, and the oak door behind it swung inward.

'Time to get warm and dry,' Cuthbert said. 'We need a fire.'

Inside the bastle it was dim, the only light coming through the open door and some vent-holes in the roof. Dust motes danced in the slanting beams. The window shutters were closed against the rain but I noticed with relief that there were no leaks forming pools on the floor, which was covered in new rush matting and scattered with fresh-cut flowering herbs that gave off a pleasing fragrance. Someone had made preparations for our visit.

Like a man familiar with the layout, Cuthbert walked to the far end of the room and bent to lift a hatch in the floor. Then he fetched a wooden ladder which had been leaning against the wall and slid it down through the opening. 'First I am going to get the horses into the stalls to dry off. You might like to try your hand at lighting a fire, Cis.'

I gazed at the empty hearth, a flat expanse of stonework in the middle of the room with a few pots and trivets arranged around the sides. A wicker basket of twigs and sticks stood nearby. Frowning, I slid off my dripping cloak and looked around for a peg to hang it on. I felt ill-at-ease and out of place, almost guilty that I had never been inside such a humble dwelling and had no idea how to light a fire or use any of the fearsome-looking implements set ready for cooking and stoking. Not for the first time I wondered whether I had done the right thing in coming to Cuthbert's manor. The rain had dampened my nervous anticipation of a secret rendezvous in the remoteness of Coverdale and I began to wish I could climb back on my horse and return to Middleham Castle where there were servants and cooks and fires and colourful hangings.

I found some wooden pegs on the wall by the open door, hung up my outer clothing and stood gazing out at the rain-lashed dale. Cuthbert had spent the first ten years of his life in a house like this, living off the land and fighting off reivers and I had never thought about it. Had his mother cooked at a fire on a hearth like this one? Had she lain with my father in a hayfield when he got her with child or had he taken her into the curtained-off sleeping area like the one I could see at the end of the room? Where had her parents been when the lord came to seduce their pretty daughter? What had happened when she found herself pregnant? Had they punished her or had my father made some arrangement for her to make a suitable marriage? I had never asked myself these questions before and all at once I wanted answers.

'Well you would not be someone to share a camp with.' Cuthbert was climbing up through the hatchway carrying two saddlebags. He strode across the room and dumped them beside the hearth. 'Where is the fire, Cis?'

The long room was furnished very simply with benches and chests; there were trestles and boards stacked neatly to one side and a store-cupboard let into the wall. The only hints of luxury were several cushions scattered about on the benches. I wondered if they had been put there especially for my visit, perhaps by the same hand that had strewn the fresh flowers. At a loss to know what to do I had placed one at my back and made myself comfortable on a wooden settle.

'There is no taper to light it with,' I said huffily, 'and nowhere to light the taper. I am no tire-woman, Cuddy.'

He picked up a square metal box with a wooden handle and a hinged lid. 'This is a tinder-box. It is for making fire.'

'Good, then you do it.' I stood up and wandered over to the saddlebags. 'What have you brought in these?'

'I wheedled some pies from the Middleham kitchen. And a manchet loaf, though they made a fuss about that. The baker said they were only for the nobility.'

'Did you not tell him your father was the Earl of Westmorland?'

'No, I told him it was for a very beautiful lady of my acquaintance and he gave it to me with a great big wink.'

'Hah!' I allowed my lips to twitch. 'Is your mother still alive, Cuddy?' I asked suddenly. 'Does she live in Coverdale?'

Cuthbert looked taken aback. 'No, she is dead. She died fifteen years ago.'

'Oh, I never knew. I am sorry. Why did you not tell me? How did she die?' I suddenly felt terrible that I had known nothing about his life away from me, not even if his mother was alive or dead. Selfishly I had not asked the questions I should have.

'They said she cut her finger on a scythe at harvest. It festered and she died. It happens in farming areas.' Cuddy was intent on building the fire, placing twigs and small pieces of wood around the flame he had made. I could not see his face but his voice sounded thick, as if his throat was constricted.

'Why was she harvesting? How old was she.'

'Everyone helps with the harvest,' he said. 'She was forty-eight. I had not seen her for many years.'

'Because you were with me?' I touched his shoulder and he nodded. 'Do you remember her? Was she pretty? She must have been pretty or else . . .' I tailed off, unsure how to finish.

'Or else our father would not have taken a fancy to her and I would not have been born.' He finished my sentence and stood up. The fire was blazing nicely. 'But because I was born he married her to a yeoman farmer who was tenant of one of the best holdings in Coverdale, so she lived a good life and had six more children. My eldest brother farms just up the dale and his wife will come and cook for you – if you stay.'

'If I stay . . .' I held my hands out to the flames. 'You do not think I should?'

'What I think is not important. It is what you think that matters.'

'That is not true. I value your opinion, and it is your house.'

'I cannot judge you if I do not know your intentions. Lord Neville will meet you here and then what?' Cuthbert pulled a wineskin out of one of the saddlebags and went to the cupboard where he found three horn cups.

'We will talk. But perhaps he will not come,' I said.

'He will come.' He put the cups down on a chest. His voice was flat, pragmatic.

'You sound very sure. What makes you think that?'

Expertly he aimed wine from the skin into the cups, one after another. 'He loves you. Anyone can see that. I think he has loved you ever since Aycliffe Tower, perhaps even before that. You are his honoured lady. He rescued you from bandits. Some men, knights in particular, cannot resist a damsel in distress.'

I shot him a sharp glance to see if he was teasing but he was concentrating on his task. 'We were young. It was a bolt from the blue. I do not know if the feelings are still there.'

'And if they are?'

I shrugged. 'The same thing will happen.' There was a silence. I waited for him to speak but he said nothing. 'You do not approve?' It was more of a statement than a question.

Cuthbert shook his head. 'I swore an oath to protect you physically, Cis, not morally.' He approached with two full cups and handed me one. 'God would not approve.'

'There are many things of which God does not approve but we do them anyway and ask his forgiveness afterwards.' I looked down into the dark red wine that filled the cup then looked up at him. 'If you do not wish us to stay in your house, Cuddy, we will go somewhere else; perhaps to a hayfield, like my father and your mother.'

He smiled broadly at that. 'My proud sister in a hayfield? I cannot contemplate it.' He raised his cup to me. 'You deal with your conscience, Cicely, and I will deal with mine. May God be good to us both.'

We drank to it and then I leaned forward and kissed his cheek. 'You are the best man I know, Cuthbert of Middleham,' I said.

'But it is only to be once.' He held my gaze sternly. 'Hilda has not been to Red Gill yet. Once we have made this place our own it will no longer be available.'

I nodded slowly. 'It will only be once,' I said.

By the time John arrived the rain had stopped and the sun was hot, drawing steam off the stubble fields around the bastle. Cuthbert and I were collecting water at the well when he rode in through a haze of mist wearing dull, yeoman's clothes and a pilgrim's hat. Cuthbert took his horse to the byre.

'Watch out for my stallion,' John called after him. 'He tends to kick when he is in a stall.' He received a wave of acknowledgement.

I was still standing by the well, a pail of water at my feet. John removed his hat and held it before him, turning the brim in his hands like a supplicant at a Halmote.

I eyed the hat. 'You do not make a very convincing pilgrim,' I ventured with a nervous laugh.

He squinted back, the sun in his eyes. 'Allow me to say the same about you. Nevertheless that is what we are, for the time being.'

'So Cuthbert has informed his sister-in-law. She is going to come and cook for us while we are here,' I remarked, picking up the pail of water.

He took it from me and we walked towards the house. 'Have you been in a bastle before?' I asked.

'I think it is something like a peel tower, is it not? I have been in one of those.' His voice held a distinctly wry note.

'So you have,' I said, putting my foot on the entrance-ladder.

Cuthbert emerged from the hatchway as we entered. 'I have unsaddled your horse, my lord,' he said rather stiffly. 'I am returning to Middleham now.' He looked directly at me. 'You know where I am if you need me.'

'Thank you, Cuddy. You have thought of everything,' I said.

'Yes, thank you, Sir Cuthbert, we are very grateful.' John's words sounded clipped. Perhaps, like me, he was anxious to be free to talk privately. We had only exchanged a couple of letters since our meeting at Nostell Priory and there was much ground to clear between us.

While we waited for the jangle of harness to indicate that Cuthbert had ridden away, John found the wineskin and cups, filled two and handed one wordlessly to me. Then he picked up a cushion, placed it beside him on the settle and patted it, inviting me to join him.

I sat down and took a sip of wine. 'There is so much to say,' I began, studying him solemnly, 'but suddenly I do not know where to start.'

He gave a rueful laugh, took another gulp of wine and set down his cup. 'Well one of us should apologize,' he said, 'and I do not think it is me.'

My instant reaction was anger because I had not been the one to make the move which first stirred passions at Aycliffe Tower. Then it came to me that I was thinking like the green girl I had been then. Now I was older and wiser. I had lived long enough with another man whose honour could no longer

346

brook the slights it had been offered, to understand the bruising effect of disparagement on a nobleman's self esteem. In John's mind the means by which I had achieved my covert departure had been a betrayal, a slap in the face of his male pride, whereas I had come to regard my actions as a justifiable way of escaping an impossible situation. Of course it also turned out to be an event in my life that had played havoc with my own self-respect, while preserving the honour of my family. It was years before I paid full penance for the episode at Aycliffe Tower. Perhaps it had still not been paid.

John obviously took my silence for obduracy and he pressed his case. 'I was not then, and never have been since, a man who played lightly with love. When I gave you mine I thought the gift was reciprocated.'

I regarded his earnest expression and felt a sharp stab of guilt. 'It was reciprocated – at the time,' I protested. 'John, it was a glorious *coup de foudre*! We were both overwhelmed. I cannot apologize for that. There was no question of a lifetime commitment.'

'Yet that is what I made.'

I could hardly believe what I heard. Blood suddenly pounded in my head. He relieved me of my cup, placed it aside and took my hand in both of his.

'You asked me why I had not married and that is the reason. You were my chosen love and still are. No one has ever compared. Unless I am wielding a sword or holding a Halmote, you fill my conscious thoughts – and much of my dreaming as well.'

He spoke with such passion that I felt driven to contest his words. 'Marie! Are you saying that I am responsible for all those raids you have led against my brother's tenants? Skirmish after skirmish, causing injuries and deaths, for twenty years, just to take your mind off me? No, John – it is a joke. I do not believe it.'

He thrust my hand away roughly and stood up, pacing away across the room, to turn on me with a thunderous expression. 'You think it is a joke? That merely confirms what the Church teaches us – that all females are daughters of Eve; light-minded, easily tempted and never to be trusted.'

As I rose to approach him, my unruly temper fired up further and I struggled to maintain a measured tone. 'And all men are sons of Adam I suppose, simple-minded, easily led and hostage to their gross desires? No – all that is nonsense, John; the babble of illiterate priests. Do not insult me with its rancour or expect me to accept that you believe it.'

We were standing eye to eye now, lips compressed, arms rigid at our sides, hands bunched into fists; the fine line between vehemence and violence was all that kept us apart and fierce as it was it suddenly dissolved in the passion generated by our blistering blue on grey gaze.

'Ah Jesu, Cicely!' John exclaimed and faster than a falcon's stoop I found his arms around me in a tight embrace, his lips on mine, his tongue seeking the moist inner rim and causing my senses to vibrate like the strings of a lyre.

Memories surged up from nowhere, carrying me back to the night when I had discovered the heart-stopping glory of two bodies melding together with the explosive effect of oil meeting fire, a sensation I had never experienced before or since. This was the man who had seized my surrender with the simple stroke of a finger on my cheek; the first man to lead me into the inferno of mutual enthralment and the subsequent joy of sated pleasure. It had started with a clash of minds and it had resulted in long languorous love-making, just as it did now. John did not take me the same way Richard did, as a lord demanding fealty from his vassal, but invited me to share in pleasure and this time I appreciated his love-making even more than I had before, when I had known nothing about it.

After we had made full use of the bed behind the blanket curtain we lay face to face in dreamy lethargy and talked in peace, as we should have done before, orchestrating our conversation with gentle stroking and soft laughs and sighs. We were cocooned in shadows because the one thing John had managed to do before our passion consumed us was to kick the entrance shut so that the fading sunlight only filtered through the smoke vents. It was when we eventually noticed that there was no smoke curling around the rafters that John left the warmth of my arms, leaping from the bed with an oath.

'The fire!' he exclaimed. 'We have let the fire go out.'

I could not help laughing and spluttered, 'No, my love – I think you will find we have just re-lit it,' to which John reacted with a low chuckle.

I pulled the covers up to my chin and watched him find his chemise and pull it on, relishing his body's fitness, the tight buttocks and the ripple of taut fighting muscles down his back and arms. I did not know his precise age but calculated that he must be over forty. Very faint streaks of white were just discernible in his flaxen hair but there was no sign of slack flesh, only the various scars gave evidence of his frequent calls to combat.

We spent five blissful days at Red Gill bastle, days when we gave no thought to feuds or factions, when we wandered up the fell-side through bracken turning russet in the shortening autumn glow, drank sparkling water from the beck and watched harriers swoop for prey along its banks. When a glorious sunrise greeted us the morning following our arrival we looked out on a world that seemed to have been created especially for us; verdant fields dotted with black-faced sheep and a sky as blue as the Virgin's veil, scattered with clouds like goose-down. The dale was our playground and we used it like children on a holiday.

Cuthbert came soon after sunrise as he expected but one look at my glowing face told him how things stood: he would be riding back to Middleham alone. He brought with him his sister-in-law whom he called Bee, and each morning afterwards she did indeed make herself as busy as a bee around the bastle, cleaning and sweeping and bringing freshly baked bread or barley bannocks and butter and cheese from her own farm dairy; there was a different pot of stewed meat or fish each day, depending on the demands of the Church calendar. She was a fount of information about the area, telling us which paths to follow and which to avoid if we wanted to stay safe; there had been lead mining on the fells and the ground was peppered with hidden shafts. 'People sometimes disappear without a trace,' she told me in a hushed voice. 'Perhaps the devil pulls them down a hole and straight to hell.'

We did not encourage too much of this folklore·because, pleased though we were with the supplies of fresh food, we could not wait for her to leave us to our own devices. As soon as she departed we saddled the horses and took easy, loping rides along the Cover Beck, stopping for a picnic of bread and cheese and ripe apples picked from the indomitable little trees growing in the shelter of the narrow ravine behind the house; the Red Gill which funnelled the fell stream that lulled us to sleep at night. The fruit grew sweeter by the day as the September sun shone down. In the afternoons we returned to the bastle and made love, delighting in the warmth radiated by the sun-kissed stone and the big bolts on the sturdy door which gave us the freedom to shed our clothes and enjoy each other in a private and secure world of our own. 'You are like these balmy days of autumn,' John said one afternoon. When I asked what he meant he gazed at me intently, and his voice was solemn. 'You are like the sweet-sharp apples we pick from the wind-blown trees. You have weathered the world and all it can throw at you and yet you are luscious and ripe and you fill my senses with delight. The sight of you as you are right now will be with me for the rest of my days.'

I drew breath sharply, for his words brought me back to harsh reality. 'You think so? Even on those days when you make love to your nubile young bride, whose body will be soft and smooth and supple? At such a time my image may shrivel and vanish from your mind.'

His expression clouded. 'You may think that if you wish but one thing I know – she will never look at me the way you are looking at me now.'

I climbed on to the bed beside him, my naked skin touching his from shoulder to thigh. 'And how is that?' I asked, kissing the hollow behind his collar-bone.

'You are untamed and beautiful and I worship you.'

He rolled onto me then and I opened to him willingly, eagerly, demandingly. He was right, at that moment, on that day, with him, I was wild and untamed in a way I knew I would never be again in my life. I felt him move in me and I whispered in his ear, 'This is the real me, the girl you carried off to a tower in the marshes and turned into a woman. You are a magician and I am your creature.'

Much later, when we had wrapped ourselves in sheets, placed the latest pot of stew on the trivet to warm and poured some wine into our cups, we pulled the cushions near to the fire and talked, reclining.

John was in thoughtful mood. 'What you said, it's not true, you know.' He did not look at me but at the wine in his cup, his eyes bleak. 'You are not my creature. And I am not a magician. If I was I would make these stolen days last forever and our love would only die when we do.'

My wine suddenly tasted sour on my tongue. 'I remember you said I had filled your thoughts for all the years since we met. Will I no longer do so now you have had your wicked way with me?'

His mouth twisted in a wry one-sided smile. 'It might be fairer to say we have had our wicked way with each other.' He nuzzled me softly, sadly. 'No, our love will die when we leave here because the world and the church will snatch it and kill it. We will return to our family enmities and we will remember that we are too closely related for cannon law. They say familiarity breeds contempt but in the case of our love it inevitably spells the end.'

'You are right; the days – the hours – of our love are numbered but I will always trust you, John, remember that. Even if there is blood between our families I will trust you not to spill that of me and mine.' Gazing into his candid grey eyes, I saw my own sorrow reflected back.

PART SIX

The Drums of War
1454–1461

31

Baynard's Castle, London & Ludlow Castle, 1454–1455

Cicely

I waited at Baynard's Castle for Richard to return from Westminster and his first council meeting as protector. Baynard's was a towering fortress on the River Thames guarding the south-west corner of the London Wall and he had acquired it from the estate of the old Duke of Gloucester. It had been refurbished by the duke who had a reputation for opulent living and was known as 'Good Duke Humphrey' by Londoners but still it was draughty and uncomfortable. We lived there because access to Westminster was easy by boat and it was of a suitable size for Richard's household and retinue. But I constantly longed to return to Fotheringhay.

The joys of the Red Gill bastle were becoming a distant memory overlain by extraordinary events and family and household matters demanding all my attention. Also, I tried to resist thinking of John. But as I gazed dolefully out over the river from a window in my grand solar at Baynard's, I had a sudden recall of his tall, muscular frame and lean, passionate face and felt desire tug at my inmost self. We had been torn from our secret hideaway by Cuthbert who brought news both disastrous and astonishing. Firstly there had been a battle at a place called Castillion in Aquitaine which had not only forced the final withdrawal of English troops from France, apart from Calais, but had also resulted in the death of Richard's old warrior-friend John Talbot, Earl of Shrewsbury. The second piece of news however was strange in the extreme and had caused Richard to summon me to join him immediately at Ludlow.

News of the defeat at Castillion had reached King Henry at Clarendon Palace in Wiltshire, during a progress he was making to dispense justice around the country. So great had been his shock and despair that he had fallen into some kind of trance, from which he had not recovered. Physicians recorded that he could see and walk and eat but he did not speak and his gaze appeared empty and disconnected; they could offer no real diagnosis or cure. Meanwhile the queen's confinement was imminent and this left the Duke of Somerset in complete control of the council.

One of Somerset's first actions in the king's name had been to order Dick of Warwick to withdraw from his wife's extensive Despenser estates in South Glamorgan which Somerset claimed as part of his own wife's inheritance. Both women were daughters of the old Earl of Warwick but by different mothers: as with the Neville feud, this was the cause of the problem.

Returning to Ludlow with Cuthbert I found Dick and Hal were there with Richard to discuss tactics against Somerset. Indeed, this summit at Ludlow resulted in a new pact between the three; now instead of being out on a limb, banished from court without support from his peers, Richard found himself in a position of some strength. He hoped he would soon be in a position to have Somerset arrested over his failure to defend France and his arbitrary control of the Great Council.

Then Queen Margaret gave birth to a son, baptised Edward with my sister Anne, Duchess of Buckingham, standing as godmother, and the status of the new prince was immediately thrown into question by renewed rumours that his sire was not the king but the Earl of Somerset, rumours compounded by the fact that King Henry was in no fit state to acknowledge the child, no matter how many times the baby was placed in his arms.

Somerset became the focus of protests in London, partly over the paternity rumour and partly because the over-taxed citizens blamed him for the kingdom's expensive failures in France. Foreign wars were popular with the citizens when they brought plunder and glory but the general who spent all their taxes and then fled home in defeat faced violent dissent. At a special meeting of the council Somerset was committed to the Tower on a charge of treason brought by the Duke of Norfolk, Richard's long-standing ally. Christmas was celebrated in a frenzy of plotting and scheming among the different factions, culminating in February with the queen demanding in a letter sent to the council that she be appointed regent for her stricken husband.

To a man the council vigorously rejected the idea of a female regent, especially a Frenchwoman, and made moves to recall parliament in order to establish a formal protectorate. A consensus gathered around Richard as the adult male with the best claim to the succession and therefore the best qualified to deputise for the crown. His appointment as Protector and Defender of the Realm was ratified on the third of April, but only after the baby prince had been invested with the cap, ring and stick of the Principality of Wales, confirming his official status as heir to the throne. This order of events had been to reassure the queen of her son's position and to pacify her fury at being denied the regency.

So I awaited the return of my husband the Lord Protector of England. Through the leaded glass of the window of the solar I saw his galley glide downriver from the Palace of Westminster and turn into the water gate at Baynard's. True to his love of display, Richard sat amidships in an elevated gilt chair under a gold-tasselled canopy and was rowed by twenty oarsmen in York livery, their blades hatched in murrey and blue. Three standards were ducked as they passed under the gate arch – the white rose of York, the falcon and fetterlock and, to the fore, an escutcheon of the arms of the Dukedom of York, three gold lions on red in a silver border. I wondered how long it would be before Richard had the College of Heralds produce a coat of arms for the new Protector of England. Behind Richard's galley there followed another, smaller craft, boasting only ten oarsmen and one standard displaying my brother Hal's green spread-eagle.

Having no intention of being outshone by Richard's flowing ermine-trimmed houppelande and gem-studded chaperon, I was dressed ready to perform my role as the Protector's lady in a gown of brocaded blue silk with trailing sable-trimmed sleeves and a headdress of jewel-encrusted gold net set on a ducal coronet. Sadly Richard's spectacular White Rose collar, which had been his proudest possession and a spectacular symbol of his investment in the future of the House of York, had had to be sold to meet our expenses. He had proved his administrative skills in Normandy and Dublin without being paid but it remained to be seen whether he would now have the chance to steer the kingdom onto what he called its 'true course' and recoup some of the debt owed to him by the crown at the same time.

For me it was a short walk from the privy apartments to the Great Receiving Chamber where friends and allies of York were gathered to hear the latest news. Richard, Hal and I arrived together, greeting each other on the steps of a dais covered in blue velvet and fitted with two gilded thrones. We did not take our seats however, until another chair had been placed for Hal beside ours. Then Richard raised his hand for silence.

'For the peace and good rule of the realm it gives me great satisfaction to announce that I have today appointed my respected and renowned brother-in-law, Richard, Earl of Salisbury, as Chancellor of England. I hope you will all join me in pledging support for the good work I am certain he will do in restoring the Exchequer to a position of strength and good management.'

There was a stamping of feet and calls of congratulation and encouragement and Hal stood up and made a short speech of thanks and commitment. Richard then announced that other new appointments would be made to the council as soon as possible and that he would open the new session of parliament the following day. The three of us then made our way to Richard's private chamber so that we could speak freely together. A chamberlain poured wine and was dismissed and we all relaxed into cushioned seats.

'You look tired, my lord,' I said, observing the dark shadows into which Richard's usually bright green eyes had sunk. Since our reunion at Ludlow, he and I had returned to a working partnership, although I knew it would never be the warm and loving relationship we had enjoyed before. I could not deny him his conjugal rights and nor did I wish to but when I announced that my eleventh child would be born sometime in late June or early July, I worried that it might arrive a little early. I would never repent my secret interlude with John but I was acutely aware of the danger of giving birth to a child which Richard could not possibly have sired.

'I would be exhausted,' he acknowledged, 'if I did not now have your brothers and nephews on my side.' He raised his jewelled cup in salute to Hal. 'I thank you heartily for agreeing to take the Great Seal, Salisbury. I have discovered that finding men to fill the highest offices in the land is not easy. Few are willing to expend their energies for the benefit of the realm when at any time the mat could be pulled unceremoniously from under their feet.'

Hal's appointment was a controversial one because it was a post usually filled by a member of the Church hierarchy, so I was surprised that he had been offered, let alone accepted, the post of Chancellor.

'It is rather disquieting,' Hal agreed, taking a judicious sip from his cup. 'Our brother Will was in the deputation that went to Windsor last week and he told me that King Henry's stupor is still profound. Yet the doctors claim he could regain his intellectual processes at any moment.'

'Or not at all,' added Richard with no obvious sign of regret.

I had also heard Will's account of that visit to Windsor. The carefully selected group of lords had been invited to attend the king at dinner time and had watched him consume a meal with agonizing slowness and a frighteningly vacant expression. He had appeared completely unaware of their presence and failed to respond to anything they said to him. It was after this unsettling audience that the council finally united behind the appointment of Richard as Protector.

'England is lucky to have two men such as you at the helm of state,' I remarked encouragingly. 'God willing, her people will soon notice a return to order and the rule of law.'

The mention of Will had reminded me of his daughter Alys, who had kindly nursed little Anne through her traumatic abduction by Harry of Exeter. Sadly I had received no correspondence from Anne herself but Alys had visited me on her way back north to be married and reported that Anne was pregnant. Her baby was due two months after mine and I knew that there would be no chance of my being admitted to Ampthill even if I had been fit to travel there, so I could only rely on Alys's assurance that there were pleasant women around her and a good midwife had been appointed. Her lying-in would be around the time of her sixteenth birthday and I prayed every day to St Margaret to grant her a trouble-free birth. At least she would be free of Harry's company because he had been summoned before the council and committed to the Tower for failing to pay substantial fines imposed for occupying Ampthill and damaging countless other properties, a sentence which I heartily applauded. I could not quite bring myself to wish him dead but I certainly felt that the country would breathe easier, the longer the Fox was denied his freedom.

The first months of Richard's protectorate brought a considerable slackening of political tension due to his rigorous application of the law to those lords who had been consistently flouting it, including the arraignment of Lord Egremont to answer for his violent raids on Hal's Yorkshire holdings. However by Christmas the king showed signs of recovering his faculties; by the following February he and the queen were back at Westminster and Somerset had been released from the Tower. The protectorate was over; Richard services on the council were no longer required and he retreated once more to Ludlow. The Wheel of Fortune had turned again.

Meanwhile I had given birth to a baby girl, born late enough to leave me in no doubt that she was legitimately Richard's.

Sadly she was also sickly and fretful, requiring constant nursing from the moment of her arrival. As soon as she and I were strong enough, I took her off to the tender care of Anicia at Fotheringhay where she joined her toddler brother Dickon in the nursery. We called her Ursula, the Little Bear.

I cannot say that I was personally sorry to see the end of the protectorate, which had meant spending much time in London at draughty Baynard's and away from the children but, of course, Richard and his affinity were furious and gathered at Ludlow for another strategy meeting in the middle of April. Sensing dangerous times ahead, I decided to join Richard and took all the younger children and their nurses and servants to Ludlow for safety.

Before dinner on the day after our arrival, family members and guests gathered in the grand first floor chamber off the great hall. Talk centered on the summons Richard, Hal and Dick had each received to a meeting of the Great Council at Leicester in May.

'I am not going,' declared Dick, waving his letter of summons high. 'To Leicester? In the Lancaster heartland? With no retinue? They jest! This is a one-way invitation to the Tower.'

'Somerset is certainly pulling no punches,' agreed his father in a slightly more moderate tone. 'No doubt he wants pay-back for the months he spent there last year.'

'It smacks of Duke Humphrey's summons to the St Edmund's Bury parliament,' said Richard grimly. 'He was ordered to attend the king and bring no retainers and look what happened to him.'

'What did happen to him, my lord?'

It was Edward who spoke; he was on the cusp of his thirteenth birthday and about to become a squire, albeit only in the service of his governor Sir Richard Croft. Of course, being Edward, he was desperate to serve someone of more exalted rank, such as his cousin Dick, but Richard had told him he must wait.

'Poor Gloucester was arrested and died soon afterwards,' Richard explained. 'He was fifty-seven and it was said that he had an apoplexy but few believe it was not murder. He took on a corrupt court party and came off worst. Edmund Beaufort was one of them – before he became Duke of Somerset and the equally corrupt Suffolk was the royal favourite at that time. Your cousin Dick is right. This summons is definitely a trap.'

Richard had still received none of the money owed to him by the crown and to add insult to injury Somerset, in the king's name, had released Harry of Exeter from the Tower declaring him to be there due to the malice of ill-wishers. Richard saw this as a personal insult and bitterly resented seeing the red rose and the wheatear flying together again.

Meanwhile Dick of Warwick was on the warpath because Somerset had reinstated his claim to Glamorgan and besieged Cardiff castle. 'I will need to send relief to South Wales before I can bring a force to your aid,' he said. 'What action do you have in mind, my lord of York?'

Richard flung one arm around Hal's shoulder, which my brother bore patiently but awkwardly. They were not bosom friends however much Richard liked to pretend they were. 'Your father suggests we should prevent this meeting of the Great Council happening at all and I am inclined to agree with him. If it does not happen we do not need to go and therefore we cannot be accused of treason for refusing.'

Warwick raised an eyebrow. 'Hmm. That is a crafty plan, my lord father. How do you propose we bring it about?'

'Will there be fighting, Uncle?' Edward asked, making thrusts with an imaginary sword.

Hal smiled at his bloodthirsty young nephew and eased himself from under Richard's arm. 'Well, young March, I think we might aim at the barber treatment – trim Somerset's beard a little but not draw any blood. We are not aiming for a fight.'

'And I think your father will consider you too young take part, Lord Edward,' remarked Sir Richard Croft, crushingly.

'And his mother most certainly will,' I declared firmly from my seat near the hearth where I sat with Elizabeth and Meg beside me. As they were eleven and almost ten respectively now, I thought it time they experienced the world of adults, however boring they claimed to find it.

I watched Edward's temper flare but was glad to see him swallow his ire, make a graceful bow of compliance to his governor and retreat to stand behind his father. Edward was learning tact as well as tactics. Edmund on the other hand was always quiet on these occasions, watching and listening. One of the small triumphs Richard had achieved as Protector had been successfully to argue that his second son should be made Earl of Rutland, in recompense for the lands and titles he had lost when France had overrun Normandy. I hoped this would do much to reduce Edmund's sense of inferiority.

Richard expanded on the proposed strategy. 'If we are to stop the council from sitting we have to prevent the king from going to Leicester. When he takes the road north he always spends the first night at St Albans Abbey. We will block his progress there but we will not make an attack and King Henry will not order one because it is not in his nature. Therefore it will be a stand-off, giving an opportunity for negotiation. That is what we need – a chance to take our case directly to the king without having to deal with his weasely side-kick. But hear this, if I could make Somerset disappear in a puff of smoke I would, believe me.'

Later that evening, after the meal was concluded, the trestles were cleared and when wine had loosened tongues I passed close to where Dick of Warwick was discussing these tactics with one of his companion knights. I did not like what I heard.

'York has tried that strategy before – bringing a large force to confront the king and relying on him to negotiate. It did not work last time and it will not do so now. Personally I vow that if Somerset is in the royal party when we confront them at St Albans I will not waste time in talking. There will be a fight and Somerset will not survive.'

32

St Albans Town, 22nd May 1455

Cuthbert

At dawn a thick mist formed over the fields where our troops were stationed behind the outer row of houses and gardens on the east side of St Albans. The town had no walls and the makeshift barricades erected against us did not look as if they would offer much resistance. Our three-thousand-strong force had been deployed in three divisions and because of my tactical skill with the longbow I had been seconded to the Earl of Warwick's retinue to captain his crack cohort of archers. We were drawn up behind the foot-soldiers who were detailed to storm the barricades while we shot over their heads to break down the defenders on the other side with showers of arrows. I could not fault Dick of Warwick's strategy or his instructions to his knights to inflict as little injury as possible on the common soldiers and concentrate on taking out the men of rank. He did not declare it publicly but all the captains knew that while York claimed only to want certain people to be stopped from abusing their positions of power beside the king, Warwick had only one aim in this confrontation – to come face to face, sword in hand, with the Duke of Somerset, the man who had robbed him of his wife's legitimate inheritance, as he saw it.

Although it meant that the archers would be shooting blind, the shrouding mist would undoubtedly assist the infantry's attack, hiding them from the defenders until the last minute and Warwick, fretfully pacing the ground between Richard's forces and his own, was anxious to get started in order to take advantage of this. First, however, we had to wait for the inevitable last-minute diplomatic efforts to prevent bloodshed. Richard had insisted on sending his herald to assure the king of his loyalty and obedience to the crown but also of his intention one way or another to remove from the king's presence the traitors by whom he was surrounded. When the herald returned with the royal reply that the only traitor the king could see around him was the Duke of York, Dick punched the air with delight, clapped his father and uncle on their armoured shoulders and declared, 'Then we fight! God give us the day!' and marched off to mount his horse.

As predicted, the barricades barely delayed our assault on the town. Once my archers had let loose their fusillades of arrows our infantry charged at the haphazard heaps of upturned carts and domestic furniture, hauling them aside and then, screaming defiance, battering and hacking their way through the defenders in the gardens beyond. Some of our more enterprising men had the idea of stopping to release pigs and chickens from their pens and coops which then ran amok and caused further havoc, before breaking through the houses to the street beyond, leaving a trail of destruction but few injured citizens, most of whom seemed to have retreated to their upper floors behind locked doors. I led the archers after the infantry. Bows slung and daggers in hand, we avoided entering the street and prowled along the row of back gardens seeking a suitable vantage point from which to bring our fire-power to bear on the real foe – the high-ranking barons and knights of the king's party. The royal forces we had encountered so far were evidently recruited from the surrounding countryside and seemed timid and badly equipped, armed mostly with scythes and billhooks and protected with ancient padded gambesons, relics from the previous century. When they turned and ran we let them go. They were not our prey on that day.

Where the houses were intersected by a crossroads, we came to a building that was one story higher than the others. The extensive stables and outhouses behind it were deserted and the rest of us took cover while two of my sturdier sergeants put their shoulders to a rear door. After several heaves they succeeded in bursting through, allowing us all to pour into the chamber beyond, a large room supported by wooden pillars, which occupied most of the ground floor. It was deserted and almost devoid of furniture but the strong smell of ale and the presence of several large barrels at one end revealed its normal function as the taproom of an inn; the furniture must have found its way onto the barricades. There was a gallery of rooms above reached by a staircase at one corner and I led the way up, hoping to find the attic floor and a way out onto the roof. If there were people cowering in the first floor bedchambers we did not disturb them as we climbed further. From a landing window, I caught sight of the painted sign that swung from the front of the building. It told us that we were occupying a hostelry called The Castle Inn.

Within ten minutes I had thirty archers deployed on the roof which overlooked a key street leading up through the market-place and into the main square of the town, an area milling with men-at-arms wearing red rose badges and fully armoured knights with shields bearing easily-recognized crests of the Lancastrian affinity. Over their heads I could just make out the top of the market cross and flying above it the unmistakable lions and lilies on the royal standard. Somewhere under that standard must be the king himself. I made a furtive sign of the cross. Never before had I taken up arms against England's anointed king and I felt as if I was breaking one of God's commandments. I glanced quickly at the men around me and wondered if the same thought had occurred to them but if they were aware that they were about to commit treason I could discern no sign of it.

By now the sun was well risen and had dispelled the mist; its beaming brilliance reflected off the polished armour of Warwick and his household knights who were massed on horseback at the far end of the street. At the entrance to the marketplace a Lancastrian mounted troop lined up and began a charge, starting at a slow trot and building up speed as they thundered between the closely shuttered houses and workshops. Their horses' iron-shod feet churned up the hard-packed dirt of the thoroughfare, forming a choking cloud of dust and when they passed beneath us we could hear the riders spluttering and coughing inside their helmets. Wisely Warwick kept his arm raised, holding his troop steady at the street's end where they could still breathe clean air, waiting for the enemy to come to them, maces, swords and shields raised against their dust-blinded attackers. Meanwhile my archers sent a shower of deadly missiles raining down on the Lancastrians, hardly able to miss their targets at such close quarters. Injured horses reared up and fell, throwing their riders and impeding those who came behind them who were forced to a halt directly beneath our deadly shower. Those with sense turned and galloped back up the street, their backs briefly making perfect targets for our armour-piercing arrows until Warwick's mounted men moved up to pursue them and I gave the order to stop firing.

Several unseated Lancastrian knights gathered swiftly around one of their number and forced their way into the shelter of the inn through the street door beneath us. The prominent member of the group displayed a ducal coronet around the band of his helmet and a portcullis on his surcote. I beckoned one of the nearest archers over to me and whispered under the earflap of his leather coif. 'Do not go out the way we came in but seek a way down through an upper window and over the outhouse roofs. Find the Earl of Warwick and tell him the Duke of Somerset is at the Castle Inn. Say I sent you. Go!'

The lad was a nimble youngster selected for his climbing skill and I watched him scramble easily over the ridge of the roof and disappear before turning to issue more orders to the rest of my men. 'Those of you with the longest range find a position from which to fire into the main square. You will not be able to see your target but fire around the area of the market cross and you should cause some consternation at least. Stop if you see any of our badges entering the square.'

As these orders were obeyed, I made my way along the parapet and back through a gable door into the roof-space. The last man up had replaced the hatch that led down into the upper floors and I eased it back slowly, fearful of attracting attention but I need not have worried. Loud voices carried up from below and the gist of the conversation was not hard to decipher. The Duke of Somerset wanted another mount.

'Fetch me Blanchard from the horse-lines!' he shouted to one of his companions. 'A horse is worse than useless in these narrow streets but that devil Warwick is mounted so I must be. And try and catch the bay! He was not badly wounded, just frightened. I cannot afford to lose a good horse. And hurry, man, hurry! I need to get back out there.'

I grinned to myself. Clearly Somerset was an angry man and angry men did not fight well. Warwick needed to get here quickly to seize that advantage. I crept back out onto the roof, hoping Somerset would draw all attention to himself so that his supporting knights would not think to wonder where the arrows that felled their precious horses had come from. If they did they would be up the stairs in moments and we would be cornered on the tiles. It would be a tricky platform to fight on.

Luckily it was not long before we heard a loud hammering from below and the squire calling out in a fearful tone. 'Your grace's horse is here but you must be quick. Warwick's knights are not far away.'

I peered over the parapet and saw the squire holding a well-armoured horse. The inn door opened cautiously and several helmeted knights stepped out onto the street; at the same time Warwick and his retinue came charging around the corner at the crossroads and with rowdy shouts plunged back down the thoroughfare, causing the Duke of Somerset's warhorse to swerve and prance, preventing him from mounting. He stepped back from the stirrup and hastily drew his sword as his own knights gathered tightly around him in a defensive semi-circle.

Warwick's horse slid to a halt a few yards away, his own knights close behind and they all dismounted. 'I would not want it said that we did not fight on equal terms, my lord of Somerset!' Warwick yelled through the visor of his helmet.

The young earl had drawn his sword and sent his horse careering off down the street with a blow from the flat of the blade. Those of his retinue followed behind and, with the herd instinct kicking in, Somerset's horse broke away and followed them. Now I could clearly see the two hostile groups lined up, facing each other across the narrow street, all visors closed, swords drawn and shields at the defensive. The Beaufort portcullis confronted the Warwick bear like a gate threatening to cage a wild animal.

'There can be no equal terms in a city street, Lord Warwick!' Somerset shouted back. 'My soothsayer has predicted I will die in a castle.'

'Ha!' Warwick retorted with scorn. 'Not in a castle, Beaufort – at the Castle Inn. Look up, my lord duke!'

It was the oldest trick in the book but Somerset fell for it. He looked up and saw the inn sign above his head but had no time to register its significance or gather his defences before Warwick was on him, catching him a brain-shaking blow on the helmet, while his house knights were engaged by the Warwick retinue. The clash of metal on metal and blade on wooden shield was suddenly deafening and I instinctively fell back from the parapet, alerted by a shout behind me.

'The king's standard has fallen, Captain!' yelled one of the archers who had been firing in the direction of the market place. 'The day must be ours!'

I hurried forward along the gutter to reach his vantage point and sure enough there was no longer any sign of the royal standard flying above the market cross. Then there was a loud clatter of hooves and I saw horses cantering fast across the road junction at the top of the street and recognized Richard's distinctive dapple-grey war-horse and, coming from the opposite direction, the green eagle standard of the Earl of Salisbury. They turned into the market place together.

'Cease firing!' I roared at the archers. 'Sling your bows! Friends in range!'

Seeing my orders obeyed, I turned back to the parapet and peered over again. Below me was mayhem. Only four knights were still on their feet and one of them was Warwick, his sword still in his hand, blood dripping from its blade. Somerset was on his knees nearby, head down and gauntleted hands feeling desperately about him, as if searching blindly for his sword. Meanwhile another knight stepped in front of Warwick, challenging him, sword and shield raised. The front of his shield was painted in a gold and blue chequer-board crossed by a horizontal red bar, which told me instantly that behind it was Lord Clifford, the Earl of Westmorland's one-time ward and squire, the same Thomas Clifford who, as a young man, had helped Sir John Neville abduct Cicely to Aycliffe Tower.

I drew an arrow from my quiver and nocked it onto my bowstring. I could easily have shot Clifford through the visor but instead I kept my metal-tipped arrow trained on Somerset, confident that I could leave the other man to Warwick as long as the duke did not rise and take the earl from behind. Although I was now sworn to York, I myself did not wish to be responsible for killing or wounding Thomas Clifford, having liked him as a lad when I had served with him on the northern march before he gained his majority and his knighthood. In my opinion he was a fine knight but I presumed Warwick would overcome him and take him for ransom.

Warwick fought like a man possessed, giving no ground or favour to his older opponent. Clifford was barely defending himself against the young earl's vicious onslaught. Meanwhile the Duke of Somerset had located his sword and was heaving himself to his feet, although it was now evident that there was blood flowing freely from a wound under his sword-arm, near the buckle of his breastplate. At this point, just as I was beginning to haul on my bowstring, I heard once more the thud of hooves on the hard ground of the street and caught the flash of yellow and green from the corner of my eye. Hal of Salisbury with his green eagle shield-crest was bearing down on the scene and, seeing his son about to be attacked by two knights at once, rode down Clifford with the metal point of his lance, taking him with a savage and deadly blow and sending him sprawling backwards, while Somerset gave a blood-curdling yell of fury and threw himself at Warwick, sword raised. He must have been disorientated however for he misjudged his slashing thrust, leaving his guard down and allowing Warwick to strike him with another cutting blow under the shield-arm while parrying Somerset's swipe with his own shield. It may not have been intentionally lethal but clearly the blade pierced a vital organ, causing Somerset to buckle over and crumple to the ground face down. Under my alarmed gaze, within seconds the combined actions of father and son had apparently taken the lives of two key members of the Lancastrian affinity. If the battle had not been over when the king's standard fell, it certainly was now.

I called my men to order and we hurriedly left the roof, returning to the empty taproom and exiting to the street through the inn door to find that the rest of Salisbury's retinue had arrived and were busy checking the wounded, removing arms and taking prisoners. Dick of Warwick was jubilant, making no secret of the fact that he had achieved his objective in triumphing over Somerset and congratulating his father for removing the threat from Clifford. Neither of them had yet noticed that the king's standard had fallen in the town square but when I told them they immediately remounted and rode in that direction, while I mustered the archers in their wake, intent on discovering if there was more work for them to do seeing off the rump of the Lancastrian force.

We found the Duke of York by the market cross where King Henry's standard had been raised, but the monarch himself was no longer there. Scores of bodies lay about on the cobbles of the square and blood flowed freely along the gutters. Only a few of the casualties seemed to be moving, uttering moans and cries of varying intensity. I immediately sent two of the archer-sergeants to check for living wounded.

The duke came forward to meet Salisbury and Warwick, his expression grim. 'His grace the king took a stray arrow in the neck and has been taken into one of the houses for treatment. It is a tanner's shop I believe, where they have the necessary tools for removing arrow-heads.' He gestured towards a large corner premises where a tanned hide hung over the door and his worried look deepened, as well it might. If the king's wounds were to prove fatal the country would be thrown into chaos and York may well be held responsible. However strongly he had felt about the weakness of the king's rule he had not intended regicide. Nor was the king the only casualty of Warwick's archers' remarkable fire-power. At Richard's feet the Duke of Buckingham was slumped helmet-less, a feathered flight protruding ominously from the left side of his jaw. One of his squires was in attendance, reassuring him that someone had gone to find a cart to carry him to his tent.

'The Duke of Buckingham is my prisoner,' Richard continued. 'Humphrey here was advising King Henry to retreat when he took an arrow himself. I have taken his bond as my prisoner and there are many other casualties of your archers, my lord of Warwick, as you see.' He gestured around him, indicating several members of the royal household, identifiable by their swan badges and red rose livery, lying wounded around the base of the steps leading up to the cross. 'These men could not protect the king or themselves from a fusillade fired over the roofs and those who should have hastened him to safety seem to have fled like cowards.'

Warwick immediately began issuing orders to members of his retinue to remove the weapons of all men lying in the square, taking the oaths of the wounded and assessing their need for help. 'Surely some of the monks will have medical skills,' he suggested. 'Shall I send my herald to ask the abbot?'

'York herald has already gone,' Richard told him. 'Give me your assessment of the military situation as it stands, my lord. The day is ours without a doubt but where is the devil whose misrule caused this unnecessary confrontation? Where is Somerset?'

'Dead,' said Warwick succinctly. 'We fought in St Peter Street and he would not surrender when clearly beaten. When Lord Clifford came to his aid my father took him out with his lance and in my own defence I was forced to strike Somerset a fatal blow.'

I could not see any sign of remorse as Warwick said this, nor did York display any. The two men exchanged meaningful nods and made the sign of the cross. 'God absolve them both,' said Richard solemnly. 'I will ask the abbot if graves may be found at the abbey. I have heard that Northumberland is also dead.'

The gates of St Albans Abbey fronted the square and various monks were now to be seen cautiously emerging, clutching bags of salves and bandages.

'I believe we may thank Almighty God that his grace the king appears to have received only a flesh-wound,' Richard told the abbot, who led the procession. 'The arrowhead is being removed in that house over there,' he indicated the tanner's shop. 'A stitch or two and immediate applications of your ointments may prevent infection.' He turned to Hal. 'Perhaps the Earl of Salisbury would accompany you to escort his grace to the abbey and also deploy a guard so that only known members of the York affinity may be granted access to him. The king must be kept secure from those traitors who have surrounded him hitherto.' Richard proclaimed this in a loud voice, making it clear to all in the square that King Henry was now under the care and protection of York.

At this point Richard's standard-bearer suddenly appeared from behind the market cross carrying not only York's crested escutcheon but also the royal standard. 'What should be done with this, your grace,' he asked Richard. 'I found it thrown onto a midden in one of the back gardens.'

The duke's face darkened. 'The traitor who discarded that should be hung, drawn and quartered!' he declared furiously. 'Never should the royal standard of England be allowed to touch the ground, let alone be foully defiled.' He glanced around and catching sight of me beckoned me over. 'Take the standard into your possession if you please, Sir Cuthbert, and see that it remains with the king. Guard the crown and the royal sword as well. We shall need to restore the king with all his regal honours to their rightful place in London as soon as his grace is fit enough to travel.'

Bowing compliance, I took the standard from the bearer, consulted briefly with my second-in-command telling him to report to the Earl of Warwick for immediate orders and followed the procession of monks who were now heading for the tanner's shop in the corner of the square. When we entered we found that the arrow had been removed and King Henry provided with a temporary dressing which he held against his neck to stem the bleeding but he looked pale and shocked and said nothing. It was the first time I had been so close to the king and I was surprised by his physical slightness. Free of their armour most knights were broad of shoulder and muscular from a lifetime of military training but although tall, King Henry had the physique of a clerk or a cleric. After the abbot had introduced him, the infirmarian immediately set about with needle and silk thread, inserting several stitches into the royal wound and applying a greenish salve before binding it neatly. I could not help admiring the stoicism of the king during what must have been a painful experience and was pleased to see him able to rise from his chair afterwards and walk slowly from the shop, leaning on his squire's shoulder for support. The heavy royal sword had already been removed from his belt and I took possession of it, shouldered the royal standard and fell into step behind my half-brother Salisbury who had placed himself at King Henry's other side. As we entered the abbey I noticed that a substantial guard in York livery was now present at the gates and I wondered what would become of a king who, although the words had not been spoken, was to all intent and purpose now a prisoner of war.

33

Baynard's Castle, London, 1455–1456

Cicely

I wrote to my sister Anne, expressing my sorrow and concern at the wounding of both her husband Humphrey, Duke of Buckingham, and her eldest son, Lord Stafford, during the confrontation at St Albans. I told her I prayed for their full recovery. She did not reply. They did recover, however, and so did young Henry Beaufort, wounded as Earl of Dorset but now the new Duke of Somerset – one of the young heirs of the St Albans fallen, who included Lord Poynings now Earl of Northumberland and John Clifford, heir to his father Thomas, Lord Clifford. Together with our estranged son-in-law Harry Holland, Duke of Exeter, and his partner-in-crime Lord Egremont, these five noble young firebrands had all publicly sworn revenge on York, Salisbury and Warwick. Richard had vowed to bring peace and justice to England but there was no denying that the battle at St Albans had made the task he had set himself vastly more difficult.

Wearing his crown and with his bandaged neck concealed under a high-collared crimson doublet, King Henry had been escorted back to London in solemn procession, unarmed but with his great sword of state carried before him by the Earl of Warwick. I watched the king ride into the city, Richard and my brother Hal close beside him and surrounded by Yorkist retainers. To the people who flocked to see him pass, their monarch must have cut a forlorn figure. However, due to the presence of Warwick, who had made himself London's darling, its citizens welcomed the royal procession with its Yorkist white rose badges. Because most of his household had scattered after the battle, King Henry did not take up residence at Westminster Palace but lodged instead at the bishop of London's palace near St Paul's church. The queen remained at Greenwich Palace with the infant Prince of Wales, where she was said to have gone into deep mourning for the Duke of Somerset. She ignored my offer of a visit to express my condolences. I was shaken by the death and injury of so many key nobles, I imagined like most of England, and wondered whether the country would dissolve into chaos, or if Richard could possibly claw it back from the brink.

On Whitsunday Richard and I walked behind the king into St Paul's for the Pentecostal Mass and hosted a feast afterwards at Baynard's Castle where it was announced that Richard would assume Somerset's roles as chief adviser to the king and Constable of England. During the following weeks, working in the king's name, he made new appointments to the posts which had previously been filled by Somerset's cronies and several prominent Lancastrian nobles came to make their peace with him. I was glad to see that although Anne had ignored my letter, her husband Humphrey managed to give Richard the kiss of peace, despite his head being copiously swathed in bandages. My brother Will Fauconberg was also prepared to build bridges, even though he had clung to his Lancastrian roots and fought with the royal party at St Albans, and the king's half-brother

Jasper Tudor, Earl of Pembroke came too, proving himself a fair-minded young man although a staunch royalist. By July a new Parliament had gathered and Richard, Hal and Dick all formally renewed their oaths of allegiance to the king before the assembled Lords and Commons in the Great Council Chamber at Westminster. Outwardly at least it looked as if peace had been restored to the kingdom.

In October, in yet another effort to show the world that York and Lancaster were reconciled, Edmund Tudor, Earl of Richmond, invited Richard and me to attend his wedding to Margaret Beaufort at her mother's home of Bletsoe Castle in Bedfordshire. This was the marriage that had been arranged by the king before his son was born, in order to bolster the Lancastrian line of succession to the English throne. Lady Margaret Beaufort was the direct heiress of the Beaufort claim and if anything happened to little Prince Edward, any sons who might be born to her would be rivals to Richard and his heirs for the succession. Edmund Tudor was the elder of the king's half-brothers who had been born secretly to his mother Queen Catherine and her second husband, the Welsh squire Owen Tudor. King Henry had ennobled Edmund as Earl of Richmond and his younger brother Jasper as Earl of Pembroke because, apart from the queen and Prince Edward, they were his closest kin. Although they were fiercely committed to the Lancastrian cause I found myself admiring both these young men for their obvious desire to bring order and unity to their brother's fractured kingdom and hoped they might provide future support for Richard in his similar aim.

In the event Richard did not attend Edmund's wedding because as autumn closed in the king began to show signs that his malady was returning; by November Richard had once again been officially appointed Protector of the Realm and was too busy to leave the seat of government. However he insisted that I make the journey to Bletsoe and take our daughters Elizabeth and Meg with me so that they might witness a dynastic marriage of the kind they would soon be expected to make themselves.

It proved a good idea because although Margaret Beaufort was only twelve years old she was a bright and intelligent girl who had been well prepared for the union by two of her older half-sisters who had made young and successful marriages to older men. On this occasion the bridegroom was twenty-six, more than twice the age of his bride but an exceptionally handsome and spirited young man who proved easily able to charm her into smiles and laughter and dance the jewelled buckles off her shoes at their wedding feast. Although I, like most mothers I knew, was opposed to brides being bedded before the age of fourteen, the church sanctioned twelve as the canonical age and a marriage was not legally binding until it had been consummated. Edmund Tudor was Earl of Richmond but his title did not carry any great estate; only when the union was declared legal would he gain possession of the Somerset lands and revenues to better support his high degree. My impression was that he would quickly charm his little bride into enjoying his company both in and out of bed.

Being as yet unaware of such legal and moral niceties, my young daughters were vastly impressed by the whole occasion and on the ride back to London conducted a girlish argument about which of them would marry the bridegroom's athletic younger brother, the dashing red-haired Jasper Tudor. Meanwhile Richard was exploiting the Tudor Welsh connections by appointing Edmund Tudor to a lieutenancy in South Wales, where Richard himself was Constable of Carmarthen, and charged him with the task of subduing the rebel Gryffydd ap Nicholas, who was defying royal decrees and raiding Welsh estates legally held by York and Buckingham. By the end of November both Tudor brothers were commanding military units in Wales, Jasper in his vast stronghold of Pembroke Castle and Edmund, having no Welsh residence of his own, ensconced with his garrison and his new young bride only a few miles away at Lamphey Castle, the fortified rural retreat of the bishop of St David's.

By the next February, however, King Henry had recovered his senses and reappeared at Westminster Palace. The council immediately revoked Richard's appointment as protector but insisted that he keep his place among their number. The queen kept her distance from London, where she was almost universally disliked, but Jasper Tudor journeyed back from Wales to lend his support to his newly recovered half-brother. Surprisingly he and the Duke of Buckingham proved invaluable allies to Richard on the council as it struggled to balance the royal exchequer and restore the rule of law.

Anne had joined her husband at court and when I learned that both she and Alice de la Pole were to be Easter guests of the queen at Greenwich, an invitation which had not been extended to me, I thought it an opportunity to try and bridge the gulf that had developed between us following the violent conflict at St Albans. I still exchanged letters regularly with Alice and suggested in one of them that after the visit she might coax my sister to come with her to Baynard's. The two of them would be arriving on Easter Monday.

On the morning of the proposed visit I had sudden misgivings. I confessed as much to Hilda as we walked together to the solar following Mass in the chapel. As well as her four-year-old boy Aiden, Hilda was now the proud mother of a little girl called Marie and her two infants shared Anicia's nursery with Dickon and Ursula. Having children of similar ages had cemented our friendship even further and she was now my closest, almost my only confidante.

'There was a time in France when Anne and I were on the best of terms,' I explained to Hilda, 'but I do not think we will ever be so again after St Albans. She seems to hold me responsible for the duke's actions, as if we women have any say in whether swords are drawn.'

'Even though her husband and son are recovered from their injuries now?' Hilda asked. 'I can imagine it might be different if they had died.'

'The Duke of Buckingham is fit and well again but I believe their son Stafford is still ailing. There is some infection in his wound that inhibits healing. Also his wife is the daughter of the Duke of Somerset, who was killed at St Albans. Although Humphrey seems able to set aside his political differences with Richard, I see there are reasons enough for Anne and her family to hate us.' As I said this I realized just what an emotional leap my sister would be making in coming to visit me.

'Now that I have children of my own I find it easier to understand the scars left by battles such as the one at St Albans,' remarked Hilda solemnly. 'Think if it had been Edward or Aidan who had been injured or, God preserve them, the duke or Cuthbert who had been killed. We would not easily forgive those responsible, would we? Foreign battles do not leave such a personal legacy. We just hate the French as a whole, not the individuals who kill our loved ones.'

Her words stopped me in my tracks for until that moment I had never truly understood the possible repercussions of the internecine warfare which constantly threatened to tear at England's foundations. More than ever I wanted to heal the rift between myself and Anne. It was as if by so doing I might prevent the delicately poised peace between Lancaster and York from tipping into the abyss.

I gazed at my companion for several seconds until I noticed her quizzical expression. 'Thank you, Hilda,' I said hurriedly. 'You have shown me that the answer is to involve the children. I will bring Elizabeth and Meg into the solar. Perhaps their presence will diffuse any atmosphere of conflict.'

So it was that later that day, when wine was served to Alice, Anne and me at the solar hearth, my two younger daughters were sitting demurely to one side with Hilda.

'How did you find the queen?' I asked Anne who was beautifully dressed in a crimson gown trimmed with sable and jet, her head encased in a jewelled turban headdress. She looked impressive but on edge, as if she was suppressing strong feelings. We had exchanged distant kisses on her arrival.

'She is well,' she replied rather stiffly. 'She is very happy with her robust little prince, my godson, and relieved that the king has returned to good health.'

I nodded and noted her deliberate mention of her status as godmother to the Prince of Wales, an honour she obviously cherished. 'Yes, his grace appears to be completely recovered. It is a relief to all of us.' I turned to Alice. 'And your son John? We so look forward to having him join our household among the duke's squires. He will have the benefit of being guided by my brother Cuthbert, Lady Hilda's husband.' I gestured in Hilda's direction and noticed as I did so that Elizabeth was gazing out of the solar window but Meg was listening intently to our conversation.

Alice smiled a little wistfully. 'It is kind of the duke to take him on but I shall miss him sorely when he leaves Wingfield. He is a wonderfully easy companion.'

'I found that when I sent a son to become squire in some other household I usually gained a potential daughter-in-law instead,' observed Anne. 'Do you have any plans for your son's marriage?' She glanced rather pointedly at the two girls not far away.

'There have been some discussions,' said Alice vaguely. 'Of course the inheritance is still uncertain.'

I smiled at her conspiratorially. We had privately been corresponding over a possible marriage between her son and Elizabeth but although Alice had been granted control of her dead husband's estates in trust for her son, the titles were presently in abeyance and I knew Richard would not consider allying one of his daughters to anyone less than an earl, even if he did hold most of Suffolk and Norfolk.

Not wishing to pursue that topic further at present I turned to Anne and took the plunge, asking gently, 'And how is my nephew Humphrey, sister? Has there been any improvement in his condition?'

Blood instantly rushed to her cheeks. 'No, not really,' she blurted, glaring at me alarmingly. 'Though I wonder you dare to ask.'

It was the reaction I had been afraid of but I knew it was a subject which had to be aired. I cast another quick glance at Elizabeth and Meg, more to remind Anne that they were there than to check on their deportment. Anne's sharp tone had attracted Elizabeth's attention away from the window. 'I can pray for him,' I said and added earnestly, 'If there is anything else I can do I hope you will tell me.'

I was taken aback by the fierceness of her response. 'You can thank the Almighty that your sons are too young to fight and tell Hal's son Warwick to curb his bloodthirsty bears.' Anne's face was contused, her voice harsh with grief as she pursued her point. 'Humphrey was defending the barricades at St Albans and heard Warwick's order to take out the commanders and let the soldiers run. Minutes later three of the bears held my son down and one ground a mace into his groin. Thank God he already has a son and heir, for there will be no more children of that marriage.'

My hope in bringing my daughters into the solar was that their presence might lighten the atmosphere. I had not anticipated the depth of Anne's anguish at the nature of her son's injury nor realized that it was Warwick she blamed as much as Richard for its cause. I thought of John's bitter anger at the violence Warwick's bears had inflicted on his nephew Jack at Middleham and all at once the full extent of the divisions within the Neville family hit me. It was not only Westmorland Neville against Salisbury Neville it was nephew against uncle, cousin against cousin and now sister against sister. But I could not brook her unbridled outburst. Anne might feel justified in venting her anger on me, but I considered it unnecessary to inflict such verbal violence on my daughters.

I felt tears of indignation prick at my eyelids. 'I am devastated by your son's injury, Anne, believe me. I had no idea of its nature. But I am also shocked and sorry that you chose to inflict such a grim description of it on my young and innocent daughters.'

Anne leaped to her feet, glaring at me. Icily, she said, 'They will hear of much worse done to people closer to them before long I fear. You Yorks have not yet suffered loss or injury from this accursed feud with Lancaster, Cicely – and I would not wish it on you – but I believe it cannot be long before you do. I did not really want to come here but Alice persuaded me. It was not a good idea after all. I bid you farewell.'

Turning on her heel, Anne crossed the room in a furious rustle of brilliant crimson silk. As she waited impatiently for the chamberlain to open the door for her, I suddenly remembered the neat way she had produced a hidden knife from her boot in Rouen. She was an indomitable woman, my sister of Buckingham. At that moment I told myself that if we were ever to meet again I would not underestimate her.

'I will go after her,' said Alice, making to rise.

'Please do not leave,' I entreated. 'I want my girls to hear more about your son John.' I beckoned Elizabeth and Meg to draw up their stools. I was hoping to distract them from dwelling too much on what Anne had said about her son's injury. They had met Alice before but not her son. 'Lady Suffolk's son will shortly join your father's henchmen at Fotheringhay. He is nearly four-teen and I hear he is very good looking.'

'Does he have red hair, my lady?' Elizabeth asked Alice sweetly.

Alice was surprised by this seemingly random question, not knowing what great effect the rufous Jasper Tudor had had on girlish dreams. 'No, Elizabeth, he is fair haired.'

'Does he read books?' asked Meg, the scholar amongst my children.

Alice nodded a little uncertainly. 'But he has to concentrate on weapons training as well. Do you like to read, Meg?'

'Yes, very much.' Meg turned to me with an apologetic expres-sion, as if she knew I was not going to like what she said next. 'My lady mother, please will you ask people to call me Margaret from now on? I do not want to be called Meg any more. It is not a name for a great lady and I am going to marry a king.'

Alice laughed. 'Well, Margaret, you certainly know what you want – and it does not hurt to be ambitious. The most my son can hope to be though is a duke.'

Meg, or Margaret as I understood we must call her from now on, turned big, round blue eyes on Alice. 'Well, I suppose a duke would do,' she said with a shrug. 'But I would rather be a queen.'

34

Fotheringhay & Ludlow, 1456–1458

Cicely

Soon after Easter in what proved to be Richard's last victory of any import in a Great Council increasingly dominated by Lancastrians once more, Dick of Warwick was appointed Captain of Calais and almost immediately he and his family departed over the channel. Meanwhile I discovered that Richard had been in negotiation with Jasper Tudor regarding a marriage between him and Elizabeth. Needless to say she was ecstatic at the idea but I worried desperately about marrying another daughter to a confirmed Lancastrian supporter, however dashing and conciliatory he may be. When I told Richard I had made advances to Alice de la Pole about a marriage with her son, John, he laughed.

'I do not think Elizabeth would be interested in marrying a commoner when she could have the king's half-brother,' he said. 'Perhaps if King Henry grants young John his titles back we might think about him for Meg. I certainly want to keep him allied to York. You have been doing good work cultivating his mother.'

I forbore to tell him that I thought of Alice de la Pole as a friend not a project and instead to change the subject I told him that Meg now wished to be called Margaret and her intention was to marry a king. I expected Richard to be amused but he thought for a moment and nodded in agreement. He said seriously, 'Stranger things have happened. Perhaps she is thinking ahead.'

A few days later I took the household and all the children back to Fotheringhay and so I was not in London when Richard made what I considered to be a grave mistake. In order to demonstrate to the people that the king was in good health and ruling the country, Richard encouraged Henry to make a summer progress around the Midlands with the queen, meeting leaders of the towns and shires and dispensing royal justice. Being thus thrown together with the king, Queen Margaret had a perfect opportunity to exert her influence. King Henry was easily swayed by minds stronger than his own and his desire to please immediately switched its focus to her. Within weeks she had persuaded him to remove the royal household and most importantly the privy seal to Kenilworth Castle and the court and its officials to Coventry, only eight miles away. In one action Queen Margaret had acquired all the tools she needed to run the country herself and rebuild the Lancastrian affinity around her new young favourites, Henry Beaufort, Duke of Somerset, John, Lord Clifford and Henry Percy, Duke of Northumberland.

This was not Richard's only setback. In Wales Edmund Tudor had been successful in garrisoning several royal strongholds against the Welsh rebels and he had taken Carmarthen Castle back from them, thus restoring the authority of the king in that part of Wales – but unfortunately Richard, the Constable of Camarthen, was at that time occupied on the northern march helping Hal chase an invading Scottish force back over the border and his Yorkist supporters in Wales interpreted Edmund's action as a Lancastrian incursion. They marched in large numbers on Carmarthen and took Edmond Tudor prisoner in a skirmish. Richard did not hear about this until he briefly joined the royal progress in the Midlands and it was several weeks before Edmund's release could be arranged. Meanwhile a wound Edmond had received in the skirmish had turned putrid and the young Earl of Richmond died of the infection before he was able to leave Carmarthen.

His thirteen-year-old countess was left at nearby Lamphey Castle in a potentially perilous situation; a widowed heiress, alone in a lawless country and six months pregnant, she needed urgent protection. Jasper Tudor had been at Kenilworth in attendance on the king and queen but as soon as he heard of his brother's death he galloped back to South Wales and took his young sister-in-law to the safety of Pembroke Castle. This sad sequence of events spelled the end of any hope there might have been for a marriage between our Elizabeth and Jasper, who blamed York retainers for his brother's death. Besides he now had responsibility for his brother's very young widow and her baby. For a thirteen-year-old girl to give birth in any circumstances was a dangerous and traumatic business and it was only many years later that I learned from Margaret Beaufort just how nearly it proved fatal for both herself and her baby. They called him Henry, not a name any of my children would ever call theirs, I was certain, except perhaps Anne, who would have no choice.

On a visit to London I had finally managed to see Anne, hearing that she had brought her two-year-old daughter to Coldharbour Inn. Had her unstable and criminally-minded husband been there I would never have managed to gain admission but he was away in the north somewhere, creating havoc with his Percy and Clifford cronies. My heart was in my mouth when I was shown to a sparsely furnished chamber where a meagre fire was burning in the grate but there was no one there and after many minutes I thought I was destined to depart disappointed. When the door opened to admit a tall woman leading a small girl I did not recognize my daughter.

Anne had, at eighteen, become the beautiful woman I had longed for her to be. All trace of her plumpness and blemishes had vanished and her deportment was superb. Tears sprang to my eyes when I beheld her long, patrician face with its noble forehead and Plantagenet green eyes set off by high cheekbones. She wore a simple white linen veil held by a circlet and a pretty grey gown trimmed with pale minerva. I held out my hands to her. 'Anne,' I said, my voice cracking with emotion. 'How wonderful!'

She took one of my hands coolly, keeping hold of her child with the other, and leaned forward to place her lips briefly on my cheek. 'My lady mother,' she murmured, then pushed the little girl forward. 'This is your granddaughter Anne. I call her Annette.'

I crouched down to the infant's level and offered her my hand but she did not take it. Instead she stood staring at me with her bright-blue eyes – my eyes, or perhaps her father's, though I did not like to think so. 'God's greeting, Annette. It is a pretty name for a pretty girl.'

She shrank back into her mother's skirts.

'Normally she is quite talkative,' said Anne. 'But she does not know you. Shall we sit?'

'Yes, thank you.' I took the chair she indicated and she took another. We faced each other across the fireplace. 'I was not sure if I would be admitted.'

'All callers are admitted when Harry is not here, as long as they leave their arms at the gatehouse.' Her tone was flat, as if she addressed a stranger. 'He is away. I do not know where and I do not care.'

'Things are not good between you, then?'

She made a dismissive noise, pushing out air. 'Things are not good between Harry and anyone. Even his cronies only put up with him because he brings them fighting men to swell their raiding parties. Harry hates the world and the world hates Harry.'

'And do you hate him too?' I simply had to ask.

This time the puffing noise was louder. 'Of course I do! Nothing has changed as far as that is concerned but he hates me back so that is fine. He wanted a son and he got a daughter. Bad luck. He will not get another. Not on me anyway.'

I looked from her to Annette, my heart in my mouth. 'But she is lovely, Anne.'

Her face softened. 'Yes. She is my one compensation for the disaster you landed me in.'

I said nothing. I no longer tried to justify Anne's marriage even to myself. I would have fought Richard far more forcefully over it had I not at the time cherished my own marriage and still hoped there might be a chance for hers. Now I could sense that while she had not made the marriage, the marriage may have made her. This Anne was a much stronger person than the tearful girl I had watched ride away across the Lincolnshire stubble.

'I gather you are planning to marry Elizabeth to another Lancastrian family. Have you learned nothing from my experience?'

I raised an eyebrow. 'How do you know that?'

Anne smiled for the first time. 'I am on Queen Margaret's

guest-list. She cannot abide Harry any more than anyone else but she needs him and his followers so she uses me as a means to deal with him. I talk to Alice de la Pole. I like her. She is a clever woman.'

'Yes, I like her too,' I said.

'Of course you do, my lady mother. You are a clever woman too. If you were Duke of York our house would not be on the cusp of war with Lancaster.'

'You still think of yourself as being of York?' I was amazed.

'More of the white rose affinity than of York. I could not support Lancaster, even though the queen thinks I do, and I will never wear the wheatear. No, I am definitely one of the white roses; what are you?'

Little Annette had let go of her mother's skirts and edged her way in my direction, still gazing at me curiously. I smiled encouragingly at her, thinking how wonderful it was that I was her grandmother. I found myself hoping that this little girl would have children of her own and them after her. I thought of John and his decision to marry at last and I understood why.

'Well of course I wear the white rose but if I had my choice I would not wear white or red. I would find one of those pink hedgerow roses and wear that.'

This time my daughter's smile was genuinely warm. 'There, you see – I said you were clever.'

She had been well informed about the marriage plans for Elizabeth and young John de la Pole. Richard changed his tune once Jasper Tudor ceased to be a contender and I had completed my tentative arrangements with Alice. By so doing Richard sealed an alliance not only with the former Duke of Suffolk's chief tenants but also, crucially, with the Duke of Norfolk and his affinity. Elizabeth had not been pleased, having expected to be a countess at least. However, soon after the wedding the king had been persuaded by the queen, encouraged by Alice of course, to at least restore the Suffolk heir to the earldom. I had already concluded that John de la Pole would never be the brightest star in the political firmament but his mother made up for that and he was obviously quite smitten by his lovely bride. I had accompanied Elizabeth to Wingfield to live with her new mother-in-law but John, her pleasant and placid bridegroom, was to remain as a squire at Fotheringhay for a year or so until they were both old enough to be bedded. I was sure that Elizabeth had every chance of making a successful marriage, in contrast to her sister Anne's disastrous experiences.

By the following spring the queen had succeeded in acquiring the king's agreement to remove all York appointees from their administrative positions and even persuaded her royal husband to sign an order sending Richard back to his post as Lieutenant of Ireland. With Hal of Salisbury tied up subduing the Scots on the northern march, Dick of Warwick busy in Calais and Richard back in Dublin, Queen Margaret could congratulate herself on having split the Yorkist affinity asunder.

However, the queen had not counted on the military skill and political cunning of Warwick whose rapidly-acquired fleet of ships now based in Calais raced to and fro across the Channel, efficiently routing the pirates who had been terrorizing shipping in the Narrow Sea and thus gained the further adulation of London merchants. The pirate loot confiscated also financed lavish entertainments at his London house on his frequent visits there, when he wooed the leaders of the guilds. The city increasingly scorned King Henry's weak rule and loathed his French queen and now they had a dashing and capable champion who was restoring their vital trade links with the Low Countries.

Thanks to Warwick, the Yorkist cause was now assured support in London.

I had refused to accompany Richard back to Dublin, which I remembered with much loathing and, to be fair, he had not encouraged me to go, agreeing that the delicate health of our two youngest children, Richard and Ursula, should not be put at risk in the damp Irish climate. So I kept an eye on our English estates, travelling regularly between Fotheringhay and Ludlow, where I observed with great pride the transformation of my two eldest boys into well-educated young noblemen, able administrators and knights of considerable skill. Their governor Sir Richard Croft told me he was particularly impressed with Edward's progress and recommended that Richard should give some thought to his eldest son's dubbing.

'Certainly he should be knighted if there is any question of him taking part in a military confrontation,' Sir Richard added. 'I mentioned it to the duke the last time he was here.'

'And what was his reaction?' I asked, annoyed that Richard had not spoken of this to me before leaving for Dublin.

'He seemed to think there was no immediate danger of conflict,' had been the reply, and in January of 1458 King Henry tried to prove Richard right on that score by calling a peace conference in London to which all Yorkist and Lancastrian magnates were summoned. It might have worked if the three young heirs of St Albans dead had not marched a large army of retainers up to the city gates and stormed the meeting demanding compensation for the killing of their fathers.

Richard, back from Dublin, ordered the portcullis at Baynard's lowered and the battlements manned with archers when he returned from the meeting at Blackfriars Abbey. 'I am taking precautions,' he explained. 'Those impertinent puppy lords have intimidated the king. Apparently we are ordered to endow a chantry at St Albans and I am to pay his widow five thousand marks in compensation for Somerset's death. It was not I who killed Somerset, it was your nephew Warwick but he is commanded to pay only one thousand marks to the Clifford family. But that is of no consequence because these are spurious awards. It was a battle, which Somerset caused and their fathers chose to fight! We owe them nothing, least of all a chantry in perpetuity for the soul of Somerset, a man who rots in hell without a doubt.'

'But will you pay, Richard, for the sake of peace?' I put the question gently, moved for once to offer physical consolation by placing my hand on his shoulder.

He turned to face me and I could see fierce determination in his hooded green eyes but to my surprise he nodded. 'I will agree to pay for the king's sake but I will simply assign five thousand marks of the debt the exchequer owes me to young Somerset. I have never received it and nor will he. Henry may be a peace-loving soul but his queen is a termagant and her followers feed her rage. There is no hope for peace in this kingdom while she leads her husband by the nose.'

'So what will you do now?' I asked, realizing with a heavy heart that the results of this so-called peace conference could affect our whole family. 'I hope you are thinking of our children's futures, Richard.'

'Tomorrow is Lady Day, the Feast of the Annunciation, but the king is calling it a Love Day. I am to hold the queen's hand and she and I are to walk behind Henry, and the Nevilles and the Percys are to follow us, also hand in hand; he wants us all to walk in procession to St Paul's for a service of reconciliation. To show the people that the royals and nobility of England are all friends.'

He paced impatiently away, his hands clasped under his forked beard and his eyes lowered as if in prayer. When he raised his head and walked back to me his expression was militant. 'But poor Henry is woefully misguided. We are not friends. Our joined hands will burn with enmity. Afterwards we shall go to Ludlow, all of us, and gather the forces of York around us. That is the only way we will be safe from Henry's scheming queen and her new favourites.'

35

Ludlow Castle, Spring 1459

Cicely

Of all the York strongholds, Ludlow Castle had the largest outer bailey, therefore when loyal retainers from the Welsh marches began to answer York's call to arms, as spring warmed the air they were able to set up camp within the security of the perimeter wall. Richard was in his element, deploying scouts, ordering supplies of weapons and arrows, touring the tented village to check on welfare, briefing his captains and above all honing his own fighting skills against the best of his knights. To his delight he was most evenly matched against his son and heir but their sparring caused an argument between Richard and Edward's governor.

'Croft does not approve of me sparring with my son, saying that only knights may challenge other knights. That may be a tournament rule but Edward needs to train for the battlefield and he will not do that by simply crashing around with the other squires,' he told me as we broke our fast together in our chamber one morning, away from the bustle of the great hall.

'When I was last here, Sir Richard recommended that Edward be dubbed, perhaps that was his meaning,' I remarked.

'Edward may be tall but he is too young,' Richard said with finality. 'I am sending Croft on a recruiting drive through my Mortimer lands. He has taught Edward all that is within his power and the lad has lost patience with his pedantry. Edward has far outstripped his fellow henchmen and needs to test himself against the best fighters but Croft holds him back. I had thought of sending Edward to Warwick but now there is no need.'

Richard looked at me seriously before he went on. 'I wrote to Dick yesterday asking him to bring men here. The king and queen have taken Prince Edward on a tour of the Midlands to raise a Lancastrian army. I believe the queen has even had the cheek to suggest that Henry abdicate in favour of their son. Yes, really – in favour of a five-year-old! I suppose she thinks to rule through him and at least Henry had the wisdom to refuse. But she has also issued commissions of array, ordering every town and village to send their young men to support the Lancastrian cause. England has never forced men into the field involuntarily, especially not into an English field. Conscription is a French custom and a bad one. Men who fight under constraint fight badly. She of all people should know that.'

'But I suppose it will boost their numbers,' I remarked. 'No general likes to be outnumbered, even by conscripts. Are you seriously thinking of confronting a royal army, Richard? You did it once before and only just escaped a charge of treason. You would not get away with it a second time.' I could see his anger building. He did not like to be questioned over tactics but I was past playing the passive wife.

'A *Lancastrian* army,' he snapped. 'And only if we can combine our forces without loss. Hal needs to avoid ambush getting here from Middleham and Dick will need fair winds across the Channel and a clear march all the way from the south coast. But I had good news from an unexpected source yesterday. John Neville has come over to our side and will bring men down from Durham.'

I nearly choked on the fine white manchet bread supplied by the castle bakery. I reached for my cup of ale and hoped Richard had not noticed the blood drain from my face. I was shocked and thrilled at the same time. It was true that since our meeting in Coverdale John had stood aloof from conflict with my brother Salisbury, restricting his military activities to confronting the Scots on the northern march, but it had never occurred to me that he would actually turn coat and throw in his lot with York, whose greatest allies – Salisbury and his son Warwick – still occupied the very Yorkshire lands that John had demanded as ransom for my release over twenty five years ago. Nor was he the only Neville to change his allegiance. After fighting with the Lancastrians at St Albans, my brother Will, Lord Fauconberg, had accepted a post as Warwick's deputy in Calais and it was mainly his nautical command which had secured the freedom of the Channel for the English merchant fleet. Affable Will was the conciliator in the family. Perhaps he had been working on John.

Richard was unaware of my distraction. His mind was too full of schemes and strategies and he began rehearsing them out loud, moving his knife, cup and trencher about the board to illustrate his planned manoeuvres. 'Dick will dock at Sandwich then march north through London, where he will pick up more men. His suggestion was to rendezvous at Warwick where Hal and I could march our armies to join him and take our combined grievances to the king at Kenilworth but I have warned him that the queen has put her Cheshire recruits under the command of Lord Audley, who is a shrewd general and would be in a good position to cut any of us off from the others. Somerset has also been gathering a sizeable force to bring up from the West Country and could do the same but if Warwick and Salisbury both bring their forces safely here to Ludlow we have a good chance of confronting the Lancastrians man for man. In those circumstances I believe we can negotiate and avoid a battle.'

I had managed to swallow my bread with the help of the ale but his last words made my heart sink. How many times had I heard that strategy from him? And it had never worked. 'Have you told Edward all this?' I asked. 'Does he even know you have mobilized Salisbury and Warwick?'

Richard stopped moving objects around and gave me a puzzled look. 'No. Why would I tell him?'

I stared back in astonishment. 'Because if anything happens to you, he will be Duke of York and command your forces. He has a right to know your mind.'

'Edward is still only a squire.'

'He is far from being "only a squire", Richard! He is the Earl of March and your heir. He is regarded by the people of his manors as their lord and he should be treated like the man he is. He is a squire only because you refuse to make him a knight.'

Richard gave an impatient shake of the head. 'It is too early to include him in our secret strategies. You know as well as I do that youths of his age are prone to uncontrolled urges.'

'So you do not trust your own son?' I heard my voice squeak with indignation. 'Do you really think that if your secret strategies, as you call them, lead to you being arraigned for treason, that Edward would not be considered a traitor as well?'

'I was not held responsible for my father's treason.'

'You were four years old when your father was executed,

Richard! Edward is seventeen! If you expect him to risk his neck for you, you have to trust him – and you have to knight him.'

'You go too far, Cicely!' he stormed. 'You have always favoured Edward too highly, considering he can do no wrong. It does not sit well with a mother to value one of her children above the others.'

Then, in Richard's eyes, I added insult to injury. 'I do not favour him any more than others do,' I said, trying to keep my tone even. 'Both Sir Richard Croft and your blue-eyed boy Dick of Warwick think that if Edward is to support you in battle then he should be knighted, which means he should be trusted. He is more than worthy.'

'By all the saints, will you hold your tongue, my lady?' Richard's volatile temper flared further and he banged the table, overturning cups and spilling ale. 'I will not be told what I should and should not do by my wife, any more than I will suffer under the illegal rule of a French harlot queen. Go back to your prayers and your embroidery and I will get on with ridding England of a powerless king and his adulterous shrew of a wife.'

My own temper was roused now and I pushed back my chair furiously and stood up. 'You should do some serious praying yourself, my lord, before you find yourself kneeling at the block! I am sorry if I have offended you.' My curtsy was as meagre and insincere as my apology. 'I will take up my sewing as you bid me but only to embroider a jupon for my son to wear at his knighting.'

'Do not dare to speak of this to Edward, Madam!' Richard called after my departing back. If I ever closed a door behind me I would have slammed it but I left it to the duty chamberlain who shut it quietly, poker-faced.

I had no intention of obeying this last order but wondered how I might manage some private conversation with Edward. Not only did he train long and hard with the other young henchmen but he also took great interest in the manors and castles along the Welsh border which formed a substantial part of his earldom of March, riding out to them frequently to preside at moot courts and inspect the financial rolls prepared by his comptroller. As a result he was well known in the area and it was noticeable that the revenues from his manors, after a serious dip a few years ago, were improving rapidly, more so than those of his father. Directly after our row Richard left Ludlow for Hereford so I made a point of accosting Edward after mass and ascertaining his plans for the day.

He was heading for Wigmore Castle, the Mortimer stronghold which was the focal point of his Welsh border fief and the fifteen mile ride there and back would give me some much-needed exercize. I asked Cuthbert if he would arrange an escort and suggested that he and Hilda might accompany me. They had recently arrived back from Coverdale, having visited their manor to commission some extensive building work there. I knew they could be relied on to keep a discreet distance from Edward and me on the way out and provide pleasant company for the ride home.

Once away from Ludlow I managed to extract Edward from among his boisterous companions and take him out of earshot of the rest of the cavalcade. Just the sight of my son on horse-back gave me a warm maternal glow. Prudently, in view of the constant threat of ambush, he was wearing half armour over a chainmail hauberk but his helmet was slung from a saddle hook and his head was bare, the morning sun shining off his bright hair. With his long body, even longer legs, he sat his warhorse in the timeless, easy fashion of the warrior class, straight-backed and taut-flanked, with one hand on his reins and the other resting on his hip. He rode at the jog, his supple frame moving with the pace of his steed, head high, expression alert, lips lightly parted over perfect white teeth in the sheer, insouciant pleasure of being alive.

'You look happy, Edward,' I remarked, relaxing into the loping stride my own palfrey took to keep up with his courser. 'Do I take that to mean you are content with your lot?'

'Content, my lady mother?' His brow creased in surprise. 'How can anyone be content with England in its present state? But I am confident that it will soon be resolved, one way or the other. York will either be trounced or triumphant and for a man of action that is an enticing prospect.'

'But you do not know your father's plans so how can you be so sanguine?'

Edward threw back his head and laughed. 'Of course I know my father's plans. He may think to keep me ignorant but I have my own information network and my own couriers who bring me letters. Why do you think I go so often to Wigmore Castle? My cousin Warwick writes to me there two or three times a week and all my retainers report to me regularly.'

'All your retainers?' I echoed, astonished. 'Who are they?'

'The lands around us are full of fighting men, my lady mother, and they all count themselves Mortimer supporters. The Earls of March have held their loyalty for centuries. I have had plenty of time. It has not been difficult to refresh their allegiance.'

My astonishment grew. 'Plenty of time? You only turned seventeen in April, Edward. You are hardly an experienced liege-lord.'

'I have been riding these hills and valleys since I was eight.

I know them like the psalms in my psalter and their people know me like they know their field-strips. Boys become men at fourteen in these parts and to them I was no different.'

I reacted to this with a pious sniff. 'I hope you have not been littering the villages with your by-blows,' I said primly. I knew I sounded like an ancient aunt but I could not bear the thought of him wasting his beauty on slatternly goose girls.

Edward gave a whoop of delight. 'There speaks the Rose of Raby – the one my Uncle Hal calls Proud Cis!'

I started to protest but was dazzled by his cheeky smile and twinkling grey eyes and experienced a sharp recall of myself at seventeen, overwhelmed by passion at Aycliffe Tower. My pride dissolved and laughter jerked into life in my belly, gradually spluttering up through my chest and out through my throat in a burst of mirth to match his. I could not remember the last time I had enjoyed myself so much.

'Oh Edward, you are incorrigible! So like my father. He could always conjure me out of the grumps.'

'That must be where my cousin Dick gets it from then. He is an ice-breaker. He can turn sour milk sweet in an instant. I swear men follow him just for the joy of his quips.'

'He does not have your charm though, Edward.' The few times I had been in Dick of Warwick's company had not made me one of his admirers. I thought him clever and charismatic but could find no kindness in him.

'Charm is for kings, not generals. Dick is the man I want beside me on the battlefield.' Edward reined in his horse to a walk. His tone had grown suddenly serious.

'*You* want on the battlefield,' I echoed, slowing my palfrey's trot. 'I do not see your father putting you in a position of command.'

'No, that is why I have chosen the Earl of Warwick to sponsor my knighthood. He is going to dub me as soon as he gets here. He understands, if my father does not, that I must be knighted if I am to take my rightful place at the forefront of any conflict with the Lancastrians.'

This conversation had taken an unexpected turn. It was suddenly apparent that both Richard and I had underestimated the maturity of our eldest son. He was not the uncontrolled youth Richard considered him to be, nor the swashbuckling young rake I admit I had briefly suspected him of being. Perhaps Richard had been misled by his experience with Harry of Exeter into believing all youths to be wild and undisciplined and I had indulged my own fancy that Edward was the reincarnation of my dashingly charismatic but undeniably selfish father, when he was actually shrewder and more tactical than either of us had realized.

I remained silent and reflective for a minute, carefully analysing my thoughts before responding to his remarkable announcement. 'Well, you do not need me to tell you, Edward, that your lord father will not approve of that arrangement, or to remind you that you are still under age and therefore subject to his command,' I said. 'Besides which you must know that he will be hurt and angered by what he will consider unforgivable disloyalty.'

Edward hung his head, though I was to discover that it was not in shame but in cogitation. It was his turn to pause our conversation and when he spoke again it was with intense gravity. 'My father must know that I hold him in the highest esteem but while he commands the present, I am the future of York. Just because the law deems me a minor does not mean I should play a minor role in our confrontation with Lancaster. Warwick understands this, and also the position we have reached. He thinks his uncle, my father, has not thought his strategy through to its logical conclusion. It is no longer possible to hold the king's advisers to blame for the parlous state of England because the king now listens only to the queen. Therefore any confrontation with Lancaster is now a direct challenge on the king. To put it bluntly, it is treason. There is no dressing it in flowery language, claiming loyalty to the king whilst accusing his advisers. Warwick sees it clearly. If the Duke of York takes up arms against Lancaster, he takes up arms against the king. If he is defeated and lives, he loses his head. If he wins, he takes the throne. There is no alternative.'

By now Edward's horse had halted, almost as if he understood the serious nature of his master's words and my palfrey followed suit. I could hardly believe that the man before me was my son, the baby I had borne less than eighteen years before, the baby son I never believed I would have. Now he was telling me that his father was leading us all into a confrontation which would mean life and a crown, or death and damnation. And the worst of it was I could see that he was right.

I took a deep breath and looked around me. We were in a lush green basin surrounded by gently sloping hills. Ahead rose the grey stone cliffs of Wigmore Castle, hazy in the distance, while a row of alders marked the course of a narrow stream where it flowed down towards Ludlow. Behind us Cuthbert brought the cavalcade to a halt in a jangle of harness. It did not seem possible that in a matter of weeks this oasis of peace might be trampled by thousands of marching feet.

Edward leaned across the gap between our horses and took my hand from the reins. 'Do not look so distressed, my lady mother. The path of life leads to a number of crossroads. Only

God knows which one will mark the end. One thing is sure though; if you do become queen you will be a wise and beautiful queen and we shall all kneel at your feet.'

Then he smiled and kissed my hand and we rode on to Wigmore.

36

Coverdale, Yorkshire & Blore Heath, Shropshire, June to September 1459

Cuthbert

In June Hilda and I returned once more to Coverdale. The masons had worked hard since our last visit and when we rode up the valley towards Coverham Abbey a fine sight greeted us at the edge of the Red Gill. Built of glittering newly cut limestone, an octagonal tower now rose at the south end of the old bastle, three stories high with glazed and shuttered windows and a pointed roof laid with stone tiles sturdy enough to withstand the fiercest winds the winter storms could hurl down the dale. I had not applied for permission to crenellate because it would have taken too long for the creaking wheels of government to grant it so although there was a parapet, from which missiles could be thrown in the event of an attack, it was not divided into merlons to make a battlement. Nevertheless the attic and upper floors of the tower would provide secure and comfortable accommodation for me and my family, leaving the ground floor cellars for storage and the old long chamber above the bastle byre for the use of my nephew Sam and his family, whom I now employed as my farm statesman or reeve. The ladder at the old main entrance had been replaced with a stone stair built against the wall and the door was now protected by an iron yett hung on a portcullis mechanism. An exterior stair-tower gave access to the new building, rising to a turret at roof-level for use as a watch-point. Its entrance was also protected by an iron yett. As I gazed proudly at what had once been a simple farm building, I decided it would not be pretentious to rename our new house a castle – Red Gill Castle.

To my everlasting joy a little sister had joined Aiden to complete our family. Dark-featured and bonny like her mother, she had been baptised Marie in gratitude to the Blessed Virgin and on our journey, despite her five-year-old protests that she was big enough to control her own mount, she rode behind me on a pillion seat. Aiden, now a lad of eight who showed unmistakable evidence of his Neville blood, being fair haired, long-boned and grey-eyed, sat easily on his sturdy fell pony for the long ride from Ludlow. In line with my new status as a landed knight, I had also acquired a burly squire called Joe Scrope, the teenage son of a Middleham horse-breeder, who was returning with us for extra protection on the road and to visit his family.

We arrived near sunset but the long summer twilight gave us time to inspect our new quarters, eat a meal and send Joe off on the three-mile ride to his home. When the two children were sleeping soundly in their new attic chamber, Hilda and I climbed up to the watch tower to view night fall over the dale. Directly below us the lichen-dappled walls of sheep folds made an irregular chequer-board pattern across the floor of the valley, while from our elevated position we could just make out the dark towers of Middleham castle dominating the rising ground on the far bank of the River Cover. The sky was inky blue, scattered with stars as bright as crystals winking in their celestial patterns. Other than the eternal sound of rushing water and the occasional bleat of a ewe calling to its lamb up on the fell pastures, the silence was all-enveloping, as if time had halted its inevitable progress.

'It seems so peaceful up here,' Hilda remarked. 'It is hard to believe there will soon be war in the land.'

I was standing behind her, gently kneading her shoulders, guessing they would be stiff from the long ride north. 'I fear it is inevitable,' I said grimly. 'But more immediately worrying for us is the fact that the Scots could swarm down over the border at any time, knowing that the fighting men of the March are mostly away, mustering south of the Humber. Tomorrow I will ride to Middleham Castle and speak to Hal. He may have information from his scouts.'

'What shall we do it the news is bad? Can we withstand an attack?' Hilda turned an anxious face up to me.

I shook my head. 'I would not risk harm coming to the children but if we get due warning you could shelter with them in Middleham and from here Sam, Joe and I could easily see off a few reivers. It would be worse if it was an army but a mass of men would be more likely to cross over on the eastern march where the passes are easier.'

Hilda shivered and I knew it was not from cold. 'Perhaps it would have been better to stay at Ludlow,' she murmured, rubbing warmth into her upper arms with her hands. 'But nowhere is really safe, is it?'

I did not respond immediately. She was right; the whole country was under the threat of violence, from French raiders on the Channel coast, from rebels in Wales, unrest in the West Country, riots in London and from the mobilised affinities of Lancaster and York tramping through the Midlands.

'At least we have built ourselves a future here, if the Almighty permits,' I said at length.

'Does that mean you will stay?' asked Hilda hopefully. 'You are nearly fifty years old, Cuthbert. Surely you cannot serve Cicely forever. You deserve to make a life for yourself now and watch your children grow.'

She had left off her coif and I bent to kiss her throat, where the delicate shoulder bone formed a hollow beneath her chin. 'A knight's vow lasts for a lifetime, sweetheart. Until I cannot set one foot before the other, I am bound to offer my service to my sister, to honour the vow I made to her father.'

'But are you honour-bound to die in her service if you have a wife and children who love you? We were not party to that vow.'

'Who says I am going to die in Cicely's service?' I asked, affecting indignation at the thought. 'I have no intention of doing so.'

'Lancaster and York will do battle, you know they will, and you will be in the thick of it. What man-at-arms dares boast that he will die in his bed?'

'A knight who is champion of the Northern March, that is who dares. Why do you doubt me?'

'I do not doubt you against the bare-legged Scots but the battle between York and Lancaster will involve many armoured knights like yourself. It will be bloody and brutal and you cannot choose your opponent. How does a knight of fifty fare against one half his age?'

'He uses his cunning and experience that is how. Have no fear, beautiful Hilda, I will come back here to you and my children.'

'So you will leave us here at and go back to Ludlow alone?' Her voice rose in alarm.

I put my arms around her and pulled her into my embrace. 'I cannot take you. Supposing there is a battle at Ludlow and York loses? The castle and the town will be overrun. I cannot bear to think what would happen then to you and the children. Here my family will protect you. When a soldier flees a battlefield it is better to be a lone wolf; easier to hide, easier to ride, easier to find the way home without hindrance.'

She was silent for several minutes, her forehead resting on my shoulder. I feared for a moment that she might break into sobs but instead she lifted her chin and gazed into my eyes, challenging me. 'You had better be right, Cuthbert of Middleham! Just remember when you are gone that if I hear news of a battle I will come up here every evening and look for you riding up the track, so do not let me down by coming back dead.'

I spent three glorious months with Hilda and the children, working through hay-making, sheep-shearing and harvesting; our wool fetched a good price through the monks' agents at Coverham Abbey and it looked as if there would be plenty of grain and fodder to see the winter through. Having been whisked off to military training at Raby by my father at the age of ten I had never been a farmer but my mother's blood must have flowed more freely during that time at Red Gill Castle because the tasks of field and byre seemed to come naturally and the sunlit sight of Hilda in a straw hat binding hay stooks with her skirts kilted up was enough to make me wish I might never leave Coverdale again.

Then at the beginning of September news came to Middleham that Warwick was starting embarkation at Calais. The Earl of Salisbury sent out his captains to round up their recruits from the dales and villages and bring them to Middleham. We would march on the feast of St Ninian, the sixteenth of September. I had recruited twenty young men from Coverdale to form a troop and we had trained once a week at Red Gill, a process which had fascinated young Aiden, who was soon wielding a wooden sword and mimicking the thrusts and feints I taught my novice swordsmen. Some of them were already good archers, having practiced regularly at the butts in Middleham provided by Hal against the time when bowmen would be needed but I feared for their lives when I first saw their ineptitude with a blade. Skill with a scythe did not transfer easily to a straight weapon. After two months under my instruction, however, I felt there was a reasonable hope of sending most of them back alive from any battle they might face.

I would not let Hilda bring the children to Middleham to watch Salisbury's army march away because I preferred to say goodbye to them in the privacy of our own home. I remembered Hilda's words to me on our first night in the tower and I wanted to hold in my mind the picture of them waving from the roof so that I could set myself the target of seeing it again. There were no tears, at least not while I was looking, and for that I was grateful, making it possible to contain my own.

The weather was set fine so we took the high route from Middleham, marching up Wensleydale then turning south, tramping through Widdale over the wild moors and fell passes before heading down the spine of England, always keeping to the hill country where population was sparse and we could avoid lands held by Lancastrian overlords. With Hal marched his two younger sons, Sir Thomas and Sir John Neville; when we finally met up with Dick of Warwick my brother would have all his sons committed to the York cause save George, who as bishop of Exeter did not carry arms. It was a heavy investment for a prudent man and he carried the worry of it in his hooded eyes. Hal was ten years older than me, entering the twilight years of a man's life, should he be lucky enough to stay alive.

We travelled at the pace of the infantry so it was a week before we approached the Midlands and had to reckon on the real likelihood of encountering Lancastrian forces. That was when I came to appreciate why Hal bore his nickname. In knightly circles Prudence may have originated as a pejorative term but if it referred to his talent for meticulous preparation and foresight then I was happy to see it amply demonstrated at this stage. The out-spread wings of the Salisbury green eagle standard seemed to overshadow every inch of the road ahead; harbingers sought out safe overnight camping grounds, quarter-masters nosed out supplies from sympathetic sources and scouts scoured our surroundings for signs of the enemy. If we were to encounter any Lancastrian army before we got to Ludlow, at least it was unlikely to take us by surprise.

The last stage of our march presented an especial risk. We either had to take a dangerously exposed route along the high ground that lay between the queen's castle at Tutbury and the Duke of Buckingham's seat at Stafford or skirt around Buckingham's territory to the north. We opted for the latter, hoping to hear news that Lord Stanley, the powerful northern baron who had recently married Hal's daughter Eleanor, would be somewhere in the vicinity with reinforcements. However, as we headed for Market Drayton we learned that, having failed to confront Warwick further south, the queen had turned about and brought her main army north to Eccleshall Castle, sending a large pincer-force west to cut us off from our aim of crossing the River Severn at Shrewsbury.

I was riding beside my brother when this message reached us. 'Unless we turn back, which I refuse to do, we cannot avoid them,' Hal said bitterly. 'What is more I cannot be sure that Stanley will bring his force to join us if he finds out there is a royal army in the vicinity. The best we can hope for is to find a good defensive position and let them come to us.'

However we did not even have that choice. As we traversed some common heathland only a few miles before crossing the Staffordshire border into relatively friendly Shropshire, we sighted a forest of red-rose pennons protruding over a high hedge towards the bottom of a gorse-studded slope to our left. At the forefront was the red and gold bee-strewn battle banner of Lord Audley, one of Lancaster's prominent local barons.

'The queen's strategy is good,' remarked Hal with grudging admiration. 'She has sent a local ally to see us off. Men will fight fiercely to defend their own territory.' He scanned the area swiftly. 'But I do not think Audley has chosen the right place to take his stand.'

Salisbury's first move was to delay developments by sending his herald, Vert Eagle, to meet the Lancastrians and ask for free passage. He knew full well it would not be granted but it gave us time to survey the ground which was soon to be a battlefield. Critically, between us and them flowed a stream with steep banks, creating a barrier that would hinder an attack from either side. However we had the wind behind us, giving our archers a slight advantage. Hal directed them to our left, giving them some shelter behind a hill and had two stakes hammered into the ground on its summit to show them where to concentrate their fire. On the right he ordered the supply wagons to be drawn up together and mounted our few cannon on them to form a barrage against attack from that side.

'It looks as if there are considerably more of them than us so we should really attack first but that stream will take all the impetus out of any cavalry charge,' he fretted. 'It is a death-trap – too wide to jump, too steep to scramble.'

'We need to make them attack us,' I suggested. 'Perhaps when Vert Eagle returns with their refusal to let us past we should pretend to retreat. That might draw them into a charge and the stream will delay and confuse them, giving us time to re-group and the archers a chance to pick them off as they cross. At least it might even up the odds.'

A rare smile lit Hal's habitually glum face. 'That is it, Cuthbert! Good man.' He turned to his two younger sons who stood at his other side. 'Tom, John, spread the word around the captains – one trumpet blast to retreat, two to turn and re-form. Go!'

When Vert Eagle cantered his horse back to our front line his flag of parley was at half-mast, indicating failure. Hal explained our strategy and a minute or two later the herald raised his trumpet to his lips and gave it one loud blast. As it became evident that our forces were turning and starting to retreat, a loud cheer could be heard from the Lancastrians and almost immediately their cavalry began to form up for a charge. Within moments they were galloping towards the perilous ditch and our archers began to fire rapidly into the target zone, felling horses and sending them crashing into the brook, which started to run with blood.

Meanwhile the herald's trumpet had sounded twice and the Salisbury infantry turned. When a second Lancastrian cavalry charge began our archers let fly once more from behind their hill and shot a number of their horses from under them before they even reached the stream, leaving the unhorsed knights to fight their way down and up the steep banks in their heavy armour. A number of them did not make it to the other side, knocked over by the fast current and dragged helplessly under the water.

On a signal from Hal his archers stopped firing and our infantry descended in a screaming horde on those Lancastrians who had successfully negotiated the stream. Holding their ground on the slope our men then fought a long and fierce battle with an enemy weakened by their struggle over the ditch and losing their footing on sloping ground in boots that were slick with blood and mud.

It was at this point that the Lancastrian commander Lord Audley led a fresh mounted assault, having somehow found a way to cross the brook on horseback. His red and gold standard flying above the mêlée immediately became the focus of some fierce but foolhardy fighting, particularly on the part of Hal's household knights, led by his youngest son Sir John and his squire Roger Kynaston, a local lad whose father was seneschal of Ellesmere Castle less than twenty miles away. I had heard on the road that there was bad blood between the Kynastons and Lord Audley and the hostility during the clash that ensued certainly reflected that. Audley and his entourage seriously outnumbered our knights and it was not long before young John was violently knocked from his horse by assaults from both sides. I looked round for Hal, certain that he would want to go to the aid of his son, but he was fully committed on the right flank pushing back another fresh advance across the ditch. I myself was too far away and on foot, fully stretched repulsing a breakaway troop of Lancastrian infantry who were intent on wiping out my Coverdale archers.

Observing what was happening elsewhere on the battlefield became impossible as brutal hand to hand fighting was going on all about me on ground that was swiftly becoming cluttered with bodies. Guts spilled gruesomely at my feet as I wrenched my sword from the belly of one pop-eyed axe-wielding attacker and plunged it straight into the throat of another but I suddenly saw out of the corner of my eye the Audley standard disappear down into the mêlée around their commander and heard a great shout go up from the Salisbury knights surrounding him.

The red-rose foot-soldiers in my vicinity noticed it too and began to yell at each other that their leader was down. A cry went up 'Retreat! Retreat!' and was passed from man to man across the heaving press. All at once I was fighting air as the Lancastrians around me turned slipping and sliding back towards the dreaded ditch, falling over each other in their haste to be first there. Fired with new energy, I was immediately engaged in pursuit and did not see the victorious young Squire Kynaston pulling his injured knight over his pommel and racing away up the hill with the captured standard streaming behind him, but I was later told the story many times of his brave slaying of Lord Audley as he stood over Hal's wounded son about to administer a deadly thrust. Kynaston had probably achieved a battlefield revenge for some incident in his family feud but, more crucially for the Yorkist cause, he had also turned the tide in a savage and bloody contest and opened the way for Hal to move the rest of his army on to Ludlow.

When reason overruled instinct, I unobtrusively extracted myself from the pursuit of the fleeing Lancastrians, having little taste for the uncontrolled blood-letting which often followed such a retreat. There were plenty of young men full of anger and blood-lust to relish such a task and I was more anxious to rally my own troop, count the casualties and find out what had happened to Hal and his two sons.

Unable to avoid trampling the bodies of men and horses, I clambered back over the ditch to find surgeons and servants already picking their way across the reeking slope seeking survivors among the hundreds of bodies strewn there and I joined them, searching for those wearing the white rose badge. Sadly there were too many to count but I did find two of my own men wounded beyond walking and marked their positions in order to send some of their companions to bring them in for treatment. There were several walking wounded among the Coverdale men who limped back to our rallying point but happily no deaths were reported and eventually I counted in a full contingent.

At this point I felt free to seek out my brother and found him under his green-eagle standard with his son Tom, receiving news of John's wounds. 'His squire Roger truly is the hero of the hour,' Tom was saying. 'He saved John from Audley's *coup de grâce*! Evil though it may be to speak ill of the dead, that man was no honourable knight. He should have taken John's offered submission but instead he laughed in his face and raised his dagger to strike. Roger was fully justified in cutting him down from behind and claiming his battle standard.'

'And it would seem that his action sealed the outcome in our favour,' Hal remarked, but he looked relieved and anxious at the same time, his drawn expression testament to an awareness that although the battle was won the war had barely started. 'How serious are John's injuries?'

Tom shrugged. 'With good treatment he will live and should be able to ride far enough to get it, at least at a walk. Roger says we can go to Ellesmere castle so we will make for there now and I will catch up with you at Ludlow in due course. Perhaps for the time being you can add my men to your command, Cuthbert?'

I readily agreed to this and Tom left to carry out his mercy mission. Higher up the hill the trumpet sounded a rallying signal which reverberated across the heath, calling the Yorkist pursuers to return to their ranks. Hal was anxious to set what remained of his force back on the road south, knowing that the rest of the Lancastrian army was only a matter of miles away and would soon be hot on our trail.

'We will find a priest and some men in Market Drayton to come and bury our dead,' he said wearily. 'Regrettably there could be as many as a thousand but we cannot stay to attend to them. I dare say that tomorrow the queen will organize disposal of the Lancastrian dead, which may be twice that number. I am told this place is called Blore Heath but looking at it now it more resembles a bloody heath. May God have mercy on their souls! I will have masses said for them when this mess is over.'

Unhappily, as we crossed the River Severn at Shrewsbury, a town friendly to York, news reached Hal that Tom and John and Roger Kynaston had failed to reach safety at Ellesmere, having been apprehended en route by Lancastrian sympathizers and taken as prisoners to the royal castle at Chester. Hal had won his battle but at a price and he greatly feared for the lives of the sons he had led into mortal danger.

'We fight for the rule of law but in its absence the vengeful queen could have them arbitrarily executed as traitors and there is nothing I can do to help them. Now that blood has been shed there is no telling where this war will go and who it will take with it.'

37

Ludlow Castle, October 12th 1459

Cicely

'NO! As God is my witness, I have not brought my men all the way from Calais in order to kneel before the king and beg for mercy!'

Dick of Warwick made the candle flames waver with the force of his angry gesticulations. Edward stood at his shoulder nodding vigorous agreement. It was youth versus maturity in the great chamber at Ludlow Castle, where all the windows were closed and shuttered and the doors locked and guarded against eavesdroppers. Dick and Edward stood in the middle of the room, confronting their fathers in a united front having abandoned their seats to emphasise their opposition, while Richard and Hal sat close together tense and red-faced, both clearly containing their anger with difficulty. Behind them stood sixteen-year-old Edmund, looking solemn and bewildered and two other men, Lord John Clinton, Richard's ever-loyal baron-tenant from Lincolnshire, and Sir Richard Grey, Lord Powys, whose mother had been a childhood friend of Richard's and the illegitimate daughter of Humphrey, Duke of Gloucester, the king's late uncle. These two faithful barons were the only noble military allies left in the Yorkist ranks. There had been no sign of Lord Stanley's promised two thousand men and to my great distress, Lord Neville, the man who had declared eternal love for me and pledged armed support for York, sent word that his men refused to take the field against the king's person.

I felt heart-sore and betrayed but kept a stony face, sitting a little apart with Cuthbert beside me. I missed Hilda, my only confidante, but took comfort in knowing Coverdale was the best place for her and the children. Although my sympathies on this occasion were with the younger generation, I also felt sorry for Richard. The ambush at Blore Heath had scuppered his best intentions. No longer could he even attempt to confront the king with what he saw as the country's grievances. The queen had cunningly sent the ambush army to Blore Heath in the name of the five-year-old Prince of Wales; and so when Hal's men had defeated it and killed its commander they had effectively spilled royal blood. The executioner's axe now hung over all the men in the room.

Over the past few weeks, matters for Richard had gone from bad to worse. Hurt though he had been by it, Edward's declaration that he wished the Earl of Warwick to be his sponsor for knighthood now seemed a mere blip compared to the failure one by one of all his strategies for a peaceful conclusion to the York/Lancaster confrontation. A public oath of obedience and loyalty to the king, made in Worcester cathedral, had been completely ignored. Then a follow-up letter which stressed his desire to avoid 'the effusion of blood' received the terse reply that King Henry would 'meet his enemies in the field'. Richard had ignored this because it did not bear the royal signature but an apparently genuine message from the king via his Windsor herald, offering a free pardon to anyone who would return to their royal allegiance within six days, made a pointed exception of the Earl of Salisbury and was therefore utterly impossible for Richard to accept.

For one wavering Yorkist supporter, however, this offer of a pardon had proved impossible to resist. Our forces had dug defences and gun emplacements in fields at Ludford Bridge on the banks of the River Teme less than a mile outside Ludlow, where they faced the royal army across only a few hundred yards of scrubland. In the small hours of the previous night Sir Andrew Trollope, a veteran commander of the French wars and a senior member of Warwick's Calais contingent, had crept across those vital yards of open land with all his men and taken with him knowledge of all York plans and strategies.

This had been the last straw for Richard and he had called his commanders away from the field for this crucial summit meeting. His proposal now was that once arrangements were made for Hal to flee to Ireland, they should all take up the king's offer and accept his pardon on their knees, eliciting Dick's instant and indignant rejection.

Although he remained seated, Richard's response was equally robust. 'Half of those men you brought from Calais followed the traitorous Trollope over to the other side, my lord of Warwick. They are probably on their knees right now, spilling our secrets. And can you have forgotten that, in addition to your father's perilous situation, your two brothers are locked up in Chester Castle, in imminent danger of being arraigned for treason? Would you be responsible for putting their heads on the block?'

Warwick stepped nearer Richard's chair to reinforce his fierce riposte. 'It would not be me who was responsible for that, my lord uncle, it would be the queen. But she knows full well that any such action would destroy the king's cause, therefore she will not do it and that is precisely why we should not give in to her spurious demands for abasement. For we all know, do we not, that the queen leads the king like an ass in a halter? And she is in no way to be trusted. Therefore no offer or promise that comes to us in the king's name is to be trusted.' He turned to his father. 'She laid a trap for you at Blore Heath, my lord, and you called her bluff then. Now we must do it again. Our only option is to fight.'

Hal frowned and rubbed his forehead distractedly. 'I would like to agree with you, Dick, but militarily we are at even more of a disadvantage here than I was at Blore Heath. Thanks to Trollope's betrayal, not only is the royal army twice the size of ours but it is better situated in open country, whereas we would be fighting with our backs to the River Teme. Name me a soldier who wants to die by drowning? If he did he would have been a sailor. In addition it is not only Stanley's and Neville's men who are wary of taking arms against the king's person. When we order an attack, our own forces may also refuse.'

Thus far I had made no contribution to the debate but since there was one important factor they all seemed to have ignored I felt bound to interject. 'If you intend to sue for peace, my lords, what do you expect to be the result? Will you not be placing your lives and those of your families and supporters at the mercy of the one person you know to be most vindictive and vengeful against York – namely the queen? I suspect you may find that the words "free pardon" apply to your bodies but not to your lands and your revenues. With one bend of the knee you will hand them all to the crown – a crown that is worn by the king but controlled by the queen, who is desperate for funds.'

It was Richard's cue to turn all his anger and frustration onto me. 'Saints' bones, my lady, do you not imagine that the spectre of attainder preys constantly on all our minds? But since we have been driven into this corner by the arbitrary and irrational actions of one woman do you think it helps us to be nagged and criticized by another?'

Given the stress my husband had been under for months, his bitter vehemence did not surprise or unduly upset me but the attack proved too much for Edward who nobly took my part, whilst also cleverly contriving to calm the atmosphere.

'I have no experience of married life but I think that is what is called a marital spat.' In his disarming way Edward grinned broadly at everyone as he said this, enjoying his own joke and his ability to do so in the face of maximum tension seemed to prick its bubble. Lips twitched involuntarily all around the room, particularly Edmund's, who put his hand hastily to his mouth to hide his mirth.

'But my lady mother is right, Dick,' Edward added more seriously, turning to address his cousin. 'Our actions and our choices affect our families as much as ourselves. Instead of insisting on a fight should we not seriously consider the other option – flight?'

There was sudden and total silence. All humour dissolved and everyone froze as if a leopard had prowled into the room.

Hal was first to break the ice. 'If I am to live, flight seems my only option but I think Edward makes a good point. Would it not be sensible for you to consider it too, Richard?'

Richard's gaze was fixed on his son, his flecked eyes gleaming in the candlelight under beetled brows. 'It is the coward's way out,' he growled. 'I am surprised to hear it suggested by a Plantagenet.'

I took a sharp breath. I had never heard Richard draw public attention to his Plantagenet heritage before; the royal line going back to the second King Henry's Angevin father. Was he beginning to think seriously of himself less as a son of York and more as a potential king of England? If so, I thought, would not the prospect of kneeling before King Henry and kissing his feet be anathema to him? I saw now that the glint in his eyes was messianic rather than morose and Edward had spotted it too because he was not displaying anger at being indirectly accused of cowardice.

Hal however took the remark another way entirely. 'Are you calling me a coward then, my lord duke, to choose a sea voyage over death by the axe?'

It was Richard's turn to smile, using my brother's family name to demonstrate his abrupt change in attitude. 'No, Hal, quite the opposite. I am seriously wondering if cowardice might be the temporary answer to all our predicaments.'

'You mean you might flee to Ireland too?' I choked on the question, unable to digest this sudden volte face.

Richard attempted reassurance. 'Not me alone, Cicely; we should all go – me, you and all our children. We can take ship from Penrhyn as usual. Word will not have reached that far of our flight from the king's forces and we will easily find transport. If we fight from the position we are in now we either die on the battlefield or on the block. If we make a run for it we can re-group and start again; us from Ireland, Dick from Calais. It is possible, even preferable.'

His whole attitude had changed; he looked and sounded more enthusiastic than I had witnessed for weeks, like a boy about to go on his first hunt. I hated to quench his fire but Edward did it anyway, albeit for different reasons.

'I agree that Ireland may be the refuge for you, my lord father, but I hope you will forgive me if I choose to go to Calais with my lord of Warwick.'

'And I think it better that I, too, accompany my son to Calais,' put in Hal quickly. 'I see your reasons for choosing Ireland, Richard, where you have revenues available from your estates but in Calais there would be more opportunity for me to further our cause.'

Richard's face clouded and, for a moment, I wondered if he was at least going to attempt to persuade Edward to change his mind but with a decisive nod he stood up. 'Very well, it seems we are all agreed on our course of action. In which case let us adjourn to make our arrangements but we need to decide on our future strategy before we leave because communication will be difficult and we cannot afford to give the men presently in the field any inkling of our intentions or they will begin to slip away themselves and that will alert the Lancastrians. I suggest we reassemble here for mass and a last meal after dark. A night departure is essential if we are to make an undetected get-away.'

I tried to catch his attention but he strode swiftly from the room with the other lords in his wake and pride prevented me from running after him. He would have to wait until his foot was almost in the stirrup before he discovered what it was I wanted to tell him. Meanwhile I had my own arrangements to make and I set off for my solar where I knew I would find Margaret. Now thirteen, under normal circumstances arrangements for her marriage would at least have been under consideration but all our attention was concentrated elsewhere, a situation which seemed to suit Margaret admirably. Always of a studious bent, she had been happily sharing Edmund's academic studies and following my direction in learning household affairs. As a result we had been spending much time together and I found her an amusing and agreeable companion.

Before I reached the stair to my chamber on the floor above

however I was stopped by Edmund, who laid a determined hand on my arm.

'May I speak with you privately, my lady mother?' he asked a little apprehensively.

I nodded, guessing what was on his mind. 'Come with me to my chamber, Edmund. We can talk there.'

Next to the solar, where Margaret and my ladies would be engaged in their various activities, was a smaller chamber which was used as an oratory. I drew Edmund in there and closed the door.

He could hardly wait to blurt out his chief concern. 'I wish to go with Edward.'

I took a seat in the window embrasure where I had received the oaths of Cuthbert and Hilda and gestured my son to another. 'Sit down, Edmund. I think your father has it in mind for you to accompany him to Ireland. After all it is his intention that the Ulster lands should be passed over to you on your majority. It is time you learned your way around them. They may provide all the revenue we have for the time being.'

His face crumpled in distress. 'But Edward and I have always been together,' he said. 'Why is he to go with Dick and Uncle Hal?'

I decided there was nothing for it but to take him into my confidence. He was sixteen. At the same age King, Henry had been considered old enough to assume his regal responsibilities.

I leaned forward and took his hands in mine, holding his gaze with what I hoped he would recognize as maternal pride. 'It is not so much why Edward is going with them but why you are going with your father. I will let you into a secret, my son. Your father does not know it yet but I will not be going to Ireland. As you know Ursula is not well and Richard still has

431

a delicate constitution. I cannot contemplate taking them on a hazardous flight across Wales and a rough sea journey to Dublin. I do not think Ursula would survive it, your brother George is too young to assume a squire's role and Margaret will stay with me of course; which leaves you alone to be squire and companion to your father. He needs you, Edmund. You are his flesh and blood. You can attend to his needs and learn from his wisdom. It is your chance to have his attention and render him service, away from Edward. And it is Edward's opportunity to make his own way in another household. Does that answer your question?'

Edmund looked at me quizzically. 'You make it sound as if I would be doing my father a favour by going with him.'

I smiled and shook my head. 'That is not just how it sounds, Edmund. That is how it is. He will need you now as he has never done before and if you use this opportunity well you will become more important to your father than any of us.'

I loved him for his next query. He was to be the only one to make any reference to it throughout the rest of the day and the night that lay ahead, before the storm broke.

'But what about you, Mother? If you stay here there will be no one to protect you. What if the Lancastrians ransack the castle?'

Edmund had suggested something that was more than just a possibility. Although the king considered himself a man of peace and reconciliation, he was a weak commander and when they learned that York, Salisbury and Warwick had absconded, the queen and her Lancastrian favourites would be furious and unlikely to make any effort to control their army. It would be open season in Ludlow to the thuggish element that inhabited every military force and I doubted if the king could or would do anything to prevent pillaging, looting and worse. In truth I did not know what I would do, other than gather my children around me and pray.

However, I did not want sensitive Edmund worrying about what he was leaving behind when he would have to concentrate on looking out for himself and his father on their dangerous flight through Wales, so I made light of his fears. 'I am sure the king will not take any action against an abandoned woman and her children. He is a man of honour who will ensure our protection and so you must not worry about us but make sure that your father reaches safety before the Lancastrians catch up with him. You must understand, Edmund, that it would be his head on the block, not mine or yours.'

He stood up, his face solemn. 'I shall go and find my father now,' he said with determination. 'If I am to be with him I must know all his plans and help in his preparations.'

I rose also, feeling a surge of pride in my second son who had spent all his life in the shadow of his older brother. Perhaps if nothing else this enforced separation might be the making of him. 'Indeed you must, my son,' I said. 'But it would be a favour to me if you would not mention my intentions to him before I have had a chance to tell him myself. When he returns from Ludford Bridge I will speak to him.'

I had been choosing my words with Edmund, treading carefully, but when I spoke at last with Margaret it was a different matter. Young as she was, she was a pragmatic and practical soul and quick to grasp the critical nature of our situation. 'Do not worry about George and Dickon,' she said, immediately adopting a big-sisterly attitude. 'I will explain everything to them, although I am sure they are already aware of some sort of crisis. You concentrate on Ursula, lady mother. She will not leave her

433

bed and she complained this morning that her throat hurt. I think she has another of her fevers coming on.'

My heart sank at that. 'I will go to her now,' I assured her, 'but later I will need you to help me with something I do not wish the others to know about. I will send someone to fetch you when I have seen what can be done for Ursula.'

Anicia now hid her grey hair under her nurse's coif and she fretted over her fragile charge, the last child in the York nursery, applying cloths soaked in cold well-water to Ursula's fevered brow.

'It is the ague again, your grace,' she told me, her brow creased with worry.

I bent and pressed my lips to my daughter's brow. They were almost burned by the heat of her skin. Unfortunately Ursula had first suffered marsh fever when she was a toddler and it returned at regular intervals, sapping her strength and laying her ever lower at each visitation. Successive physicians had provided no cure and one had even predicted to Richard that he did not expect her to survive many more attacks. Anicia however had procured a variety of mixtures from apothecaries in both Ludlow and Fotheringhay which had produced hopeful results and used herbal remedies she prepared herself to cool the heat of the little girl's blood when the ague struck.

I summoned a hovering servant to take over the old nurse's task and took her aside to explain the latest developments. 'There is no knowing what will happen tomorrow, when the Lancastrians gain access to the town, Anicia, as they are bound to do,' I warned. 'If you have friends in the town with good bolts on their doors you would be well advised to take shelter with them for I fear the castle will be no refuge for any servant of York.'

The nurse stared at me, aghast. 'I could not leave the child, your grace,' she said. 'The fever is always at its worst on the second day. With your permission I will stay with you. Surely not even the Lancastrians would make war on a sick child?'

I shrugged helplessly. 'Who knows what the Lancastrians will do, Anicia. All we can be sure of is that the queen will be after Yorkist blood. Perhaps, should any Lancastrian come near us with evil intent, God will forgive us if we pretend that Ursula's malady is extremely infectious.'

38

Ludlow Castle, October 1459

Cicely

R ichard did not return to the castle from Ludford Bridge
until nearly midnight, accompanied by Hal, Dick, Edward
and Edmund and a handful of loyal household knights who
had agreed to accompany them on their separate journeys. A
fire still burned in the hearth in the great chamber where food
and wine had been laid out on trestles. The men were dispirited,
thirsty and hungry after a day spent more or less play-acting,
trying to rouse their troops to a fight they knew would not take
place and contemplating a long ride at speed through the rest
of the night. I acted as butler and kept their cups filled as Richard
vented his spleen.

'I could not believe my eyes when King Henry paraded
between the lines for the third time just before dusk,' he declared
after he had drained his cup at a gulp. 'They were using him
like an armoured puppet. I swear someone was behind him
moving his arms and legs.'

While Richard marched up and down restlessly, Hal was
conserving his energy, sitting in a carved oak chair and sipping
steadily, between bites of pigeon pie. 'His appearances may have

had something to do with you spreading a rumour that the king had died,' he remarked sardonically. 'What possessed you to do that?'

Richard paused at the table in his perambulations and selected a slice of the pie. 'The men were so disheartened. I thought it might give them cheer to think that they were not being asked to fight their anointed sovereign.' He took a bite and chewed with an aggressive jerk of his jaw.

Dick gave a derisive snort. 'Instead the sight of their sovereign beckoning to them from his army's lines made half of them throw down their arms and race to join him. If we had not already decided to leave, that was a sight which would certainly have convinced me to run.' He turned to his group of knights who were foraging eagerly among the platters. 'Yes, friends, fill your bellies. Who knows where we shall find our next meal. I have sent a message and money to Sir John Dinham in Devon to acquire us a ship but there is no knowing how long it will take or even if the courier will get through. Dinham will give us shelter though, provided we can reach his house.'

As I filled Richard's cup for the second time, I murmured in his ear, 'I must talk to you urgently and privately, my lord.'

He glared at me with knitted brows. 'Why? The horses are ready. I take it you have prepared the children for the journey. We ride after mass.'

I received the distinct impression that he regarded us as troublesome appendages. 'No. I very much fear that I cannot come with you, my lord. Ursula has a high fever and Dickon is not yet strong enough to race through Wales on horseback for a night and a day. Edmund will go with you. The rest will stay with me.'

I kept my voice firm but low so that the others might not

hear but Richard's response was loud and hoarse with strain. 'Dear God, woman, do not defy me now! It is all arranged. It is bad enough to leave my men. I cannot leave you and my children as well. I will carry Ursula on my pommel.'

I put the wine jug down on the trestle beside us and laid a hand on his arm. 'Be calm, my lord. This is not defiance. Ursula is too sick to move. The other children cannot go without their mother and I will not leave her.'

The room had gone quiet as it became obvious to everyone that there was a crisis. Richard's chest heaved as he fought to control his anger and his stress and I waited for him to succeed, as I knew he would, for the sake of appearances.

His cup slopped wine onto the floor as he put it down and considered the full implications of my announcement. 'Then I cannot go either,' he said flatly. 'In all honour I cannot leave my wife and family to the mercies of that rabble out there.' He made a vague, flapping gesture towards the window and we all knew he meant the twenty-thousand-strong Lancastrian army encamped only a mile from the castle on the other side of Ludford Bridge.

Edward had moved nearer to us and cleared his throat to speak but his father rounded on him, venting his anger and cutting him off. 'If you think to make one of your fatuous light-hearted quips Edward, kindly desist. Now is not the time for humour.'

Edward took a step backwards in surprise but rallied swiftly. 'On the contrary, my lord, I was humbly going to suggest that honour need not demand that you sacrifice yourself for poor little Ursula.' He gestured towards Hal who was frowning at him over the rim of his cup. 'Do not forget that my aunt of Salisbury will also be left behind in England. Surely honour demands that you and my father flee the injustices of the council but at the same time you also demonstrate your faith in King Henry's justice by committing your wives and families to his grace's personal care, as hostages if you like, to guarantee the loyalty of your intentions.'

Edward paused to let his words sink in and Richard and Hal both studied him briefly before turning their questing gaze upon each other. Neither spoke but it was clear they were giving serious consideration to Edward's submission.

'A letter of explanation could be given to Vert Eagle to deliver to the king's hand,' Edward went on. 'According to the chivalric code, in the hands of a herald it will not be intercepted.'

I held my breath, inwardly blessing Edward. This was the very argument I had been going to make to persuade Richard that he must go, although, shamefully, I had not thought of including Hal's wife Alice in the plea. With all her children grown and flown, she remained alone at her home at Bisham in Bedfordshire but would doubtless suffer as much as I as a result of her husband's declared treason. The idea was more palatable to Richard because it came from his son rather than his wife but still Richard sat balefully silent for some while before raising an eyebrow at Hal to signify that he should speak first.

'That was well said, Nephew,' Hal began. 'You have summed up my thoughts and prayers precisely and I hope your father will agree that what appears at first as dishonourable, is in fact the only honourable course of action.'

Receiving a nod from Richard, Hal concluded, 'Now I think it is time to hear mass, place ourselves in the hands of God and take to the road.' He consumed his last morsel of pie and gazed lovingly at the remains left on the table. 'That was an excellent pie, Cis,' he remarked, standing up and smiling at me. 'I hope someone will pack up the rest and put it in my saddlebag.'

While the men heard mass in the castle's exquisite round chapel, I gathered all the younger children except Ursula from their beds, ensured they put on warm clothes and had them ready in the inner court to make their farewells as the service ended. Young Dickon looked dazed and bewildered, bleary-eyed at being roused from a deep sleep. I doubt if he truly understood the significance of this midnight departure but he dutifully bent his knee to receive Richard's blessing then stood for the embrace of his two big brothers and waited with tears welling in his dark eyes as they followed each other down the family line. George was more demonstrative, flinging his arms around Edward in particular, as if he feared he would never see him again, while Margaret looked up at her father with a clear-eyed gaze as he placed a paternal hand on her head and asked God to be with her.

'And may He also be with you, my lord father,' she said earnestly. 'For I think you will have much need of His loving care.'

As she said this, in the dancing light of the torches I thought I saw a tear glisten in Richard's eye. Then I watched Edward make a particularly grave bow to his sister, kiss her hand respectfully and receive a whispered comment in his ear which, to my surprise, made his eyes widen in surprise. When I asked Margaret later what she had said to make him start she replied serenely, 'It was in Greek, lady mother. That is why he was surprised.' But she did not tell me what it was in Greek that she had said.

Last to bid farewell to his siblings was Edmund, who spent several minutes reassuring Dickon that he was only going to Ireland with their father for a short while and would be back in no time with a tame leprechaun for his little brother. 'What is a leprechaun?' Dickon asked, beguiled.

'I do not really know,' admitted Edmund. 'A little man in a big hat I believe but I am going to learn all about Ireland and I will make sure to find out and bring you one as a pet.'

Dickon screwed up his small face in doubt. 'I do not think I would like a little man as a pet, Edmund. I would rather have a horse.'

I stifled a smile. Although only just seven, Dickon was excessively fond of horses and had earned praise for his riding from no less a task-master than my brother Cuthbert. He yearned to graduate from a pony to what he called 'a proper horse' but his physical slightness and my reluctance to put too much strain on his underdeveloped body proscribed it.

There was a back exit through Ludlow's outer curtain wall known as Mortimer's gate, after one of Richard's more infamous ancestors who had made many hasty exits to avoid trouble and eventually died on the block. It had occurred to me lately that too many of his relatives had done so. This tower-gate provided access to a bridge over the River Corve and the routes west to Wales and south to Wigmore and the Black Mountains. More importantly the Lancastrians had not blockaded it, being fully occupied on the other side of the town on the far bank of the River Teme, into which the Corve flowed. I walked beside Richard's horse as he rode across the outer bailey towards this back gate, followed by the rest of the escapees and their followers. Every horse in the cavalcade was equipped with bulging saddle-bags for they took no sumpters due to the need for speed. It was my last chance to speak to my husband out of earshot of others.

'I do not know where I shall be, Richard. It depends what

the king decides to do with us but I shall endeavour to get word to you somehow,' I told him.

'My spies report regularly to their contacts. I am certain they will keep me informed of your whereabouts,' he replied gruffly. 'I cannot bear to think of you facing Henry's smug toadies when they enter Ludlow tomorrow, Cicely. If they harm a hair of any of your heads . . .' He did not finish because he did not know how, or even if, he would be able to revenge himself against them. Lancaster was in the ascendant, York was on its knees; there was no denying it.

'They will not dare,' I declared with a confidence I did not feel. 'We still have plenty of supporters Richard. Lancaster cannot afford to stir the York hive too much lest the bees go berserk.' I reached up and drew his hand down from its grip on the reins. 'York and Neville will rise again, you will see. Let the winter do its worst then spring will turn all in our favour.'

I saw the gleam of his teeth in the moonlight. 'You northerners have so much drive,' he remarked. 'Sometimes I think Warwick has too much.'

'You can never have too much energy, my love, and Dick will be good for Edward. Together I believe they will prove far too much for poor King Henry.'

'Well, we shall see.' We had reached the gate-tower and he swung his leg over the saddle and jumped down, sweeping me into his arms. 'We cannot part on bad terms, Cicely. I pray that we meet again in brighter and better circumstances.' He bent and kissed my lips, hard. 'God go with you and protect you, as I cannot.'

'And may His Holy Might further your cause, my dear lord,' I said fervently. 'We *will* meet again.'

'Do not doubt it.' He put his foot in the stirrup and remounted. 'I will look after Edmund,' he said.

I smiled up at him, hoping the moon lit my face. 'And let him look after you,' I said. 'He can, you know.'

He rode forward and ducked under the low arch of the gate. Hal and Dick came next and I signalled a solemn farewell to them with a bow and a hand-gesture but blew kisses to Edward and Edmund as they trotted past me. Edmund waved forlornly back, riding alongside his brother for the last time before their paths divided on the other side of the bridge but Edward's blown kisses were jubilant; even in these desperate circumstances he gave the impression of an eager young man setting off on a great new adventure without any doubts or fears. The arched vault of the gatehouse echoed with the clatter of iron-shod hooves and then they were all through. Suddenly there was silence save for the creak of saddle-leather and a series of soft, equine grunts as a dozen horses negotiated the steep earthen path which led down the wooded escarpment to the river and the bridge – and escape.

I waited a few minutes, listening anxiously for any sounds of conflict which might indicate that they had met opposition but none came. Looking up at the dark sky, studded with diamond stars, I had mixed feelings about the bright gibbous moon that stood like a gleaming misshapen lantern, high in the heavens. It would light them on their way but might also reveal them to unwelcome observers. I sent up a prayer to St Christopher to grant them safe conduct and shivered in the chill October air. As I turned to hurry back across the drawbridge to the inner court a familiar figure stepped out to meet me. It was Cuthbert; dear, faithful, worried-looking Cuthbert.

Before he could speak I greeted him warmly, taking his hand and planting a kiss on his stubbled cheek. 'I should have known you would not be far away, Cuddy. At least they went off safely – no sounds of ambush at the bridge. Now I want you to leave too. You must go back to Hilda and the children and pray that when the Lancastrians come to Middleham, which they certainly will, they do not interfere with the tenant farmers. Put on a smock, Cuddy, and revert to your mother's roots. They will stand you in much better stead than your Neville connections in these coming months.'

The moonlight shone in his eyes, reflecting their genuine anguish. 'I never thought to hear you denigrate your family name, Cis,' he said sorrowfully.

'Sadly in England's present state the Nevilles do not scintillate, on either side of the struggle. The best of them have just set off for Calais though it is far from certain whether they will get there or if they will return, it could be months, years before they do. I will pray constantly for my husband and sons of course but God knows that in my heart it is Edward on whom I pin my hopes.'

Cuthbert shook his head and the badge on his draped hat caught the moon's rays. 'He is over-young to carry such a burden,' he observed. 'But what will you do, Cis, when the Lancastrians enter the town tomorrow? I should be standing at your side through good and bad times, as your father made me promise.'

I smiled and pointed to the gleaming badge. 'No, Cuddy, you should be protecting your wife and children. I insist that you ride away from Ludlow tonight but before you do, take off that badge I beseech you! You should not even be found with it about your person. Give it to me and I will keep it safe for you. If I send it back, you will know that I have need of you. I know you will come.'

He dipped his head and I unpinned the enamelled white rose from his hat and slipped it into the purse on my belt. Later I would transfer it to the hem of my chemise into which Margaret and I had already sewn a number of gold and silver coins. I foresaw a time when a small bribe to the right person might prove extremely useful.

'Now, find your squire and your horse, Cuddy, and go back to Coverdale. And may God and all his angels guard you and your family.'

After speaking to Cuthbert, I had obeyed Richard's instructions to tell the Ludlow constable of his lord's departure and advised him to muster his men at dawn, leave the castle open and march them down to spread the word at Ludford Bridge. I had then placed all my personal jewellery and keepsakes in the strong-room and put the key in the purse I would later wear on a belt hidden under my outer clothing. I did not know whether the iron-clad door would withstand a Lancastrian onslaught but it was the best I could do.

To my surprise, when I lay down in the magnificent ducal chamber that night for what might be the last time, I actually slept, waking only as the first light of dawn broke through the unshuttered windows. Most of my ladies had wisely decided to return to their homes or if that was not possible to friends nearby, but two of them had elected to stay with me. They had slept on mattresses in the ante-room and soon arrived to help me dress in the plain brown kirtle and warm riding heuque I had decided would be unpretentious and practical garb for wherever the events of the day took me. Afterwards I went to the children's quarters and selected similarly modest attire for them, neat and plain, without fuss or ornament. I had chosen clothes suitable for riding because I could not imagine that I or the children would be allowed to remain long at Ludlow. In fact I half expected us to be taken to some royal castle as prisoner-hostages and dreaded that it might be in the custody of the queen, who I feared would be a pitiless gaoler. Revenge being best served cold, I did not expect to spend a comfortable winter. I had one single hope: that being a mother herself she would not inflict any suffering on my children.

I sent my two ladies to see if there was any hope of breakfast and they reappeared with jugs of ale, some hard cheese and day old bread, reporting the kitchen empty and the ovens cold. Clearly the Ludlow lords were not the only ones to have made a surreptitious exit from the castle overnight. We dipped the hard bread in the ale and tried to nibble a little of the cheese but Ursula would eat nothing and although Margaret tried to persuade Dickon, he simply shook his head, his huge round eyes and vivid pallor betraying his state of high anxiety. George seemed to have adopted his father's habit of pacing the floor when he was worried and barely stopped to drink a cup of ale and swallow a crust or two of bread. He only spoke to complain that he should have been allowed to go with Richard and Edmund and insisted on wearing his precious short sword, even though I told him that it would probably be taken from him, never to be seen again.

Eventually I suggested that we all go the castle chapel and pray for the safety of the absent men. Anicia picked up Ursula, wrapped in her blankets, carrying her like a baby, and followed us as we emerged through the great hall arch and down the grand stone stairway into the inner court. Alarmingly we could hear the first sinister rumbles of action coming from the direction of the town; muffled shots of small-arms fire and massed male voices raised in shouts of rage and aggression. I did not hesitate but ushered the children quickly towards the castle chapel, the one place which I hoped would remain inviolate, even if the rest of the stronghold was ransacked.

The delicately carved stone archway at the entrance to the chapel of St Mary Magdalene drew us into its reassuringly calm interior. Its unique circular nave had recently been extended into a rectangular chancel so that the building now echoed the shape of the fetterlock depicted with a falcon on the distinctive York insignia. Its interior walls were freshly decorated with colourful bible stories and hagiography, surrounding us in a circle of benediction as we passed through the nave and into the chancel where, to my surprise, candles blazed and the castle chaplain knelt at the altar in prayer.

'I knew you would come here to find sanctuary, your grace,' the priest said when he turned to greet us. 'God will sustain and protect you within the circle of His holy house.'

Then he said mass and we all prayed and waited. Ursula's fever had dropped a little overnight but she was torpid and appeared to fall asleep when Anicia sat with her on her knee in the sedilia while the rest of us knelt, huddled close together at the altar rail.

In the end neither the king nor the queen came to Ludlow Castle that day. Instead it was my brother-in-law Humphrey Duke of Buckingham who entered the chapel in full armour accompanied by his son, my nephew Sir Henry Stafford. The chaplain hurried forward to meet them at the chancel arch, begging them humbly not to enter the sanctuary bearing arms. I, too, rose and urged the children to come with me so that we met the two knights together as a group. It was then that I remembered George's small sword, which still hung in its scabbard from his belt.

'You have my assurance, Sister, that we come in peace,' said Humphrey, bowing punctiliously along with his son. He had immediately noticed the sword hanging at George's side. 'But I do not think we can lay down our arms while we confront an armed son of York.'

With his right hand on the hilt of his own sword, he held out his left hand for George's, an implacable expression on his face. I nodded in response to my son's anguished and enquiring look and George sullenly unbuckled his sword and handed it over.

'Thank you. Now I think we can agree that York has officially surrendered to Lancaster.' Humphrey stood back, indicating that I should pass in front of him. 'To avoid offence to the Almighty, let us conduct the rest of our business in the nave. I think you will find any other room in the castle uncomfortably lively. My men are justifiably angry at being cheated of a chance to avenge the death and injury inflicted by York on Lancaster at St Albans and so, although I have tried to restrict looting in the town of Ludlow, I have felt powerless to deny them enjoying some of the spoils of war in a castle so cravenly abandoned by its suzerain.'

In other words, I thought bleakly, it was a free-for-all at Ludlow Castle. Through the open door of the chapel the sound of troops rampaging was unmistakable. Smoke hung over the inner court and drifted towards us, making our eyes smart, and men wearing helmets and gambesons bearing red-rose badges could be seen running across the inner court yelling Lancastrian war cries and waving looted articles. Seeing George's red-faced fury and Margaret's attempts to comfort Dickon, who was trembling with shock, I found my voice for the first time.

'I hope you will not subject the children to the horror of seeing their home torn apart by vandals, my lord,' I said hoarsely, forcing back angry tears. 'They are innocent bystanders in the vicious feuds of their elders.'

Humphrey beckoned me aside and spoke low so that the children would not hear. 'Their lives may not be forfeit for treason as their father's and brothers' are but they are guilty by birth and association and will be held under house arrest; as will you, Cicely. When the king heard that you remained in the castle he ordered that the children be made wards of my wife, your sister Anne, and for the time being you and they will be held at Maxstoke Castle. Arrangements are being made for horses to transport you there immediately. My son Henry here will escort you.'

My immediate reaction was relief that we were not to be placed under royal control; then I frowned and gestured at Ursula, who was still in Anicia's arms, lying white-faced and apparently unconscious. 'As you see, Ursula is ill and unable to ride, even on a pillion-seat. I hope your men have not set fire to all the carts in the stables.'

He favoured me with a grim smile. 'They are more likely to have commandeered them to transport their loot from the castle. However, one will be requisitioned. Is there a key to lock the chapel?'

'The chaplain has it.' I gestured to the priest, who stood at the chancel arch wringing his hands. 'But none of us will abscond, if that is what you fear.'

Humphrey grimaced and shook his head. 'That is not my concern. I worry more that the men may not stop at slaking their thirst for revenge on your home. Once they broach the contents of your cellars, in drunken fury they may turn their mood of attrition on you.' He gestured at Margaret who sat with her arm around Dickon. 'I think your daughter's marriage prospects are now much reduced anyway but I would hate them to be ruined entirely.'

I stared at him, horror-struck. Until that moment I had not considered the possibility that Margaret, not yet even truly a woman, might be subjected to the kind of ugly and uncontrolled ravishment so often inflicted on defenceless females in time of war. I found myself stuttering with panic as I urged him to take the key from the chaplain. 'Lock us in then and leave us to our prayers, my lord duke.'

'I fear they are all you have left, Cicely,' Humphrey said and, bowing abruptly, left my side.

He and his son left the chapel and we all heard the key turn in the lock. The priest made his way back to the altar where we presently heard his voice raised in a sung mass. I walked over to the arched wall niche where Anicia had sat down with Ursula. 'She will sleep all day, your grace,' said the nurse, showing me the flask of herbal elixir she had kept hidden somewhere about her person. 'I gave her another dose. I thought it best.'

I could not help wishing that I, too, could swallow some of Anicia's potion and escape the reality of what was to come. First we had to escape the castle unmolested and although I was grateful that our gaoler was to be my sister Anne rather than the queen, I was not confident that it would be an easy sentence. The journey to Maxstoke Castle would take the best part of three days through hostile Lancastrian territory and although Henry Stafford and his men-at-arms might be able to protect us from attack or abduction, there was no guarantee that it would bother to defend us from the abuse and rotten vegetation a hostile local population might hurl. Hatred could be vicious when it was stoked by rumour and propaganda from a victorious affinity against its defeated enemy. Anne had been turned against us at St Albans and there was no telling how much she might hate us now; I was horribly conscious of the fact that the worst enemies were often relatives.

'What will happen to us, my lady mother?' asked George, who had walked up behind me, thumbs tucked defiantly in his empty sword belt. 'I am sorry that I cannot defend you now that they have taken my sword.'

'We are going to stay with your Aunt Buckingham,' I told him in as calm a voice as I could muster; one which also carried to Margaret and Dickon now that the dreadful noise from the castle was muted by the locked door. 'She will keep us safe until your father comes back to us. Now let us all return to the chancel and take comfort from the holy mass. It is all we can do until it is time to leave.'

39

Maxstoke Castle, October 1459 – July 1460

Cicely

A nne's antipathy towards York was even worse than I had anticipated. We had been at Maxstoke Castle for over a week before she even visited our quarters.

It had been a miserable journey from Ludlow. Rain had begun to fall before we left, which may have put out the fires lit by the looters but soaked us within minutes of mounting our horses. I was grateful that at least the cart in which Ursula travelled with Anicia was covered but the rest of us remained wet or damp until we reached Maxstoke three days later. I tried to encourage Richard to share the cart but he threw such a temper tantrum that I gave in to his determination to ride all the way. However, as I feared, the result was a cough which persisted until spring. None of us really recovered from that ride for months.

Partly that was due to our accommodation. Maxstoke was not so much a castle as a fortified mansion but our hostess, or gaoler to describe her more accurately, refused to allow us to set foot in her home and so we were confined to the gatehouse. This was a large, square structure with two stories above the gate arch and a pair of taller, battlemented towers flanking it.

Like the rest of the castle, it was built of red sandstone. There were guardhouses on either side of the gateway and the constable's quarters were on the first floor of the main building. Our accommodation was above this, consisting of one great chamber and the two smaller chambers at the top of each of the towers. Good enough for prisoners of war, it had to be acknowledged, but hardly comfortable living for the sister, nieces and nephews of the castle's chatelaine, especially as there were no guarderobes or latrines available. We were supplied with two close-stools which were not emptied nearly enough and only the fact that the rooms were bone-achingly cold prevented the smell of human excrement becoming unbearable. These conditions caused me to worry dreadfully about the children's health and for the first week I asked constantly to speak to my sister but she did not come.

Sir Henry Stafford had barely addressed a word to me during the journey and, having shown us to our quarters, never put in another appearance. Our communication was done through the castle constable, a pleasant enough young knight called Sir Christopher Deyne, who had an irritating habit of meeting every request with the ambiguous comment 'I will do my best'. His best, it seemed, was never good enough.

Then after a sennight, suddenly and unannounced, there she was at the door of our chamber, my sister Anne, Duchess of Buckingham. I was shocked at her appearance because she was clad all in black, the only relief being a wimple of unbleached linen which all but matched the hue of her complexion. From its frame her eyes stared, swollen and bloodshot but with piercing grey Neville irises, almost the only feature that told me it was definitely her.

'Anne, you have come. Thank you.' I went to kiss her cheek

but she put a hand up to ward me off and moved past me into the room.

'I have not come to speak to you, who are married to the man who cost me my son. I have come to see the children.' She strode across the bare flagstones to the west window which overlooked the house and courtyard, where Margaret, George and Dickon were playing a game, but she did not greet them. 'I demand that you keep these shutters closed,' she said, reaching over their heads and firmly pulling the heavy wooden shutters together. 'I do not want York children spying on our activities.'

Having no idea who this lady was and indignant at her suggestion, Margaret protested, 'We were not spying. We were playing spot the object.'

'Well play something else!' snapped the duchess.

'There is nothing else to do,' Margaret pointed out reasonably. 'My brothers have no books or toys and I have no needles or threads.'

I thought Anne might hit her, so angry did she look, and I hurried over to protect my daughter. But after frowning fiercely, my sister gave a loud sniff and turned on me. 'Quite the little madam, is she not? Just like her mother. Did no one teach her manners?'

I shrugged. 'Margaret spoke nothing but the truth. They are bored. Children need stimulation, as I am sure you know.'

'Margaret,' echoed Anne. 'That is a very Lancastrian name for a daughter of York.'

'Margaret is thirteen. She is named after the queen. But boredom is not their only problem. There is the matter of their health.'

Anne sniffed even louder and raised her sleeve to her nose. 'There is a bad smell. You should keep the place clean. I am sure Margaret can scrub the floor, even if she is named after the queen.'

'We can keep the place clean, Sister, but we cannot empty the close-stools because we are not allowed out. They have only been cleared once since we have been here. Also we need to wash our underclothes but there is not enough water and we have nothing else to wear. And it is cold. We have no heat. That is why I am worried for their health.' I dropped to my knees at her feet and clasped my hands. 'I beg you not to visit the sins of the father on the children.'

Anne turned her back. 'Do not be melodramatic, Cicely,' she snapped. 'I will see what I can do.'

I remained kneeling, determined to drive my message home. 'That is what your constable says every day. I know we are your prisoners but I am still your sister. Do you want your niece to die, Anne?'

She swung round and her face was twisted in a snarl. 'It is only months since my son – your nephew – died of the wounds he received at St Albans. He lived in pain and humiliation for three years. Do you remember how he was injured, Cicely?'

I felt my eyes fill with tears. 'Of course I remember how he was injured. It was appalling.' Her brief and contentious visit to Baynard's Castle with Alice de la Pole still rankled but I was not going to let her know that at this stage. 'But I did not know he had died and I am very sorry for your loss. All this conflict is not of my making or yours, yet it has torn our family apart and put our men at each other's throats. Must we also be enemies?'

She looked down at me as if I was simple-minded. 'Yes, we must. That is how the world works. Do not hope for sympathy from me.'

I watched the hem of her fine black worsted skirts stir the dust on the floor as she swept across the room and out of the door. The sound of the key turning evoked vivid memories of my detention in Brancepeth Castle and the grim realization that I had been imprisoned three times in my life and each time it had been at the hands of a member of my own family. Later that day a workman came to nail the shutters closed on the window that overlooked my sister's living quarters. That meant our large gatehouse chamber was lit by only one window in the east wall, leaving much of the room in deep shadow even in the middle of the day. We were given no candles, only smoky tapers and as winter closed in I had to ration the use of our two lamps in order to preserve enough oil to keep one burning constantly for Ursula because the little girl was terrified of the dark.

However, during the next few weeks, as a result of Anne's visit there were a few small improvements in our living conditions. The gongfermour came every second day to clear the close stools, a brazier was supplied though not always enough charcoal to burn in it and, to Margaret's delight, paper, pens and ink came in a parcel specifically addressed to her from her aunt, who also sent books and sewing materials from time to time. Although Anne had seemed disapproving when they came face to face, Margaret had obviously made a favourable impression on her.

At the beginning of December, Sir Henry Stafford came to escort me the twelve miles to Coventry to appear before a special Parliament, which had been summoned by the king to arraign Richard, Hal and Dick for high treason. 'You have the right to appeal for your husband's pardon,' Sir Henry told me as we rode. 'Not that I imagine there is any hope of it being granted.

456

A Bill of Attainder has already been passed against York and all his supporters, which demands forfeit of all their estates in perpetuity and of their lives if they should return to England.'

It was no more than I had expected but hearing the words spoken made my heart sink. In the event, whether by error or design I arrived too late to make the plea for a pardon because there had been an eight-day deadline for appeals and the Bill had been passed twelve days before. However I did make a suitably humble appearance before the lords gathered in the chapter house of St Mary's Priory in Coventry, who magnanimously granted me a maintenance sum of one hundred crowns from the ten thousand crowns per year of revenue the royal exchequer had seized from the combined York, Salisbury and Warwick estates. As I rode back to prison, I reflected glumly that the queen would certainly not lack the wherewithal to fund a royal army to confront any force that my husband, son, brother and nephew might manage to raise to make their return. Of my children only Anne and Elizabeth now appeared to have a future and I learned later that Elizabeth had written letters to us from Wingfield, letters which my sister had confiscated and burned. For the rest of us life stretched ahead looking bleak and impoverished and not a day went by that I did not question whether Richard had thrown away his considerable assets for nothing and with them the prospects of all his children. But especially I bitterly regretted what I believed could have been the brilliant future of my golden boy Edward and longed for news from Calais.

Christmas went almost unnoticed in the Maxstoke gatehouse. Anne had departed to join her husband at the court celebrations in Coventry and left no instructions for any cheer to be delivered to her prisoners but the constable made arrangements for us to be escorted to the nearby Augustinian priory to make our confessions and hear the Christmas mass. On our return journey in the gathering dusk it began to snow and when we awoke the following day the world was covered in a blanket of white. For the next month we spent our time huddled around the brazier and even our regular exercise was curtailed because the castle wall-walk was treacherous with ice. Understandably the children, especially the two boys, became fractious and moody and George, in particular, flew into pointless rages in which he screamed abuse against his father and older brothers, blaming them for being free when he was not. Margaret tried pointing out to him that being in exile and under sentence of death could hardly be counted as freedom but he was not mollified.

'I would rather be dead than bored to death,' he yelled back at her. 'Why are you not bored too?'

'Because I read every book that comes through the door,' she countered. 'You are merely getting a taste of what it is like to be a noblewoman, confined to the solar and the lying-in chamber. For me, knowledge is power and I will use it.'

'That is stupid,' said George scornfully. 'Power is rank and land, and we have lost all ours.'

I listened to them arguing and sighed. Both were right in their own way but I feared that unless our fortunes changed for the better, Margaret might never make the kind of marriage that would utilise her emerging intellect. I recalled that at one time there had been correspondence between Richard and the Duchess of Burgundy regarding a marriage to her son and heir but it seemed unlikely now that there would ever be such an exalted union for either of my dowerless daughters. It occurred to me that the veil might tempt the studious Margaret, if there was a convent that would take her. In these troubled times the veil began to seem increasingly attractive to me.

When the snow melted, Anne returned and came to bring us news, little of which was good from our point of view. Most of our Welsh manors had been granted to Jasper Tudor, Earl of Pembroke, and those nearest to Anglesey to his father Owen Tudor. In return they had been given the duty of ensuring that Richard would never be able to return to England through Wales. From what I knew of Jasper Tudor, he would approach that task with military thoroughness. Meanwhile the young Duke of Somerset had been given Dick of Warwick's command of Calais; but first of all he had to get there and Dick was making it extremely difficult for him. There had been a battle in the Pale around Calais and Somerset had been beaten back.

When Anne told me this, I could not completely hide a smile, causing her to snap at me. 'You will not smile when you hear that your precious son Edward was in the thick of the fighting.'

I tried not to show alarm. 'But you are not telling me he was injured.'

She shrugged. 'Not as far as I know. He took some prisoners but Somerset took Guisnes Castle, the land-gate to the Pale, so it will not be long before he is hurling Warwick and March into the Channel.'

'Time will tell,' I said, crossing my fingers in the folds of my skirt.

It was only later that I learned what she was not telling me; that, far from being ejected from Calais, Hal, Dick and Edward had left my brother Will Fauconberg to hold the outpost and sailed to a meeting with Richard in Waterford in the south of Ireland. There they made plans to launch a two pronged invasion of England in the summer, Richard from the north and

Hal, Dick and Edward from the south. On their way back, the Calais contingent had sailed freely past Dartmouth where a new and vastly expensive English fleet commissioned under its High Admiral, Harry of Exeter, did not sail out to intercept them because not enough men could be found prepared to crew the ships and fight under Harry's erratic command – this news when I heard it induced a rare smile.

It was high summer before I received another visit from my sister and this time she seemed distinctly anxious. 'Humphrey has gone to Northampton with the king,' she said. 'Warwick and your precocious son have to be stopped from marching north.'

I could hardly catch my breath to speak. 'They are in the country? Since when?'

Anne scowled. 'They landed in Kent in June and have been causing trouble ever since. Warwick seems to have the Londoners under some kind of spell. The guilds opened the gates to him and all the Lancastrian nobility who were in the city at the time had to take refuge in the Tower. I believe the Duchess of Exeter is among them. Now your brother Salisbury has them under siege.'

'Anne is besieged in the Tower?' My mind, stale from incarceration, was unable to take it all in. I had to resist a terrible urge physically to shake more information out of my sister. 'Where is Edward?'

'Marching north with Warwick.' Suddenly, and without warning, Anne's stern expression crumpled and tears began to flow down her cheeks. 'It is dreadful, Cicely! Your brother has your daughter under siege in London and your nephew and son are marching to confront my husband somewhere outside Northampton. How has our family come to this?'

She was distraught and for the life of me I could not stop myself taking her in my arms. I held her as she broke down in gasping sobs of distress on my shoulder. It was as if a dam had burst and all the emotion of months and years was pouring from her. Across the room I saw Margaret put down her book and rise from her chair in surprise.

'What is wrong with her?' she asked.

'Life, war and the futility of both,' I answered, still hugging Anne's shaking shoulders. 'Have you a kerchief, Meg?'

'It should be you who is crying, my lady mother,' she said, pulling a square of white linen from her sleeve. Even in prison Margaret could be relied on to have a clean kerchief.

I took it from her and pressed it into Anne's hand. 'Your aunt is crying for the news she fears to get from a battle she cannot prevent. Perhaps we should all be doing the same.'

When Anne had soaked the kerchief with her tears, she blew her nose and tucked it up her sleeve. 'I will have it washed and returned,' she said to Margaret, her expression rather sheepish. No reference was made to her storm of weeping but, on leaving, she gave me the faintest of rueful smiles and said, 'I hope neither of us will need to wear black again, Cicely.'

Anne had not worn black since the year of mourning for her son had ended and the fine blue silk gown and jewelled head-dress she wore now made me painfully conscious that I still wore the same dull brown kirtle I had donned on my last day at Ludlow. All our clothes would have been threadbare, had it not been for Margaret's skill with a needle.

'Please keep me informed, Sister,' I begged, hoping that at last we had struck a chord of empathy. 'Pray do not let me suffer in ignorance.'

All through the following day I heard nothing and I fretted, wondering if there had been a battle and if so, what had been the outcome. It had rained almost without ceasing and at noon the next day we heard the drawbridge winding down and Dickon spotted a mud-caked courier waiting to cross over the moat. Still we heard nothing but in the afternoon when the rain had dwindled to a damp drizzle we went out onto the wall-walk for some fresh air. George was the first one to notice something amiss.

'Look, lady mother. The flag is halfway down the pole. Does that mean someone has died?'

From the battlemented roof of one of the gatehouse towers sprouted a flagpole and George was right, the standard was flying at half-mast; a gold shield slashed with a blood-red bend, topped with a ducal cap and surrounded by the blue garter sash. It could only mean that Humphrey of Buckingham was dead and my sister was back in black. I made the sign of the cross and whispered a prayer for Humphrey's soul. I had never considered him an enemy and now I mourned for my sister who, although plunged into a dynastic marriage at fourteen, had somehow made it a love-match.

It was days before I discovered how Humphrey had died outside the king's tent as the Lancastrian camp was overrun by Warwick's crack Kentish fighters. King Henry had been captured alone in his tent and later taken to London in formal procession by Dick and Edward. It was the first word I had received that York's cause was in the ascendant and my beloved son was safe and uninjured.

All the same, I could not celebrate because those were dark days for all of us at Maxstoke. Ursula, who had weathered the winter without a recurrence of the ague, had been taken ill again and this time her condition deteriorated so fast that there was no time for anything to be done about it. Although the young constable acquired what Anicia needed for her herbal cures and sent for a physician, by the time he reached us it was too late. Weakened during our imprisonment, the fever had seemed to burn her up overnight and she died in Anicia's arms as dawn broke.

40

Coverdale, Yorkshire, Summer 1460

Cuthbert

Huge snowdrifts kept Coverdale cut off from the rest of the world until spring. I spent my time digging fodder out of haystacks to feed the over-wintering stock crowded into the ground floor of the old bastle and fuel out of the woodpile to keep us from freezing in the tower. But at least deep snow lessened the likelihood of Lancastrian incursion into Salisbury-held lands.

In April, however, the expected summons came for all tenants to present themselves at Middleham Castle. Since the Duke of York had purchased my manor off the Earl of Salisbury, I had not expected to be included in this summons but the messenger came anyway, with a letter specifically addressed to me.

—§§—

To Sir Cuthbert of Middleham, lord of Red Gill Manor, greetings,

Although you are not a tenant of the attainted Earl of Salisbury's estate, as a tenant of York and a known member

of the treasonous Yorkist affinity you are nevertheless
summoned by order of his grace King Henry to report to
Middleham Castle. Present yourself at noon on the feast of
St Mark and I will endeavour to see you privately.

Your friend and debtor,
John, Baron Neville, Lord of Middleham

Written this twentieth day of April, 1460

—§§—

Lord of Middleham! So John Neville had succeeded at last in acquiring Middleham Castle from the attainted Salisbury estates! I decided that the fact that he called himself my debtor showed that he had not forgotten his sojourn at Red Gill Bastle with Cicely, or who had made it possible.

I went to Middleham Castle on the day specified, hoping to gain news of Cicely and the rest of the York family but I did not expect it to be good. It was a vast ant-heap of a fortification, its many towers and buildings crammed tightly within its soaring curtain. The smoke-darkened walls dominated the town, dwarfing the surrounding houses like a threatening thundercloud.

Lord Neville met me in the constable's room above the gatehouse and I could see his surprise at my appearance when I walked in. I had taken Cicely's advice and embraced the style of a yeoman farmer and so I wore a leather jack over a coarse but clean brown tunic and hose tucked into sturdy leather boots. I had also grown a full beard and jammed a wide-brimmed felt hat down over my long, grey-streaked hair. On an occasion such as this, when I was uncertain of my security, I wore a gambeson beneath my tunic and a dagger hidden in my boot. I had not announced myself as a knight and I had not been searched by the guards therefore neither had been found.

John had aged considerably in the eight years since our last meeting. He was bare-headed, his pale hair faded to white and his complexion weathered and crisscrossed with fine lines; deeper furrows ran between his nose and mouth. I had passed a clerk leaving the chamber as I went in so he was alone with a pile of ledgers and scrolls on the table in front of him but he rose and moved around it to greet me.

'Good day, Sir Cuthbert,' he said solemnly. 'You have come, so I can legitimately enter your presence in my list of attendances, therefore you should not be further inconvenienced by the Middleham receivers. I feel I owe you that at least, even though we may fight under different banners.'

I pulled off my hat and made him a brief bow of acknowledgement. 'God give you good day, my lord. For a time we thought you might come over to York but it did not happen; it was disappointing,' I said bluntly.

He spread his hands ruefully. 'York did not stand a chance, even with the two thousand men I brought to Ludlow. It did not seem worth turning my coat to fight with a side that could not win.'

I had not had John Neville down as a good-time man but now I knew that was what he was. I shrugged, quashing the temptation to ask why in that case he had signalled his possible support at all. 'Next time, perhaps?' I suggested.

'Perhaps.' He moved across to a chest on which stood cups and a jug. 'May I offer you wine?' He held the spout of the jug over a cup, awaiting my reply before tipping it.

'Yes, if you please.'

'Where is Cicely now?' He handed me the filled cup.

'I believe she is living with her sister, the Duchess of Buckingham, but I do not know under what circumstances.'

His eyebrow flicked upwards. 'Awkward, I imagine. The Buckingham heir died recently of the wounds he received at St Albans and her husband is the king's commander in chief, as you know. Why did Cicely not go to Ireland with the Duke of York?'

I explained about the health of the youngest children. 'But she was not happy in Dublin when they were there before,' I added. I made no mention of the very obvious signs of a rift in the York marriage, thinking it might feed what I saw as his unnecessary and continuing obsession with Cicely.

'Do you think York will try to return to England?'

I stared at the red rose badge on his shoulder. 'If I knew the answer to that I would hardly tell you,' I pointed out.

'Will you join him if he does?'

'Perhaps.'

He half-smiled at the tit-for-tat reply. 'It seems these wars between the roses are fought on perhapses.'

'It is a pity they are fought at all. Too many good men die unnecessarily as a result.' I took a gulp of wine.

John studied me seriously over the rim of his cup. When he lowered it he said, 'One of my retained knights is Sir Gerald Copley. He asks for you everywhere he goes; says you abducted his sister and boasts that he will kill you in revenge.'

'Is he here in Middleham?' I asked, hoping the alarm I felt did not show.

John made a face. 'No. I do not find him pleasant company. I sent him to Sheriff Hutton. I take it you would rather he did not discover your whereabouts.'

'Correct. I fear for my wife's safety if he finds out.'

'Yes, I see. Well, the queen has recently issued another order of array, in her son's name of course, so I imagine most fighting men will be heading south quite soon. Personally I do not like conscription.'

'I do not like the way conscripts fight,' I said. 'Why has she done that?'

'I imagine it is a precaution, in case York and Warwick attempt an invasion.'

'Can a man invade his own country?'

'A traitor is considered an alien.'

'The Duke of York is a cousin of the king. Do you consider King Henry an alien?'

He did not answer that but walked back around his desk and sat down. When he spoke again the subject had changed.

'When you next see Cicely, will you give her a message for me?'

'I will, of course, but it may not be for months, or even years,' I replied. 'I hope it is not urgent.'

His lips twitched. 'No, it is not urgent. Just tell her that I have a son now and he is called Ralph. He is five years old. I hope she will be pleased.'

I nodded. 'Yes, I think she will be.' I placed my empty cup back on the chest. 'With your permission I will take my leave now, my lord. Thank you for the wine.'

Lord Neville inclined his head. 'Goodbye, Sir Cuthbert. I am glad to have met with you. I am sorry we cannot be friends. In different circumstances I think we might have been.'

I reserved judgement but I thought about his last words as I rode home. He was a Neville and a northerner, as was I. Yet I had chosen to pledge my allegiance to the Duke of York, who was a southerner, a Plantagenet nobleman of the old school. Richard dealt fairly with his feoffees and followers but at the same time assumed an inherent superiority. He prided himself on being a lawgiver, an administrator, as well as a soldier. He could be noble and magnanimous. He was admirable but not attractive. I realized that the half of me that was a northern commoner, my maternal inheritance, liked a touch of flamboyant charm in those he was asked to serve. I had pledged my loyalty to York because of Cicely, not because of Richard; the Neville half of me was glad to be one.

It was August before the news from the south began to stir my sense of knightly obligation. I would go frequently to Middleham to gather news and come back more unsettled every time. In June the townsfolk secretly celebrated the landing of Dick of Warwick and Edward of York in Kent and then in July they openly cheered on hearing news of their victory over the Lancastrian army at Northampton.

Following Northampton the king had become effectively a prisoner in the Tower of London and the queen and prince had fled into Scotland. England held its breath, wondering what would happen next, waiting for Richard to come from Ireland.

Walking around the barmkin in the evening to shut the chickens and ducks in their coops for safety against marauding foxes, Hilda asked, 'Has there been good news or bad?'

I had spent an hour in the Spread Eagle Inn that day. 'The latest news is momentous,' I told her, 'more momentous even than the achievement of Dick and Edward at Northampton. Richard is coming back to claim the throne. A Parliament has been summoned for October. Cicely has been in London for a month now and I believe that any day I could receive a summons from her. If I do, Hilda, I shall not be able to stop myself from going; unless of course you stop me.'

Hilda said nothing immediately but took my hand and led me to a mounting block set against the side wall of the bastle. We sat down on its steps side by side, gazing out across the barmkin at the view of the dale. Our backs were against the still-warm stone and the sun was setting below the ridge of the high moor, spraying the sky with wisps of pink cloud. The hillsides were patched with russet-coloured bracken and dotted with boulders that had long ago lost their hold on the steep crags higher up. As always, the beck behind us sang its gurgling tune as it tumbled over the rocks in the Red Gill.

I thought she was going to ask me how I could leave this place, which was so beautiful, whether in snowfall, sunshine or sunset, but she did not. Instead she posed different questions altogether. 'Do we want our children to be yeoman farmers or gentlefolk, Cuddy? Should they learn how to shear sheep and make cheese or wield a sword and run a household? At the moment they are going to be neither cheese-maker nor sword-wielder.'

I turned to her with knitted brows. 'I thought you wanted them to put down roots in the north-country,' I said.

'We can do both,' she answered. 'Cicely would take me back into her service and Aiden could become a page. You have more years to give in her service too and Marie could make a good marriage. It is very likely that Cicely is going to be queen, Cuthbert! We would be mad to turn our backs on such an opportunity for our children.'

'Are you saying that we should *all* go to London?'

'I am saying that we should all follow Cicely, wherever that takes us. We can come back to Red Gill from time to time and your nephew will run it perfectly meanwhile, with a little more help.' She made an expansive gesture. 'This dale will not go away. It will always be here.'

I thought of myself at Aiden's age, being taken from Coverdale into the princely household at Raby. There had been so much to learn and so many wonders to see and hear. I should not deprive my son of the same opportunity that my father had given me. And Marie was the daughter and granddaughter of knights. She should marry into her own class. Hilda was right. If Cicely called me we should all go.

I planted a kiss on her lips and tweaked the peak of her housewife's coif. 'You will have to look out your finery, my lady,' I said. 'And I will have to get a shave and a hair cut.'

Two weeks later, a courier wearing the York crest brought a package. Cicely must have gathered her London household again at Baynard's Castle I thought as I tore at the falcon and fetterlock seal. Something heavy fell into the palm of my hand. It was the white rose brooch she had unpinned from my hat on our last night at Ludlow. Her message read:

—ξξ—

<u>From Cicely, Duchess of York to Sir Cuthbert of Middleham,
greetings.</u>

The Wheel of Fortune has turned, my faithful brother. Edward is with me in London and Richard is on the way from Ireland. He has asked me to meet him at Hereford in the middle of September. We will travel together in procession to Westminster, where a Parliament has been summoned and where he says he will claim the throne. I need you with me,

Cuddy, and Hilda too, if she will come. Send me your answer by return and pin this brooch again to your hat. Wear it with pride. By God's good grace, when we meet again the House of York will be in its rightful place at last.

Take care on the journey. Many still wear the red rose.

Your loving sister,

Cicely

PS You may not have heard that sadly our little Ursula died during our imprisonment at Maxstoke Castle. We took her for burial beside Henry, William and John at Fotheringhay. The Lord giveth and the Lord taketh away.

<u>Written at Baynard's Castle, London, this day August 24th 1460.</u>

41

Cicely

It was very strange to be living in the royal apartments at Westminster, almost like playing in a masque. At any moment I expected someone to come and take away my costume and jewellery and tell me that the entertainment was over; and that was still perfectly possible.

We had ridden in a glorious procession to London surrounded by hundreds of liveried men-at-arms and a phalanx of York knights with the white rose prominent on their banners. Richard had provided a splendid litter for me, like a great gilded tester bed slung between four pairs of white horses and hung with blue velvet curtains. He rode ahead of it in full armour on a dapple-grey charger with red and gold trappings, the great sword of state borne before him as if he had already been crowned. I told him how I much preferred to ride on a horse and that it was unlucky to assume the crown before the coronation but, as so often in those days, he was in no mood to listen. His belief in the power of pomp and show drove him on remorselessly. He had festered in the Dublin Pale and on his Ulster estates for nearly a year, receiving a constant flow of information from his spy network in England and straining at the invisible fetters that kept him in Ireland. Being attainted and put under sentence of death for treachery had been the last straw. He no longer wanted simply to reorganize the government of England and reclaim his lands and revenues. He no longer saw it as his duty to rule but as his right. He wanted to rid the country of its useless king and poisonous queen.

'Henry's grandfather was driven to take the throne by King Richard's ill-judgment and now the tables have turned,' he had declared when he explained his intentions to me before we left Hereford. 'The Beaufort claim has always been blighted by the stain of bastardy and Henry's reign has been ruined by weak leadership, incompetence and female interference. I have always had the better claim and will make a better ruler. It has been proved time and again. Moreover I have defeated him in battle. I am king both by right and conquest.'

I bit back the urge to point out that it was not Richard but Dick and Edward who had defeated King Henry's army because I agreed that his claim to the throne was better. Through both his mother and his father his lineage ran direct from King Edward the Third, which was more than could be said for Henry who, even though his father had been king before him, might be said to have a more direct claim on the French throne than on the English one through his de Valois mother. Besides, I was not averse to becoming Queen of England. Neville ambition coursed in my blood. Short of being admitted to the gates of Heaven, no man or woman ever reached higher than the throne. I am not sure that even my aspiring father ever envisaged that for me.

I was more than delighted that Cuthbert and Hilda were willing to join me at Baynard's and had the York steward arrange accommodation for them and a place for their son as a page in his own house. I always preferred to keep ladies close to me whom I knew I could trust and, having shared my childhood, Hilda had always been foremost in that role. For his part Cuthbert, ever the faithful knight and brother, also served me well as a conduit of affairs in Richard's inner court.

It was Edmund who described to me the sequence of events on the tenth of October when his father walked into the Parliament to claim the throne. During the year since that ignominious midnight departure from Ludlow, Edmund had matured very much in the image of his father. He had not yet quite reached my height but when we conversed his flecked green eyes met my gaze with refreshing candour and he expressed himself with clarity and brevity, uncomplicated by political nuance as Edward's remarks often were now, reflecting his cousin Dick's influence, I surmised. In addition I noticed that in his father's presence Edmund was was usually to be found standing quietly at his shoulder and they frequently exchanged hushed confidences. Even when Edward was also present it was to Edmund that Richard turned for a small service or confirmation of a fact. Officially he was still an underage squire but he was also playing his role as Earl of Rutland, his father's aide and confidant, with increasing skill.

He came back alone from Westminster Hall looking dejected, bending his knee before my chair and casting a frown at the companions gathered around me. 'My lord father sent me to you,' he said. 'May I speak privately with your grace?'

As soon as we were alone he pulled up a stool beside me and leaned close. 'I hope it will not upset you too much, my lady mother, if I tell you that my father was not acclaimed king today as he expected to be. I fear he overestimated his position, even among those lords who are allied to York.'

I had more or less anticipated this news, partly because of the gloomy expression on Edmond's face and partly because I had never been as optimistic as Richard that his fellow peers would easily rid themselves of their anointed monarch, ineffective and hag-ridden though he might be.

I folded my hands in my lap and nodded. 'Tell me exactly what took place, Edmund.'

His account was solemn and meticulous. 'We rode round to the Great Hall of Westminster; the streets were very quiet, as if London was empty. There were eight of us in my lord father's retinue and we dismounted and walked into the building in procession, my father preceded by his bearer carrying the great sword of state. To our surprise the hall was empty except for several ushers, one of whom told us that the two Houses were sitting separately and directed us to the lords' session in the Painted Chamber. King Henry was not there; the throne stood unoccupied on a dais at one end of the room but the lords present were seated around a long table, including my uncle of Salisbury and our cousin of Warwick. Some of the Lancastrian earls were absent; Exeter, Northumberland, Devon, Somerset.'

'I am glad Exeter was not there,' I remarked as he paused to draw breath.

'They say he is in Scotland with the queen, trying to raise an army,' Edmund commented. 'I was surprised to see Edward there. I thought he would be considered under age for parliament. Anyway, my lord father did not wait to be greeted. He bowed to the assembly then marched straight past the table. Lord Bourchier, who had been speaking, fell silent and they all watched my father walk up to the dais, mount the steps and put his hand on the arm of the throne, as if to take his seat. Then he turned and waited to be encouraged to do so, to be acclaimed king, but no voice was raised. Even Edward did not speak, although I saw him open his mouth as if to do so then close it again. He looked surprised but not nearly as surprised as our father who nevertheless declared in a loud voice that he claimed the throne as the heir of King Richard the Second. Then the Archbishop of Canterbury stood up and asked him if he would like to see the king. My father looked furious and said – these are his exact words I think – "There is no one in the realm who should more fitly come to me than I to him."'

Edmund gazed at me curiously. 'What do you think, lady mother? Did he do the right thing?'

I sighed and shook my head. 'I do not know, my son. As we rode through the border towns, all the Welsh marcher lords were encouraging him to claim the throne but the nobles think very differently here in London. It is a solemn and serious matter to dethrone an anointed king to whom you have knelt and sworn allegiance. It is an apostasy which can reverberate down through the hierarchy, perhaps encouraging petty vassals to disassociate themselves from their overlords. What do you think, Edmund?'

He sucked his teeth pensively, then took a deep breath and said something which touched and astonished me. 'I think my lord father has suffered too much rejection. For years he has served the crown with skill and honour and been cheated of his dues by corrupt officials; he has suffered the torture of being attainted and discarded like a worthless rag and yet he is the noblest and the worthiest man in the kingdom. Now his closest allies, his brother-in-law and nephew, even his son and heir, have failed to speak up for him. If I had been a member of the

House of Lords today, even if I had stood alone, I would have hailed him as my king.'

My eyes filled with tears as I gazed on his earnest face. I reached out, took both his hands in mine and raised them to my lips. 'Bravo, Edmund,' I said huskily. 'No man has a truer or more loyal son than you are to your father.'

He clasped my hands tightly and leaned forward to kiss my cheek. 'No man has a truer or more loyal wife than you are to my father. I believe that if women were allowed in the House of Lords you would have raised your voice with me.'

I smiled ruefully, wondering what he would say of me if he knew the truth. 'But women are not allowed,' I said, 'and I will not have the opportunity. I do believe however that your father would make an admirable king. What is he doing now?'

'At the suggestion of the archbishop he has gone with the other lords to Blackfriars to discuss what is to be done. He told me that despite this setback he is still preparing for his coronation on All Saints Day. That is in three weeks' time.' He pushed back his stool and stood up, bowing and flicking back his thick dark-honey hair in a way that reminded me vividly of his father as a young man. 'Now I must leave you, lady mother. I am to go to Blackfriars and wait to escort my father back to the palace. I am sure he will want to tell you all this himself when he returns.'

After he had gone I sat for several minutes pondering his belief that I would have joined in his acclamation of Richard as king. It did not surprise me that Edward had not raised his voice when the others did not. His silence had disappointed Edmund but then he was not his father's heir. It would not have helped Edward's own cause or that of his father if he had been the only one to acclaim him king. Had any of the others spoken up I was sure that he would have done so too and probably Hal and Dick as well. I would not have said so to Edmund but I thought Richard should have taken time to sound out opinion among his fellow peers before plunging in with his claim as he did. I believed that a king should rule with the sworn consent of his peers, not merely because he had the right. If his peers felt they could not swear allegiance because they had already done so to another, then he would have a job persuading them otherwise.

At this time Edward was still living in the Earl of Warwick's household at the Erber Inn and that evening Dick and he came to Westminster Palace together with Tom Neville and his wife Maud. Dinner was just over. We had dined in our great chamber quietly with several of Richard's household knights and their ladies who now mingled around the hearth while hippocras, mead and sweetmeats circulated.

Since our arrival in London I had found no opportunity for conversation with Edward so I was delighted when he came straight to my side and lured me off to a cushioned seat in a window embrasure. 'I wore the beautiful silk jupon you made for me at my knighting, my lady mother,' he said, after kissing my hand and cheek. 'As you intended. I wish you had been there.'

I sighed. 'You cannot wish that more than I do, Edward. Tell me where and when it was and who was your other sponsor?'

One of his heart-stopping smiles lit his face. 'Dick was the main sponsor of course but my second was your brother Will. There – I knew that would please you. He has been Dick's number two in Calais for the past couple of years and has been a magnificent supporter of the York cause.'

'So I gather. Was the ceremony held in Calais castle?' I asked.

'Not entirely. I bathed and held my vigil in the castle chapel but the actual dubbing was done on the harbour quay before we boarded to cross to England. It was Dick's idea. He said the men should witness it so they would know they were following a true knight into battle. I think, dear lady mother, they would have had a very clear view of your magnificent white rose embroidery when I knelt before them all for Warwick's accolade.'

I studied his face, so mobile and expressive at that moment, although I knew he had the ability to keep his emotions well hidden if the need arose. 'And what went through your mind when you held your vigil, Edward? I assume it to be a time for reflection and self-examination and not easy for a man of action like you.'

A shadow crossed his eyes. 'You are right, I found it a great challenge. You may be surprised to hear that I thought a great deal about you and my brothers and sisters who were left behind when we fled. I have not told you of my sorrow when I heard of Ursula's death. You must have been heartbroken.'

To my consternation I felt sudden tears fill my eyes and spill down my cheeks. For a minute I could not speak and Edward impulsively put his hand on my arm. 'You have been through so much, my mother. I hope one day I can make it up to you. Was it very terrible being a prisoner?'

I nodded, took a deep breath and found my voice. 'Ursula's death was the worst part. But all my children are precious to me and you particularly, Edward. You have had to become a man so young. I am in awe of what you have achieved.'

He gave a dismissive shrug. 'I have achieved nothing until I see you as queen and my father as king. And I will do it, with Dick's help.'

I was about to ask him why he had not spoken up when

Richard had claimed the throne but raised voices across the room drew our attention.

'I hope by querying my silence today you are not suggesting that I have not supported you through thick and thin in your fight for justice, my lord duke?' It was Warwick's voice raised in anger. 'Do not forget that it was Edward and I who made it possible for you to return to England when we defeated the king's army at Northampton. It would have been more than mere courtesy to ask whether we would support your claim to the throne before you actually made it.'

Edward removed his hand from my arm and turned to look. Richard had been sitting comfortably with a cup of wine in one hand but now he stood up abruptly. 'It was because I assumed you would want to glean maximum advantage from your glorious victory that I did not consider it necessary to seek your opinion, my lord.' His tone was hard, his expression guarded, but his temper was under control.

'It was high-handed to assume anything of the kind, especially when it concerns deposing a king who has occupied that throne for thirty-eight years and to whom we have all vowed allegiance. I, my brother Tom and your son Edward are all agreed on this. You have over-stepped the mark, my lord duke.' Warwick's attitude was dangerously aggressive, his stance wide, one hand on his dagger-sheath.

Edward rose but did not move away and my eyes widened when I saw Edmund move between Dick and Richard and stoutly defend his father. 'Calm yourself, sir, I beg you,' he said firmly to Warwick. 'For we all know that York has the true and only right to the crown and my father is the true and rightful king. Henry of Lancaster has not been king for thirty-eight years, he has been a usurper.'

Edward suddenly strode across the room and put his hand on Edmund's shoulder. 'Hold hard, little brother. Dick and Tom are our friends and cousins. We do not tell them what they do and do not know and will and will not do.' He then swept a bow to Warwick and snatched two cups from a passing servant's tray. 'You have made it clear where you stand on the matter of the crown, Dick, so let us drink to the fact that our attainders are rescinded and you have Middleham Castle back again. They tell me John Neville led his garrison out of the gates Friday last.' He placed one of the cups in Warwick's hand and drew him away from his brother and father, arm about his shoulder.

I had drawn a kerchief from my sleeve to wipe away the remnants of my tears and now Edward's sudden mention of John Neville made my stomach lurch. Cuthbert had told me of his meeting with him at Middleham when John had been granted tenure of the castle in return for withholding his army from York at Ludford Bridge. I had remarked that bringing his men to a confrontation and then standing aside from it seemed to be a favourite strategy of John's. Sitting on the fence was certainly one way of ensuring you were never on the wrong side but it could hardly be considered the mark of a reliable ally. Now he was suffering the consequences – and he would suffer severely because the possession of Middleham and Sheriff Hutton had been his lifetime's ambition.

Tucking my kerchief away, I wandered over to speak to Maud who was seated beside the buffet with Hilda. 'Dick seems very hot-tempered these days,' I murmured in her ear. 'Has he lost faith in Richard, do you think?'

'I would say that he is pinning his hopes on Edward, rather than losing faith in the duke,' Maud replied in a whisper. 'I think you would hear a different tune from my lord of Warwick if it was Edward claiming the throne.'

I frowned. 'Edward? He is only eighteen.'

'Yes but he is a man.' Maud caught Edward's eye over Warwick's shoulder and blew him a kiss, which was returned with the added bonus of a wink. 'And man enough to have notched up a significant victory on the battlefield already. He is a very popular lad your son, Cicely; especially in London. Do not underestimate the importance of popular acclaim.'

I watched the two cousins raise their cups to each other and drink. 'I do not but I am afraid Richard has always prized obedience over adulation.'

Barons, bishops and lawyers agonized for days over Richard's claim to the throne, while he persisted in continuing his costly and complicated arrangements for a coronation ceremony at Westminster Abbey. King Henry spent much of his time at prayer in the chapel of the bishop of London's palace where he was lodged and four hundred miles away in Scotland Queen Margaret negotiated for arms, men and money to launch a counter attack in the name of their son, Prince Edward.

In the end the lords came to Richard with a compromise. Henry was to remain king for his lifetime and Richard was to be officially recognized as heir to the throne and appointed Protector of the Realm. This time he did not make the mistake of failing to consult anyone. He called a meeting in the great chamber. Hal had gone north to reclaim his Yorkshire estates and keep an eye on the Scottish March so he was not there but for once I was included, as was the new Chancellor, Hal's son George Neville, bishop of Exeter who, apart from his priest's tonsure, was a man something after the style of his brother Dick, pugnacious and with a sharp intellect.

Richard began by running through the main points of the proposed Act of Settlement and concluded with his own scathing opinion of it. 'They call it an Act of Settlement but of course it settles nothing.'

He appeared in a remarkably buoyant mood nevertheless, striding about the room waving the scroll on which the terms of the Act were penned in a neat, clerk's script. 'However I am inclined to accept it, not because I like it but because it will never work. King Henry may have signed it but he will sign anything; that is why I am made protector – again! But the lady who calls herself queen will never agree to it because it disinherits her son and so she will have to be dealt with on the battlefield. Her misguided followers who were scattered after Northampton have gathered their forces in Northumberland and are waiting for the Scottish reinforcements she has acquired by giving away two of our key border strongholds, Berwick and Roxburgh, both of them vital to England's security, but the Frenchwoman would not know or care about that. The Scots will be gloating over their prizes and doubtless supplying her with undisciplined mercenaries and faulty guns in return, like the one which recently exploded and killed their own king.

'So as soon as we have annihilated Margaret's sorry attempt to regain her husband's side, it would be my intention to rescind this heinous Act and get down to the real business of returning England to peaceful unity and the rule of law. I ask for your comments.'

There was a short silence while people digested what truly was an extraordinary speech. What Richard had effectively said was that he would accept the lords' compromise because within a few months it would have no relevance since he would have made himself king by conquest anyway.

Dick of Warwick was the first to speak. 'As I understand it, my lord duke, what you are saying is that having failed to get there by law you will fight your way to the throne and by using the word "we" you are inviting us to assist you to do so.' He was seated between Edward and his brother Tom and put a hand on each of their shoulders.

When Richard smiled his face lit up and he looked ten years younger than his forty-nine years. 'Precisely, my lord of Warwick, only do not tell the House of Commons or they will never pass this piece of nonsense and we shall be delayed getting into the field as a result.' He waved the scroll then threw it dismissively onto the table beside his empty chair and sat down.

'It is not just the Frenchwoman and her cronies we have to dispatch though, is it my lord father?' It was Edward's turn to speak. 'There is also Jasper Tudor in Wales. One of us must raise our marcher lords to stop him joining her army in the north and as Earl of March I think that is my prerogative. Will you give me the command?'

There was a tense pause, during which I sent up a prayer to St Michael to clear Richard's paternalistic view of Edward as a youth and not a man. The future of their relationship hung on his reply but it seemed that Edmund had the matter in hand. He leaned over from his habitual position behind his father's chair and murmured something in his ear. Richard looked up at him, frowned then gave a sharp nod in Edward's direction.

'You are the obvious choice for that task, Edward – and the sooner the better, then you can bring your men to confront the Lancastrians wherever we find them. As soon as Parliament passes the Act, I will march our army north to meet the Earl of Salisbury, which will leave the security of London in your capable hands, my lord of Warwick.'

For a few seconds Dick had looked as if he was going to dispute Edward's sole command of the Welsh campaign but the mention of the London command cleared his frown. I breathed an initial sigh of relief and then the truth hit me. This was not Ludlow, when the Lancastrians had been the aggressors. This time there would be no last minute escape; the whole York affinity including my husband, three of my brothers and, worst of all, my two eldest sons were going to war – to fight for the crown of England. Their mere survival was not an option. In my heavy heart I knew that I would spend much of the next weeks and months on my knees, praying for their victory.

42

Sandal Magna Castle, Yorkshire, December 1460

Cuthbert

For all Richard's regal magnificence and his air of supreme confidence, his troops did not arrive at his fortress of Sandal Magna in good heart. I had responded to Cicely's plea to join the Yorkist army which marched out of London in early December and from the start I had been far from convinced that it was fit to take on the highly experienced fighting men of the northern border. I did not see how soldiers who only weeks before had been dying cloth or making pies in the workshops of London would be any match for those northern warriors. Nor were many of their captains trained commanders. Richard had numbers behind him but few quality marching-men.

The Earl of Northumberland and Lord Clifford, two of the young Lancastrian heirs who had inherited after their fathers were killed at the Battle of St Albans, would have been busy recruiting along the wild lands between Scotland and England where men's skills with sword and claymore were matched by their sharp wits and cunning.

Moreover as we entered the Lancastrian heartland near

Worksop some of our harbingers were set upon and systematically cut down by their Lancastrian equivalent. When we came upon their butchered bodies we realized that some had been tortured before they were killed and had no doubt spilled information about our numbers and battle-readiness. It was bad enough to know myself that we were outnumbered, ill-prepared and poorly supplied and even worse to know that the enemy was now also aware of it.

I felt enormous relief when the great fortress of Sandal Magna loomed on the horizon, high on its hill above the town of Wakefield. This was York territory and the locals were as glad to see us as we were to see them, for since the death of Lord Egremont at Northampton they had been subject to much harassment by avenging raiders from the Percy strongholds of Spofforth and Healaugh thirty miles north. On Richard's orders, once the men were fed and billeted, I set about getting our big guns placed and organizing details to dig defensive ditches around the ramparts. Sandal was a well-fortified castle but its footprint was small and ten thousand men had to be squeezed into every nook and cranny of its steep motte and baileys. Some troops were obliged to camp outside the walls, defended only by the big guns and the ditch defences, so the gates would need to open for them to come and go from the castle, for duties or for refuge should the need arise; I made sure that the operation of the gates, especially closing them and raising the drawbridge, were swift and decisive actions.

Then on Christmas Eve, as Bishop George Neville was celebrating mass in the castle chapel, an alarm bell rang from the watch on the roof of the great round tower keep. A parley party was arriving under a white flag. Richard and his retinue had hardly reached the great hall before the Lancastrian deputation strode in, having left their swords and helmets at the guardhouse. Ahead of the herald who bore a white flag with a red rose set prominently at its centre Henry Beaufort, the urbane young Duke of Somerset, marched up to the dais, accompanied by his contemporary and ally Lord Clifford.

By any standards it was an extraordinary confrontation. The difference in age between the chief antagonists was substantial – by my reckoning about twenty-five years. Both were in half armour and wore over their cuirasses crested jupons which were remarkably similar, scattered with English lions and French lilies, demonstrating vividly the close family relationship between the two rival parties for the throne. Here was a great-grandson of King Edward the Third face to face with a great-great-grandson of the same king, both of whom had a claim on that doughty monarch's throne. It was York versus Lancaster, maturity versus youth, resolve versus guile. Good-looking though he was with his thick auburn hair and bright blue eyes, I did not feel inclined to trust Henry Beaufort an inch.

The younger man made a sharp, military bow. 'My lord duke, we come in peace on the eve of Christ's birth.'

I could not help noticing that while Somerset held Richard's gaze with a steady look, Lord Clifford was scanning the hall, taking note of the occupants. When he reached Hal of Salisbury, he paused as if he had found what he was looking for. Then his eyes roved to Edmund, who stood as usual at Richard's elbow and afterwards across to me. I frowned back at him. Not only had this young man's father been killed by Hal at St Albans but he had also been involved in Cicely's abduction to Aycliffe Tower. There was a lot of history between Clifford and Neville.

Richard did not return the other duke's bow. 'You have already disturbed our Christmas peace, Somerset. Say what you have come to say and take your leave.'

'As you wish. Here is my proposal.' The young duke turned and nodded at his herald who cleared his throat and raised a scroll to read from it.

'His grace the Duke of Somerset has the honour to command the army of his grace the Prince of Wales. We are camped at your gates and have your castle under siege in his name. But in view of the season it is suggested by that most puissant prince that both sides refrain from hostilities until Epiphany so that all may celebrate the birth of our Lord in His holy peace.'

Richard's face remained set in stone. He waited a considerable time before responding and then spoke in a voice that was clipped and clear. 'The heir to the throne is the only puissant prince to bear the title Prince of Wales. I am heir to the throne by Act of Parliament and therefore titular Prince of Wales. I do not recognize the high command of your army, nor do I consider an eight-year-old boy old enough to make treaties or truces. However, I do rejoice in the birth of our Lord and will agree to a suspension of hostilities until Epiphany. Until then, let us all go with God.'

The parley party nodded their heads and turned on their heels but not before the Duke of Somerset had aimed a flourish of his hand and a mocking smile at Richard and Lord Clifford had treated me to a lifted brow and a hard stare, which I found impossible to interpret. Why Clifford glared at me as if he had a personal grudge was a mystery, since we had never met.

Richard kept his eyes on the Lancastrians until they left the

490

hall, closely escorted by armed guards, then he turned to us. 'Those young firebrands bear a grudge against all of us,' he observed with a lop-sided smile. 'But what they do not know is that their twelve-day truce will give our latest ally a chance to bring an extra two thousand men to Sandal. Lord Neville of Brancepeth has pledged his support to York.'

This was news indeed. I sucked my teeth in surprise but said nothing, remembering my conversation with that same Lord Neville at Middleham when 'perhaps' had been the word of the day. Hal however voiced reservations similar to my own. 'Can we trust him, Richard? Do not forget he was crucially late at Ludford Bridge.'

'Yet he held back when the Percys threatened your Tom's wedding procession at Heworth Moor,' the duke reminded us. 'Rest assured, Hal, that he has sympathy for the York cause, even if you and he have clashed over property for years.'

Hal stroked his chin. 'Well we can certainly use his men when the time comes. It is one thing to celebrate Christmas but we cannot stay behind these walls for long afterwards. We do not have enough supplies for ten thousand, let alone twelve.'

While that was true enough, I had another reason altogether to ponder the consequences of John Neville's defection to York. I had been assuming that as a tenant knight of the Brancepeth Nevilles my blood-thirsty brother-in-law Sir Gerald Copley would be recruited to their banner and fight on the other side but now it seemed he might be on ours. In view of what John had told me at Middleham, I would rather have been on a battlefield face to face with someone who had sworn to kill me than have him at my back.

Christmas was hardly a celebration, although a lot of wine

and ale was consumed as men sought to drown their apprehension about what was to come. Despite the arranged truce, the gates of the castle were kept firmly closed except for when the troops camped out on the ramparts were able to enter and leave for religious services and meals. However, strict rationing meant that the meals were not plentiful and many of these men took to foraging about the countryside to supplement their diet, a practice with which I sympathized but the foragers were very vulnerable to attack and, truce or no truce, there were several clashes with Lancastrian scouts which cost the lives of men we could ill afford to lose.

Immediately below the hill on which Sandal Magna Castle stood was an area called Wakefield Green. It was a wide stretch of common land used in summer by the people of the town for grazing their stock but during those tense winter days of truce it became a taunting ground for the Lancastrians. Detachments of troops would march to and fro under red rose banners or practice manoeuvres there, always ensuring that they were just out of arrow-shot.

One such incident drew Richard out onto the battlements and tipped him into a rare fit of rage. For half an hour around noon on Holy Innocents Day, December the twenty-eighth, about four hundred men paraded prominently in murrey and blue York livery, giving the impression that they were reinforcements bound for the castle, except that none were expected and they did not attempt to gain entry. Then all at once they ripped off their York colours, stamped them into the ground and raised the battle standard of Sir Anthony Trollope, the very Captain who had turned his coat at Ludlow and taken his men across to the Lancastrians. It was the kind of schoolboy jape that probably amused the youthful commander of the present

Lancastrian army and was calculated to infuriate the Duke of York, which it unquestionably did.

'I swear that cowardly devil's disciple Trollope shall die!' Richard stormed. 'How dare he trample the York colours? As God is my witness I will personally sink a dagger into his black heart!'

The following day a message came through to Sandal Magna that Lord Neville had camped the previous night only twenty miles away with his two thousand men. 'We cannot wait for Epiphany,' Richard fretted. 'We have not enough food for another two thousand and we cannot afford to lose those men. While the weather stays dry, I am going to tell Lord Neville to advance. We will do battle tomorrow.'

Hal, as always, advised prudence. 'Suppose Somerset's scouts intercept your messenger. He would get warning of our intentions. Neville is coming anyway. We should wait until we see him.'

'We should wait until he is actually among us with weapons drawn,' I warned. 'Otherwise we are putting a lot of trust in his good faith.'

'But my father is right.' Edmund's sudden interjection took us all by surprise. Aware of his youth and inexperience, he normally kept silent during strategical discussion. Now he added, 'We cannot last another week until Epiphany and Lord Neville's arrival will give us the advantage. Now is the time.'

Tom Neville spoke up for Edmund. 'I agree. We should spring on them tomorrow. Waiting is not good for morale.'

Hal and I exchanged glances but, disappointingly, he did not put up any further objection. 'But Lord Salisbury is right too, we should not risk sending a message today,' I urged, echoing his earlier caution.

However, a mood of eager anticipation had suddenly pervaded the atmosphere, causing everyone else to clasp hands and confirm the plan, exchanging exclamations of elation and encouragement. I was not certain I had even been heard.

43

Wakefield Green, Yorkshire, 30th December 1460

Cuthbert

All our fighting men were told to be armed and ready by dawn and so the castle had been a hive of activity late into the night, with knights and squires checking weapons and armour, artillerymen running supplies of gunpowder and shot out to the battery under cover of darkness and foot-soldiers sharpening their pikes and halberds. Due to the terrain and our intention to make the first charge, it would not be a battle where archers could cut down the enemy without inflicting casualties on our own men and so snipers were to be placed on the castle battlements to pick off unwary Lancastrian units who strayed too near the walls but otherwise the bowmen would be deployed as infantry and issued with body-armour and weapons suited to the vicious hand-to-hand fighting such a battle guaranteed.

I was among the advance cavalry lining up in the lower bailey, waiting for the gates to open when a cry came down from the watch high above on the keep roof. 'Enemy movement on Wakefield Green! Troops advancing in numbers from the Lancastrian camp!'

Already mounted on his dappled grey stallion Richard gave

a brisk nod to his bearer who raised the York ducal standard with its labelled royal arms quartered with those of his Mortimer mother and his Castilian grandmother. This was the signal for the gates to be opened, the portcullis raised and the drawbridge lowered, all in the smooth two-minute operation I had rehearsed with the mechanics. Herald trumpeters blew a fanfare as we cantered three abreast under the gatehouse arch and down the steep road that swept round the hill to the flat ground known as Sandal Field. There we took up our positions for the first charge, watching as the Lancastrian cavalry were scrambling to do the same on Wakefield Green, between us and the River Calder.

'Our numbers look pretty even,' shouted Edmund, who had been roughly counting heads. Our visors were still up and like any lad before his first battle the seventeen-year-old looked flushed and excited at the prospect of putting all his training into practice, though inside he would be terrified that he would not prove worthy.

I turned to look behind us where a hundred horsemen were lining up in their gleaming armour and colourful heraldry but I rose in my stirrups to peer over their heads, seeking the sight that I most wanted to find – the black bull's head and white-on-red saltire cross that would signal the arrival of the Brancepeth Nevilles. It was not there and I knew we could not wait. If we were to achieve the advantage we sought we would have to charge before the Lancastrians were ready and it would not be long before they were. In fact I was impressed with their uncanny intuition about our intentions; as if they had known what our plans were.

Unobtrusively I placed myself close behind Edmund, knowing Cicely would expect me to shadow him as closely as possible.

It was bitingly cold. The frost-wilted grass crunched under our horses' hooves and their breath and ours rose like steam. I stole another look over my shoulder – still no sign of our reinforcements. The flag went up for preparation to charge. I crossed myself and slammed my visor shut. The very sound of it caused my warhorse to sidle and snort and I leaned back in the saddle to halt him. Then Richard moved his lance from vertical to horizontal and with the dip of the standard the first line of cavalry edged into a slow trot. Within moments we were cantering and as we drew closer I saw that the opposition was also on the move. The thunder of hooves grew louder and I thanked St George for the studs in the horse-shoes, which the blacksmiths had sweated blood to fit the previous day. Without them my destrier and all the others around me would have been slipping and sliding on the icy ground. Couched in my gauntleted hand the lance felt finely balanced and thrummed with a familiar vibration which matched the pounding of blood in my veins. Through the slits in my visor I selected an approaching horseman to aim at, set my teeth and waited for the bone-jarring crunch of collision.

There was definite contact but it was impossible to know whether the lance had found a vital spot because impulsion carried us past each other and into the next line of cavalry. All I knew was that my shield had taken the force of his lance while mine drooped from my arm, shattered and useless, which was the sign of a good impact. I hurled it away and unhooked the mace from my saddle. For close fighting on horseback it was my weapon of choice and I brought it crashing down on the nearest red rose badge I could see. Not for the first time the thought shot through my mind that it was never sensible to attach your badge to your fighting shoulder for the studded metal ball made contact and my opponent's battleaxe flew from his hand. Wheeling my horse around and ducking under his neck I swung it back-handed at the Lancastrian's steel-clad shin and saw the greave dent like a plough-share as the injured knight toppled from his horse. There was one soldier who would not walk off the battlefield I thought and blocked a sword slash with my shield, whipping my mace up to swing it under the raised arm that had made it. Once again there was a clang as the mace scraped steel but before I could ascertain the damage I was past that opponent and wheeling back to look for Edmund.

Finding a small gap in the mêlée I risked lifting my visor to look once more towards the castle hoping to see the black-bull standard, but instead I saw something which made my blood freeze. Our infantry were still streaming out of the castle gate but to either side of them Lancastrian foot-soldiers could be seen charging out of woodland and bearing down on their flanks. Within minutes not only would we be greatly outnumbered but we would also be cut off from any retreat to the castle. Also, as the gates were open Lancastrian forces were peeling off to make an incursion into the fast-emptying castle. Not only had John Neville failed us once more but my gut feeling that our battle plan had been leaked was proving right.

'God damn you, John Neville!' I shouted out loud. He had not come when we needed him and even if he did bring his men up now it was certain that he would see York in a hopeless situation and turn away. In the second that this thought ran through my mind I turned my head and saw Richard's horse rear up and throw him from the saddle. Blood was spurting from under the stallion's chamfron where a blade had slit his nostril. I drove my spurs into my destrier's sides to try and smash my way through to Richard's aid but found myself blocked by a knight whose shield-crest I instantly recognized – five gold caltrops on a blue ground. Sir Gerald Copley. He must have come down from the north in Northumberland's or Clifford's army for he wore the red rose on his shoulder.

'Stand, bastard! You are going to die!' he screamed.

I did not stop or make a reply because, despite his deadly challenge, I knew instinctively that he would not allow me to make any kind of stand. My horse was already at a charging trot and I urged him on, swinging him to the right when he was a yard from Copley and raising my shield. His sword blow slammed into it, giving me a split second to bring my mace down on his horse's forehead. The chamfron rang like a bell and the horse staggered but it did not fall. I wheeled my destrier to take advantage of Copley's exposed rear and dealt him a passing blow on the back plate of his cuirass but I had to reach out to do so and could not get my full force into it. Now my back was to him but his charger was still stunned and would not respond to his furious kicks and yanks on the reins.

'Did no one teach you how to ride a horse, Copley?' I yelled, circling his stricken steed. 'You are not driving an ox-cart!'

Surrounded as we were by the resounding clash of arms and the shrill shrieks of wounded men I doubt if he heard my jibe but it gave me satisfaction to make it. However, fighting a man on a stationary horse from the advantage of a moving one seemed to dull my lust for combat and instead of rushing in to take advantage of my mobility, I held back for a few moments, steeling myself to make the deadly blow that would rid me of a mortal enemy. I could not free my mind of the thought that this was my wife's brother, the boy with whom she had shared a nursery and whose mother had been her mother. Paradoxically

I found I could almost enjoy his screeching frustration as his great horse shook its damaged head and tried and failed to obey his clumsy aides. But as I watched a mounted man-at-arms wearing the white rose appeared from the surrounding crush with his battle-axe raised, slammed into Copley's horse and dealt its rider a crushing blow to the back of the head. I saw Gerald's helmet split. The impact of the collision unbalanced his injured horse and down they went together in a welter of flailing hooves. I was spared the inevitable sight of his spilled brains as Copley disappeared under the iron-shod feet of his assailant's mount.

I made the sign of the cross and turned away, unexpectedly grateful to the unidentified man-at-arms who had saved me from making the gruesome choice of killing or being killed by my wife's brother. After that I began to fight automatically, using a lifetime of experience at practice and skirmish to block and parry, wheel and charge, until at last I reached the place where I had seen Richard part company with his horse and where his standard still flew. He was on foot, back to back with Edmund and with his dismounted retinue surrounding them, all ferociously fighting off a series of red rose contenders for the honour of killing the Duke of York and capturing his banner. I plunged into the fray, wielding my mace with a vicious energy I had not known was still in my armoury. At length I managed to smash and dance my horse through to the Yorkist circle which, recognizing the bend on my Neville shield, parted to let me in.

'Take my horse, Richard!' I screamed over the screech of metal on metal as I battered off a foolish knight who seemed to be fighting without a shield and soon succumbed to my side-swipes. 'We are surrounded. We have to retreat now!'

'No retreat,' he yelled back. 'Take Edmund up with you, Cuthbert, and get him out of here. That is an order!'

'I – will – not – leave – you,' panted Edmund, who was clearly exhausted, handling his sword like a slippery fish and staggering under his full armour-plate.

One of the circle-knights managed to slice through the hamstring of a horse whose rider made the mistake of getting too close and sprang back as it came crashing down beside him. As the knight pounced on its winded rider Richard took advantage of the diversion to turn on his young son and shout fiercely at him through his visor. 'Do not dare to disobey me, Edmund! You heard Cuthbert. We are surrounded. You have fought well. Go now and go with God.'

'I do not go willingly, my lord father. May God protect *you!*' Edmund's voice choked as he put his foot in my stirrup and somehow I managed to haul him up in front of me. I could feel my horse sag at the weight of two men in armour, even if one of them was a comparative lightweight, and I knew we could not go far. 'You take the left hand side and I will take the right,' I shouted at the part of Edmund's helmet where his ear would be. 'We will have to fight our way out of this.'

Richard's retinue opened up to let us out of their ring and closed back around their lord. They were all on foot now and must have known they were fighting for their lives as knights fell one after another, slain, wounded or exhausted. I saluted them solemnly as dead men and urged my charger into as much pace as he could muster. Jinking and swerving we slashed our way out of the throng of fighting men and headed for the woods lining the banks of the River Calder which skirted the battlefield to the west. Having studied the terrain from the castle battlements I knew there was a bridge which led to the town of

Wakefield and that if we could get there I would find a temporary refuge for Edmund among the Yorkists who made up the bulk of the inhabitants.

It was a case of pushing my tired horse to his limits of speed because, although I could not see behind us due to the trees, I could hear the thunder of hooves on our trail and they had the terrifying sound of a hue and cry, as if our pursuers knew exactly who we were and were determined to stop us. As we broke out of the woods on the other side my heart lifted.

'There it is, Edmund. There is the bridge to Wakefield. We will find friends there.' But my brave horse could go no further. The poor beast simply stopped and shuddered and then sank from beneath us. His great heart must have failed. 'We will have to run. Take off your helmet and surcote and head for the bridge and I will watch our backs,' I told Edmund as we picked ourselves up.

The youngster obeyed orders. When he pulled off his helmet, his face was ashen but he did not speak or delay. He had the air of one who was beyond thought, almost beyond hope. He knew he had left his father to die on the battlefield and now he thought there was little chance of staying alive himself. But he was too young to die. I was determined to prove him wrong. I rolled up his surcote and helmet and flung them into the river. In this perilous situation, it was unwise to be identified as a son of York.

He was nearly at the bridge when two horsemen broke out of the trees and immediately put up a shout. 'Stop, Yorkist coward! Stop and surrender!'

I could see Edmund hesitate and stumble on the word 'coward' and screamed at him 'Do not listen! Keep running!' as I stepped out in front of the galloping horses. Both riders wore the same crest on their surcôtes, the blue and gold chequer-board and red bar of the Cliffords, and I put myself in the way of the leading horse because I hoped it might swerve and unseat its rider. It was a desperate action against what I feared was about to be a calculated act of vengeance for I recognized the young baron who had accompanied Somerset to the parley on Christmas Eve and had stared so hard at me. Unfortunately this horse did not swerve. It had been well-trained and simply flung me aside like a rag doll and galloped on. With a clanging thud, I landed face down in the hoof-churned grass of the riverbank, dazed and completely winded.

For a full minute everything went dark and I struggled to get a single breath into my lungs. My head felt as if it would burst inside my helmet but I could not move a muscle to take it off. Fortunately the visor was still down and it kept my face out of the mud so that when I did manage to draw breath there was enough air leaking through the slits to serve my starved lungs. I could not see because I could not lift my head but I could hear shouts at the bridge.

'Who are you, coward? Name yourself!' I took it to be Clifford's voice. A sudden vision came to me of the scene at St Albans when Dick of Warwick had been fighting this man's father, unaware that the Duke of Somerset was coming at him from behind. It had been my brother Hal who had impaled the senior Clifford with his lance, enabling his son Dick to deal a fatal blow to Somerset. I tried to cry out that York was not to blame for the senior Clifford's death but I had not enough breath even to croak.

To my everlasting shame I could do nothing to prevent what happened next but by the devil's aid I managed to lift my head enough to observe a deed that would for ever be seared on my memory. Edmund had said nothing but threw his sword at Clifford's feet in a gesture of surrender and should have expected capture and ransom but there was no chivalry present on the arch of that bridge.

'Bah! I need no name for I know who you are.' Clifford had his dagger out and his blood up. 'You were at York's shoulder at the parley. Your father slew mine and I will slay the accursed son of York!'

His dagger, sharp as a barber's razor, sliced through the flesh of Edmund's smooth throat; I saw the lad's young blood flow and his eyes widen in shock before his body crumpled against the bridge railing and slumped to the ground. My neck could support the weight of my helmet no more. It dropped back into the mud and my whole body was wracked with a silent scream.

I was witness to a murder but they thought that I was dead – killed in the crash with Clifford's horse. Nevertheless they came to make sure. Clifford's accomplice put the toe of his steel-plated foot under my cuirass and tried to roll me over but found my armoured body too heavy. So he bent and lifted my head then dropped it back. 'Neck's broken,' he said, 'but I'll have the sword.'

'No!' Clifford's tone was peremptory. 'That is the Bastard of Middleham; one of the finest knights my father ever fought alongside. His sword should be buried with him. If you want to remember the day we killed York's son, take his. Come, let us go. The day is ours. We have work to do.'

They left me and I slowly started to breathe again. When I dared to lift my head, I saw them disappearing into the woods, the squire leading his horse with Edmund's body slung over the saddle. Slowly I sat up, wiped the mud from my visor and removed my helmet. Then, as if he knew I was alive, my own horse came back from the dead. He raised his head, looked around then heaved and kicked himself to his feet. Man and horse stood staring at each other in shock across an expanse of muddy grass. I nodded at him encouragingly and he began plodding towards me, taking one step at a time, testing his legs. I did the same, astonished to find that they worked. I took his reins and swung myself into the saddle. As we crossed the bridge he shied at the sight and smell of blood on the planking where Edmund had bled to death and I began to sob.

44

Baynard's Castle, London, January to March 1461

Cicely

Those winter months were dark indeed. If it had not been for Margaret I do not think I would have emerged sane from that black time. The mere thought of what the fiendish Lancastrians had done to my family sent me deep into the pit of despair and I thought about it almost every minute of every hour of every day. I had not seen them with my own eyes but York herald's description had been enough to stamp a picture in my mind and whenever I closed my eyes I could see the severed heads protruding above York's Micklegate Bar and, worst of all, for some reason Edmund's was always smiling at me.

'Why does he smile?' I groaned at Margaret when we were together in the chapel at Baynard's Castle. This was where I spent much of my day but if during my prayers I ever chanced to close my eyes they immediately flew open in alarm. 'My sweet, innocent Edmund! What is there to smile about, being murdered at seventeen?'

'Perhaps he is smiling because he is innocent and therefore he is with the saints in heaven.' Margaret murmured her words of comfort on her knees beside me as she almost constantly was. 'Or perhaps he does not want you to be sad.'

At not quite fifteen years old, she had given herself the task of mothering her mother and gratefully I let her, weeping in her arms and begging her not to leave my side. She must have wondered why I hardly mentioned Richard or Hal in my lamentations, especially as she mourned her father at least as much, if not more, than her brother, but I could not forgive Richard for taking Edmund into the thick of the battle and I could not forgive Hal for killing Clifford's father at St Albans and sowing the seeds of revenge in the young heir's mind. Theirs were the other two heads that my fevered mind's eye saw rotting on the Micklegate Bar but theirs were grinning in the rictus of death, not smiling the way Edmund's was. His smile was for me alone, a smile of love and tenderness which I did not deserve and could not abide.

I had learned of the dreadful defeat and of the deaths of my menfolk on the eve of Epiphany and for the first time in my life I had swooned with shock, unable to stomach the idea that their heads had been severed from their bodies and displayed on pikes as traitors. But it was Cuthbert who related the whole horrifying tale of the battle and its aftermath.

I had barely recognized him when he arrived back at Baynard's in the middle of January. He had been forced to travel by night and on a circuitous route in order to avoid Lancastrian fiefs and strongholds and when he entered my solar I took him for a stranger until I saw Hilda run into his arms with cries of joy. His hair had turned completely white and he was so thin his clothes hung off him like the rags on a scarecrow. Moreover his demeanour was utterly forlorn, his face pale and unshaven and his eyes red-rimmed and constantly downcast. As soon as he extricated himself from Hilda's embrace he flung himself at my feet, craving my forgiveness in a voice that was hoarse with grief.

'I am sorry, Cicely. I could not save him. Forgive me. I could not save your boy!'

I stood up and forced him to rise. When I put my arms around him I could feel the bones of his shoulders through his jacket. Never far away, my tears flowed freely down my cheeks as I drew him to a window seat and beckoned Hilda to follow. 'It could never be your fault, Cuddy, never!' I croaked. 'Tell me; please tell me of my poor Edmund's death.'

In halting words he related the events of that fateful day and the terrible details he had discovered of its aftermath. There were long pauses in Cuthbert's narrative while he blinked back tears and tried to compose himself but this was the gist of his tale and how I learned of the dreadful ignominy inflicted on my husband by drunken and vengeful Lancastrians in the great hall of his own castle.

'They found him dead on the battlefield and carried his body in triumph up to Sandal Magna along with Edmund's. There they hacked off Richard's head, crowned it with a paper crown and impaled it on a pike, waving it around like a puppet while spitting on it and mocking "the man who dared to think himself a king!" Then they cut off Edmund's already almost-severed head and mocked him as "the son of the would-be king!". The next day they brought our loved ones' remains to Pontefract where they threw them into unmarked graves.

'But our poor brother Hal suffered torture. Having been captured, naturally he expected to be held for ransom but at Pontefract he was shown Tom's body, which had also been taken from the battlefield, and forced to watch as his son's head was hacked off. Then Hal himself was publicly denounced as a traitor and summarily executed in the castle bailey. There was no trial, no justice, just a jeering crowd, an axe and a tree-stump. They sang bawdy songs as all four heads were waved aloft on pikes and then taken to York in procession, there to be exposed to the crows and the ravens on the Micklegate Bar.'

'I learned of this heartless and bloody vengeance from the people with whom I took shelter in Wakefield and then I was forced to flee through the back garden as Lancastrian soldiers hammered at the front door, seeking Yorkist refugees.'

Cuthbert looked exhausted as he ended his story and we pressed food and wine on him, which he barely tasted. Later, in a private moment between him and me, he also revealed John Neville's terrible treachery.

'I never saw Lord Neville come because it happened when I was taking Edmund from the field but apparently he did march in from the north with two thousand men to the cheers of our embattled forces, who saw him as their salvation. But then, under their very eyes, he crossed the line and joined the Lancastrians. Queen Margaret had promised him Middleham and Sheriff Hutton. It was Richard's death knell, Cicely.'

'Do not call that Frenchwoman queen, Cuddy,' I snapped, my heart plummeting deeper in my already grief-stricken breast. 'I pray to God that she will rot in hell and that John Neville will suffer the torture of having his son die before him at another man's hand.'

My mind was reeling and I struggled to breathe. It did not seem possible that John had crossed the line. I could not fathom how the man I had loved and who I thought had loved me could have knowingly made himself the cause of my husband's death and worse than that, effectively an accomplice to my son's murder. Had his love turned to hate? Was this his idea of revenge?

His sadistic way of showing me that I had not won when I betrayed his love at Aycliffe Tower? Had we shared love at Coverdale so that he could ultimately betray me in his turn? And for what? For his son to inherit a couple of castles and a strip of England? It did not seem possible. We had parted friends. I had thought him a tender lover and honourable man. Instead he had revealed himself as a vengeful, greedy creature who had made me a notch on his bedpost and then stabbed me in the back. It was too much for me to bear. I thought that nothing now could drag me out of the pit of despair.

As his father had commanded, Edward had been marshalling his supporters on the Welsh border ready to take on Jasper Tudor's army when it set out from Pembroke to join the Lancastrian forces. After their gory triumph at Wakefield the red-rose banners had moved south and at the beginning of February Edward's and Jasper's armies clashed at a place called Mortimer's Cross near Wigmore Castle resulting, praise be to God, in another glorious victory for Edward. Jasper successfully fled the field but his father Owen Tudor, King Henry's step-father, was captured and taken to Hereford with other prisoners. In another mass blood-letting, without trial or sentence, all of them had been beheaded in the market place there.

With my own grief still raw I considered that Edward could be forgiven for seeking Owen's execution as revenge for the death of his own father and brother at Wakefield but in a letter he informed me that he had not ordered the executions.

'I would not regard the beheading of Owen Tudor as adequate revenge for the death of my father and brother I assure you. I was away chasing Jasper Tudor, a man I consider far more important prey than his ageing rapscallion of a

father. But the deed is done now and when I am king I shall grant Owen's Welsh manors to William Herbert, who has been my staunchest ally and support in the West . . .'

The name William Herbert and the granting of Owen Tudor's manors meant nothing to me but Edward's assertion 'when I am king' stirred me out of my lethargy. Of course, under the Act of Settlement, he was now the heir to the throne, but this letter implied that he had decided not to wait for the death of King Henry but to take the crown by force of arms, and since Dick of Warwick was still in London preparing to hold the city against the advancing Lancastrians, he had made the decision without consulting his cousin and mentor. While my desolate spirits soared at the drive and energy and military skill Edward had displayed, I wondered how Dick and his fellow magnates would regard the prospect of paying homage to such a young and untried king. I decided to pay a visit to the Erber, the imposing London residence of the Earl of Warwick.

I had not been abroad in the streets since hearing of the losses at Wakefield and I was surprised at how quiet they were. It was as if the citizens were cowering behind closed doors fearful of what might be to come. Posted all over Cheapside were bills and pamphlets declaiming against the Lancastrians and warning Londoners that their properties and livelihoods were gravely at risk if the 'raiders from the north' marched through the gates. I detected Warwick's propaganda machine at work, bolstering his own position as London's defender and stressing the dangers of a rampaging Lancastrian army let loose in a city of rich merchant warehouses.

Dick was magnanimously welcoming but received me in the great hall where he conducted his business, which bustled with servants and military personnel coming and going on their duties and clerks and couriers dealing with the earl's surfeit of correspondence.

'My poor bereaved aunt,' he boomed in a voice that carried into the rafters. 'I humbly crave your grace's pardon. We have not yet commiserated together over the appalling deaths of our loved ones but as you see,' he waved his black-velvet-clad arm to encompass the grand and crowded chamber, 'there are many calls upon my time.' He walked around his table of business, took my hand and kissed it. 'You are greatly distressed I have no doubt but the news from Hereford is good.'

'Indeed I am and it is,' I acknowledged, thinking wryly that dark rings under inflamed eyes framed by a widow's wimple and barbe hardly indicated that I was about to dance a galliard. 'And it is news from Edward that brings me here, not commiserations. May I speak with you privately, my lord?'

Dick did not look eager to oblige but nevertheless guided me quickly through his privy door and into a small ante-room. 'Have you heard from Edward today?' I enquired, reaching into my sleeve-pocket for his letter.

'Not today but I gather men are flocking to his banner following his splendid victory at Mortimer's Cross. Why do you ask?'

'Let me read you a paragraph from a letter I received from him today.' I said. When he heard the key phrase 'when I am king' his face did not alter but I thought I heard his tongue click behind his teeth. 'Has Edward broached the matter of claiming the throne outright with you, Dick?' I asked baldly, re-folding the letter.

He rubbed his nose thoughtfully, couching his elbow in his other hand. 'We have not spoken together since before the duke

512

was killed as you know but no, he has not mentioned it to me in his letters. It is certainly a possibility.'

'He is so young. After years of ineffectual rule the kingdom needs firm government. Is he really ready to take on the responsibilities of kingship?'

Dick shrugged and his lips twitched. 'Your son is a prodigy, my lady. Besides, he would not be alone. He would have me beside him.'

'So you would support him?'

'Yes I would and I would not be the only one. There is no doubt he has the right. But first we have to deal with the ever-growing horde of Lancastrians who are marching down from the north, ravaging the country as they go. The Frenchwoman has told them they can have victors' spoils if they fight their way to London and I have the task of stopping them, otherwise the city will be ransacked. So, much though I would love to debate the merits and demerits of your son as King of England, if you will forgive me, I have more urgent matters to attend to.'

This interview had not made me anymore favourably disposed towards Warwick than I had been before but at least I had the reassurance of one very powerful magnate that he would support Edward's claim to the throne if, indeed, he intended to make it.

Nor did my opinion of my nephew improve after he led a large force against the Lancastrians in the middle of February and clashed with them once again at St Albans. This time Londoners were really given reason to panic because their blue-eyed hero failed to see off the much-feared horde and was forced to retreat further north with the remnants of his army, thus leaving their golden city wide open to Lancastrian rape and pillage. For me however, the most serious consequence of this defeat had been that Warwick had taken the king to the battle and managed to lose him. King Henry had been found by Lancastrian officers in his usual state of dazed bewilderment sitting under an oak tree somewhere and been reunited with his wife and son, which meant that he could no longer be held in London as a useful hostage against Lancastrian good behaviour.

Once again I put aside my state of mourning because now I could foresee that if the leading Lancastrians entered London – Somerset and Exeter in particular – they would have no compunction in using my two younger boys as hostages in their turn, bringing terrible pressure to bear on Edward and Dick when they united to confront their enemies again, to say nothing of the terror it would inflict on George and Dickon.

The two boys answered my summons from the schoolroom with their different attitudes to life reflected in their dress. Although only eleven George already had his own distinct ideas about what he wore and had perched his cocky black felt hat at a jaunty angle and pinned a bright blue cockade on it, making little concession to the solemnity of mourning, and he had insisted that the tailor put wide puffed sleeves on his tight-waisted and full-skirted black doublet, whereas eight-year-old Dickon, less flamboyant and more prone to chill than his brother, looked swamped in a rather clerical black gown relieved by a dark fur lining and a fur-edged cap. They both bent the knee and kissed my cheek before I bid them pull up stools to sit beside me.

'I am sending you to Bruges,' I said, watching their reactions carefully. George seemed to glow with excitement and Dickon was the first to protest.

'To Bruges!' he echoed in alarm. 'But why?'

'Because the Lancastrians defeated the Earl of Warwick at

St Albans and although the earl got away, there is no knowing now whether London will open the gates to the enemy. If they do, it would be better if you two sons of York were not in the country.'

'What do you think they might do to us, lady mother?' enquired George rather nervously, as if he was not sure if he wanted to hear the answer. 'Would they kill us like they killed Edmund?'

How I wished children were not so painfully direct! 'No, George, but they might use you to force Edward and Dick to do things they do not wish to do. Do you understand?'

'You mean use us as hostages?'

'Yes, possibly. Basically until the Lancastrians are routed you would be safer in Bruges. The Duke of Burgundy will protect you and he has a court full of artists and intellectuals who will teach you many things that you cannot learn here.'

'I do not want to leave you, mother,' said Dickon flatly. 'Who will protect *you*?'

'Well you cannot anyway, Dickon,' George scoffed. 'You are not even strong enough yet to wield a sword.'

'That is not true!' cried Dickon, incensed. 'I have a wooden one.'

'That is enough,' I scolded. 'Thank you for worrying about me Dickon but I have a whole household of people to protect me and most of all your Uncle Cuthbert. You will sail on Friday with Anicia to look after your everyday needs and your tutor to guide your studies. I will send gifts for your host Duke Philip and his wife the Duchess Isabella. I want you to write to me every week, both of you. I will miss you terribly but let us pray it will not be for long. Soon Edward and Dick will come back to London and it will be safe for you to return.'

I said this with a smile but there was no reason to hope that the situation would improve soon. The boys sailed as planned amid reports flooding in from the towns surrounding London that the Lancastrian army was running riot, plundering and raping and even raiding churches and abbeys, stealing precious chalices and relics for their gold and jewels. This terrifying activity made Londoners more determined than ever that none of them should be admitted to the city, not even the king and particularly not 'the Frenchwoman'. I heard that my sister Anne, now Dowager Duchess of Buckingham, came with a deputation to the Mayor and Aldermen to plead for the gates to be opened but she did not visit me which was no surprise, nor were her efforts on behalf of the Lancastrians successful. Londoners simply did not believe that promises of good behaviour would be fulfilled and declared that they would wait for the return of the Duke of York and the Earl of Warwick.

It seemed that a battle at the gates of London was almost inevitable as we learned that Edward and Dick had now united their forces near Oxford and were marching south-east together. Margaret and I knelt in the chapel and prayed that God would bring them victory, for another disaster like Wakefield did not bear thinking about. Then we heard that unexpectedly the Lancastrians had retreated back into Bedfordshire in the hope of persuading Londoners that they meant them no harm. Only days later Edward and Dick slipped past them and rode into London at the head of a vast army to be welcomed by gates thrown wide open and the deafening cheers of the citizens.

After he had seen his men safely camped in Clerkenwell Fields Edward came straight to Baynard's Castle. Margaret and I were in the courtyard to greet him as he rode in wearing a smile nearly as wide as the Thames and a new blue jupon over his armour bearing the image of a white rose surrounded by the sun's golden rays. Many of his followers had silver badges of a similar design. When we had greeted each other amid the applause of the household, Edward went to change into more comfortable apparel and a meal was served to us privately in front of a roaring fire in the great chamber.

Margaret mentioned the new badge. 'What does it signify, Edward?' she asked.

'Did you not hear about the remarkable omen before the battle at Mortimer's Cross?' Edward asked in amazement. 'I thought the story would have been all round the country with the speed of a thunderbolt.' He leaned forward eagerly. 'Let me have the pleasure of telling you about it then. We had word that Jasper Tudor was bringing his force from Pembroke to Ludlow and we waited for them at a place I had chosen long ago as the perfect location for a battle if Wigmore Castle was ever to come under threat from the south. I had fought a battle there a dozen times in my head so I knew exactly how to go about it. It is in a valley where two roads cross and the locals now call it Mortimer's Cross because they call me Lord Mortimer.'

'But you are Duke of York now,' Margaret put in a little irritably. 'Surely they realize that.'

Edward laughed. 'The people of the Welsh March pledged their loyalty to the Mortimers hundreds of years ago and are averse to change. I do not care what they call me so long as they follow me with a will, which I am glad to say they do. Anyway when we got there at dawn it was freezing and to keep them warm I set the men to digging ditches and making traps and when the clouds suddenly cleared in mid morning there were seen to be three suns in the sky. All fighting-men are superstitious and Welshmen particularly so and someone started a rumour that this was a sign of God's displeasure. I did not want them all downing weapons and heading for the hills so I leaped up on a rock and made a rousing speech about how the three suns were a sign of the Holy Trinity – Father, Son and Holy Ghost – and that they signified that the Almighty was with us and would help us to win the battle.' He spread his arms wide to emphasize his point. 'Which of course He did. So I have adapted the white rose and surrounded it with the sun's rays as my personal badge of affinity. I am the Sun of York! Good, is it not?'

As Margaret clapped and nodded her agreement, I gazed at this son of mine who seemed so genuinely possessed of divine grace. He was so quick of mind and eye, so confident and sure, that people simply did not doubt his ability to achieve whatever he said he would. I had no doubt that he would sally forth to his next confrontation with the Lancastrians surrounded by God's rays of grace and men who would follow him to the ends of the earth. I would never show disloyalty by saying so in public but I could not help seeing a quality in my son which had never been evident in his father. Apostasy had been Richard's downfall but I did not believe that Edward's followers would ever consider betraying him.

I sat back for a few minutes, watching and listening as he and Margaret laughed and joked together and thought for the first time how alike they were, both in looks and character. They had been separated a great deal as children but I hoped that Edward would come to realize what a great confidant he might make of his sister and she of him. However I was jolted out of my reverie when I heard Margaret suddenly pose the question I had been avoiding like a bat avoids a torch flame.

'Are you going to be king, Edward? Everyone in London seems to think you are.'

Edward rolled his eyes. 'Who knows? But God only gives a man one life and I intend to make the most of mine, so I will not refuse a crown if it is offered to me.'

'If the lords have any sense they will offer it,' said his sister.

Edward regarded her with a lop-sided smile, head on one side. 'Do you know, Meg, I rather think they might.'

I was reminded that four years earlier Edward had refused to adhere to Margaret's request to be called by her full name. 'The world may call you Margaret.' He had said the word in a comic pompous voice. 'But I shall always think of you as Meg. So I shall call you Meg and you can call me Ned. It will remind us that we are special to each other – blood kin. But, Meg, when I am king and you are a queen, please do not call me King Ned.' The idea had caused them to collapse into giggles. At the time there had been no question of Edward ever being king.

The following day we were all leaving the chapel after hearing masses for the souls of Richard and Edmund when the steward came to tell us that a deputation had arrived from the Great Council and asked to meet with Edward. 'I took them to the Great Hall, your grace,' he said to me. 'There are quite a number of them, including the Archbishop of Canterbury, the Earl of Warwick and your brother, Lord Fauconberg.'

Edward and I exchanged glances. His face, already solemn after the requiem masses, went quite pale and I saw him briefly grab Margaret's hand and squeeze it.

'Have one of the casks of Bordeaux tapped,' I told the Steward. 'And Lent or not, tell the cooks to make some honey wafers. We may have something to celebrate.'

A group of some twenty lords and bishops were gathered in the centre of the great hall wearing long furred gowns against the stiff March breezes. Their cheeks and noses were rosy after the short walk from Blackfriars, where they had met earlier that morning. We paused in the arched entrance and I glanced briefly at Edward.

'Do you want to go first?' I asked him in a low voice.

He shook his head. 'No, let us walk together, you, me and Meg. We will see what they have to say.'

As we approached the group I briefly caught the eye of my brother Will, tall at the back. I had not seen him for years and noticed that his beard was streaked with grey. Then the Archbishop of Canterbury stepped forward. Thomas Bourchier was the brother of Richard's sister Isabel's husband Viscount Bourchier and the random thought crossed my mind that probably everyone in this room was related to each other either directly or by marriage. Because, like the two branches of Nevilles, the Bourchiers and the Buckinghams had a common grandparent and so, like me, most of them were closely related to someone in the Lancastrian command. York and Lancaster were not factions. Sadly they were family.

The cross on the archbishop's chest glittered with a pattern of diamonds and his mitre was slightly askew, as if he had donned it hastily. He held in his hand a rolled vellum scroll on which there was, as yet, no seal. He cleared his throat as he unrolled it and then began to read.

'After much deliberation and consultation with the Commons, the peers of the Great Council of England have decided that Edward, Duke of York, three times great grandson of the puissant King Edward the Third, is by right of birth and descent their true king and on this day, the fourth of March fourteen hundred and sixty one, wish to offer to the said Edward, Duke of York, the crown and throne of England

520

which, in due course, they entreat him to come to the Abbey of St Peter at Westminster to accept.'

The archbishop lowered the scroll and a profound silence fell as every eye in the hall focused on Edward. He took one step forward and I could feel my heart pounding so hard in my chest that I imagined the sound must reach the ears of everyone about me. Then Edward turned to me without speaking and dropped to his knees. I knew the reason. He had said to me once that I would make a wise and beautiful queen and that he and everyone else would kneel at my feet. Now he was about to accept the crown and afterwards, as the highest in the land, he would never kneel to me or to anyone.

He wore no hat and I reached out and put my hands on his golden head. 'God bless you, Edward,' I said. 'My son. My king.' Then I cupped his smooth, boyish chin in my palm and leaned down to kiss his cheek.

To my astonishment I tasted the salt of tears and knew intuitively that the boy who had so suddenly become a man was weeping for his father. Gently, with my thumb, I wiped the tear away and gave a slight shake of my head. He could grieve later, when the throne was secure. Now was not the time for tears.

Edward stood up and stepped forward, taller and lighter of foot than anyone else in the room. 'My lords,' he said and I was pleased to hear his voice emerge loud and firm, 'I accept your offer and will come with you to Westminster to accept the crown and the throne of England.'

Later in the day, after Edward had been sworn in as England's lawgiver and enthroned on the King's Bench at Westminster Hall, Margaret and I sat together in the chancel at Westminster Abbey and watched as the abbot and monks brought out the crown and sceptre of Edward the Confessor and offered them to his namesake. Taking the crown, the new, young Edward placed it reverently on his own head and then sceptre in hand he walked to the throne, sat down and addressed the congregation loudly and clearly.

'At the request of the Lords and Commons I have accepted the crown of England but this is not a coronation. Sixty-two years ago Henry of Lancaster usurped the throne of Richard the Second. I am the descendant of King Richard's heir, Edmund Mortimer, Earl of March, and as such I am your rightful king. I vow to you in this holy place that I will serve you diligently and faithfully. But I will not be crowned by the archbishop or receive the divine right of kingship by anointment with the holy chrism until I have driven the present usurper Henry and his wife out of the kingdom or else brought them to my royal justice charged with treason. May God bless our realm and all its worthy citizens!'

Because of the lump in my throat I could not cheer his speech as the congregation then did, loud and long. The peers present formed a queue to pay homage to their new king but the line was short. There were so many dukes, earls and barons who were not there and who were even now mustering their next army to throw their might against this untried eighteen-year-old monarch and commander. This was the beginning of a reign but it was not the end of the war.

My thoughts turned to Richard, who had spent so much of his life fulfilling what he saw as his duty to serve and support a king who had failed so utterly to understand the process of government. If Richard had not died at Wakefield, would he now be sitting on the throne in Westminster Abbey taking the homage of his peers? Somehow I could not imagine it. Now more than ever I saw Edward as more Neville than Plantagenet.

When I was born, my father had been older than Richard was when he died. I had never known him as a young man but my mother had adored him and told me that he was the kind of man who could turn black clouds into blue sky. Edward certainly had Ralph Neville's imposing height, his fair hair and his dancing grey eyes and I believed he also had his charisma. It was as much his Neville blood as his Plantagenet breeding that had won him this place on the throne of England. Would the Neville blood with its fighting flair and its charismatic charm keep him alive and fit to reign? I offered a silent prayer that it be so.

Beside me Margaret bent her head to whisper her thoughts. 'If our father had not died you might be queen now, lady mother. Do you regret that?'

Behind my clasped hands I gave her a sideways smile. 'I am a Neville and I think, like Edward, that if a crown had come my way I would not have refused it.'

Outside the sun shone on Edward's procession as he walked to the river to board the barge that would take him back to Baynard's. 'King Edward! King Edward! God save King Edward!' The cheers and calls of the crowd echoing off the abbey walls told me that the people of London believed as I did, that after years of discord, disruption and war, surely with this golden king on the throne England could now look forward to peace and prosperity?

EPILOGUE

Berkhamstead Castle, Hertfordshire
June 24th 1580

Wearing a pristine white lace ruff, a blue pearl-buttoned doublet and puffed white breeches paned with bright blue silk, Sir Edward Carey, Keeper of the Queen's Jewels, made his way to the rose garden of Berkhamstead Castle. In one hand he held a beribboned basket containing a white satin cushion and in the other a sharp pruning knife.

Having outlived all of her children except Elizabeth and Margaret, Cicely had caused the rose garden to be planted when she retired to Berkhamstead to live out her twilight years. It contained only red and white roses and had been carefully maintained, even after she died on May 31st 1495 at the age of eighty. Sadly, after her death, the rest of the castle was allowed to fall into disrepair, abandoned by its royal owners.

Nearly a hundred years later, Queen Elizabeth I granted the castle to Sir Edward, who was permitted to use stone from the crumbling walls to build himself a house in the hunting park. On that bright midsummer day he set down the basket, selected a rose and cut it from the bush with his knife. He trimmed its leaves and laid it on the white satin cushion before picking up the basket and setting off for the stables. The only rent required for the castle was that each year, on the feast day of St John the Baptist, Sir Edward should bring to court one perfect red rose, in memory of the queen's great grandmother Cicely Neville, the Rose of Raby.

AUTHOR'S NOTE

The civil disturbances during the fifteenth century in
England were so many and varied that it would be foolish
to try and tell a story that encompassed all the battles and
family feuds that constituted what we now call the Wars of the
Roses. My decision to concentrate on the York/Neville connection was dictated by my fascination with Cicely Neville and
the way the Wheel of Fortune turned so abruptly and violently
for her and her family. And what an outstanding family it was
– and a contentious one! Her father married twice and she was
the youngest of his twenty one (or twenty-two, depending on
which records you consult) legitimate children and not a day
can have gone by without some sort of disagreement or difference of opinion and of course the oldest of them would have
flown the nest and had their own children long before the
youngest were even born. So definitely not a family such as we
are used to today.

However, as soon as I started my research, I realized that the
size of the family was the least of my problems. For although
there is detailed Neville genealogy available, I discovered that
the early records from Raby Castle had been entrusted to the
county archive in Durham, which had gone up in flames in the
nineteenth century. So I had to rely on aural history and family
legend to construct a picture of Cicely's early life, before she

became a national figure. Incidentally there are differing opinions as to the spelling of her name. Some spell it Cecily and she signed herself Cecylle in a rather crabbed hand but I have chosen to employ the spelling Cicely, as used at Raby Castle in their guides and documents. Both Raby and Brancepeth castles are still in private hands and occupied by their owners. Raby is open to the public (www.rabycastle.com) and is the magnificent home of direct descendants of the Nevilles, and although it has been extensively developed and renovated through the centuries it still has the same footprint as it had in Cicely's time. Brancepeth is smaller but equally well preserved and has changed hands a number of times over the years but remains in private ownership. The two Neville palaces in Yorkshire are now both ruins. Little remains of Sheriff Hutton Castle, but Middleham is a very atmospheric place to visit, particularly if you are a follower of the history of Richard III, who spent some of his teenage years there as well as much of his married life – a period not covered in *Red Rose, White Rose*.

Sir John Neville is quite a mysterious character in history but I have fleshed him out from the sketchy mentions to be found. The relationship I have given him with Cicely is fictitious but it is a fact that he did not marry until he was well over forty, which is late for medieval times, and he did marry his nephew's twelve-year-old widow. Their son eventually inherited the earldom of Westmorland.

I would love to have met Cicely's father, Ralph Neville, the first Earl of Westmorland, and I see Sir John Neville as a slightly flawed version of him. Since he was clearly very fertile, Ralph probably did have illegitimate children although there is no record of them but there is a son called Cuthbert listed as 'died young' among the children of his marriage to Joan

Beaufort. I have simply chosen to give him a different mother and use him as the co-narrator of the novel in order to bring another voice into story and enable me to take the narrative onto the battlefield, where obviously Cicely would not have gone. Hilda Copley is an entirely fictitious character, as is her obnoxious brother Gerald and Hilda's first husband, Master Simon Exeley.

Cicely's eldest full brother was baptised Richard but for convenience I have concocted a family name of Hal in order to reduce the number of Richards in the novel which I considered would be too confusing for the reader. For the same reason the Earl of Warwick is called Dick and Cicely's youngest son is known as Dickon. But it is entirely possible that the name Richard would have been an embarrassment at court during the early years of King Henry IV's reign.

There was a Neville manor called Aycliffe which was eventually held by Sir Thomas Neville but that is all I know about it. I made it a tower in a bog because the modern town of School Aycliffe does stand on the edge of a 'wetland' which has been drained and turned into a nature reserve.

The breakdown of relations between the Duke of York and King Henry VI is well documented, as are their characters and that of Queen Margaret of Anjou. I hope I have not taken any 'liberties' with them, or with the battles I have described which took place as a result.

The characters of Cicely's children are from my imagination but based on their documented adult actions. I have absorbed recent opinions about the legitimacy of King Edward IV but take the view that 'my' Cicely would have been far too proud to have an affair with a mere archer! Also there seems to me to be no proof that the Duke of York could not have been his father and every reason to believe that he was. Edward just happened to inherit the looks, height and character of his grandparent, which plenty of people do.

The marriage of Anne of York and Henry (Harry) Holland definitely took place and was reported to be acrimonious, just as he was described by contemporaries as ill-tempered, violent and erratic. Anne eventually achieved an annulment from him, which was unusual in those times, and when he died she was granted wardship of their daughter and all his lands and revenues. So she was far from stupid and I'm happy to say made a second marriage (probably a love match) to a mere knight, which produced another daughter, one of whose descendants was used to supply the DNA that finally identified the 'body in the car-park' as definitely being that of Anne's brother, King Richard III.

I could find no record of Edward of York's knighting, which is surprising as it is a documented rite of passage for most high-ranking noblemen. So it is my own imagination which gave the honour to his cousin, the Earl of Warwick and made it the subject of a bitter row between Cicely and her husband. The fact remains that despite being only eighteen, he must have been knighted before taking a command at the Battle of Northampton and then going on to lead his army into the Battle of Mortimer's Cross, which were the defining conflicts that won him the offer of the crown. I have chosen to end this account of Cicely's early life at this stage because after this the historical focus turns to Edward's choice of a wife. Elizabeth Woodville and her family take centre stage in history during the next stage of the Wars of the Roses and there are many battles and turns of fortune to come.

I hope I have answered the historical questions readers may

have after reading *Red Rose, White Rose* but if there are any I have overlooked I would love to hear from you on Twitter (@joannahickson) or Facebook (Joanna Hickson) where I will readily attempt to answer them.

THE AGINCOURT BRIDE

The epic story of the queen who founded the Tudor dynasty, told through the eyes of her loyal nursemaid. Perfect for fans of Philipa Gregory.

Her beauty fuelled a war.
Her courage captured a king.
Her passion would launch the Tudor dynasty.

When her own first child is tragically still-born, the young Mette is pressed into service as a wet-nurse at the court of the mad king, Charles VI of France. Her young charge is the princess, Catherine de Valois, caught up in the turbulence and chaos of life at court.

Mette and the child forge a bond, one that transcends Mette's lowly position.

But as Catherine approaches womanhood, her unique position seals her fate as a pawn between two powerful dynasties. Her brother, The Dauphin and the dark and sinister, Duke of Burgundy will both use Catherine to further the cause of France.

Catherine is powerless to stop them, but with the French defeat at the Battle of Agincourt, the tables turn and suddenly her currency has never been higher. But can Mette protect Catherine from forces at court who seek to harm her or will her loyalty to Catherine place her in even greater danger?